A

Regency

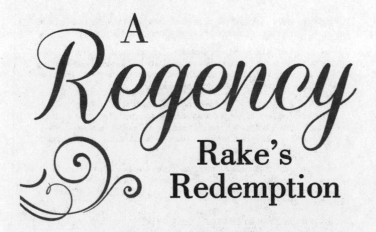

Rake's Redemption

LOUISE ALLEN

MILLS &
BOON

Published in Great Britain 2015
by Mills & Boon, an imprint of Harlequin (UK) Limited,
Eton House, 18-24 Paradise Road, Richmond, Surrey, TW9 1SR

A REGENCY RAKE'S REDEMPTION © 2015 Harlequin Books S.A.

Ravished by the Rake © 2011 Melanie Hilton
Seduced by the Scoundrel © 2011 Melanie Hilton

ISBN: 978-0-263-91761-1

052-0915

Harlequin (UK) policy is to use papers that are natural, renewable and recyclable products and made from wood grown in sustainable forests. The logging and manufacturing processes conform to the legal environmental regulations of the country of origin.

Printed and bound
by CPI Group (UK) Ltd, Croydon, CR0 4YY

**ROM
Pbk**

Ravished by the Rake

LOUISE ALLEN

Louise Allen loves immersing herself in history. She finds landscapes and places evoke the past powerfully. Venice, Burgundy and the Greek islands are favourite destinations. Louise lives on the Norfolk coast and spends her spare time gardening, researching family history or travelling in search of inspiration. Visit her at www.louiseallenregency.co.uk, @LouiseRegency and www.janeaustenslondon.com.

Chapter One

7th December 1808—Calcutta, India

It was blissfully cool, Dita assured herself, plying her fan in an effort to make it so. This was the *cool* season, so at eight o'clock in the evening it was only as hot as an English August day. Nor was it raining, thank heavens. How long did one have to live in India to become used to the heat? A trickle of sweat ran down her spine as she reminded herself of what it had been like from March to September.

But there was something to be said for the temperature: it made one feel so delightfully loose and relaxed. In fact, it was impossible to be anything *but* relaxed, to shed as many clothes as decency permitted and wear exquisitely fine muslins and lawns and floating silks.

She was going to miss that cat-like, sensual, indolence when she returned to England, now her year of exile was over. And the heat had another benefit, she thought, watching the group of young ladies in the reception room off the great Marble Hall of Government House:

it made the beautiful peaches-and-cream blondes turn red and blotchy whereas she, the gypsy, as they snidely remarked, showed little outward sign of it.

It had not taken long to adapt, to rise before dawn to ride in the cool, to sleep and lounge through the long, hot afternoons, saving the evenings for parties and dances. If it had not been for the grubby trail of rumour and gossip following her, she could have reinvented herself, perhaps, here in India. As it was, it had just added a sharper edge to her tongue.

But she wanted so much now to be in England. She wanted the green and the soft rain and the mists and a gentler sun. Her sentence was almost done: she could go home and hope to find herself forgiven by Papa, hope that her reappearance in society would not stir up the wagging tongues all over again.

And if it does? she thought, strolling into the room from the terrace, her face schooled to smiling confidence. *Then to hell with them, the catty ones with their whispers and the rakes who think I am theirs for the asking. I made a mistake and trusted a man, that is all. I will not do that again.* Regrets were a waste of time. Dita slammed the door on her thoughts and scanned the room with its towering ceiling and double rows of marble columns.

The *Bengal Queen* was due to sail for England at the end of the week and almost all her passengers were here at the Governor's House reception. She was going to get to know them very well indeed over the next few months. There were some important men in the East India Company travelling as supercargo; a handful of army officers; several merchants, some with wives and daughters, and a number of the well-bred young men who worked for the Company, setting their feet on the ladder of wealth and power.

Dita smiled and flirted her fan at two of them, the Chatterton twins on the far side of the room. Lazy, charming Daniel and driven, intense Callum—Mama would not be *too* displeased if she returned home engaged to Callum, the unattached one. Not a brilliant match, but they were younger brothers of the Earl of Flamborough, after all. Both were amusing company, but neither stirred more than a flutter in her heart. Perhaps no one would ever again, now she had learned to distrust what it told her.

Shy Averil Heydon waved from beside a group of chaperons. Dita smiled back a trifle wryly. Dear Averil: so well behaved, such a perfect young lady—and so pretty. How was it that Miss Heydon was one of the few eligible misses in Calcutta society whom she could tolerate? Possibly because she was such an heiress that she was above feeling delight at an earl's daughter being packed off the India in disgrace, unlike those who saw Lady Perdita Brooke as nothing but competition to be shot down. The smile hardened; they could certainly try. None of them had succeeded yet, possibly because they made the mistake of thinking that she cared for their approval or their friendship.

And Averil would be on the *Bengal Queen*, too, which was something to be grateful for—three months was a long time to be cooped up with the same restricted company. On the way out she'd had her anger—mostly directed at herself—and a trunk full of books to sustain her; now she intended to enjoy herself, and the experience of the voyage.

'Lady Perdita!'

'Lady Grimshaw?' Dita produced an attentive expression. The old gorgon was going to be a passenger, too, and Dita had learned to pick her battles.

'That is hardly a suitable colour for an unmarried girl. And such flimsy fabric, too.'

'It is a sari I had remade, Lady Grimshaw. I find pastels and white make me appear sallow.' Dita was well aware of her few good features and how to enhance them to perfection: the deep green brought out the colour of her eyes and the dark gold highlights in her brown hair. The delicate silk floated over the fine lawn undergarments as though she was wearing clouds.

'Humph. And what's this I hear about riding on the *maidan* at dawn? Galloping!'

'It is too hot to gallop at any other time of day, ma'am. And I did have my *syce* with me.'

'A groom is neither here nor there, my girl. It is fast behaviour. Very fast.'

'Surely speed is the purpose of the gallop?' Dita said sweetly, and drifted away before the matron could think of a suitably crushing retort. She gestured to a servant for a glass of punch, another fast thing for a young lady to be doing. She sipped it as she walked, wrinkling her nose at the amount of arrack it contained, then stopped as a slight stir around the doorway heralded a new arrival.

'Who is that?' Averil appeared at her side and gestured towards the door. 'My goodness, what a very good-looking man.' She fanned herself as she stared.

He was certainly that. Tall, lean, very tanned, the thick black silk of his hair cut ruthlessly short. Dita stopped breathing, then sucked down air. No, of course not, it could not be Alistair—she was imagining things. Her treacherous body registered alarm and an instant flutter of arousal.

The man entered limping, impatient, as though the handicap infuriated him, but he was going to ignore it. Once in, he surveyed the room with unhurried assurance. The scrutiny paused at Dita, flickered over her face, dropped to study the low-cut neckline of her gown, then moved on to Averil for a further cool assessment.

For all the world like a pasha inspecting a new intake for the seraglio, Dita thought. But despite the unfamiliar arrogance, she knew. Her body recognised him with every quivering nerve. *It is him. It is Alistair.* After eight years. Dita fought a battle with the urge to run.

'Insufferable,' Averil murmured. She had blushed a painful red.

'Insufferable, no doubt. Arrogant, certainly,' Dita replied, not troubling to lower her voice as he came closer. *Attack*, her instincts told her. *Strike before you weaken and he can hurt you again.* 'And he obviously fancies himself quite the romantic hero, my dear. You note the limp? Positively Gothic—straight out of a sensation novel.'

Alistair stopped and turned. He made no pretence of not having heard her. 'A young lady who addles her brain with trashy fiction, I gather.' The intervening years had not darkened the curious amber eyes that as a child she had always believed belonged to a tiger. Memories surfaced, some bittersweet, some simply bitter, some so shamefully arousing that she felt quite dizzy. She felt her chin go up as she returned the stare in frigid silence, but he had not recognised her. He turned a little more and bowed to Averil. 'My pardon, ma'am, if I put you to the blush. One does not often see such beauty.'

The movement exposed the right side of his head. Down the cheek from just in front of the ear, across the jawbone and on to his neck, there was a half-healed scar that vanished into the white lawn of his neckcloth. His right hand, she saw, was bandaged. The limp was not affectation after all; he had been hurt, and badly. Dita stifled the instinct to touch him, demand to know what had happened as she once would have done, without inhibition.

Beside her she heard her friend's sharp indrawn breath. 'I do not regard it, sir.' Averil nodded with cool dismissal and walked away towards the chaperons, then turned when she reached their sanctuary, her face comically dismayed as she realised Dita had not followed her.

I should apologise to him, Dita thought, *but he ogled us so blatantly. And he cut at me just as he had that last time.* Furthermore, he apologised only to Averil; her own looks would win no compliments from this man.

'My friend is as gracious as she is beautiful,' she said and the amber eyes, still warm from following Averil's retreat, moved back to hers. He frowned at the tart sweetness of her tone. 'She can find it in herself to forgive almost anyone, even presumptuous rakes.' Which is what Alistair appeared to have grown into.

And on that note she should turn on her heel, perhaps with a light trill of laughter, or a flick of her fan, and leave him to annoy some other lady. But it was difficult to move, when wrenching her eyes away from his meant they fell to his mouth. It did not curve—he could not be said to be smiling—but one corner deepened into something that was almost a dimple. Not, of course, that such an arrogant hunk of masculinity could be said to have anything as charming as a dimple. That mouth on her skin, on her breast...

'I am rightly chastised,' he said. There was something provocative in the way that he said it that sent a little shock through her, although she had no idea why. Then she realised that he was speaking to her as a woman, not as the girl he had thought her when he had so cruelly dismissed her before. It was almost as though he was suggesting that she carry out the chastisement more personally.

Dita told herself that one could overcome blushes by sheer force of will, especially as she had no very exact idea what she was blushing about now. He did not recognise her; even if he did, what had happened so long ago had been unimportant to him, he had made that very clear at the time. 'You do not appear remotely penitent, sir,' she retorted. Sooner or later he would realise who he was talking to, but she was not going to give him the satisfaction of acknowledging him and thinking she attached any importance to it.

'I never said I was, ma'am, merely that I acknowledged a reproof. There is no amusement in penitence— why, one would have to either give up the sin or be a hypocrite—and where's the fun in that?'

'I have no idea whether you are a hypocrite or not, sir, but certainly no one could accuse you of gallant behaviour.'

'You struck first,' he pointed out, accurately and unfairly.

'For which I apologise,' Dita said. She was not going to act as badly as he. Even as she made the resolution her tongue got the better of her. 'But I have no intention of offering sympathy, sir. You obviously enjoy fighting.' He had always been intense, often angry, as a youth. And that intensity had miraculously transmuted into fire and passion when he made love.

'Indeed.' He flexed the bandaged hand and winced slightly. 'You should see the other fellow.'

'I have no wish to. You appear to have been hacking at each other with sabres.'

'Near enough,' he agreed.

Something in the mocking, cultured tones still held the faintest burr of the West Country. A wave of nostalgia for home and the green hills and the fierce cliffs and the cold sea gripped her, overriding even the shock of seeing Alistair again.

'You still have the West Country in your voice,' Dita said abruptly.

'North Cornwall, near the boundary with Devon. And you?' He did not appear to find the way she had phrased the statement strange.

He misses it, too, she thought, hearing the hint of longing under the cool tone. 'I, too, come from that area.' Without calculation she put out her hand and he caught it in his uninjured, ungloved, left. His hand was warm and hard with a rider's calluses and his fingertips rested against her pulse, which was racing. Once before he had held her hand like this, once before they had stood so close and she had read the need in his eyes and she had misunderstood and acted with reckless innocence. He had taken her to heaven and then mocked her for her foolishness.

She could not play games any longer. Sooner or later he would find out who she was, and if she made a mystery of it he would think she still remembered, still attached some importance to what had happened between them. 'My family lives at Combe.'

'You are a Brooke? One of the Earl of Wycombe's family?' He moved nearer, her hand still held in his as he drew her to him to study her face. Close to he seemed to take the air out of the space between them. *Too close, too male. Alistair. Oh my lord, he has grown up.* 'Why, you are never little Dita Brooke? But you were all angles and nose and legs.' He grinned. 'I used to put frogs in your pinafore pocket and you tagged along everywhere. But you have changed since I last saw you. You must have been twelve.' His amusement stripped the eight years from him.

'I was sixteen,' she said with all the icy reserve she could manage. *All angles and nose.* 'I recall you—and your frogs—as an impudent youth while I was growing up. But I was sixteen when you left home.' *Sixteen when I kissed you with all the fervour and love that was filling me and you used me and brushed me aside. Was I simply too unskilled for you or too foolishly clinging?*

A shadow darkened the mocking eyes and for a moment Alistair frowned as though chasing an elusive memory.

But he doesn't seem to remember—or he is not admitting it. But how could he forget? Perhaps there have been so many women that one inept chit of a girl is infinitely forgettable.

'Sixteen? Were you?' He frowned, his eyes intent on her face. 'I don't…recollect.' But his eyes held questions and a hint of puzzlement as though he had been reminded of a faded dream.

'There is no reason why you should.' Dita pulled her hand free, dropped the merest hint of a curtsy and walked away. *So, he doesn't even remember! He broke my foolish young heart and he doesn't even remember doing it. I was that unimportant to him.*

Daniel Chatterton intercepted her in the middle of the room and she set her face into a pleasant smile. *I am not plain any more,* she told herself with a fierce determination not to run away. *I am polished and stylish and an original. That is what I am: an original. Other men admire me. It is good that I have met Alistair again—now I can replace the fantasy with the reality.* Perhaps now the memories of one shattering, wonderful hour in his bed would leave her, finally.

'Never tell me that you do not idolise our returning adventurer, Lady Perdita.' Apparently her expression was not as bland as she hoped. She shrugged; no doubt half the room had heard the exchange. She could imagine the giggles amongst the cattery of young ladies. Chatterton gestured to a passing servant. 'More punch?'

'No. No, thank you, it is far too strong.' Dita took a glass of mango juice in exchange. Was the arrack responsible for how she had felt just now? Without it perhaps she would have seen just another man and the glamour would have dropped away, leaving her untouched. As she raised her drink to sip, she realised her hand retained the faintest hint of Alistair's scent: leather, musk and something elusive and spicily expensive. He had never smelled like that before, so complex, so intoxicating. He had grown up with a vengeance. But so had she.

'If you mean Alistair Lyndon, the insolent creature who spoke to Miss Heydon and me just now, I knew him when he was growing up. He was a care-for-nothing then and it seems little has changed.' Now she was blushing again. She *never* blushed. 'He left home when he was twenty, or thereabouts.'

Twenty years, eleven months. She had bought him a fine horn pocket comb for his birthday and painstakingly embroidered a case for it. It was still in the bottom of her jewel box where it had stayed, even when she had eloped with the man she had believed herself in love with.

'He is Viscount Lyndon, heir to the Marquis of Iwerne, is he not?'

'Yes. Our families' lands march together, but we are

not great friends.' Not, at least, since Mama was careless enough to show what she thought of the marquis's second wife, who was only five years older than Dita. With some friction already over land, and no daughters in the Iwerne household to promote sociability, the families met rarely and there was no incentive to heal the rift.

'Lyndon left home after some disagreement with his father about eight years ago,' she added in an indifferent tone. 'But I don't think they ever got on, even before that. What is he doing here, do you know?' It was a reasonable enough question.

'Joining the party for the *Bengal Queen* passengers. He is returning home, I hear. The word is that his father is very ill; Lyndon may well be the marquis already.' Chatterton looked over her shoulder. 'He is watching you.'

She could feel him, like the gazelle senses the tiger lurking in the shadows, and fought for composure. Three months in a tiny canvas-walled cabin, cheek by jowl with a man who still thrived, she was certain, on dangerous mischief. It wouldn't be frogs in pinafore pockets these days. If he even suspected how she felt, *had* felt, about him, she had no idea how he would react.

'Is he, indeed? How obvious of him.'

'He is also watching me,' Chatterton said with a rueful smile. 'And I do not think it is because he admires my waistcoat. I am beginning to feel dangerously *de trop*. Most men would pretend they were not observing you—Lyndon has the air of a man guarding his property.'

'Insolent is indeed the word for him.' He did not regard her as his property, far from it, but he had bestowed his attention upon her just now and she had snubbed him, so he would not be satisfied until he had her gazing at him cow-eyed like all the rest of the silly girls would do.

Now Dita turned slightly so she was in profile to the viscount and ran a finger down Daniel Chatterton's waistcoat. 'Lord Lyndon might not admire it, but is certainly a very fine piece of silk. And you look so handsome in it.'

'Are you flirting with me by any chance, Lady Perdita?' Chatterton asked with a grin. 'Or are you trying to annoy Lyndon?'

'Me?' She opened her eyes wide at him, enjoying herself all of a sudden. She had met Alistair again and the heavens had not fallen; perhaps she could survive this after all. She gave Daniel's neckcloth a proprietorial tweak to settle the folds, intent on adding oil to the fire.

'Yes, you! Don't you care that he will probably call me out?'

'He has no cause. Tell me about him so I may better avoid him. I haven't seen him for years.' She smiled up into Daniel's face and stood just an inch too close for propriety.

'I shall have to try that brooding stare myself,' Chatterton said, with a wary glance across the room. 'It seems to work on the ladies. All I know about him is that he has been travelling in the East for about seven years, which fits with what you recall of him leaving home. He's a rich man—the rumour is that he made a killing by gem dealing and that his weakness is exotic plants. He's got collectors all over the place sending stuff back to somewhere in England—money no object, so they say.'

'And how did *he* get hurt?' Dita ran her fan down

Daniel's arm. Alistair was still watching them, she could feel him. 'Duelling?'

'Nothing so safe. It was a tiger, apparently; a man-eater who was terrorising a village. Lyndon went after it on elephant-back and the beast leapt at the howdah and dragged the *mahout* off. Lyndon vaulted down and tackled it with a knife.'

'Quite the hero.' Dita spoke lightly, but the thought of those claws, the great white teeth, made her shudder. What did it take to go so close, risk such an awful death? She had likened it to a sabre wound; the claws must have been as lethal. 'What happened to the mahout?'

'No idea. Pity Lyndon's handsome face has been spoiled.'

'Spoiled? Goodness, no!' She forced a laugh and deployed her fan. *His face? He could have been killed!* 'It will soon heal completely—don't you know that scars like that are most attractive to the ladies?'

'Lady Perdita, you will excuse me if I tear my brother away?' It was Callum Chatterton, Daniel's twin. 'I must talk tiresome business, I fear.'

'He's removing me from danger before I am called out,' Daniel interpreted, rolling his eyes. 'But he'll make me work as well, I have no doubt.'

'Go then, Mr Chatterton,' she said, chuckling at his rueful expression. 'Work hard and be safe.' She stood looking after them for a moment, but she was seeing not the hot, crowded room with its marble pillars, but a ripple in the long, sun-bleached grass as gold-and-black-striped death padded through it; the explosion of muscles and terror; the screaming *mahout* and the man who had risked his life to save him. Her fantasy of Alistair's eyes as being like those of a tiger did not seem so poetic now.

She turned, impulsive as always. She should make

amends for her remark, she should make peace. That long-ago magic, the hurt that had shattered it, had meant nothing to him at the time and it should mean nothing to her now. Alistair Lyndon had haunted her dreams for too long.

But Alistair was no longer watching her. Instead, he stood far too close to Mrs Harrison, listening to something she was virtually whispering in his ear, his down-turned gaze on the lady's abundantly displayed charms.

So, the intense young man she had fallen for so hard was a rake now, and the attention he had paid her and Averil was merely habitual. A courageous rake, but a rake none the less. And he was just as intrigued to find his plain little neighbour after all these years, which would account for his close scrutiny just now.

It smarted that he did not even seem to remember just what had happened between them, but she must learn to school her hurt pride, for that was all it could be. And he had found a lady better suited to his character than she to talk to; Mrs Harrison's reputation suggested that she would be delighted to entertain a gentleman in any way that mutual desire suggested.

Dita put down her glass with a snap on a side table, suddenly weary of the crowd, the noise, the heat and her own ghosts. As she walked towards the door her bearer emerged from the shadows behind the pillars.

'My chair, Ajay.' He hurried off and she went to tell Mrs Smyth-Robinson, who was obliging her aunt by acting as chaperon this evening, that she was leaving.

She was tired and her head ached, and she wished she was home in England and never had to speak to another man again and certainly not Alistair Lyndon. But she made herself nod and wave to acquaintances, she made herself walk with the elegant swaying step that disguised the fact that she had no lush curves to flaunt, and she kept the smile on her lips and her chin up. One had one's pride, after all.

Alistair was aware of the green-eyed hornet leaving the room even as he accepted Claudia Hamilton's invitation to join her for a nightcap. He doubted the lady was interested in a good night's sleep. He had met her husband in Guwahati buying silk and agreed with Claudia's obvious opinion that he was a boor—it was clear she needed entertaining.

The prospect of a little mutual *entertainment* was interesting, although he had no intention of this developing into an *affaire*, even for the few days remaining before he sailed. Alistair was not given to sharing and the lady was, by all accounts, generous with her favours.

'There goes the Brooke girl,' Claudia said with a sniff, following his gaze. 'Impudent chit. Just because she has a fortune and an earl for a father doesn't make up for scandal and no looks to speak of. She is going back to England on the *Bengal Queen*. I suppose they think that whatever it was she did has been forgotten by now.'

'Her family are neighbours of mine,' Alistair remarked, instinct warning him to produce an explanation for his interest. 'She has grown up.' He wasn't surprised to hear of a scandal—Dita looked headstrong enough for anything. As a gangling child she had been a fearless and impetuous tomboy, always tagging along at his heels, wanting to climb trees and fish and ride unsuitable horses. And she had been fiercely affectionate.

He frowned at the vague memory of her wrapping her arms around his neck and kissing him. That had been the day before he packed his bags and shook the dust of Castle Lyndon from his shoes.

He had been distracted with grief and humiliated anger and she had tried to comfort him, he supposed. Probably he had been abrupt with the girl. He had been drinking, too, the best part of a bottle of brandy and wine as well, if his very faint recollection served him right. But then his memory of that day and night were blurred and the dreams that still visited him about that time were too disturbing to confront. Dita… No, the dreams had not been of an affectionate kiss from a tomboy but of a slender, naked body, of fierce passion. Hell, he still felt guilty that his drink-sodden nightmares could have produced those images of an innocent girl.

Alistair glanced towards the door again, but the emerald silk had whisked out of sight. Dita Brooke was no longer a child, but she had most certainly developed into a dangerous handful for whichever man her father was aiming to marry her off to.

'You think her lacking in looks?' It was amusing to see the venom in Claudia's eyes as she thought about the younger woman. He had no intention of asking her to speculate about the scandal. Given the repressive English drawing rooms he remembered, it had probably been something as dreadful as being caught kissing a man on the terrace during a ball. Dull stuff.

'No figure, too tall, her face lacks symmetry, her nose is too long, her complexion is sallow. Other than that I am sure she is tolerable.'

'A catalogue of disasters to be sure, poor girl,' Alistair agreed, his fingertip tracing lazy circles in Claudia's palm. She made a sound like a purr and moved closer.

She was right, of course, all those things could be said of Lady Perdita. Little Dita Brooke had been as plain and ungainly as a fledgling in a nest. And yet, by some alchemy, she had overcome them to become a tantalising, feminine creature. Poise, exquisite grooming and sheer personality, he supposed. And something new—a tongue like an adder. It might be amusing to try his luck as a snake charmer on the voyage home.

Chapter Two

'Steady, Khan.' Dita smoothed her hand along the neck of the big bay gelding and smiled as he twitched one ear back to listen to her. 'You can run in a minute.' He sidled and fidgeted, pretending to take violent exception to a passing ox cart, a rickshaw, a wandering, soft-eyed sacred cow and even a group of chattering women with brass bowls on their heads. The Calcutta traffic never seemed to diminish, even at just past dawn on a Wednesday morning.

'I wish I could take you home, but Major Conway will look after you,' she promised, turning his head as they reached one of the rides across the *maidan*, the wide expanse of open space that surrounded the low angular mass of Fort William. Only one more day to ride after today; best not to think about it, the emotions were too complicated. 'Come on, then!'

The horse needed no further urging. Dita tightened her hold as he took off into a gallop from almost a standing start and thundered across the grass. Behind her she heard the hoofbeats of the grey pony her *syce* Pradeep rode, but they soon faded away. Pradeep's pony could never catch Khan and she had no intention of waiting for him. When she finally left the *maidan* he would come cantering up, clicking his tongue at her and grumbling as always, 'Lady Perdita, *memsahib*, how can I protect you from wicked men if you leave me behind?'

There aren't any wicked men out here, she thought as the Hooghly River came in sight. The soldiers patrolling the fort saw to that. Perhaps she should take Pradeep with her into the ballroom and he could see off the likes of Alistair Lyndon.

She had managed about three hours' sleep. Most of the night had been spent tossing and turning and fuming about arrogant males with dreadful taste in women—and the one particular arrogant male she was going to have to share a ship with for weeks on end. Now she was determined to chase away not only last evening's unsettling encounter, but the equally unsettling dreams that had followed it.

The worst had been a variation on the usual nightmare: her father had flung open the door of the chaise and dragged her out into the inn yard in front of a stagecoach full of gawking onlookers and old Lady St George in her travelling carriage. But this time the tall man with black hair with her was not Stephen Doyle, scrambling out of the opposite door in a cowardly attempt to escape, but Alistair Lyndon.

And Alistair was not running away as the man she had talked herself into falling for had. In her dream he turned, elegant and deadly, the light flickering off the blade of the rapier he held to her father's throat. And then the dream had become utterly confused and Stephen in a tangle of sheets in the inn bed had become a much younger Alistair.

And that dream had been accurate and intense and so arousing that she had woken aching and yearning and had had to rise and splash cold water over herself until the trembling ceased.

As she had woken that morning she had realised who Stephen Doyle resembled—a grown-up version of Alistair. Dita shook her head to try to clear the last muddled remnants of the dreams out of her head. Surely she hadn't fallen for Stephen because she was still yearning for Alistair? It was ludicrous; after that humiliating fiasco—which he had so obviously forgotten in a brandy-soaked haze the next morning—she had fought to put that foolish infatuation behind her. She had thought she had succeeded.

Khan was still going flat out, too fast for prudence as they neared the point where the outer defensive ditch met the river bank. Here she must turn, and the scrubby trees cast heavy shadow capable of concealing rough ground and stray dogs. She began to steady the horse, and as she did so a chestnut came out of the trees, galloping as fast as her gelding was.

Khan came to a sliding halt and reared to try to avoid the certain collision. Dita clung flat on his neck, the breath half-knocked out of her by the pommel. As the mane whipped into her eyes she saw the other rider wrench his animal to the left. On the short dusty grass the fall was inevitable, however skilled the rider; as Khan landed with a bone-juddering thud on all four hooves the other horse slithered, scrabbled for purchase and crashed down, missing them by only a few yards.

Dita threw her leg over the pommel and slid to the ground as the chestnut horse got to its feet. Its rider lay sprawled on the ground; she ran and fell to her knees beside him. It was Alistair Lyndon, flat on his back, arms outflung, eyes closed.

'Oh, my God!' *Is he dead?* She wrenched open the buttons on his black linen coat, pushed back the fronts to expose his shirt and bent over him, her ear pressed to his chest. Against her cheek the thud of his heart was fast, but it was strong and steady.

Dita let all the air out of her lungs in a whoosh of relief as her shoulders slumped. She must get up and send for help, a doctor. He might have broken his leg or his back. But just for a second she needed to recover from the shock.

'This is nice,' remarked his voice in her ear and his arm came round her, pulled her up a little and, before she could struggle, Alistair's mouth was pressed against hers, exploring with a frank appreciation and lack of urgency that took her breath away.

Dita had never been kissed by a man who appeared to be taking an indolently dispassionate pleasure in the proceeding. When she was sixteen she had been in Alistair's arms when she was ignorant and he was a youth and he had still made her sob with delight. Now he was a man, and sober, and she knew it meant nothing to him. This was pure self-indulgent mischief.

Even so, it was far harder to pull away than it should be, she found, furious with herself. Alistair had spent eight years honing his sexual technique, obviously by practising whenever he got the opportunity. She put both hands on his shoulders, heaved, and was released with unflattering ease. 'You libertine!'

He opened his eyes, heavy-lidded, amused and golden, and sat up. The amusement vanished in a sharp intake of breath followed by a vehement sentence in a language she did not recognise '…and bloody hell,' he finished.

'Lord Lyndon,' Dita stated. It took an effort not to slap him. 'Of course, it had to be you, riding far too fast. Are you hurt? I assume from your language that you are. I suppose you are going to say your outrageous behaviour is due to concussion or shock or some such excuse.'

The smouldering look he gave her as he scrubbed his left hand through his dusty, tousled hair was a provocation she would not let herself rise to. 'Being a normal male, when young women fling themselves on my chest I do not need the excuse of a bang on the head to react,' he said. He wriggled his shoulders experimentally. 'I'll live.'

Dita resisted the urge to shift backwards out of range. There was blood on his bandaged hand, the makings of a nasty bruise on his cheek; the very fact he had not got to his feet yet told her all she needed to know about how his injured leg felt.

'Are *you* hurt?' he asked. She shook her head. 'Is my horse all right?

'Pradeep,' she called as the *syce* cantered up. 'Catch the *sahib*'s horse, please, and check it is all right.' She turned back, thankful she could not understand the muttered remarks Lyndon was making, and tried to ignore the fact that her heart was still stuck somewhere in her throat after the shock. Or was it that kiss? How he *dared*! How she wanted him to do it again.

'Now, what are we going to do about you?' she said, resorting to brisk practicality. 'I had best send Pradeep to the fort, I think, and get them to bring out a stretcher.' At least she sounded coherent, even if she did not feel it.

'Do I look like the kind of man who would put up with

being carted about on a stretcher by a couple of sepoys?' he enquired, flexing his hand and hissing as he did so.

'No, of course not.' Dita began to untie her stock. Her hands, she was thankful to see, were not shaking. 'That would be the rational course of action, after all. How ludicrous to expect you to follow it. Doubtless you intend to sit here for the rest of the day?'

'I intend to stand up,' he said. 'And walk to my horse when your man has caught it. Why are you undressing?'

'I am removing my stock in order to bandage whichever part of your ungrateful anatomy requires it, my lord,' Dita said, her teeth clenched. 'At the moment I am considering a tourniquet around your neck.'

Alistair Lyndon regarded her from narrowed eyes, but all he said was, 'I thought that ripping up petticoats was the standard practice under these circumstances.'

'I have no intention of demolishing my wardrobe for you, my lord.' Dita got to her feet and held out her hand. 'Are you going to accept help to stand up or does your stubborn male pride preclude that as well?'

When he moved, he moved fast and with grace. His language was vivid, although mostly incomprehensible, but the viscount got his good leg under him and stood up in one fluid movement, ignoring her hand. 'There is a lot of blood on your breeches now,' she observed. She had never been so close to quite this much gore before but, by some miracle, she did not feel faint. Probably she was too cross. And aroused—she could not ignore that humiliating fact. She had wanted him then, eight years ago when he had been a youth. Now she felt sharp desire for the man he had become. She was grown, too; she could resist her own weaknesses.

'Damn.' He held out a hand for the stock and she gave it to him. She was certainly not going to offer to bandage his leg if he could do it himself. Beside any other consideration, the infuriating creature would probably take it as an invitation to further familiarities and she had the lowering feeling that touching him again would shatter her resolve. 'Thank you.' The knot he tied was workmanlike and seemed to stop the bleeding, so there was no need to continue to study the well-muscled thigh, she realised, and began to tidy her own disarranged neckline as well as she could.

'Your wounds were caused by a tiger, I hear,' Dita remarked, feeling the need for conversation. Perhaps she was a trifle faint after all; she was certainly oddly light-headed. Or was that simply that kiss? 'I assume it came off worst.'

'It did,' he agreed, yanking his cuffs into place. Pradeep came over, leading the chestnut horse. 'Thank you. Is it all right?'

'Yes, *sahib*. The rein is broken, which is why the *sahib* was not able to hold it when he fell.' The *syce* must think he required a sop to his pride, but Alistair appeared unconcerned. 'Does the *sahib* require help to mount?'

He'll say no, *of course*, Dita thought. *The usual male conceit.* But Lyndon put his good foot into the *syce*'s cupped hands and let Pradeep boost him enough to throw his injured leg over the saddle.

It was interesting that he saw no need to play-act the hero—unlike Stephen, who would have doubtless managed alone, even if it made the wound worse. She frowned. What was she doing, thinking of that sorry excuse for a lover? Hadn't she resolved to put him, and her own poor judgement, out of her head? He had never been in her heart, she knew that now. But it was uncanny, the way he was a pale imitation of the man in front of her now.

'What happened to the *mahout?*' she asked, putting one hand on the rein to detain Lyndon.

'He survived.' He looked down at her, magnificently self-assured despite his dusty clothes and stained bandages. 'Why do you ask?'

'You thought he was worth risking your life for. Many *sahibs* would not have done so.' It was the one good thing she had so far discovered about this new, adult, Alistair. 'It would be doubly painful to be injured and to have lost him.'

'I had employed him, so he was my responsibility,' Lyndon said.

'And the villagers who were being attacked by the man-eater? They were your responsibility also?'

'Trying to find the good side to my character, Dita?' he asked with uncomfortable perception. 'I wouldn't stretch your charity too far—it was good sport, that was all.'

'I'm sure it was,' she agreed. 'You men do like to kill things, don't you? And, of course, your own self-esteem would not allow you to lose a servant to a mere animal.'

'At least it fought back, unlike a pheasant or a fox,' he said with a grin, infuriatingly unmoved by her jibes. 'And why did you put yourself out so much just now for a man who obviously irritates you?'

'Because I was riding as fast as you were, and I, too, take responsibility for my actions,' she said. 'And you do not irritate me, you exasperate me. I do not appreciate your attempts to tease me with your shocking behaviour.'

'I was merely attempting to act as one of your romantic heroes,' he said. 'I thought a young lady addicted to novels would expect such attentions. You appeared to enjoy it.'

'I was shocked into momentary immobility.' Only, her lips had moved against his, had parted, her tongue had touched his in a fleeting mutual caress... 'And I am not *addicted*, as you put it. In fact, I think you are reading too many novels yourself, my lord,' Dita retorted as she dropped the rein and turned away to where Pradeep stood holding Khan.

Alistair watched her walk, straight-backed, to her groom and spend a moment speaking to him, apparently in reassurance, while she rubbed the big gelding's nose. For all the notice she took of Alistair he might as well not have been there, but he could sense her awareness of him, see it in the flush that touched her cheekbones. *Momentary immobility*, his foot! She had responded to his kiss whether she wanted to admit it or not.

The *syce* cupped his hands and she rose up and settled in the saddle with the lack of fuss of a born horsewoman. And a fit one, he thought, appreciating the moment when her habit clung and outlined her long legs.

In profile he could see that Claudia had been right. Her nose *was* too long and when she had looked up at him to ask about the *mahout* her face had been serious, emphasising the slight asymmetry that was not apparent when she was animated. And a critic who was not contemplating kissing it would agree that her mouth was too wide and her figure was unfashionably tall and slim. But the ugly duckling had grown into her face and, although it was not a beautiful one, it was vividly attractive.

And now he need not merely contemplate kissing her, he knew how she tasted and how it was to trace the curve of her upper lip with his tongue. The taste and feel of her had been oddly familiar.

He knew how she felt, her slight curves pressed to his chest, her weight on his body, and oddly it was as though he had always known that. It was remarkably effective in taking his mind off the bone-deep ache in his thigh and the sharp pain in his right hand. Alistair urged the bay alongside her horse as Dita used both hands to tuck up the strands of hair that had escaped from the net. The collar of her habit was open where the neckcloth was missing and his eyes followed the vee of pale skin into the shadows.

Last night her evening gown had revealed much more, but somehow it had not seemed so provocative. When he lifted his eyes she was gathering up the reins and he could tell from the way her lips tightened that she knew where he had been looking. If he had stayed in England, and watched the transformation from gawky child into provocatively attractive woman, would the impact when he looked at her be as great—or would she just be little Dita, grown up? Because there was no mistaking what he wanted when he looked at her now.

'We are both to be passengers on the *Bengal Queen*,' he said. It was a statement of the obvious, but he needed to keep her here for a few more moments, to see if he could provoke her into any more sharp-tongued remarks. He remembered last night how he had teased her with talk of chastisement and how unexpectedly stimulating that had been. The thought of wrestling between the sheets with a sharp-tongued, infuriated Lady Perdita who was trying to slap him was highly erotic. He might even let her get a few blows in before he…

'Yes,' she agreed, sounding wary. Doubtless some shadow of his thoughts was visible on his face. Alistair shifted in the saddle and got his unruly, and physically uncomfortable, imaginings under control. Better for now to remember the gawky tomboy-child who had always been somewhere in the background, solemn green eyes following his every move. 'You will be anxious to get home, no doubt,' she said with careful formality. 'I was sorry to hear that Lord Iwerne is unwell.'

'Thank you.' He could think of nothing else to say that was neither a lie nor hypocritical. From the months'-old news he had received from Lyndonholt Castle there was a strong chance that he was already the marquis, and try as he might to summon up appropriate feelings of anxiety and sadness for his father, he could not. They had never been close and the circumstances of their parting had been bitter. And even if his father still lived, what would he make of the hardened, travelled, twenty-nine-year-old who returned in the place of the angry, naïve young man who had walked away from him?

And there was his stepmother, of course. What would Imogen be expecting of the stepson who had not even stayed to see her wed?

She was in for a shock if she thought he would indulge her or had any tender feelings left for her. She could take herself off to the Dower House with her widow's portion and leave the Castle for the bride he fully intended to install there as soon as possible. And that bride would be a gentle, obedient, chaste young lady of good breeding. He would select her with care and she would provide him with heirs and be an excellent hostess. And she would leave his heart safely untouched—love was for idealists and romantics and he was neither. Not any more.

'A rupee for your thoughts?' Dita said, her wary expression replaced with amusement at his abstraction. It almost had him smiling back, seeing a shadow of the patient child in an unusual young lady who did not take offence at a man forgetting she was there. But then, she was probably relieved his attention was elsewhere. 'Are you daydreaming of home?'

'Yes,' he agreed. 'But the thought was hardly worth a rupee. Ma'am, it was a pleasure.' He bowed his hatless head for a moment, turned his horse towards Government House and cantered off.

For a moment there he had been tempted to stay, to offer to escort her back to wherever she was living. He must have hit his head in that fall, Alistair thought, to contemplate such a thing. He was going to be close to Dita Brooke for three months in the narrow confines of the ship, and he had no intention of resuming the role of elder brother, or however she had seen him as a child. He was not going to spend his time getting her out of scrapes and frightening off importunate young men; it made him feel old just thinking about it. As for that impulsive kiss, she had dealt with it briskly enough, even if she *had* responded to it. She was sophisticated enough to take it at face value as part of the repertoire of a rake, so nothing to worry about there.

Alistair trotted into the stable yard of Government House and dismounted with some care. The Governor General was away, but he was interested in plant hunting, too, and had extended a vague invitation that Alistair had found useful to take up for the few weeks before the ship sailed.

Damn this leg. He supposed he had better go and show it to the Governor's resident doctor and be lectured on his foolishness in riding so hard with it not properly healed. But the prospect of weeks without energetic exercise had driven him out to ride each day for as long as the cool of the morning lasted. No doubt Dita had been motivated by the same considerations.

Which led him to think of her again, and of violent exercise, and the combination of the two was uncomfortably vivid. No, his feelings were most definitely not brotherly, any more than those damnably persistent dreams about her were. 'Bloody fool,' he snapped at himself, startling the *jemahdar* at the front door.

Intelligent, headstrong, argumentative young women with a scandal in their past and a temper were not what he was looking for. A meek and biddable English rose who would give him no trouble and cause no scandal was what he wanted and Dita Brooke had never been a rosebud, let alone a rose. She was pure briar with thorns all the way.

Chapter Three

$\mathcal{A}$s Alistair limped up the staircase to the first floor he thought of Dita's threat to apply a tourniquet around his neck and laughed out loud at the memory of her face as she said it. The two men coming out of an office stopped at the sound.

'Hell's teeth, Lyndon, what's happened to you?' It was one of the Chatterton twins, probably Daniel, who had been flirting with Perdita last night. 'Found that tiger again?'

'My horse fell on the *maidan* and I've opened up the wound in my thigh. I'd better get a stitch in it—have you seen Dr Evans?' Stoicism was one thing, being careless with open wounds in this climate quite another.

'No, no sign of him—but we only dropped in to leave some papers, we haven't seen anyone. Let's get you up to your room while they find Evans. *Daktar ko bulaiye,*' one twin called down to the *jemahdar.*

That was Callum, Alistair thought, waving away the offer of an arm in support. The responsible brother, by all accounts. 'I can manage, but come and have a *chota peg* while they find him. It's early, but I could do with it.'

They followed him up to his suite and settled themselves while his *sirdar* went for brandy. 'Horse put its foot in a hole?' Daniel asked.

'Nothing so ordinary. I damn nearly collided with Lady Perdita, who was riding as if she'd a fox in her sights. I reined in hard to stop a crash and the horse over balanced. She wasn't hurt,' he added as Callum opened his mouth. 'Interesting coincidence, meeting her here. My family are neighbours to hers, but it is years since I have seen her.'

'Did you quarrel in those days?' Daniel asked, earning himself a sharp kick on the ankle from his brother.

'Ah, you noticed a certain friction? When we were children I teased her, as boys will torment small and unprepossessing females who tag around after them. I was not aware she was in India.'

'Oh, well, after the elopement,' Daniel began. 'Er… you did know about that?'

'Of course,' Alistair said. Well, he had heard about a scandal yesterday. That was near enough the truth, and he was damnably curious all of a sudden.

'No harm in speaking of it then, especially as you know the family. My cousin wrote all about it. Lady P. ran off with some fellow, furious father found them on the road to Gretna, old Lady St George was on hand to observe and report on every salacious detail—all the usual stuff and a full-blown scandal as a result.'

'No so very bad if Lord Wycombe caught them,' Alistair said casually as the manservant came back, poured brandy and reported that the doctor had gone out, but was expected back soon.

'Well, yes, normally even Lady St George could have

been kept quiet, I expect. Only trouble was, they'd set out from London and Papa caught them halfway up Lancashire.'

'Ah.' One night, possibly two, alone with her lover. A scandal indeed. 'Why didn't she marry the fellow?' Wycombe was rich enough and influential enough to force almost anyone, short of a royal duke, to the altar and to keep their mouths shut afterwards. A really unsuitable son-in-law could always be shipped off to a fatally unhealthy spot in the West Indies later.

'She wouldn't have him, apparently. Refused point blank. According to my cousin she said he snored, had the courage of a vole and the instincts of a weasel and while she was quite willing to admit she had made a serious mistake she had no intention of living with it. So her father packed her off here to stay with her aunt, Lady Webb.'

'Daniel,' Callum snapped, 'you are gossiping about a lady of our acquaintance.'

'Who is perfectly willing to mention it herself,' his twin retorted. 'I heard her only the other day at the picnic. Miss Eppingham said something snide about scandalous goings-on and Lady Perdita remarked that she was more than happy to pass on the benefits of her experience if it prevented Miss Eppingham making a cake of herself over Major Giddings, who, she could assure her, had the morals of a civet cat and was only after Miss E.'s dowry. I don't know how I managed not to roar with laughter.'

That sounded like attack as a form of defence, Alistair thought as Daniel knocked back his brandy and Callum shook his head at him. Dita surely couldn't be so brazen as not to care and he rather admired the courage it showed to acknowledge the facts and bite back. He also admired Wycombe's masterly manner of dealing with the scandal. He had got his daughter out of London society and at the same time had placed her in a situation where it would be well known that she was not carrying a child. Three months' passage on an East Indiaman gave no possibility of hiding such a thing.

But what the devil was Dita doing running off with a man she didn't want to marry? Perhaps he was wrong and she really was the foolish romantic he had teased her with being. She certainly knew how to flirt—he had seen her working her wiles on Daniel Chatterton last night—but, strangely, she had not done so with him. Obviously he annoyed her too much.

But, whatever she thought of him, the more distance there was between them mentally, the better, because there was going to be virtually none physically on that ship and he was very aware of the reaction his body had to her. He wanted Perdita Brooke for all the wrong reasons; he just had to be careful that wanting was all it came to. Alistair leaned back and savoured the brandy. Taking care had never been his strong suit.

'Perdita, look at you!' Emma Webb stood in the midst of trunks and silver paper and frowned at her niece. 'Your hair is half down and your neckcloth is missing. What on earth has occurred?'

'There was an accident on the *maidan*.' Dita came right into the room, stripped off her gloves and kissed her aunt on the cheek. 'It is nothing to worry about, dearest. Lord Lyndon took a fall and he was bleeding, so my neckcloth seemed the best bandage.' She kept going, into the dressing room, and smiled at the *ayah* who was pouring water for her bath from a brass jug.

'Oh?' Her aunt came to the door, a half-folded shawl

in her hands. 'Someone said you were arguing with him last night. Oh dear, I really am not the good chaperon my brother expected.'

'We have not seen each other since I was sixteen, Aunt Emma,' Dita said, stepping out of her habit. 'And we simply picked up the same squabble about a frog that we parted on. He is just as infuriating now as he was then.'

And even more impossibly attractive, unfortunately. In the past, when she had told herself that the adult Alistair Lyndon would be nothing like the young man she had known and adored eight years ago, she had never envisaged the possibility that he would be even more desirable. It was only physical, of course. She was a grown woman, she understood these things now. She had given him her virginity: it was no wonder, with no lover since then, that she reacted to him.

It was a pity he did not have a squint or a skin condition or a double chin or a braying laugh. It was much easier to be irritated by someone if one was not also fighting a most improper desire to…

Dita put a firm lid on her imagination and sat down in eight inches of tepid water, an effective counter to torrid thoughts. It was most peculiar. She had convinced herself that she wanted to marry Stephen Doyle until he had tried to make love to her; then she had been equally convinced that she must escape the moment she could lay her hands on his wallet and her own money that was in it.

She was equally convinced now that Alistair Lyndon was the most provoking man of her acquaintance as well as being an insensitive rake—and yet she wanted to kiss him again until they were both dizzy, which probably meant something, if only that she was prone to the most shocking desires and was incapable of learning from the past.

'I think everything is packed now,' Emma said with satisfaction from the bedchamber. 'And the trunks have gone off to the ship, which just leaves what you need on the voyage to be checked. Twelve weeks is a long time if we forget anything.' She reappeared as Dita stepped out of the bath and was wrapped in a vast linen sheet. 'I do hope Mrs Bastable proves as reliable as she appears. But she seems very happy to look after you and Miss Heydon.'

Averil was going to England for the first time since she was a toddler in order to marry Viscount Bradon, a man she had never met. *Perhaps I should let Papa choose me a husband*, Dita thought. *He couldn't do much worse than I have so far.* And her father was unlikely to pick on a pale imitation of Alistair Lyndon as she had done so unwittingly, it seemed. 'It isn't often that we see brides going in that direction,' Lady Webb added.

'Do you think me a failure?' Dita asked, half-serious, as her maid combed out her hair. 'After all, I came over with the Fishing Fleet and I haven't caught so much as a sprat.' *And do I want to marry anyway? Men are so fortunate, they can take a lover, no one thinks any the worse of them. I will have money of my own next year when I am twenty five...*

'Oh, don't call it that,' her aunt scolded. 'There are lots of reasons for young ladies to come India, not just to catch husbands.'

'I can't think of any,' Dita said. 'Other than escaping a scandal, of course. I am certain Papa was hoping I would catch an up-and-coming star in the East India Company firmament, just like you did.'

'Yes, I did, didn't I?' Lady Webb said happily. 'Darling George is a treasure. But not everyone wants to have to deal with the climate, or face years of separation for the sake of the children's health.' She picked up a list and conned it. 'And you will be going home with that silly business all behind you and just in time for the Season, too.'

That silly business. Three words to dismiss disillusion and self-recrimination and the most terrible family rows. Papa had been utterly and completely correct about Stephen Doyle, which meant that her own judgement of men must be utterly and completely at fault. On that basis Alistair Lyndon was a model of perfection and virtue. Dita smiled to herself—no, she was right about him, at least: the man was a rake.

10th December 1808

'Two weeks to Christmas,' Dita said as she hugged her aunt on the steps of the *ghat*. 'It seems hard to imagine in this climate. But I have left presents for you and Uncle on the dressing table in my room, and something for all the servants.' She was babbling, she knew it, but it was hard to say goodbye when you had no idea if you would ever see the person again.

'And I have put something in your bag,' Emma said with a watery smile. 'Goodness knows what happens about Christmas celebrations on board. Now, are you sure you have everything?'

'I went out yesterday,' her uncle assured her, patting his wife on the shoulder and obviously worried that she would burst into tears. 'You've got a nice compartment in the roundhouse below the poop deck, just as I was promised. That will be much quieter and the odours and noise will be less than in the Great Cabin below. It is all ladies in there as well, and you will be dining at the captain's table in the cuddy with the select passengers.'

'But those wretched canvas partitions,' his wife protested. 'I would feel happier if she was in a cabin with bulkheads.'

It had been a subject for discussion and worry for weeks. 'The partitions give better ventilation,' Dita said. 'I felt perfectly secure on the outward passage, but that was in a compartment forward of the Great Cabin and it was so very stuffy.' And revoltingly smelly by the time they had been at sea for a month.

'And all your furniture is in place and secured,' her uncle continued. *All* made it sound as though she was occupying a suite. The box bed that was bolted to the deck was a fixture, but passengers were expected to supply anything else they needed for their comfort in the little square of space they could call their own. Dita had a new coir mattress and feather pillow, her bed linen and towels, an ingenious dressing chest that could support a washbasin or her writing slope and an upright chair. Her trunk would have to act as both wardrobe and table and her smaller bags must be squashed under the bunk.

'And there are *necessaries* for the passengers' and officers' use on this ship,' Lord Webb added. Which was a mercy and an improvement on a slop bucket or the horrors of the heads—essentially holes giving on to the sea below—that had been the only options on the outward passage.

'I shall be wonderfully comfortable,' Dita assured them. 'Look, they want us to go down to the boats now.'

Plunging into the scrimmage of passengers, porters, beggars, sailors and screaming children was better than dragging out this parting any longer, even if her stomach was in knots at the thought of getting into the boat that was ferrying passengers to the ship. It hurt to part with two people who had been understanding and kindly beyond her expectations or deserts, and she feared she would cling and weep and upset her aunt in a moment.

'I love you both. I've written, it is with the Christmas presents. I must go.' Her uncle took her arm and made sure the porter was with them, then, leaving her aunt sniffing into her handkerchief, he shouldered his way to the uneven steps leading down into the fast-running brown water.

'Hold tight to me! Mind how you go, my dear.' The jostling was worse on the steps, her foot slipped on slime and she clutched wildly for support as the narrow boat swung away and the water yawned before her.

'Lady Perdita! Your hand, ma'am.' It was Alistair, standing on the thwarts. 'I have her, sir.' He caught her hand, steadied her, then handed her back to one of the Chatterton twins who was standing behind him.

'Sit here, Lady Perdita.' This twin was Callum, she decided, smiling thanks at him and trying to catch her breath while her uncle and Alistair organised her few items of hand baggage and saw them stowed under the plank she was perched on. 'An unpleasant scrum up there, is it not?'

'Yes.' She swallowed hard, nodded, managed a smile and a wave for her uncle as the boat was pushed off. Alistair came and sat opposite her. 'Thank you. I am the most terrible coward about water. The big ship is all right. It is just when I am close to it like this.' She was gabbling, she could hear herself.

'What gave you a fear of it?' Alistair asked. He held her gaze and she realised he was trying to distract her from the fact that they were in an open boat very low in the water. 'I imagine it must have been quite a fright to alarm someone of your spirit.'

'Why, thank you.' Goodness, he was being positively kind to her. Dita smiled and felt the panic subside a little.

'Presumably you got into some ridiculous scrape,' he added and the smile froze as the old guilt washed through her.

Without meaning, to she gabbled the whole story. 'I was walking on the beach with my governess when I was eight and a big wave caught me, rolled me out over the pebbles and down, deep.' She could still close her eyes and see the underneath of the wave, the green tunnel-shape above her, trapping her with no air, beating her down on to the stones and the rocks. 'Miss Richards went in after me and she managed to drag me to the beach. Then the next wave took her. She nearly drowned and I couldn't help her—my leg was broken. The poor woman caught pneumonia and almost died.'

'Of course you couldn't have helped,' Callum said firmly. 'You were a child and injured.'

'But Lord Lyndon is correct—I had disobeyed her and was walking too close to the water. It was my fault.' No one had beaten her for her bad behaviour, for Miss Richards had told no one. But the guilt over her childish defiance had never gone away and the fear of the sea at close quarters had never left her.

'It has not prevented you from taking risks,' Alistair said dispassionately.

'Lyndon.' Chatterton's tone held a warning.

Alistair raised one eyebrow, unintimidated. 'Lady Perdita prizes frankness, I think.'

'It is certainly better than hypocrisy,' she snapped. 'And, no, it did not stop me taking risks, only, after that, I tried to be certain they were my risks alone.'

'My leg is much better.' Alistair delivered the apparent *non sequitur* in a conversational tone.

'I cannot allow for persons equally as reckless as I am,' Dita said sweetly. 'I am so glad you are suffering no serious consequences for your dangerous riding.'

'We're here,' Chatterton said with the air of a man who wished he was anywhere rather than in the middle of a polite aristocratic squabble.

'And they are lowering a bo'sun's chair for the ladies,' said Alistair, getting to his feet. 'Here! You! This lady first.'

'What? No! I mean I can wait!' Dita found herself ruthlessly bundled into the box-like seat on the end of a rope and then she was swung up in the air, dangled sickeningly over the water and landed with a thump on the deck.

'Oh! The wretched—'

'Ma'am? Fast is the best way to come up, in my opinion, no time to think about it.' A polite young man was at her elbow. 'Lady Perdita? I'm Tompkins, one of the lieutenants. Lord Webb asked me to look out for you. We met at the reception, ma'am.'

'Mr Tompkins.' Dita swallowed and her stomach returned to its normal position. 'Of course, I remember you.'

'Shall I show you to your cabin, ma'am?'

'Just a moment. I wish to thank the gentleman who assisted me just now.'

The ladies and children continued to be hoisted on board with the chair. Most of them screamed all the way up. *At least I did not scream*, she thought, catching at the shreds of her dignity. What had she been thinking of, to blurt out that childhood nightmare to the men? Surely she had more control than that? But the tossing open boat had frightened her, fretting at nerves already raw with the sadness of departure and the apprehension of what was to come in England. And so her courage had failed her.

Dita gritted her teeth and waited until the men began to come up the rope ladder that had been lowered over the side, then she walked across to Alistair where he stood with Callum Chatterton.

'Thank you very much for your help, gentlemen,' she said with a warm smile for Callum. 'Lord Lyndon, you are *so* masterful I fear you will have to exercise great discretion on the voyage. You were observed by a number of most susceptible young ladies who will all now think you the very model of a man of action and will be seeking every opportunity to be rescued by you. I will do my best to warn them off, but, of course, they will think me merely jealous.'

She batted her eyelashes at him and walked back to Lieutenant Tompkins. Behind her she heard a snort of laugher from Mr Chatterton and a resounding silence from Alistair. This time she had had the last word.

Chapter Four

Dita sat in her cabin space and tried to make herself get up and go outside. Through the salt-stained window that was one of the great luxuries of the roundhouse accommodation she could see that they were under way down the Hooghly.

Every excuse she could think of to stay where she was had been exhausted. She had arranged her possessions as neatly as possible; thrown a colourful shawl over the bed; hung family miniatures on nails on the bulkhead; wedged books—all of them novels—into a makeshift shelf; refused the offer of assistance from Mrs Bastable's maid on the grounds that there was barely room for one person, let alone two, in the space available; washed her face and hands, tidied her hair. Now there was no reason to stay there, other than a completely irrational desire to avoid Alistair Lyndon.

'Perdita? We'll be sailing in a moment—aren't you coming on deck?' Averil called from the next compartment, just the other side of one canvas wall.

Courage, Dita, she thought, clenching her hands into

tight fists. *You can't stay here for three months.* She had grown up knowing that she was plain and so she had learned to create an aura of style and charm that deceived most people into not noticing. She was rebellious and contrary and she had taught herself to control that, so when things went wrong it was only she who was hurt. Or so she thought until her hideous mistake with Stephen Doyle meant the whole family had had to deal with the resulting gossip. And in India she had coped with the talk by the simple method of pretending that she did not care.

But I do, she thought. *I do care. And I care what Alistair thinks of me and I am a fool to do so.* The young man she had adored had grown up to be a rake and the heir to a marquisate and she could guess what he thought about the girl next door who had a smirched reputation and a sharp tongue. *Hypocrisy.* Had the tender intensity with which he had made love to her eight years ago been simply the wiles of a youth who was going to grow up into a rake? It must have been, for he showed no signs of remembering; surely if he had cared in the slightest, he would recall calling her his darling Dita, his sweet, his dear girl…

'I'm coming!' she called to Averil, fixing a smile on her face because she knew it would show in her voice. 'Just let me get my bonnet on.' She peered into the mirror that folded up from the dressing stand and pinched the colour into her cheeks, checked that the candle-soot on her lashes had not smudged, tied on her most becoming sunbonnet with the bow at a coquettish angle under her chin and unfastened the canvas flap. 'Here I am.'

Averil linked arms with the easy friendliness that always charmed Dita. Miss Heydon was shy with strangers, but once she decided she was your friend the reserve melted. 'The start of our adventure! Is this not exciting?'

'You won't say that after four weeks when everything smells like a farmyard and the weather is rough and we haven't had fresh supplies for weeks and you want to scream if you ever see the same faces again,' Dita warned as they emerged on to the deck.

'I was forgetting you had done this before. I cannot remember coming to India, I was so young.' Averil unfurled her parasol and put one hand on the rail. 'My last look at Calcutta.'

'Don't you mind leaving?' Dita asked.

'Yes. But it is my duty, I know that. I am making an excellent marriage and the connection will do Papa and my brothers so much good. It would be different if Mama was still alive—far harder.'

In effect, Dita thought, *you are being sold off to an impoverished aristocratic family in return for influence when your family returns to England.* 'Lord Bradon is a most amiable gentleman,' she said. It was how she had described him before, when Averil had been excited to learn that Dita knew her betrothed, but she could think of nothing more positive to say about him. *Cold, conventional, very conscious of his station in life*—nothing there to please her friend. And his father, the Earl of Kingsbury, was a cynical and hardened gamester whose expensive habits were the reason for this match.

She only hoped that Sir Jeremiah Heydon had tied up his daughter's dowry tightly, but she guessed such a wily and wealthy nabob would be alert on every suit.

'You'll have three months to enjoy yourself as a single lady, at any rate,' she said. 'There are several gentlemen who will want to flirt.'

'I couldn't!' Averil glanced along the deck to where

the bachelors were lining the rail. 'I have no idea how to, in any case. I'm far too shy, even with pleasant young men like the Chatterton brothers, and as for the more... er...' She was looking directly at Alistair Lyndon.

As if he had felt the scrutiny Alister looked round and doffed his hat. 'Indeed,' Dita agreed, as she returned the gesture with an inclination of the head a dowager duchess would have been proud of. Alistair raised an eyebrow—an infuriating skill—and returned to his contemplation of the view. 'Lord Lyndon is definitely *er.* Best avoided, in fact.'

'But he likes you, and you are not afraid of him. In fact,' Averil observed shrewdly, 'that is probably *why* he likes you. You don't blush and mumble like I do or giggle like those silly girls over there.' She gestured towards a small group of merchants' daughters who were jostling for the best position close to the men.

'*Likes* me?' Dita stared at her. 'Alistair Lyndon hasn't changed his opinion of me since that encounter at the reception, and the accident we had on the *maidan* only made things worse. And don't forget he knew me years ago. To him I am just the plain little girl from the neighbouring estate who was scared of frogs and tagged along being a nuisance. He was kind to me like a brother is to an irritating little sister.' *And who then grew up to discover that she was embarrassingly besotted by him.*

'Well, you aren't plain now,' Averil said, her eyes fixed on the shore as the *Bengal Queen* slipped downriver. 'I am pretty, I think, but you have style and panache and a certain something.'

'Why, thank you!' Dita was touched. 'But as neither of us are husband-hunting, we may relax and observe our female companions making cakes of themselves without the slightest pang—which, men being the contrary creatures they are, is probably enough to make us the most desirable women on board!'

Dinner at two o'clock gave no immediate opportunity to test Dita's theory about desirability. The twenty highest-ranking passengers assembled in the cuddy, a few steps down from the roundhouse, and engaged in polite conversation and a certain jostling for position. Everyone else ate in the Great Cabin.

Captain Archibald had a firm grasp of precedent and Dita found herself on his left with Alistair on her left hand. Averil was relegated to the foot of the table with a mere younger son of a bishop on one side and a Chatterton twin on the other.

'Is your accommodation comfortable, my lord?' she ventured, keeping a watchful eye on the tureen of mutton soup that was being ladled out to the peril of the ladies' gowns.

'It is off the Great Cabin,' Alistair said. 'There is a reasonable amount of room, but there are also two families with small children and I expect the noise to be considerable. You, on the other hand, will have the sailors traipsing about overhead at all hours and I rather think the chickens are caged on the poop deck. You are spared the goats, however.'

'But we have opening windows.'

'All the better for the feathers to get in.'

Dita searched for neutral conversation and found herself uncharacteristically tongue-tied. This was torture. The way they had parted—even if he had no recollection of it—made reminiscence of their childhood too painful. She was determined not to say anything even remotely provocative or flirtatious and it was not proper to discuss further details of their accommodation.

'How do you propose to pass the voyage, my lord?' she enquired at last when the soup was removed and replaced with curried fish.

'Writing,' Alistair said, as he passed her a dish of chutney.

The ship was still in the river, its motion gentle, but Dita almost dropped the dish. 'Writing?'

'I have been travelling ever since I came to the East,' he said. 'I have kept notebooks the entire time and I want to create something from that for my own satisfaction, if nothing else.'

'I will look forward to reading it when it is published.' Alistair gave her a satirical look. 'I mean it. I wish I had been able to travel. My aunt and uncle were most resistant to the idea when I suggested it.'

'I am not surprised. India is not a country for young women to go careering around looking for adventures.'

'I did not want to *career around*,' Dita retorted, 'I wanted to observe and to learn.'

'Indeed.' His voice expressed polite scepticism. 'You had ambitions of dressing up as a man and travelling incognito?'

'No, I did not.' Dita speared some spiced cauliflower and imagined Alistair on the end of her fork. 'I am simply interested in how other people live. Apparently this is permissible for a man, according to you, but not for a woman. How hypocritical.'

'Merely practical. It is dangerous'. He gestured with his right hand, freed now of its bandage.

Dita eyed the headed slash across the back, red against the tan. 'I was not intending to throw myself at the wildlife, my lord.'

'Some of the interesting local people are equally as dangerous and the wildlife, I assure you, is more likely to throw itself at you than vice versa. It is no country for romantic, headstrong and pampered young females, Lady Perdita.'

'You think me pampered?' she enquired while the steward cleared the plates.

'Are you not? You accept the romantic and headstrong, I note.'

'I see nothing wrong with romance.'

'Except that it is bound to end in disillusion at the very best and farcical tragedy at the worst.' He spoke lightly, but something in his voice, some shading, hinted at a personal meaning.

'You speak from experience, my lord?' Dita enquired in a tone of regrettable pertness to cover her own feelings. He had fallen in love with someone and been hurt, she was certain. And she was equally certain he would die rather than admit it, just as she could never confess how she felt for him. How she had once felt, she corrected herself.

'No,' he drawled, his attention apparently fixed on the bowl of fruit the steward was proffering. 'Merely observation. Might I peel you a mango, Lady Perdita?'

'They are so juicy, no doubt you would require a bath afterwards,' she responded, her mind distracted by the puzzle of how she felt about him now. Had she ever truly been in love with him, and if so, how could that die as it surely had, leaving only physical desire behind? It must have been merely a painful infatuation, the effect of emotion and proximity when she was on the verge of womanhood, unused to the changes in her body and her feelings. It would have passed, surely, if she had not stumbled into his arms at almost the moment she had realised how she felt.

But if it was merely infatuation, why had she been so

taken in by Stephen? Perhaps one was always attracted to the same looks in a man…Then she saw the expression on Lady Grimshaw's face. Oh goodness, what had she just said?

'Bath,' Alistair murmured. He must have seen the look of panic cross her face. 'How fast of you to discuss gentlemen's ablutions, Lady Perdita,' he added, loudly enough for the elderly matron's gimlet gaze to fix on them intently.

'Oh, do hush,' she hissed back, stifling the giggle that was trying to escape. 'I am in enough disgrace with her already.'

Alistair began to peel the mango with a small, wickedly sharp knife that he had removed from an inner pocket. 'What for?' he asked, slicing a succulent segment off the stone and on to her plate.

'Existing,' Dita said as she cut a delicate slither and tried it. 'Thank you for this, it is delicious.'

'You have been setting Calcutta society by the ears, have you?' Alistair gestured to the steward who brought him a finger bowl and napkin. 'You must tell me all about it.'

'Not here,' Dita said and took another prim nibble of the fruit. Lady Grimshaw turned her attention to Averil, who was blushing at Daniel Chatterton's flirtatious remarks.

'Later, then,' Alistair said and, before she could retort that he was the last person on the ship to whom she would confide the gossip that seemed to follow her, he turned to Mrs Edwards on his other side and was promptly silenced by her garrulous complaints on the subject of the size of the cabins and the noise of the Tompkinson children.

Dita fixed a smile on her lips and asked the captain

how many voyages he had undertaken; that, at least, was a perfectly harmless topic of conversation.

When dinner was over she went to Averil and swept her out of the cuddy and up on to the poop deck.

'Come and look at the chickens, or the view, or something.'

'Are you attempting to avoid Lord Lyndon, by any chance?' Averil lifted her skirts out of the way of a hen that had escaped from its coop and was evading the efforts of a member of the crew to recapture it.

'Most definitely,' Dita said. 'The provoking man seems determined to tease me. He almost made me giggle right under Lady Grimshaw's nose and I have the lowering suspicion that he has heard all about the scandal in England and has concluded that I will be receptive to any liberties he might take.'

The fact that she knew she would be severely tempted if Alistair attempted to kiss her again did nothing to calm her inner alarm.

'Forgive me for mentioning it,' Averil ventured, 'but perhaps if one of the older ladies were to hint him away? If he has heard of the incident and has wrongly concluded that you... I mean,' she persisted, blushing furiously, 'if he mistakenly thinks you are not...'

'I spent two nights in inn bedchambers with a man to whom I was not married,' Dita said. 'An overrated experience, I might add.'

It had been a dreadful disillusion to discover that the man she had thought was perfect in looks and in character was a money-hungry boor with the finesse of a bull in a china shop when it came to making love.

The realisation that she had made a terrible mistake had begun to dawn on her by the time the chaise hired with her money had reached Hitchin. Stephen had no longer troubled to be charming, to be witty, to converse or to show the quick appreciation of her thoughts he had always counterfeited before. He had fretted about pursuit and asked interminable questions about her access to her funds. When the postillions, who quite obviously realised that an elopement was afoot, became impertinent he blustered ineffectually and Dita had to snub them with a few well-chosen words.

By the time they had stopped for the first night Dita decided she had had enough and declared that she would hire another chaise and return alone. It was then that she discovered that Stephen was quite capable of forcing her into the inn and up to a bedchamber and that he had removed all the money from her luggage and reticule.

The effort to keep him from her bed involved a sleepless night and a willingness to stab him with a table knife after he had run the gamut from trying to charm her, to attempting to maul her, to a desperate attempt to force her.

The second day had been worse. He had been furious and sulky and every pretence that this was anything but an abduction had gone. Papa had caught up with them as they had arrived in Preston and by that time she was so exhausted by lack of sleep that she had simply flung herself on his chest and sobbed, unconscious of the audience in the inn yard and uncaring about his anger.

Averil was blushing, but it did not stop her putting the question she was obviously dying to ask. 'Is it really horrid? You know, one hears such things.'

'With the wrong man it is,' Dita said with feeling. And that had been without the actual act taking place. She shuddered to think what it would have been like if Stephen had forced her. 'With the right one—' She stopped on the verge of admitting that it was very pleasurable indeed.

'I am sure it would be wonderful,' she said, as if she did not know. There was no point in making Averil fearful of her own nuptials, even if she suspected that her betrothed had no finesse to speak of. Dita shivered a little, wondering what would happen if another man tried to make love to her.

Oh, but she had enjoyed Alistair's impertinent kiss on the *maidan*. The cockerel in the chicken coop flapped up on to the perch and crowed loudly, ruffling his feathers and throwing his head back. 'Yes, you are a fine fellow,' she said to him and he crowed again. Male creatures were all the same, she told herself. They needed feminine admiration and attention all the time. And Alistair had sensed she had enjoyed that meeting of lips, she was certain. No wonder he was so confident about teasing her. It would be well to exercise considerable caution if he was to not to guess the way she felt about him now—which could be summed up in three words: desirable, treacherous, trouble.

'Let us walk,' she said firmly. 'We must exercise every day, it will help keep us healthy.'

They strolled round and round the poop deck, both of them sunk, Dita guessed, in rather different thoughts about wedding nights. The view was not particularly diverting, for the river banks were hardly higher than the water, here in the delta of the Ganges, and mud banks, fields covered in winter stubble and herds of buffalo were all that could be seen between the small villages that dotted the higher ground.

'I had better go and unpack,' Averil said after a while. 'I can see now why I was advised to bring a hammer and nails to hang things up. I cannot imagine how I am ever going to fit everything in and still live in that space. It is a quarter the size of my dressing room at home!'

Dita could well believe it. For all that she was unpretentious and unspoiled, Averil was used to considerable luxury. She wondered what she would make of the chilly Spartan grandeur of her betrothed's home. But doubtless her own money would go a long way to making it comfortable.

When her friend went below Dita leaned her forearms on the rail and let herself fall into a daydream. Soon the rhythms of shipboard life would assert themselves and the passengers would develop a routine that could become quite numbing until landfalls, quarrels or hurricanes enlivened things. On the way out she had read her way through a trunk full of books, determined to keep her mind off her problems with light fiction. Now she was equally determined to face the reality of her future. There was only one problem, Dita realised: she had no idea what she wanted that to be.

'That was a big enough sigh to add speed to the sails.'

She turned her head, but she had no need to look to know who that was, lounging against the rail beside her. Her biggest problem, in the flesh.

'I was trying to decide what life will be like when I return to England,' she replied with total honesty. 'What I want it to be like.' *Whatever was the matter with me when I was sixteen? Perhaps all girls that age believe themselves in love without receiving the slightest encouragement.* Only she had received rather more than a little encouragement. She sighed again, thinking of the girl newly emerged from childhood, suddenly realising the boy she had idolised had turned into a young man, just as she was becoming a woman.

'Will the scandal be forgotten?' Alistair asked.

Dita blinked at him. Most people politely pretended they knew nothing about it, to her face at least. Only the more catty of the young women would make snide remarks, or the chaperons hint that she needed to be particularly careful in what she did.

'You know about it?'

'You eloped and your father caught up with you after two nights on the road and you refused to marry the man concerned.' Alistair shifted so that his elbow almost met hers on the rail. Her breath hitched as though he had touched her. 'Is that a fair summary?'

'Fair enough,' Dita conceded.

'Why did you refuse?'

'Because I discovered he was less than the man I thought he was.'

'In bed?'

'No! What a question!' The laugh was surprised out of her by his outrageous words. She twisted to stare at him. No, this was not the boy she remembered, but that boy was still there in this man. The trouble was, every feminine instinct she possessed desired him. Him, Alistair, as he was now.

He was waiting for her answer and she made herself speak the truth. 'He was after my money. Which wouldn't have been so bad if he hadn't been a bore and a lout into the bargain. He must be a very good actor.' *Or I must have been blinded by the need to escape the Marriage Mart, the restrictions of life as a single young woman.*

'Or you are a very poor judge of men?' Alistair suggested.

'Perhaps,' Dita conceded. 'But I have *your* measure, my lord.'

He was staring out to sea and she could study his

profile for a moment. She had been correct when she had told Daniel Chatterton that the savage slash of the scar on his face would only enhance his attractiveness. Combined with the patrician profile and his arresting eyes, it gave him a dangerous edge that had been missing before.

Then he turned his head and she looked into his eyes and realised that the edge had been there already: experience, intelligence, darkness. 'Oh yes?'

She straightened up, pleased to find she could face him without a blush on her cheeks; it had felt for a moment as though every thought was imprinted on her forehead. Alistair turned so he lounged back against the rail, shamelessly watching her. She tried not to stare back, but it was hard. He looked so strong and free. Bare-headed, the breeze stirred his hair and the sun gilded his tanned skin. *I want him. He fills me with desire, quite simple and quite impure.*

'You have a great deal in common with that creature there.' She nodded towards the cockerel's cage. 'You are flamboyant, sure of yourself and dangerous to passing females.'

There was no retort, not until she was halfway across the deck and congratulating herself on putting him firmly—safely—in his place. His crack of laughter had her pursing her lips, but his words sent her down the companionway with something perilously close to an angry flounce.

'Why, thank you, Dita. I shall treasure the compliment.'

Chapter Five

After their exchange on the poop deck Dita did her best to avoid Alistair without appearing to do so, and flattered herself that she was succeeding. It did not prevent the disturbing stirring in her blood when she saw him, but it gave her a feeling of safety that, in the restless small hours, she suspected was illusory.

She was helped by the captain relaxing his seating plans at dinner. Having clearly established precedent, he acknowledged that to keep everyone tied to the same dining companions for three months was a recipe for tedium at best and squabbles at worst.

Breakfast and supper were informal meals and by either entering the cuddy with a small group, or after he was already there, Dita ensured she was always sitting a safe distance from Alistair.

During the day, when she was not in her cabin reading or sewing alone or with Averil, she sought out the company of the other young women on deck. They were all engaged in much whispering and secrets, making and wrapping Christmas gifts, teasing each other about who was giving what to which of the men.

They irritated her with their vapid conversation, giggling attempts to flirt with any passing male and obsession with clothes and gossip, but they provided concealment, much, she thought wryly, as one swamp deer is safer from the tiger in the midst of the herd.

Alistair had no way of realising that this was not her natural habitat, she thought, as she watched him from under the tilted brim of her parasol while Miss Hemming confided her plan to get Daniel Chatterton alone under the stars that evening.

It was on the tip of her tongue to point out that Mr Chatterton was already betrothed, and had been for years to a young woman who awaited him in England, and that with the amount of cloud cover just now there would be no stars to flirt beneath. But she bit her lip and kept the tart remarks to herself. Alistair bowed slightly as he passed the group, accepting both the wide-eyed looks, nervous titters and her own frigid inclination of the head with equal composure.

Now, why is Dita so set on avoiding me, I wonder? Those chattering ninnies are boring her to distraction and in five days I cannot believe we have not sat next to each other for a meal simply by chance. That kiss on the maidan? *Surely not. Dita has more spirit than to flee because of that, even if she knows I want to do it again. And more. And I'll wager so does she.*

'Oh, Lord Lyndon!' It was one of the Misses Whyton, indistinguishable from each other and with a tendency to speak in exclamations.

He stopped and bowed. 'Miss Whyton?'

'What is your favourite colour, Lord Lyndon?'

Ah, Christmas gifts. He had hoped to escape that by the simple expedient of not flirting with any of the little peahens, but it was obviously not working. 'Black,' he drawled, producing what he hoped was a sinister smile.

'Ooh!' She retreated to her sister's side, a frown giving her face more expression than it usually bore. Apparently whatever she was making would not work well in mourning tones.

He glanced across and saw Dita's head bent over a book. Now, it would be amusing to surprise her with a Christmas gift. What a pity he had no mistletoe to accompany it.

Or, perhaps he could improvise; he certainly had the berries. Smiling to himself as he plotted, Alistair strolled along the main deck to where the Chatterton twins and a few of the other young men had gathered. With the captain's permission they were going to climb the rigging. After a few days out most of them were already feeling the lack of exercise and it seemed an interesting way of stretching muscles without overly shocking the ladies. Wrestling, sparring or singlestick bouts would have to be indulged in only when a female audience could be avoided.

Daniel and Callum had already taken off their coats and were eyeing the network of ropes as they soared up the main mast. 'It looks easy enough,' Daniel said. 'Climb up on the outside and you are leaning into the rigging the whole way.'

'Until you get to the crow's nest,' his brother pointed out. 'Then you have to swing round to the inside and climb up the hole next to the mast.'

'Bare feet,' Alistair said. Like the other younger men he was wearing loose cotton trousers. He heeled off his shoes as he looked up. 'I tried this on the way out.'

He squinted up at the height and added, 'Smaller ship, though!'

'We cannot all get up there at once, not with a sailor already in the crow's nest,' Callum pointed out, and the others moved off to stand at the foot of the smaller foremast, leaving the Chattertons and Alistair in possession of the main mast.

'We three can if we move out along those ropes the sailors stand on to bundle up the sails,' Daniel pointed out. 'And don't snort at me, Cal, I don't know the name of them and neither do you, I wager.'

'Sounds as though that will work.' Alistair took a yard in his hand and swung up to stand on the rail. 'Let's try it.'

The tarred rope was rough under the softer skin of his arches, but it gave a good grip and his hands were toughened by long hours of riding without gloves. It felt good to reach and stretch and use his muscles to pull himself up and to counteract the roll of the ship, one minute dropping him against the rigging, the next forcing him to hang on with stretched arms and braced legs over the sea.

The newly healed wound in his thigh reminded him of its presence with every contraction of the muscle, but it was the ache of under-use and weakness, not the pain of the wound tearing open. His right hand was not fully right either, he noticed with clinical detachment, and compensated by taking more care with the grip.

The wind blew his hair off his face and ripped through his thin shirt and Alistair found he was grinning as he climbed. Daniel appeared beside him, panting with effort as he overtook. From below Callum called, 'It isn't a race, you idiot!'

But Daniel was already twisting around the edge of

the rigging to hang downwards for the few perilous feet up into the crow's nest. Alistair heard the look-out greeting Chatterton as he reached the top spar of the mainsail himself and eyed the thin rope swinging beneath it. It was a tricky transfer, but if sailors could do it in a storm, he told himself, so could he. There was an interesting moment as the sail flapped and the foot rope swayed and then he was standing with his body thrown over the spar, looking down at the belly of the sail.

Callum appeared beside him. 'I wouldn't want to do this in a gale at night!' he shouted.

'No. Damn good reason not to get press-ganged,' Alistair agreed as he twisted to look back over his shoulder. The young women had stopped all pretence of ignoring the men and were standing staring up at them. Dita, hatless, was easy to pick out, her face smoothed into a perfect oval by the distance.

'We have an audience,' he remarked.

'Then let's get down before Daniel and make the most of the admiration,' Callum said with a grin.

Going down was no easier, as Alistair remembered. As he glanced down at the ladies, and to set his feet right on the rigging, the scene below seemed to corkscrew wildly, as though the top of the mast was fixed and the ship moved beneath it.

'Urgh,' Callum remarked, and climbed down beside him. 'Remind me why this is a good idea.'

'Exercise and impressing the ladies, if that appeals.' Alistair kept pace with him as the rigging widened out. His leg was burning now with the strain, but it would hold him. He'd be glad to relax his hand, though. 'It is Daniel who is betrothed, is it not?'

'Yes,' Callum agreed, somewhat shortly. 'A childhood friend,' he added after another rung down. 'I'm not looking for a wife myself, not yet while I don't know whether the Company wants me to come back out or work in London.' After another two steps down he seemed to unbend a trifle. 'What about you?'

'I certainly require a wife,' Alistair agreed. 'There's the inheritance to think of. I shall no doubt be braving the Marriage Mart this Season in pursuit of a well-bred virgin with the requisite dowry and connections, not a thought in her brain and good child-bearing hips.'

Callum snorted. 'Is there no one below us right this minute with those qualifications? What about Lady P—?'

He broke off, obviously recalling that Dita fell scandalously short of one of Alistair's stated requirements. 'Er, that is—'

'That is, Lady Perdita has enough thoughts in her brain to keep any man in a state of perpetual bemusement,' Alistair said, taking pity on him. 'I have had my fill of troublesome women, I want a placid little English rose.'

And besides, he thought as he jumped down on to the deck and held out a hand to steady Callum, *she certainly hasn't got child-bearing hips. She's still the beanpole she always was.*

A beanpole, he was startled to realise, who stood regarding him with wide-eyed interest. So, she was not above getting in a flutter over displays of male prowess. How unexpected. How stimulating. She came up to him as he shrugged back into his coat and he braced himself for gushing admiration.

'That looks wonderful!' Dita exclaimed, her eyes fixed on the crow's nest and not on him, or any of the men. 'I would love to do that.'

'No! Of course you can't, you're a girl!' It was the

response that had become automatic through years of her tagging along behind him. 'A lady,' he corrected himself as the wide green eyes focused on his face, and he was conscious of an odd feeling of disappointment.

'That's what you always said,' she retorted. 'You always snubbed me, and I always got my way. I climbed the same trees, I learned to swim in the lake—I even rode a cow backwards when you did. Do you remember?'

'Vividly,' Alistair said. 'I got a beating for that. But what you did when you were eight has nothing to do with this. Besides anything else, you couldn't climb rigging in skirts.'

'That is a very good point,' she said, bestowing a smile on him that left him breathless. Before he could think of a response she turned away.

Dita Brooke had obviously been taking lessons in witchcraft, he concluded, wondering whether he was foolishly suspicious to read a promise of trouble into that radiant smile.

'Ooh! Lord Lyndon, you must be ever so strong to do that!' One of the merchants' daughters, he had no idea which, gazed at him in wide-eyed adoration.

'Not at all,' he said, lowering his voice into a conspiratorial whisper. 'I get dizzy at heights and had to be helped by Mr Chatterton there. Fine physical specimen, and all that money, too...' He let his voice trail off in admiration and watched with wicked pleasure as she hurried off to hang on Callum's arm.

Alistair sauntered back to his cabin to wash. He took care not to limp and reflected that unless he wanted to become a circus turn it would be better to confine vigorous exercise to the early morning before the ladies were about.

It was not until he had stripped off his shirt and was pouring water over his head that he identified the strange feeling of disappointment that had hit him during that brief exchange at the foot of the mast. Dita had wanted the adventure, the experience, but for the first time, she did not want it in order to follow him.

But why should she? he thought. He was no longer thirteen, she was no longer eight, and she was most certainly not the troublesome little sister he had always thought of her as. But she was going to be trouble for someone.

Dita retreated to her cabin and piled all the items from on top of her trunk on to the bed so she could open it. She was restless and impatient and they had only been at sea a few days; she needed exercise and adventure and she was going to get it, even if it meant getting up an hour early.

The fact that the close proximity of Alistair Lyndon was contributing to the restlessness could not be helped. She closed her eyes and let her memory bring back the sight of him, his thin shirt flattened against his back by the wind, the muscles in his forearms standing out like cord as he gripped the ropes, the curiously arousing sight of his bare feet. He had always been tall, but the lanky youth had filled out into a well-muscled man.

She had watched him like a hawk for any signs of weakness from his wounds, but he had shown nothing, not until he had strolled away and she had seen what she doubted anyone else had: the effort not to limp. He should take it more easily.

Then she gave herself a little shake. Alistair could look after himself and there was no point in torturing herself with worry about him. She should think about her own plans. Alistair was right, she could not climb in skirts and she couldn't climb at all if the captain realised what she was about, so it was a good thing that she had packed her Indian clothes.

Dita dug out a pile of cottons and laid them on the bed. She had beautiful *shalwa kameezes* in silk, but she had stowed those in the trunks below decks. In her cabin luggage she had kept the simple cotton ones for lounging in comfort in the privacy of her cabin.

She shook out a pair of the trousers, tight in the lower leg, comfortably roomy around the waist and hips: perfect for climbing. And she had a *kurta*, the loose shirt that reached well down her thighs. That would give her plenty of room to move. All she had to do was to wake at dawn.

The deck was cool and damp under her bare feet, still not dry after the early morning holystoning it had received. Most of the crew on deck were gathered near the main mast, with few close to the shorter of the three masts nearest the stern.

Dita dropped her heavy plait of hair down inside the *kurta*, used a coil of rope as a step and climbed on to the rail, her hands tight on the rigging, her eyes fixed on a point above her head and not on the sea. Her heart pounded and for a moment she thought her fear of the water would root her to the spot, but it was far enough below.

No one had noticed her in the early light, they were too busy with their tasks and she had deliberately chosen garments dyed the soft green that, improbably, cow dung produced.

She stepped on to the first horizontal rope in the rigging that tapered upward to the crow's nest and grimaced at the tarry smell and the roughness under her hands and feet. But it felt secure and after a moment she began to climb, slowly and steadily, not looking down.

It was harder than it had looked when the men had done it, but she had expected that. After several minutes she rested, hooking her arms through the ropes and letting her body relax into the rhythm of pitch and roll. Perhaps that was far enough for today; there was a burn in her muscles that warned her they were overstretched and when she risked a downwards glance the deck seemed a dizzying distance below.

Yes, time to get down. As she hung there, deciding how much longer to rest, a figure came out on to the deck. Even foreshortened she recognised Alistair in his shirtsleeves. He seemed to be holding a pole of some kind. He turned as though to climb the companionway to the almost deserted poop deck and as he did so he glanced up.

Dita froze. Would he would recognise her?

'Get down here this instant!' He did not shout, but his voice carried clearly.

Defiant, Dita shook her head and began to climb. She had rested; she could do it and she was not going to come down just because Alistair told her to. A rapid glance showed he was climbing after her and she kept going. But she was slow now, slower than he was, and he reached her as she neared the top where the rigging narrowed sharply.

'Dita, don't you dare try to get into the crow's nest!'

She glanced down to the wind-tousled black head on a level with her ankles, suddenly very glad he was there. 'I have no intention of trying,' she admitted. 'I'll just have a rest and then I'll come down.'

'You are tired?' His face was tipped up to her now,

and the world below him—one moment the sea, the next the hard and unforgiving white deck planks—twisted and turned in the most disconcerting manner.

'Just a little.'

'Hell. Keep still and hang on.'

'I have no intention of doing anything else. Alistair! What on earth are you doing?' He climbed up beside her and then swung over so his body bridged hers and his hands gripped the rope either side of her wrists.

'Stopping you falling off. Your face has gone the nasty shade of green I remember from when you climbed the flagpole on the church tower.'

'Oh.' She certainly felt green now. 'Alistair, you can't do this, I'll push you off.'

'There's hardly any bulk to you,' he said. 'Put one foot down. Good, now the other.'

Awkwardly they began to descend. When the ship swung one way his body crushed hers into the rigging, even though she could feel him fighting to keep his weight off her. When it went the other way she knew his arms would be stretched by the extra extension her body created. She glanced over to his right hand and watched the way his knuckles whitened and the tendons stood out under the strain.

His breath was hot on her neck, her cheek, her ear, and she could feel his heartbeat when his chest pressed into her back. And, as her mind cleared and she gained enough confidence to think of other things, she realised that he was also finding this proximity stimulating—with his groin crushed into her buttocks with every roll of the ship there was no disguising it.

The realisation almost made her lose concentration for a moment. She was enjoying the feel of his body so close too, frustrating though it was to be pinned down like this, unable to do anything but place hands and feet at his command. *I remember how his body felt over mine on a bed. I remember the scent of his skin and his hands on my...*

'We're at the rail. Slide round in front of me and jump down,' Alistair ordered, shaking her out of her sensual reverie.

Dita very much doubted her legs were up to jumping, but she had too much pride to argue. With an awkward twist she swung down from the rigging and landed on the deck on all fours with an inelegant thump. 'Thank you.'

Alistair's face as he straightened up beside her showed nothing but anger. If he had enjoyed being so close to her, it did not show now. 'You idiot! What the blazes do you think you were doing? You could have been killed.'

'I doubt it.' They were attracting attention from some of the deck hands; Dita turned on her heel and walked away towards the cuddy, her shoulders braced against the coming storm. Behind her she could hear the slap of Alistair's bare feet on the deck.

The space was empty, she was relieved to see, and the stewards had not begun to lay the table and set out breakfast. There was little hope of outdistancing Alistair and reaching the roundhouse, although she was going to try—he could hardly pursue her into that all-female sanctuary. Dita lengthened her stride, then his grip on her shoulder stopped her dead in her tracks. His hand was warm and hard and the thin cotton caught in the roughness of his palm. Struggling would be undignified, she told herself.

'I should go and change,' Dita said, her back still turned.

'Not until you give me your word you will not try that

damn-fool trick again.' The thrust of his hand as he spun her round was not gentle, nor was the slap of his other palm as he caught her shoulder to steady her. 'Are you all about in your head, Perdita?'

She tipped up her chin and stared back into the furious tiger eyes with all the insolence she could muster. 'Perdita? Now that *is* serious—you never called me that unless you were very angry with me.' Alistair's eyes narrowed. 'Let me see. The last time must have been when I borrowed your new hunter and rode it.'

'Stole,' he said between gritted teeth. 'And *tried* to ride it. I can recall hauling you out of the ditch by your collar.'

'And you called me *Perdita* for a week afterwards.' She remembered his strength as he had lifted her, the fear in his voice for her—and how that had changed to anger the moment he realised she was unhurt. He had never failed to rescue her then, however much she annoyed him.

'And it is not funny!'

She must have been smiling at the memory. He took a step forwards; she slid back, still in his grasp.

'And I am very angry now and I am not fifteen and you are not a child and a fall from a horse is not the same as plunging into the sea from a great height.'

'No,' she agreed. The door was quite close. If she just edged a little more to the right and ducked out of his grip… She needed to distract him. 'You enjoyed that.'

His brows snapped together as he took the step that brought them toe to toe. 'What do you mean?'

'We were pressed very close together. Did you think I would not notice, or not understand? I am not an innocent.' What had possessed her to say that? The fact that he was obviously thinking of her as a child to be extracted from scrapes, even though his body was well aware of her age? *He really does not remember that last night*, she thought. He had been drinking, a little, when she had gone into his arms; she had tasted the brandy on his lips, but he had not been drunk.

'No, you're not, are you?' Alistair agreed, his voice silky as he moved again, turning them both so that he was between her and the door. Once she had been small and lithe enough to slip from his hands, evade his clumsy adolescent attempts to control her. Now he was a mature man, with a man's strength, and he was not going to let her go. Not until he was ready. She was angry and a little frightened and, it was disturbing to realise, aroused by the fact. 'You would be wise to behave as though you were.'

'I mean—' Dita bit her tongue. But she was not going to explain herself to Alistair and tell him that her only experience was their eager, magical, lovemaking. If he chose to believe that she had lost her virginity to Stephen Doyle, that was up to him. She could hardly accuse him of failing to understand her, when she couldn't forgive herself for going off with the man. 'I mean, why should I trouble to pretend, with you?'

'Is that an invitation, Dita?' He was so close now that she had to tip her head back at an uncomfortable angle to look up at him. He gave her a little push and she was trapped against the massive table.

'No,' she said with all the composure she could muster. 'It is an acknowledgement that we were… friends, once, a long time ago and I do not think you have changed so much that you would deliberately hurt me now.'

'And an *affaire* would hurt?' He lowered his head so his mouth was just above hers. His lids were low over those dangerous eyes and she stared at the thick fringe of spiky black against his tanned cheek. Not a young man's fresh skin any more. There were small scars, fine lines at the corners of his eyes. Her gaze slid lower. He hadn't shaved yet that morning and the stubble showed darker than she remembered. Alistair's mouth was so close now that she could kiss him if she chose.

I do not choose, she told herself fiercely. 'Naturally.' *And an* affaire *is all you would consider, isn't it? You've as much pride as I have and you wouldn't offer to marry another man's leavings. And I am not the girl I was, the one who was dazzled by you and had no idea what the fire was she was playing with that night. I am the woman who desires you and who knows that to surrender would be my undoing and the last blow to my reputation. I* must *be sensible.*

She made herself shrug, then realised that her hands had come up to clasp his upper arms, her fingers pressed against the bulge of muscle. Dita made herself open her hands and pressed them instead to his chest. Pushing was hopeless, but it gave her at least the illusion of resistance.

'A dalliance with you, Alistair, would doubtless be delightful—you have so much experience, after all. But I have my future to consider. In this hypocritical world *you* may dally all you wish and still find yourself an eligible bride. I must do what I may to repair my image. One slip, with my name and my money, might be overlooked. Two, never.'

'You are very cool about it, Dita. Where's the impulsive little creature I remember?' His right hand moved up her shoulder and she stiffened, refusing to give in to the shiver of need running through her. Between her legs the intimate pulse throbbed with betraying insistence and she made herself stand still, expecting him to cup her head and hold her for his caress. Instead his hand curled round her neck and pulled the long plait out of the back of her shirt.

'Where's the intense, straightforward young man of my memory?' she countered as he twisted her hair around his hand and tugged gently.

'Oh, he is still intense,' Alistair said. 'Just rather less straightforward.' He was close enough for her to see the pulse in his throat, exposed by the open-necked shirt. Close enough to smell the fresh linen and the soap he had used that morning and the salt from the sea breeze and the sweat from that rapid climb to reach her.

Dita closed her eyes. He was going to kiss her and she was not strong-willed enough to stop him, nor, in her heart, did she want to. One kiss could not matter; it would not be of any importance to him. He pulled gently on the plait and she swayed towards him, blind, breathless, and felt his warmth against her upper body in the thin cotton. His knuckles brushed her cheek, his breath feathered over her mouth and she tipped her face up, remembering the feel of his lips on hers, the sensual slide of his tongue as he had explored her mouth while he sprawled on the ground.

Nothing happened. Confused, Dita opened her eyes and looked straight into his dark, amused amber gaze where her reflection was trapped like a fly. Alistair flicked the tip of her nose with the end of her plait and stepped back. She swayed and threw out her hands to grip the edge of the table to keep from falling

'As always, I will do my best to keep you out of trouble, Dita my dear.' He sauntered to the head of the companionway leading down to the lower deck and the Great Cabin and paused at the top. 'The stewards are on their way, Dita. What are you waiting for?'

Chapter Six

What am I waiting for? A kiss? An apology? The strength to walk over there and slap that beautiful, assured, sardonic face? Whatever it was, she was not going to let him see how shaken she felt, how close she was to reaching for him. Dita blinked back angry tears, furious with herself and with Alistair.

'Waiting for? Why, nothing.' It was quite a creditable laugh and really should have been accompanied by the flutter of a fan. 'I had thought you might have wanted a reward for your gallant rescue just now, but obviously you are not as predictable as I thought you were.' The door to the roundhouse was mercifully close. 'I will see you at breakfast perhaps, my lord.'

Something showed in his face, just for a second. Admiration? Regret? Dita got safely through the door and ran, her hand pressed against her mouth to stifle the furious sob that was struggling to emerge.

'Dita!' Averil's startled cry stopped her dead in her tracks. 'What on earth are you doing dressed like that?'

Dita pushed back the canvas flap of her own cabin

and pulled her friend inside. 'Shh!' The walls were the merest curtains, enough for an illusion of privacy only. She pulled Averil down to sit beside her on the bed. 'I have been climbing the rigging,' she muttered.

'No! Like that?' Averil whispered back.

'Of course, like this. I could hardly do it in a gown, now could I?'

'No. I suppose not. I was going to come and see if you were ready for a walk before breakfast. I thought if the other ladies weren't out there we could walk faster and stretch our legs.'

'Without having to stop every minute to exclaim over an undone bonnet ribbon or bat our eyelashes at a man?' Dita stood up to pull off the *kurta* and Averil modestly looked away as she tugged off the trousers. 'Pass my chemise, would you? Thank you.' Her stomach was churning with what she could only suppose was a mixture of unsatisfied desire and sheer temper.

'Did you really climb up? All the way? What if someone had seen you?' Averil clasped her hands together in horror.

'Someone did.' Dita unrolled a pair of stockings and began to pull them on. She had to tell someone, pour it all out, and Averil was the only person she could trust. 'Alistair Lyndon. And he climbed up after me and made me come down.'

'How *awful*!' Averil got up to help lace Dita's light stays.

'I was glad to see him, if truth be told,' she admitted, prepared to be reasonable now that Averil was aghast. 'Or, rather, I was glad when he came after me. My first instinct when he told me to come down was to climb higher and then I wished I hadn't! It is much harder work than I realised and my legs were beginning to shake and when I looked down everything seemed to go round and round in circles.'

'What did he say when you reached the deck again? Was he angry? I would have sunk with mortification, but then you are much braver than I am.' Averil bit her lip in the silence as Dita, words to describe what had happened next completely deserting her, shook out her petticoats. 'It was rather romantic and dashing of Lord Lyndon, don't you think?'

It was and she would have died rather than admit it, even if what had happened next was anything but romantic. 'He lectured me,' Dita said, her head buried in her skirts as she pulled her sprig muslin gown on. Instinct was telling her to dress as modestly as she could. 'He thinks of me as a younger sister,' she added as she pinned a demure fichu over what bare skin the simple gown exposed. 'Someone to keep out of trouble.'

And that's a lie. That teasing near-kiss and the feeling of Alistair's hard, aroused body pressed against her had told her quite clearly that whatever his feelings were, they were not brotherly. He had felt magnificent and just thinking about it made her ache with desire. What would he have done just now if she had bent her head and kissed his bare throat, trailed her tongue down over the salty skin to where she could just glimpse a curl of dark hair?

She remembered the taste of him, the scent of his skin. But there had not been so much hair on his chest eight years ago. *He's a man now*, she reminded herself. What if she had reached out and cupped her hand wantonly over the front of his trousers where his desire was so very obvious?

'What a pity,' Averil surprised her by murmuring as

she stood up to tie the broad ribbon sash. 'Perhaps he'll change his mind. It is a long voyage.'

'He will do no such thing,' Dita said. 'He knows about my elopement. Bother, I must have an eyelash in my eye—it is watering. Oh, thank you.' She dabbed her eyes with Averil's handkerchief. 'That's better.' *I am not going to weep over him, not again. Not ever.*

'But you are Lady Perdita Brooke,' Averil protested. 'An earl's daughter.'

'And Alistair is about to become a marquis, if he isn't one already. He can look as high as he likes for a wife and he won't have to consider someone with a shady reputation. If we were passionately in love, then I expect he would throw such considerations to the wind. But we are not, of course.' *Merely in lust.* 'Not that I want him, of course,' she lied. *Marriage isn't what either of us wants; sin is.*

'I can't imagine why not,' Averil said with devastating honesty. 'I would think any unattached woman would be attracted to him. He *might* fall in love with you,' she persisted with an unusual lack of tact. Or perhaps Dita was being better at covering up her feelings than she feared.

'Love?' Dita laughed; if Averil noticed how brittle it was, she did not show it. 'Well, he had plenty of opportunity when we were younger.' She brushed out her hair and twisted it up into a simple knot at her nape.

Not that it had occurred to her that what she felt for him was more than childish affection, not until that night when he had been so bitterly unhappy and she had reached out to him, offering comfort that had become so much more. But now she realised that he had hardly cared who he was with, let alone been concerned about her feelings, whatever endearments he had murmured as he had caressed the clothes from her body. If he had, he would never have rejected her so hurtfully afterwards.

It was a blessing that he had not understood, simply seen the innocent love that burned in her eyes, the trust that had taken her into his arms.

She could still feel the violence with which Alistair had put her from him that last day, the rejection with which he had turned his face from her. He had been upset about something, desperately, wordlessly upset, and he had been drinking alone, something that she had never seen him do before, and her embrace had been meant only to comfort, just as the eight-year-old Dita would hug her idol when he fell and cut his head. But it had turned into something else, something the sixteen-year-old Dita could not control.

He had yanked her into his arms, met her upturned lips in a kiss that had been urgent on his part, clumsy and untutored on hers. And then it had all got completely, wonderfully, out of control and she had discovered that, however innocent she was, he was not and that he could sweep away her fears, melt them in the delight of what he was teaching her body—until he had pushed her from him, out of his bedchamber, his words scathing and unjust.

For several months she had thought she had driven him away by her actions, had shocked him with her forwardness. After a while she had made up stories to console herself and blank out what had really happened; then she overheard her parents talking and learned that he had left after a furious quarrel with his father.

'When Alistair left home,' she told Averil as she stuck in combs to hold her hair, 'I had this fantasy that his father had refused to allow him to pay his addresses to me. Wasn't that foolish? There was absolutely no reason why we wouldn't have been a perfectly eligible couple then. In reality, they had a row over Alistair taking over one of the other estates, or something equally ridiculous to fall out about.'

'So you were in love with him then?' Averil asked.

'I fancied I was!' Dita was pleased with the laugh, and her smile, as she made the ready admission. 'I was sixteen and hopelessly infatuated. But I grew out of it and I would expire of mortification if he ever found out how I had worshipped him, so you must swear not to tell.' Hero worship, affection, calf love and desire: what a chaos of feelings to try to disentangle.

'I wouldn't dream of it,' Averil assured her. 'I would hate it if a man guessed something like that about me.'

'So would I,' Dita assured her as she adjusted her shawl. 'So would I.'

They managed a brisk walk around the deck, which Dita thought would account for any colour in her cheeks, and then went straight in to breakfast. Alistair was already at table, seated between the Chattertons; Dita deliberately sat opposite. The men half-rose, greeted them and resumed their conversation.

'I was going to try some singlestick exercises early this morning, but I got distracted,' Alistair said, continuing his conversation with Callum.

So that was what he was doing, up so early. Dita accepted a cup of coffee and took a slice of toast.

'I think I'll do that every morning,' he went on, without so much as a glance in her direction to accompany the warning. 'Why don't you two join me? We could box, wrestle, use singlesticks.'

'Good idea,' Callum agreed, with a nudge in the ribs

for Daniel who was grumbling about early rising. 'We will be sure to avoid the ladies by doing that.'

And that put an end to any dawn exercise on her part, Dita recognised, slapping preserve on her toast with a irritable flick. It was easier to be angry with Alistair than to confront any of the other feelings he aroused in her.

'What a charming picture you two ladies make.' Alistair again, smiling now. Beside her Averil made a small sound that might have been pleasure at the compliment, or might have been nerves. 'So English in your muslins and lawns and lacy fichus.'

'You do not like Indian female dress, my lord?' Dita enquired. She was not going to allow him to needle her and she rather thought he knew exactly why she had changed into something so blandly respectable. It had been an error to show him that she cared for his opinion. She had morning dresses that would make him pant with desire, she told herself, mentally lowering necklines and removing lace trim from the contents of her trunk.

'It is suitable for Indian females, but not for English ones to ape.'

'But English gentlemen resort to Indian garb to relax in, do you not? Why should ladies not have the same comforts? But of course,' she added, 'you do not appreciate the wonderful freedom of casting off one's stays.'

Averil gave a little gasp of horrified laughter, Callum went pink and Alistair grinned. 'No, but I can imagine,' he said, leaving her in no doubt he was thinking of garments he had unlaced in the past.

She was not going to rattle him, she realised, and all she was succeeding in doing was embarrassing Averil and scandalising Callum Chatterton, who was too nice and intelligent a man to be teased.

'And how do you ladies intend passing the day?' Callum enquired, changing the subject with rather desperate tact.

'I am making Christmas gifts,' Averil confided. 'I thought that all of us who dine in the cuddy make up a house party, as it were. On Christmas Eve after supper it would be delightful to exchange little tokens, just as though we really were at a Christmas house party, don't you think?'

'Gifts for *everyone*?' Daniel asked, chasing some tough bacon around his plate.

'It would be invidious to leave anyone out, I think.' Averil frowned. 'Of course, it is not easy to prepare for this sort of thing, not knowing everyone who is of the party. But twenty small gifts are not so very hard to come up with.'

'Twenty-one with the captain,' Dita pointed out. 'I think it is a charming idea, but we should let everyone know we will do it, don't you think? In case there is anyone who had not thought of gifts and is embarrassed.'

'Oh. I had not considered that. If there are people with nothing suitable to exchange, it would indeed put them out.' Averil's face fell.

'If you mention it now, then anyone who needs to do last-minute shopping can go to the bazaars when we call at Madras,' Alistair suggested. Averil beamed at him and Dita found herself meeting his eyes with something like gratitude for his thoughtfulness to her friend.

'That was a kind thought,' she said across the table when Averil was distracted by Daniel teasing her about what she could possibly give the captain. 'Thank you.'

'I do occasionally have them,' he said laconically. 'Miss Heydon is a charming and kind young woman and I would not like to see her embarrassed.'

'I do not accuse you of being unkind,' Dita began. That had felt like an oblique slap at her, the young woman he had no compunction about embarrassing.

'You, my dear Dita, are a feline. You walk your own path, you guard your own heart and you will not yield to anything but your own desires. Miss Heydon is a turtle dove—sweet, loyal, affectionate. Although,' he added, glancing along the table to where Averil was fending off Daniel's wit with surprising skill, 'she has more intelligence and courage than at first appears. She would fight for what she loves.'

'Whereas you think me merely selfish?' Dita's chin came up.

'And intelligent and courageous and quite surprisingly alluring. But you are going to find it hard to bend that self-will to a husband, Dita.'

'Why should I?' *Alluring?* The unexpected compliment was negated by the fact he found it surprising that she should be attractive. She sliced diagonally across the slice of toast with one sweep of her knife. 'Men do not have to compromise in marriage. I cannot imagine *you* doing so, for example, even for a woman you love.'

Alistair gave a harsh laugh. 'What has love got to do with it? That is the last thing I would marry for. Excuse me.' He pushed back his chair and left the table.

How had he let that betraying remark escape? Alistair wondered as he strode down to his tiny cubicle off the Great Cabin. Or was it only his acute consciousness of his own ghosts that made him fear his words would expose him?

Love brought blindness with it and rewarded trust with lies. It had blinded him, humiliated him—he was not going to give it a chance again. Physical love was easy enough to take care of, even if one was fastidious and demanding, as he knew himself to be. Alistair grimaced as he sat on his bunk and tried to remember what he had come down here for. Not to run away from Dita Brooke, he sincerely hoped, although the wretched chit was having the most peculiar effect on his brain.

Easier to think about sex than about emotion—and Dita seemed to produce emotional responses in him he rarely experienced: anxiety, protectiveness. Possessiveness, damn it. Yes, better to think about sex and she certainly made him fantasise about that, too.

He had dreamed about her for years, erotic, arousing, frustrating dreams that had puzzled him as much as they had tormented him. They had been too real. Had he really thought about the girl he had grown up with in that way and suppressed it so the desire only emerged when he was asleep? Now it was damnably hard not to indulge in waking dreams about the adult woman.

Three months' celibacy was not something he would seek out, he had to admit. He was a sensual man by nature, but he prized control and he was not going to seek relief either here on board or in any of their ports of call. Fortunately there was no one on the *Bengal Queen* who attracted him in that way. No one except Lady Perdita Brooke, of course.

Hell. How could he feel responsible for her—a hangover from all those childhood years, he supposed—and yet want to do the very things he would kill another man for trying with her?

She was so responsive, with all the intensity and passion of the child grown into the woman. Her reckless riding, the way she had flung herself from her horse and run to him, her uninhibited attempts to care for him.

That kiss. Alistair fell back on to the bed and relived those stimulating seconds.

He had enjoyed that, irresponsible as it had been. And so had Dita. And being Dita, when she thought he was offering to do it again she had wanted it, as filled with passionate curiosity for risk and experience as she always had been. Passion. A shiver ran through his long frame as he thought about passion and Dita.

Damn it, no. By all accounts she had been hurt enough by her own recklessness—the last thing she needed was an *affaire* with him. And the last thing *he* needed when he arrived in London for the Season was the rumour that he had been involved with the scandalous Lady Perdita. He was hunting for a bride as pure as the driven snow and for that he had to preserve the mask of utmost respectability that was expected in this artificial business. He owed it to his name. And he owed it to his own peace of mind not to become embroiled with a mistress who would expect far more than he was prepared to give.

Alistair sat up abruptly. He was leaping to conclusions about what Dita might expect. She knew he was no saint. His mouth curled into a sensual smile. If Dita wanted to pay games—well, there were games they could play, games that would be just as much fun in their own way as those innocent sports of their childhood.

Alistair left the cabin half an hour later, notebooks under one arm and his travelling inkwell in his hand. He had told Dita that he was going to write a book; now he must see whether he could produce prose that was good enough and turn his travels into something that would hold a reader's attention.

There was a lady seated at the communal table in

the middle of the cabin, a sewing box open and items strewn around. Ah, yes, Mrs Ashwell, the wife of newly wealthy merchant Samuel Ashwell. He had seen her at work before, it was what had prompted his idea about mistletoe for Christmas.

'That is very fine, ma'am,' he observed.

She was instantly flustered. 'Oh! You mean my artificial flowers? I used to be… I mean, I always used to make them, for myself and friends, you understand. I enjoy the work…'

In other words, she had been an artificial flower maker before her husband made his money. He, no doubt, wished his wife to hide the fact, but she enjoyed the creativity. The products were as good as any society lady would buy.

'Can you make mistletoe?' Alistair asked. 'A spray of it that a lady might put in her hair?'

'Why, yes, I suppose so. I never have, but it should be straightforward.' She frowned and rummaged in her work box. 'This ribbon is the right green. But I would need white beads for the berries and I have none.'

'I have.' Alistair went back into his cabin and unlocked the small strong box he had bolted to the deck. 'Here.' He handed her a velvet bag. 'Use all of them if you can.' Now, how to recompense her for what would be a considerable amount of fiddling work without giving offence by offering payment?

'And thank you. You have rescued me from the embarrassing predicament of having no suitable gift for a lady. I do hope, when you are in London next, you will do me the honour of leaving your card? I would very much like to invite you and Mr Ashwell to one of the parties I will be giving.'

'My lord! But…I mean…we would be delighted.' He left her ten minutes later, flushed and delighted. If only pleasing a woman was always that easy.

Chapter Seven

20th December 1808—Madras

The *Bengal Queen* dropped anchor opposite Fort St George close to the mouth of the Kuvam River and the harassed ship's officers set about sorting out the groups of passengers. Some wanted to go ashore to shop in Madras; there were men who were eager to hire a boat and go upstream to shoot duck and the East India Company supercargo—very senior men indeed—demanded to be taken ashore to transact Company business with all speed.

'I really do not think we should go ashore without a gentleman to escort us,' Mrs Bastable said for the fourth time since breakfast. 'And Mr Bastable is clerking for Sir Willoughby and will be in the Company offices all day. Perhaps we could join the Whytons.'

Averil and Dita exchanged looks. The thought of a morning in the company of the Misses Whyton was excruciating. 'Um…I think they are already a very large group. I asked the Chattertons,' Dita said, 'but Daniel is committed to the shooting party and Callum is going to the offices with Sir Willoughby.' She surveyed the rest of the available men without much enthusiasm. 'I suppose I could ask Lieutenant Tompkins, if he is off duty.'

'A problem, ladies?'

Dita turned, her heart thumping in the most unwelcome manner. 'Merely a question of an escort to the markets, Lord Lyndon. Please, do not let us detain you—I am sure there are ducks awaiting slaughter.'

'I was not intending to join the shooting party and I have my own shopping to do.' He appeared to take their acceptance for granted. 'Are you ready?'

'Yes, we are. Thank you so much, my lord.' Mrs Bastable had no hesitation snatching at this promise of escort. 'Oh dear, though, there's that dreadful chair to negotiate.'

'Safest way down,' Alistair said. 'Let me assist you, ma'am. There you are.'

Averil and Dita watched their chaperon being whisked skywards. 'She's landed safely,' Averil announced. 'Look.'

'No, thank you.' Dita remained firmly away from the rail.

'Why do you climb the rigging if you won't look over the side?' Alistair demanded as Averil sat down in the bos'un's chair with complete unconcern.

'The further I get from the sea, the happier I am,' Dita said and turned her back firmly on the rail and all the activity around it. She fixed her gaze on Alistair's mouth, which was a reckless thing to do for the sake of her emotions, but was a great help in taking her mind off small boats and open water. 'Don't ask me to explain it, I know it is irrational.'

'That is no surprise, you are female after all,' Alistair

remarked. She glanced up sharply and met a look that was positively lascivious.

Dita opened her mouth, shut it again with a snap at the expression in his eyes and took two rapid steps back. Alistair followed her, gave her a little push and she sat down with a thump in the chair.

'Why, you—' He flicked the rope across the arms and signalled to the sailors hauling it up. Seething, Dita found herself in the flat-bottomed boat being helped out by Averil.

'You devious, underhand, conniving creature,' she hissed as Alistair dropped into the boat from the ladder.

'It worked,' he said with a grin as he sat down beside her. 'And I take it back—you *are* irrational, but not because you are female. But I cannot apologise for any looks of admiration—you do look most charming.'

Dita sorted through the apology and decided she was prepared to accept it. 'Thank you. But you really are the most provoking man,' she added. 'I don't recall you being so—except when you wouldn't let me do something I wanted to, of course.'

'Which was most of the time. You always wanted to do the maddest things.'

'I did not!' The boat bumped alongside the *ghat*. 'You wretch! You are doing it again, arguing in order to distract me.'

'I have no idea why you are complaining,' Alistair said, as he got out on to the stone steps and held out his hand to Mrs Bastable, who glanced from one to the other with a puzzled frown. 'You have made the transition from ship to shore without turning green in the slightest.'

They were enveloped in the usual crowd of porters jostling for business, trinket sellers, garland merchants and beggars. Alistair dropped into rapid, colloquial

Hindi as he cleared a way through for the ladies to climb the steps; by the time they had reached the top they had two of the more respectable men at their heels.

...double that when we get back here with all our packages intact, Dita translated when she could hear more clearly. Coins changed hands, the men grinned and set off.

'I told them I wanted the best general market,' Alistair said as they followed, skirting a white-clad procession bearing a swathed body towards the burning *ghats*.

'Oh, I can never get used to that,' Mrs Bastable moaned, turning her head away. 'I so long for the peace of a green English churchyard.'

'But not yet, I hope,' Alistair murmured. Dita caught his eye and stifled a choke of laughter. Now that she had recovered from his trickery she discovered that today she was quite in charity with the man, which was dangerous. She reflected on just how dangerous as she picked her way round potholes and past a sacred cow that had come to a dead halt beside a vegetable stall and was placidly eating its way through the wretched owner's produce.

'And cows that stay in a field would be nice,' she remarked.

The market they were guided to was down the usual narrow entrance that opened out into a maze of constricted alleys, lined on each side with tiny stalls and booths, many of them with the owner sitting cross-legged on the back of the counter.

'Do you know what you want?'

'Not fish!' Mrs Bastable turned with a shudder from the alley to their left, its cobbles running with bloody water, the flies swarming around the silvery heaps.

'Down here.' Averil set off confidently down another lane and they soon found themselves amidst stalls selling spices, baskets of every kind, toys, small carvings and embroidery. 'Perfect!'

Soon their porters were hung around with packages. Mrs Bastable fell behind to haggle over a soapstone carving and Alistair stayed with her to help.

'We'll be in the next alley on the right,' Averil called back. 'I can see peacock-feather fans. They are charming and useful,' she said as they stood examining them. 'We could buy a dozen between us; they will do very well for gifts.'

'Yes, I—what's that?' Both swung round at the sound of screams and running feet and a deep-throated snarling. The alleyway cleared as though a giant broom had swept through it. Men leapt on to counters, dragging women with them as a small boy ran down, screeching in fear, followed by a dog, snarling and snapping, its mouth dripping foam.

'Up!' Dita grabbed Averil and thrust her towards the fan seller, who took her wrists and dragged her on to the narrow counter amidst a heap of feathers. Time seemed to slow to a crawl as the boy and the dog hurtled towards her and she realised there was no room on any of the stalls now and the alley was a dead end. Dita snatched the child as he reached her and clambered up a pile of baskets as though it were a stepladder until they were perched on the top of the teetering heap, the dog leaping and snarling at the foot.

'Hilo dulo naha,' she murmured to the boy as he clutched her, his dirty, skinny little body wrapped around hers. But he needed no warning to keep still and, as their fragile sanctuary began to tilt with an ominous cracking sound, he seemed to stop breathing.

The dog leapt at them, clawing at the baskets. It was mad, there was no mistaking it. Dita tried to put out of her mind the memory of their *jemahdar* who had been bitten. His death had been agonising and inevitable. She had to stay calm. If the baskets collapsed—*when* they collapsed—she would throw the boy to Averil and pray she was strong enough to hold him. And she would try and get behind the baskets…

Something flew through the air and hit the dog and it turned, yelping. Alistair, a long, bloody knife in his hand, came down the alley at the run and kicked out as the dog leapt for him, catching it under the chin. As it spun away he lunged with the knife, but his foot slipped on rotting vegetables in the gutter and he went down on to the snapping, snarling animal.

Dita screamed as she slid down the baskets and thrust the little boy into Averil's reaching arms. As she hit the ground, groping for the stone he had thrown, Alistair got to his feet. The dog, throat cut, lay twitching in the gutter.

'Did it bite you?' Frantic, she seized his hands, used her skirts to wipe the blood away. 'Are you scratched? Have you any cuts on your hands?'

Alistair dropped the knife and caught at her wrists. 'I'm all right. Dita, stop it.'

'You fell hard, you might not have felt a bite.' She tried to see if there were any tears in his coat or the light trousers he wore. 'Alistair, don't you know what happens if you've been bitten, even a graze—'

'Yes, I know. I am all right,' he repeated. 'Dita you are getting covered in blood. What the devil were you thinking of, scrambling up there with that child?'

'There was nowhere else to go,' she protested as the alley began to fill up. One man, a fish seller by the state of his clothes, picked up the bloody knife and walked away with it. A woman, weeping loudly, ran and snatched the child from Averil. The noise was deafening.

'It wouldn't bear the weight of both of you.' Alistair released her and she began to shake. 'It was going to collapse at any moment.'

'I know that. I couldn't leave him!'

'Most people would have.' Someone brought a bowl of water and Alistair plunged his hands into it. Dita held her breath until they emerged, the skin unbroken. His coat was stained, but she could see no evidence of teeth marks on it, or tears in his trousers.

Alistair gestured for more water. When it was poured he took her hands in his and washed them and she thought back over the crowded, terrified, minutes. 'You came to rescue the child,' she said. 'You must have gone for the knife the moment you heard him scream, or you wouldn't have got here with it when you did.'

'Well, that's two of us who are sentimental,' he said, his voice harsh, but his eyes as he looked at her held admiration and the shadow of fear, not for himself, but for her. 'Don't do that to me again, Dita. My nerves won't stand it. The mast was bad enough, this—'

They stood, their hands clasped in the reddening water and the noise of the crowd faded. Dita wondered if she was going to faint. Alistair was staring at her as though he had never seen her before.

'Dita! Dita, are you all right?' She looked round, dazed and a little dizzy, to see her friend supporting their weeping chaperon. 'I don't think Mrs Bastable can walk back.'

'Rickshaw,' Alistair snapped at their two porters. 'Two. Can you help Lady Perdita, Miss Heydon?' As Averil's hand came under her elbow he scooped Mrs Bastable up and followed the porters out of the market.

'Oh, my,' Averil said with a laugh that broke on a sob. 'She's gone all pink. At least it has stopped her weeping.'

'Are you all right?' Better to think about Averil than what might have happened to the child, to Alistair, to her.

'Me? Oh, yes. I've feathers sticking in me and doubtless any number of bruises, but if it wasn't for you I don't know what would have happened. You are a heroine, Dita.'

'No, I'm not,' she protested. 'I'm shaking like a leaf and I would like to follow Mrs Bastable's example and have hysterics right here and now.' *I wish he was holding me. I wish...*

Mrs Bastable sank into the rickshaw with a moan. 'I'll get in with her,' Averil said. 'I have a vinaigrette in my reticule and a handkerchief.'

Dita held on to the side of the other rickshaw while Alistair got Averil settled. She would like to sit down, but she didn't think she could climb in unaided. Her legs had lost all their strength and the bustling street seemed to be growing oddly distant.

'Don't faint on me now.' Alistair scooped her up, climbed into the rickshaw and sat down with her still in his arms.

'Can't I?' she murmured against his chest. 'I would like to, I think. But I never have before.'

'Very well, if you want to.' There was the faintest thread of amusement in his voice and he shifted on the seat so he could get both arms around her as it tilted back and the man began to trot forwards between the shafts.

'Perhaps I won't. This is nice.' *That was he said when he kissed me on the* maidan. *Nice.* 'Where's my bonnet?'

'Goodness knows. Lie still, Dita.'

'Hmm? Why?' *He is very strong, all those muscles feel so good.* His chest was broad, his arms were reassuring and his thighs…she really must stop thinking about his thighs.

'Never mind.' He was definitely amused now, although there was something else in his voice. Shock, of course. Alistair wasn't made of stone and that had been a terrifying few minutes.

'You are all right, aren't you?' she asked after a moment, the panic spiking back. 'You would tell me if you had been bitten or scratched?'

'I am all right. And I would tell you if I had been bitten.' Alistair added the lie as he bent his head so his mouth just touched the tangled brown mass of her hair. He was still shaken to find that his skin was unbroken and his stomach cramped at the thought of those few seconds after the dog had collapsed twitching into the gutter and he had looked, felt, for any wound on his body and on hers.

It was good that he was holding Dita, because he suspected his hands would shake if he was not. Never, in his life, had he been more afraid—for himself, for another person. She thought he had grabbed the knife when he heard the screams because he wanted to save the child and he could not tell her the truth, that he had reacted purely on instinct: she was where those screams had come from.

'Something smells of fish,' she said. She still sounded drugged with shock; the sooner she was in bed, warm, the better. Despite the heat she was shivering.

'I do. That was a fish-gutter's knife and I ran through those puddles by their stalls to get it.'

She chuckled and he tightened his arms and made himself confront the nightmare that was gibbering at the back of his brain. If he had been bitten, then he would have shot himself. He had seen a man die of the bite of a mad dog and there didn't seem to be any worse way to go. But what if it had bitten Dita? What if he had arrived just too late? The vision of her slender white throat and the knife and his bloody hands and the dog's foaming muzzle shifted and blurred in his imagination.

'Ouch,' she murmured and he made himself relax his grip. All his young life it seemed he had looked out for Dita, protected her while she got on with being Dita. Eight years later and, under the desire he felt for her, he still felt the need to do that—but would he have had the courage to do for her what he would have done for himself? Would it have been right?

'Alistair? What is wrong?' She twisted round and looked up at him, her green eyes dark with concern, and he shook himself mentally and sent the black thoughts back into the darkness where they belonged. The worst hadn't happened, they were both all right, the child was safe and he had to keep his nightmares at bay in case she read them in his face and was frightened.

'Our wardrobes are wrecked, I smell of fish and now you probably do too, we haven't finished our Christmas shopping, Mrs Bastable is still wailing—it is enough to send a man into a decline.'

Her face broke into a smile of unselfconscious amusement and relief. 'Idiot.'

It was the least provocative thing to say, the least flirtatious smile, but the desire crashed over him like a wave hitting a rock. He wanted her, *now*. He wanted her hot and trembling and soft and urgent under him. Somehow he knew how she would feel, the scent of her skin, of her arousal. He wanted to take her, to bury himself in her heat and possess her. He wanted her with all the simple urgency of a man who had felt death's breath on his face and who had tasted more fear in a few seconds than he would surely ever feel for the rest of his life.

She was still looking at him; her wide mouth was still smiling and sweet and her eyes held something very close to hero worship. Alistair bent and kissed her without finesse, his tongue thrusting between lips that parted in a gasp of shock, his hands holding her so that her breasts were crushed against him; the feel of soft, yielding curves against his chest, against his heart, sent his body into violent arousal.

Dita must have felt his erection and she could not escape the message of a kiss that was close to a brutal demand, but she did not fight him. She melted against him, her mouth open and generous, her tongue tangling with his, her hands clinging while he tasted and feasted and felt the need and the primitive triumph surge through him. He had killed the beast for her and now she was his prize.

The seat tilted sharply, almost throwing them out of the rickshaw as the man lowered the shafts to the ground. Alistair grabbed the side with one hand and held tight to Dita with the other, shaken back into reality and the realisation that he had damn near ravished a woman in a rickshaw on the streets of Madras.

'Hell.'

She stared at him, apparently shocked speechless by what they had just done, then scrambled down on to the ground unaided and went to the other rickshaw.

Alistair got out, paid the drivers, found the boat, paid off the porters and oversaw loading the parcels before he turned to the three women. By then, he hoped, he would have himself under control again. Mrs Bastable was leaning on Averil's arm, fanning herself, but looking much more composed. Averil smiled. Dita, white-faced, just looked at him with no expression at all, although if either of the others had been themselves they could not have failed to see her mouth was swollen with the force of his kisses. She had said nothing, he realised.

He got them into the boat, the three women in a row, and sat down opposite them so he could look at Dita. She sat contemplating her clasped hands, calm while they were rowed out, calm when he helped her into the chair, last of the three so he could get up the ladder and be there when she landed on the deck.

'I'll take Lady Perdita to her cabin,' he said to Averil and picked her up before either of them could react.

'Second on the left,' she called after him. 'I'll come in a moment.'

If there was anyone in the cuddy he didn't see them. He fumbled a little with the ties on the canvas flap, uncharacteristically clumsy with delayed shock, then he had her inside and could put her on the bed.

'I'm sorry,' he said as she raised her eyes to meet his. 'It happens, it's a male reaction to danger, fear—we want sex afterwards. It doesn't mean anything… It wasn't you. Don't think it was your fault.'

'Oh.' She arched her brows, aloof, poised, the acid-tongued lady from Government House despite her stained, torn gown and tumbling hair and bruised mouth and shaking hands. 'Well, as long as it wasn't *me*. I would hate to think I was responsible for that exhibition.' He could not read her eyes as she watched him and her smile when it came did not reach them. 'Thank you for saving my life. I will never forget that.'

'Dita?' Averil said from outside. 'May I come in?'

'Ma'am.' He opened the flap and stepped out, holding it for her to enter. 'I'll have the parcels sent down to the cuddy.'

'Oh, Dita.' Averil sat down on the trunk. 'What a morning. Mrs Bastable is resting and I've asked the steward to make tea.'

'Thank you. A cup of tea would be very welcome.' Incredibly she could still make conversation. Alistair had kissed her as though he was starving, desperate—for her. And she had kissed him back with as much need and desire and with the certainty that he wanted her. And then he said it wasn't *her*. That any woman would have provoked that storm of passion. That kissing her as she had always dreamt he would kiss her meant absolutely nothing to him. He needed sex as Mrs Bastable had needed to have hysterics.

That time when they had made love fully, gloriously, he had looked at her as she had smiled up at him dreamily afterwards and told her harshly to get out, to go, all his tenderness and passion hardening into rejection and anger.

Alistair had saved her life, risked a hideous death, behaved like the hero she had always known him to be—and stamped on her heart all over again.

'Oh, don't cry!' Averil jumped up with a handkerchief. *She must have an inexhaustible supply*, Dita thought, swallowing hard against the tears that choked her throat.

'No, I won't. It is just the shock. I think I will lie down for a while. That would be sensible, don't you think?'

'Yes.' *Poor Averil, she doesn't need another watering pot on her hands.* 'You get into bed and I'll bring your tea and tuck you in. I'll put all our shopping in my cabin; you just rest, dear.'

Chapter Eight

24th December 1808

They rounded the southern tip of India and headed across the ocean towards Mozambique as dinner was served on Christmas Eve. The stewards had brought a load of greenery on board from Madras and the Great Cabin and cuddy were lavishly decorated with palm fronds and creepers.

The ladies cut both red and gold paper into strips to weave amongst it and there were garlands of marigolds that had been kept in the cool of the bilges and were only a little worn and wilted if one looked too close.

'At least that reduces the look of Palm Sunday in church that all those fronds produced,' Averil observed as they made table decorations to run down the length of the long board.

The captain had decreed a return to formality and precedence, Dita noticed as the stewards began to set out place cards with careful reference to a seating plan. It meant she would be sitting next to Alistair. She had been avoiding any intimacy ever since their return on board ship, despising herself for cowardice even as she did so.

She had tried not to be obvious about it: she owed the man her life, after all. But it was torture to be close to him. She wanted to touch him, to have him take her lips again, and yet she knew that the passion he had shown her would have been the same for any woman. It was not much consolation that he appeared to have been avoiding her, too.

'We can put out the presents now,' Averil said. 'The place cards will help.' Dita made herself concentrate on the task at hand. The stewards were having a difficult time of it, trying to lay an elaborate formal setting while ladies ducked and wove between them, heaping up little parcels that slid about with the motion of the ship, but the mood was good natured and, as Miss Whyton said, sorting out the gifts could only add to the jollity.

Dita juggled her pile of packages, squinting at labels and tweaking ribbons while she tried to avoid thinking about the fact that there was one person she had no gift for. Alistair wouldn't notice, she tried to tell herself, not with such a pile of parcels in front of him. But she suspected he would. It was not that she wanted to snub him, but she had had no idea what to give him. A trivial token was just that: trivial. She could not insult the man who had saved her life with a trinket. A significant gift—and she was a good enough needlewoman to make a handsome waistcoat from the silks in her trunk if she applied herself—would cause comment.

There was only one thing and it nagged at the back of her mind until the last teetering pile was stabilised with tightly rolled napkins.

'Just time to get changed,' Averil said as they all

stood back to admire the effect, then Dita followed her to their cabins.

The jewellery box was locked in her trunk and she lifted it out and set it on the bunk. Emeralds for dinner, she decided, and lifted out the necklace and earrings and set them aside.

Her hands went back to the box, hesitated, then she lifted out the top tray, then the items below until it appeared to be empty. There was a pin to be pulled, a narrow panel to be pushed and then the secret drawer slid out. In it was a slim oblong package wrapped in tarnished silver paper. The amber velvet ribbon was frayed and the label, *Alistair, Happy Birthday with love from Dita XXX*, was crumpled.

It was almost nine years since she had wrapped it up. The stitches might be embarrassingly clumsy—she should check. Certainly it needed rewrapping. Dita hesitated, then lifted out the package, slid it into her reticule just as it was, and reassembled the box before she locked it safely away.

The cuddy was filling up as she returned and the noise level was rising, helped by bowls of punch and glasses of champagne. The doors had been thrown open to the deck so the sea breezes could mitigate the heat of twenty-one bodies, hot food and scurrying stewards and some of the sailors had been posted on the deck to play fiddles and pipes.

'Lady Perdita.' Captain Archibald bowed over her hand and handed her wine.

'You look, if I may be so bold, utterly stunning, Lady Perdita.' Daniel Chatterton appeared at her side, his gaze frankly appreciative as he took in her amber silk gown and the glow of the emeralds. 'You look so…uncluttered—' he glanced towards some of the other ladies, weighted down with jewellery and feathers '—and that shows off your beauty.'

There was no denying the pleasure his words gave her. She had deliberately set out to dress her hair without ornament, only one long brown curl brushing her shoulder. The emeralds were simply cut and simply mounted to achieve their effect by their size and quality and her gown shimmered in the light.

But it was not Daniel Chatterton she had dressed for. It was a satisfying statement of the polished style she had made her own and it was a defiant gesture to Alistair. *See what you spurn.*

He was on the opposite side of the cabin, talking to Averil, making her laugh and blush, and Dita allowed herself a moment's indulgence to admire the dark tailcoat, the tight breeches, immaculate striped stockings, exquisite neckcloth. He would look perfectly at home in a London drawing room, she thought. Then he moved and the play of muscle disturbed the cut of the coat and the look he swept round the crowded room held the alertness of the hunter. *He isn't quite civilised any more*, she thought, and found she was running her tongue over dry lips.

The gong sounded, the patterns shifted and broke up as people went to their places, the chaplain said grace and then went below decks to do the same in the Great Cabin, and Alistair was holding her chair for her. She smiled her thanks and he smiled back. No one looking at them could have imagined that kiss in the rickshaw, she thought. It almost seemed like a dream now. But, of course, he didn't want her, so there would be nothing in his look to betray him.

* * *

The meal passed in a noise-filled blur. The food was good, but too rich, the wine flowed too freely, Alistair made unexceptional, entertaining small talk, first to her, then to his other partner. Dita nodded and chatted and smiled and plied her fan and drank a second glass of wine and wondered if the room was spinning or whether it was her head.

Finally the dishes were cleared, fruit was set out, more wine was poured and the captain raised his glass. 'A toast, my lords and gentlemen, to the ladies who have created this festive table.'

The men rose and drank, the ladies smiled and bowed and the captain picked up his first present, the signal for them all to begin.

There were shrieks and laughter and people calling their thanks down the length of the board. It would be impossible, Dita thought, to notice if someone had omitted to give you a present unless you were looking for one gift in particular. The Chattertons waved and mouthed *Thank you* for the watercolour sketches she had done of them. Averil seemed delighted with the notebook she had covered in padded silk and the captain was most impressed with her drawing of the *Bengal Queen*'s figurehead.

Her own collection of gifts was delightful, too. Thoughtful, handmade presents from some people, well intentioned but prosaic ones from others. The Chattertons had given her a pair of beautiful carved sandalwood boxes, Averil a string of hand-painted beads. There was nothing from Alistair.

Dita carefully folded up the wrapping paper, handed it to a steward and glanced around the table. No, no unclaimed gift, nothing had fallen to the floor. He had not given her a present—that would teach her to be complacent and expect something.

'What a clever idea these knots made into paper-weights are,' she remarked to Alistair with a bright smile, holding out her own gift from the captain. 'You have a different knot, I see.'

'Yes,' he agreed as he pushed back his chair. 'Please excuse me.'

Dita watched him leave the cuddy. He had gone down to the Great Cabin, she realised, hearing the noise coming up the companionway from the company below. Why? Was he going to come back? On the impulse Dita got to her feet and followed him. She would give Alistair her gift even if he scorned it. It was that or throw it over the side.

There was a passage at the foot of the steps formed by the screens that divided up the cabins down on this deck. To her right she could hear the passengers in the Great Cabin toasting each other amidst much laughter. A small boy ran out astride a hobby horse, a toy trumpet in one hand. He stared at her, then rushed back.

This was foolish. She could hardly confront Alistair with her tattered little parcel in front of everyone down here; she would go back and lay it at his place. Even as she thought it he emerged from the same opening that the child had run through.

'Dita?'

'I have a gift for you.'

'And I one for you. Come down here.' Alistair led her past several doors and along the cramped passageway, lit only by a few lanterns. They turned a corner and were quite alone, even the noise from the Great Cabin fading into a murmur like the sea. In the shadows he seemed larger than ever and somehow mysterious.

'I realised there would be one thing missing from a traditional Christmas, beside a flaming Yule log and snow.' He held something in his hand, a spray of foliage that caught the light with a myriad of soft creamy orbs.

'Oh, how lovely! Mistletoe—where on earth did you get it?' Dita reached for it, but he held it just out of her reach.

'Magic.'

She could believe that. The ship pitched and she stumbled towards him and was caught in his free arm. 'Will you trust me with a kiss now?'

'I thought you didn't want me. You said you did not.'

'I said that the way I kissed you then was simply a reaction to danger, to fighting. It was wrong to have done it like that, then. But I would have to be dead not to want to kiss you, Dita.'

'Oh. I see. I thought—' *So he does want me, just as I want him.* 'Yes.' Her heart soared and she did not hesitate now. Trust him? It was herself she could not trust, here in the semi-darkness, but she was not going to fight the way she felt. He was so close, and what she could not see clearly she could read with every other sense. He smelled of wine and smoke and she leaned a little closer to inhale clean, hot male and the scent that was his alone. His breathing was slow and calm, but she could detect just the slightest hitch in it as though he was controlling it consciously. And touch—solid, strong male in clothing she wanted to rip from his body.

Around her waist his hand held her steady and she fought the need to press against it, to feel those long fingers move on her skin. She wanted them on her, all over her. In her. Dita blushed in the shadows, hot with desire and shaken by her own imaginings and memories.

Alistair's free hand moved and touched her hair and she felt him fasten the mistletoe sprig in amongst the heaped curls before he drew her to him with both hands.

'Just a kiss,' he murmured as he bent his head.

'Yes,' she agreed and reached up her own hands to touch his hair. It was soft and strong, thick and rebellious under her fingers and she recalled the unruly length of it when he had been younger, long enough for him to tie back with a cord when he was outside. When they had been in bed together she had untied the cord and run her fingers into the silk of it. 'I like this short, it feels like fur.' She stroked as she would a cat and he pushed against the caress, his eyes hooded and heavy.

Just a kiss, a Christmas kiss. The taste of him when he touched his mouth to hers had her closing her eyes and opening her lips. The darkness was arousing, gave an edge of danger now she could not see him, only feel and smell and taste. Alistair kissed her as deeply as he had in the rickshaw, but with no desperation, as leisurely as he had on the *maidan*, but with no mockery; she sighed into his mouth as their tongues met and tangled and stroked, sharing the wet heat and the intimacy and the trust.

Just a kiss, he had said. Dita wanted more, more of him. She pressed close, feeling the ache as her breasts crushed against the silk of his waistcoat, the heat as his erection pressed against her and she rocked into him, moaning now because a sigh was not enough for the need inside her. The man knew how to tantalise and prolong as his young self had not.

'Dita.' He lifted his head and she caught his ear between her teeth as he bent to kiss her neck, his hands sliding up to cup her breasts. Stephen had done that and she had recoiled and his hungry grasp had hurt her; now the pressure made her want to rub herself shamelessly against Alistair. It was an effort not to bite and she forced herself to concentrate on licking, nibbling, probing the intriguing whorls of his ear.

'Perfect,' Alistair murmured as his fingers found the edge of her bodice and began to stroke the aureole of her nipple. Her breast ached and swelled, heavy and tight in the silken bodice, and she moved under his hands, restless, needing to be free of corsets and camisole, needing his hands on her bare flesh.

He bent to kiss the swell of her breast above the silk, his teasing fingers fretting at the nipple until it was tight to the point of an exquisite pleasure that was almost pain. Dita gasped and Alistair lifted his head, his eyes glinting in the lantern light. 'Did I hurt you?'

'No. No…kiss me.'

It was almost too much, the heat of his mouth on hers, the demanding pressure, the tug at her breast that went deep, deep into her belly, down to where she felt the heat building and twisting into something that made her arch to rub against him—but that only made the ache worse. Her back was against the panelling now, Alistair's weight pressing her, the thick length of his erection just where she needed him to be.

There was something behind her, digging into her back, and she shifted, felt it move and the wall vanished.

Alistair caught her as she stumbled back. 'The door must have been unlocked,' he said as she stared about her, confused. 'It's an empty cabin.' There was just enough light to see. Alistair reached outside, lifted a lamp from the wall and came in, closing the door behind him. She heard the click of the key as he stood there, the light spilling out over the bare deck, the unmade bed with its coir mattress. 'Alistair—'

'Yes,' he said, putting down the lantern and coming to pull her into his arms. 'What do you want, Dita?'

'I don't know.' She tugged at his waistcoat buttons. 'You.'

'I want you, too,' he said as she undid the last of them and began to pull his shirt from his waistband. 'I only meant to kiss you: I should have known it wouldn't stop there. Trust me a little more, Dita? Trust me to pleasure you?'

'Yes,' she said, not quite understanding what he was asking, what it meant. 'I need to touch you. *Aah…*' Her hands slid around his waist against the hot skin and she stood there, resting against him, catching her breath and feeling him tense under her caress.

That evening so long ago, there had been no time to simply hold each other. He had reached for her, she had stumbled into his arms, thinking to give comfort for whatever was causing him such pain, finding her innocent intentions going up in a blaze of scarce-understood desire in the arms of a young man who had been, it seemed, as desperate as she had been and who had somehow found the control to be gentle despite their urgency.

Alistair moved and lifted her and then they were lying on the bunk and her skirts were around her thighs and her hand was cupped around his erection through his trousers and he groaned as he stroked up her legs. She trembled as he pressed them apart, opened her, slid his fingers into the slick folds that parted for him with no resistance. She had fought Stephen off before he touched her with such intimacy; now she had no shame and no fear, only the desperate need for this man.

That time before she had been passive and uncertain under his seeking hands and urgent mouth; now she wanted to touch him, all of him.

'Touch me,' he said against her mouth, echoing her thoughts, and she struggled to understand for a moment. She was touching him… Then she found the fall of his trousers and somehow undid them, slid her hand inside, found the hot, hard length of him and closed her fingers. 'More. Dita…'

She squeezed and stroked and he shuddered and slipped one finger inside her as she clung to him. Then another, and his thumb found a place that felt hard and tight with tension and stroked and she cried out until he stopped her mouth with his, pressing into her circling hand, stroking and squeezing until she screamed silently, arching upwards as everything broke inside her and he surged in her grasp and shuddered above her and the world spun out of its orbit.

'Dita, sweetheart. Are you all right?'

'Hmm?' She was on a bed, in a strange cabin, with Alistair, and he had made love to her—and she had made love to him and it had been everything she remembered yet different. 'Yes. Yes, I am quite all right.'

He was sitting up, putting his clothing to rights and she lay there, just looking at him in the lamplight. Beautiful, mysterious, male. Even more mysterious now he had let her come so close to him again. As close, almost, as it was possible to be. Alistair gave her his handkerchief and got up, his back turned, while she tidied herself and got unsteadily to her feet.

'Are you all right?' He turned to look at her in the lamplight and she smiled. 'That wasn't what I really want, you know that.' He reached out and began to put her hair into order. 'There. I'll leave the mistletoe in place for some other lucky fellows to snatch a kiss.'

'What *do* you want?' she asked, ignoring her hair, not caring about any other men and their kisses.

'To make love with you, fully. But I won't take that risk, Dita. You said it yourself—one slip would be fatal to your reputation. This was certainly a slip—but I think we'll get away with it.' He pulled her closer. 'Was it all right for you, our loving, even though it was not complete?'

She answered him truthfully. 'You gave me more pleasure just now than Stephen did in two days and nights.' *You gave me as much pleasure as that boy had done, so long ago, even though I ache because I need you inside me.*

Alistair laughed and caught her to him for another kiss. As they stood there, her arms twined round his neck she said, 'Do you want your gift?

'Of course!' He sounded eager, almost the young Alistair that the present had been intended for all those years ago.

'Where is my reticule?' They found it on the floor and she pulled out the package and handed it to him and watched as he flattened out the crumpled label.

'Happy birthday?'

'I was going to give it to you the day you left home. I tossed it into the secret drawer of my jewellery box when I realised you were gone. Then I found it again, quite recently. I thought it might amuse you.' She shrugged, 'I will not vouch for the embroidery—I think I will have improved since I was sixteen.'

'You were sixteen when I left?' He frowned at her. 'I suppose you must have been. Dita, did we quarrel, that last day? There was something, some memory in the

back of my mind that I cannot catch hold of. Dreams
like smoke. A kiss? But that cannot be right: I would
not have kissed you.' She thought he muttered, *Let alone
more*, but she was not certain. 'God, I was drunk that
night. The whole thing was such a hellish mess I can't
recall properly.'

'Yes, we quarrelled,' she lied. *He does not recall
making love, his anger, the things he said afterwards. He
must have been beside himself.* 'And I cried and you…
I left.'

'Ah.' The tarnished silver paper flashed in the light
as he turned it over in his hands. 'What are you going
to give me for my birthday this year if I open this now?'

'It depends upon what you deserve,' she said, and
tried to keep her voice light to match his tone.

'Mmm.' The low growl held a wealth of promise as
the paper tore away to reveal the comb case, wavy stripes
of amber and gold and black on one side, on the other a
tiger, copied painstakingly from a print in her father's
library. The stitching was a little uneven, the sewing not
quite smooth.

'You made me a tiger?' Alistair slid the comb out
and then back, turning the case in his hands. 'You had
powers of prediction?'

'No. I always thought you had tiger's eyes,' she confessed. 'When I was a little girl I used to dream you
would turn into a tiger at night and stalk the corridors
of the castle.'

Alistair stared at her from those same uncanny amber
eyes. 'I frightened you that much?'

'No, of course not. I thought it was exciting. You
know you never frightened me, even when you were
angry with me. You looked after me.'

'I did, didn't I.' There was a silence that was strangely

awkward while he stood there, quite still except for the restless fingers that turned the comb case over in his hands. Then, just as she opened her mouth to break it, he pushed the gift into his pocket and took up the lantern.

'We shouldn't have done that, Dita,' he said flatly. She stared at him as he turned the magic of their love-making into an ill-judged romp with his matter-of-fact words. 'You look a little ruffled—we had best go up the companionway at the end here and account for that with some sea air. Ready?'

It was as though another man entirely had come into the cabin: brisk, efficient and practical. 'A good idea,' Dita said, chilled, and followed him as he stepped with wary care into the corridor.

Chapter Nine

Alistair looked from the charming, slightly clumsy piece of embroidery in his hands and up to the generous mouth he had kissed until it was red and swollen. And then up again and into the green eyes that were Dita's, just as they always looked, unchanged even though he had taken her with careless lust. He had seen the sophisticated, adult Dita at Government House and somehow she and the girl in his memory had seemed separate individuals; now, with her gift in his hand, the two slid together, became one.

It had been very strange, that feeling that they had done this before, that she had lain in his arms, that his lips had tasted the tender skin of her breasts, stroked those long, slim legs. It must be because he had known her so well. And those frequent dreams: confused, erotic, troubling dreams touched with anger and betrayal, all mixed with the memories of how he had left home.

The last thing he needed was her becoming in some way attached to him. Lovemaking was all very well, but perhaps he had underestimated her experience. His brain felt as though he had a fever, but one thing was clear: Dita might not be a virgin, but she was inexperienced. The man she had eloped with had obviously been a clumsy boor and now he had shown her a glimpse of what lovemaking could be like. He suspected he had given her her first orgasm.

Alistair led her up the companionway and on to the foredeck. Other passengers had come out, too, but they were laughing and talking and listening to the sailors playing, not paying any attention to two of their number who appeared to have strayed a little further along the deck to catch the warm breeze.

'There—safe,' he said, giving his neckcloth a final tug.

'Indeed.' Dita was a good actress, he thought with gratitude. Her voice was cool even though she looked flushed and a little…a little *loved*. He had thought her still a skinny beanpole, but now he had caressed those slight curves he knew he had been wrong: she was perfect and made for his touch. Her skin glowed under its slight golden tan, her lower lip pouted with a fullness that held the promise of passion with its potential still unfulfilled. Dita raised one hand and curled the loose ringlet around it and his body tightened at the memory of those slender fingers circling his flesh, the ache to sheathe himself in her tight, wet heat.

Perhaps he had been worrying unnecessarily and she was sophisticated enough for these kind of games. He would wait and see.

Some of the passengers had begun to dance a country jig. Alistair caught Dita's hand and almost ran down to join them, whirling her into the end of the line next to the elder Miss Whyton and Lieutenant Tompkins.

'Mistletoe!' Miss Whyton cried as Dita was spun

past her, on down between the row of dancers by the lieutenant. 'Wherever did you get that?'

But she was safely down to the other end now and Alistair made himself focus on the steps as he caught her hands and waited for their turn to dance to the other end.

By the time the fiddler drew out the last chord everyone was flushed and laughing, the ladies fanning themselves, the men pretending to pant with exertion. Alistair saw Callum Chatterton admire Dita's hair ornament and then snatch a kiss, followed by his brother. A positive queue of gentlemen formed.

'I will lend it to you,' Dita said to Daniel, 'and then you may go and make mischief.'

Averil began to unfasten it for her, then stopped, the spray in her hands, and stared. Alistair strolled a little closer.

'But these berries are pearls, Dita! *Real* pearls—you could make an entire necklace there are so many.'

Callum took the spray out of her hands and turned it close in front of his eyes. 'And fine ones at that. You should have them locked in the strongbox, Lady Perdita, not be dancing a jig on the open deck in something this valuable.'

'How lovely they are.' Mrs Bastable came over to join the group, her arm linked through that of her taciturn husband. 'But you ought to replace the pearls with glass beads, for safety. Who gave them to you, dear?'

'Someone I was friends with a long time ago.' Dita said. 'I don't think I know him any more.' She looked up from the mistletoe and caught Alistair looking at her. Her eyes were bleak. 'Excuse me. I will take your advice and lock them away.'

Alistair held the door to the cuddy open for her and she paused on the threshold. 'I would have lain with you for glass beads, or none,' she said in a vehement whisper. 'You had no need to buy me with pearls. I am not a professional. Nor am I an innocent girl who has no idea what is happening when a man kisses her. Don't behave as though we have just done something regret-table; something *silly*. If you want someone to patronise, go and flirt with Dotty Whyton.'

'Damn it!' The accusation was so unfair, and yet such an accurate stab at his conscience, that Alistair let go of the door and it slammed, shutting them off from the others.

'Give them back, then,' he said, smiling, not troubling to keep that devil out of his eyes.

'No.' She put up her chin. 'I shall keep them to remind myself of the folly of passion. They will make a very lovely necklace.'

They were fortunate with the weather, everyone agreed. The wind held, the storms were not severe and they reached Cape Town a week ahead of Captain Archibald's most optimistic prediction.

'I will be so glad to stretch my legs on a surface that does not go up and down,' Averil said as she tied her bonnet ribbons under her chin and tried to see the result in the small mirror that hung on her wall.

'The land will go up and down just as much as the ship seemed to,' Dita told her from her perch on Averil's bunk. 'You have got your sea legs now. What do you intend to do today? The captain says we have two days here.'

'Lord Lyndon has asked me to form one of a party

going to the Company's gardens. Apparently they have the most wonderful collection from all over the world, and a menagerie as well. But surely he has asked you, too?'

'He did, but I have shopping to do, so I refused.' Dita met Averil's questioning gaze with a look of bright interest. 'I saw the gardens on my way out. They are very fine—you will enjoy yourself.'

'I am sure I will.' Averil stuck a hatpin in her pincushion and fidgeted about tidying her things. Dita waited for the next question.

'Shopping for two days?'

'I have something to take to the jewellers and then I must collect it the next day.'

'Is there something wrong between you and Lord Lyndon?' Averil went slightly pink; she was not given to intrusive personal questions.

'Yes,' Dita said. There was no point in lying about it.

'Since Christmas Eve.' Averil nodded to herself. 'That is what I guessed. Whatever is the matter?'

'We had a…a misunderstanding.' *Or, at least, I misunderstood. I thought he cared for me and wanted to make love to me because of that. How naive! He wanted to make love and so he* seemed *to care and once he had, then he was all cool practicality.* It was a mercy he had held back from entering her. She was shamefully aware that she would not have stopped him.

'I thought you liked him very well.'

'I do…did. I find him too…attractive for prudence with a man like that.'

'Oh.' Averil fiddled some more, dropped her gloves and blurted out, 'Did he overstep the mark?'

'Overstep it? Yes, I think you could say he over-leapt it. I should have known better—' Dita broke off, but the sound she heard had been from above their heads, not from anyone returning to the roundhouse, and the windows were closed.

'Dita—you didn't *sleep* with him?'

'Absolutely no sleeping occurred. Oh, I am sorry, I should not be so flippant. No, if you mean did anything occur that might lead to, say, pregnancy. I was more intimate with him than I should have been, and, it is fair to say, we are both regretting that now.'

'So he kissed you very passionately?' Dita reminded herself that Averil was a virgin, and a well-behaved one at that, and nodded. 'But if you are both regretting it, could you not put it behind you now?'

'It is one thing both of you regretting something at the same time,' Dita said, jamming her own hat on her head as she got to her feet. 'That indeed might lead to eventual harmony. What is not...flattering is when the man shows every sign of wanting to run a mile within moments of the encounter.'

'Oh, no! How—'

'Humiliating, is the word you are looking for. The fact that this is, of course, the most sensible and prudent outcome does not help in the slightest.'

'No, I can see that.' Averil gathered up her parasol, reticule and shawl and opened the canvas flap. 'What a pity. I thought he was perfect for you.'

Perfect. He is beautiful and insanely courageous and intelligent and apparently rich and he makes love like an angel and he...he is no angel. An angel would bore me.

'Lady Perdita, Miss Heydon. Good morning.' It was Dr Melchett, a tough old survivor of everything India could throw at a man. Except possibly tigers, Dita thought.

'Good morning, Dr Melchett. Are you going with the party to the gardens?'

'I am not, Lady Perdita. I have seen them several times and I have every intention of buying gifts for my godsons. Might I escort you ladies, if you are also looking for bargains? Ostrich feathers, for example?'

'Thank you, I would be glad of your company, sir. Miss Heydon is bound for the gardens, so I will be your only companion.'

He was a dry and witty escort, Dita discovered, and the perfect antidote to troubling and handsome young men. He tempted her into buying a huge ostrich feather fan and plumes for her next court appearance and then enchanted her by taking her to a wood carver to buy amusing carved animals for his godchildren.

'Oh, look.' It was a small oval box, no bigger than a large snuffbox, with Noah's Ark carved in low relief on the lid. When the lid was opened it was full of minute animals, each in exquisite detail and so small that she could sit the elephant on her little fingernail.

Dita played with it for several minutes before she found the pair of tigers and remembered Alistair and her reason for coming shopping.

'Is there a good jeweller's shop, do you know, Doctor?' Reluctantly she slid the lid closed and handed the box back to the dealer. She already had a number of larger carved animals for nephews and nieces and they were all too young for anything so delicate.

'You are not intending to buy gemstones? You would have done better in India. There is one along here, I seem to recall. Ah, yes, here we are.'

'I need a necklace stringing,' she explained as the jeweller came to greet them. 'These. They are already drilled.' She poured the pearls out on to the velvet pad on the counter. 'Can you do it for tomorrow? I want them in one simple string.'

'I can do it for tomorrow morning, madam.' He produced his loupe and picked up a handful. 'These are very fine and well matched. Indian?'

'Yes.' They agreed a price and she let the doctor take her arm and find a carriage back to the ship.

'Your mistletoe pearls?'

'They are.' She gazed out of the window, willing the doctor to change the subject.

'Interesting young man, that. And generous.' So he had guessed who had given them to her.

'We knew each other as children.' *Talk about something else. Please.*

'And yet you are no longer friends.' The old man rested his clasped hands on the top of his walking cane and regarded her with faded blue eyes. 'A pity to fall out with old friends. When you reach my age you appreciate the value of all of them.'

'It is his birthday tomorrow,' Dita said. There was a lump in her throat for some reason. 'I… Perhaps I should buy him a present.'

'What would he like, do you think?' Doctor Melchett sat up straight, a twinkle of interest in his eyes.

'I do not know. He can afford whatever he wants and it is too late to make anything.'

'Then give him simplicity and something to make him smile. He does not smile enough, I suspect.'

'The Noah's Ark!'

'That would make me smile if a lovely young lady gave it to me,' the old man said with a chuckle, pulling the check string and ordering the carriage back to the shopping district.

* * *

After breakfast Dita waited until Alistair strolled out on to the deck alone. If he snubbed her, she did not want an audience.

'Happy birthday.' She could have sworn she had made no sound as she walked towards him where he leaned against the rail, but he did not start at the sound of her voice right behind him. Nor did he look round.

'Thank you.' She waited, despite her instinct to turn on her heel, and eventually he shifted until he faced her. 'You are speaking to me again?'

'And you to me. Kindly do not imply I have been sulking.' She drew down a deep breath: this was not how she had meant this encounter to go. 'You are the most infuriating man. I was determined to be all sweetness and light and in less than a dozen words you have me scratching at you.'

'Sweetness and light?' He smiled and she found herself smiling back with wary affection. *Thank you, Dr Melchett.* 'That I would like to see.'

'I would like to forget Christmas Eve, to put it behind us. I wish we could just be friends again and not think about who was to blame or who said what.'

His smile was wicked. 'I would suggest that staying in plain view of at least three fellow passengers at all times might be a good idea if that is your plan. You might want to be *just friends*, Dita, I would be a liar if I said I did. And I am not sure I believe you either.'

'Have you no self-control?' she snapped, then threw up her hands. 'I am sorry. Doubtless you are right. It was both of us, I know that. Can we not forget it?'

'We could pretend to forget it,' Alistair said, watching her. Could he sense how aroused he made her feel, just standing there? She had kissed his mouth, just there.

Those long, clever fingers had touched her there and there and… 'Would that do?' he asked. Something in his expression made her doubt he intended pretending for very long.

'It will have to, I suppose.' Dita brought her hands out from behind her back to reveal the box. 'This is for your birthday. It is quite useless—its only purpose is to make you smile.'

'That seems a good purpose.' He reached out and took it, his fingers scrupulously avoiding touching hers. 'Local work?'

'Yes. Best to open it over a flat surface and out of the breeze, I think.'

It was reward enough, just to sit and watch his face, intent over the box, his fingers delicately lifting each tiny creature on to the table, arranging them in pairs, finding the miniature gangplank that could slope up to the box. 'Here is Noah.' He lifted the final piece out and looked up at her, smiling. She swayed towards him a little, drawn by the curve of his lips.

'Thank you, this is exquisite.' He lifted a finger and touched her cheek. 'It makes you smile, too. I hated that I killed your smiles, Dita.'

'You did not,' she said, stiffening. He had only to touch her, it seemed, and her self-control wilted. Attack seemed the only defence. 'You have an exaggerated idea of the influence you have over me. If I have seemed sombre, it is no doubt because I have been reflecting on the folly of allowing myself to be attracted to a personable rake.'

'Attracted?' That smile was back. He must practise it to have such a devastating effect, she thought, fighting down equal measures of panic and arousal.

'Do stop fishing for compliments, Alistair.' Dita

pushed back her chair and stood up and he rose, too, the movement of his linen coat scattering the tiny animals across the table. 'Of course *attracted*. I would hardly make love with a man for whom I felt no attraction.'

'Wouldn't you? I really have no idea what you might do, Dita, if the fancy took you.' The amusement had drained out of his expression, leaving it bleak and arrogant.

'You are suggesting that I would—' *What? Sleep with any man I fancied, on a whim?* She almost asked the question, then bit it back; she did not want to hear him say *yes*.

'That so-called chaperon of yours, sweet lady though she is, just isn't up to your weight, Dita.'

'I am not a damned horse!'

Alistair's eyes narrowed into an insolent scrutiny that had her balling her fists at her sides in an effort not to slap him. 'No. You don't need a jockey, you go fast enough as it is. What you need, Perdita my love, is a husband.'

'Perhaps I do,' she said with every ounce of sweetness she could get into her voice. 'Perhaps, somewhere, there is a man who is not patronising, arrogant, domineering or interested only in my money or my body. On the evidence so far, however, I am finding that hard to believe.'

Behind them the door opened, bringing with it the sea air and the sound of shouted orders to the men in the rigging. Dita whirled round and walked out, almost colliding with Dr Melchett on the threshold. She managed a thin-lipped smile as she passed, intent on reaching the prow of the ship before anyone, anyone at all, spoke to her.

Chapter Ten

'Happy birthday, my lord.'

Alistair looked up from collecting up the tiny animals. It took steady fingers and had to be done before they were scattered and damaged, whatever else he wanted to do. Like kicking the panelling or getting drunk. 'Doctor Melchett. Thank you, sir. How did you—? Ah, yes, you knew Lady Perdita bought the Ark for me, I assume.'

'I went shopping with her yesterday,' the older man said as he sat down opposite Alistair. 'Charming young lady. Intelligent, lovely and high spirited.'

'She is certainly all those things.' Alistair continued to slot each fragile piece into place.

'You did not like her gift?'

'Very much; it is a work of art.' Dr Melchett was silent. Alistair recognised the technique: keep quiet and eventually your opponent will start babbling. He considered playing the game and saying nothing, but that would be disrespectful to an old man. 'Lady Perdita is not certain she likes me.'

'Ah.' The doctor fumbled in his pocket, brought out

a snuffbox and offered it to Alistair. He didn't use the stuff himself, but he recognised the friendly overture and took a pinch. 'Difficult thing, love,' Melchett mused.

'What?' A minute elephant went skidding out of his hand and across the table.

The doctor picked it up and peered at it. 'Love. Old friends, aren't you?'

'Yes. Not lovers.' He examined the last half-hour in painful detail and shrugged. 'We were friends, as children, as much as one can be with a six-year age gap. We have apparently grown out of it.'

'Love, lovers, in love, loving… So many shades of meaning to that word.' Melchett sighed. 'You were fond of her as a boy?'

'She was a burr under my saddle,' Alistair said evenly as he slid the box lid closed. 'A pestilential little sister.' He grinned reluctantly, remembering. 'I suppose I was fond of her, yes.'

'And you still want to protect her.'

No, he did not want to protect her—he wanted to make love to her for the rest of the voyage. 'Lady Perdita requires protecting from herself, mainly,' Alistair said as he put the box in his pocket. 'But of course I keep an eye on her; she is the daughter of neighbours, after all.'

Melchett got to his feet. 'That's the ticket: neighbourliness. Now you know what it is, you won't fret over it so much.' He chuckled. 'Nothing like a proper diagnosis for making one feel better. Don't let me disturb you,' he added as Alistair stood. 'Have a pleasant birthday, my lord.'

What the devil was that about? Neighbourliness? Diagnosis indeed! He didn't need medical assistance to know that he was suffering from a mixture of exasperation and frustration. And just a tinge of guilt.

He wanted Dita: wanted her in bed, under him, around him. He wanted her screaming his name, wanted her begging him to make love to her again, and again. Alistair took a deep breath and thought longingly of cold rivers.

He also wanted to box her ears half the time. That was nothing new—he had spent most of his boyhood in that frame of mind, when she wasn't making him laugh. Not that he had ever given in to the temptation: one did not strike a girl under any circumstances, however provoking she was.

Unfair that, he thought with a slight smile. *Spanking, now...* The word brought a vision of Dita's small, pert backside delightfully to mind.

Which brought him neatly back to the guilt. It was not an emotion he was much prone to. He certainly hadn't felt guilt over leaving home. Since then he had done few things that caused him regret; all experience had some value. The problem was, he saw with a flash of clarity, he was not feeling guilty over wanting to make love to Dita, he was feeling guilty because he couldn't be sorry about it.

Damn it. It would be a good thing when she was home safely, despite her best efforts otherwise, and when she *was* home he hoped she would do her utmost to find a decent husband, although her list of requirements from this paragon probably meant the man did not exist. He could watch this while he searched for a wife—who should be easy to identify when he met her. She would be precisely the opposite of Lady Perdita Brooke in every particular.

'If I never see St Helena again it will be too soon,' Mrs Bastable remarked as the island vanished over the horizon. 'A more disagreeable place I cannot imagine, and the food was dreadful.'

'There's Ascension next; we can pick up some turtles and have splendid soup,' Alistair remarked from his position on the rail, surrounded by a group of ladies, amongst whom the elder Miss Whyton was prominent. 'And from there, if we have good fortune, perhaps only another ten weeks sailing.'

'The Equator soon,' Callum Chatterton added. 'But no sport to be had there—we got everyone who had never crossed before on the way out from Madras.'

Alistair ducked under the sailcloth and sat down on one of the chairs under the awning that sheltered Dita, Averil and Mrs Bastable. He chose one opposite her and not the vacant one by her side, much to her relief. Then she realised that from where he was sitting he could meet her eyes. He seemed intent on doing just that. She held the amber gaze and her breath hitched, shortened, as his lids drooped sensually and the colour seemed to darken.

'How are you entertaining yourselves?' he asked, his tone at variance with the messages his eyes were sending. 'I find I am growing blasé about flying fish and whales.'

'I still have needlework,' Averil said. 'There is all the table linen for my trousseau. The light on deck is so good it makes doing white-work monograms very easy.'

'I intend to carry on reading,' Dita said. 'Novels,' she added, daring him to comment.

'Sensation novels?' Alistair enquired, ignoring her challenging look.

'Of course. I packed the most lurid novels I could find and I am devouring them shamelessly. I have an ambition to write one and I am reviewing plots to see what has not been covered. Perhaps I shall become an eccentric spinster novelist.'

'How about a story set on a pirate ship?' Alistair suggested, his expression so bland she could not tell if he was teasing her or not.

'Oh, yes, what a wonderful idea, and quite fresh, I think.' Dita cast round their little group for inspiration. 'My heroine—who will look just like Miss Heydon— has been carried on board by the villain—a tall, dark, dastardly character with a scar on his cheek—' Alistair raised one eyebrow, which she ignored '—who has chained the hero in the foul bilges.'

'How is she going to escape his evil intent?' Averil asked, missing this byplay.

'The hero escapes, but, single-handed, even he cannot overpower the villain,' Dita said, improvising wildly. 'So he must haunt the ship, stepping in only to save her at critical moments.

'There will be storms, sea monsters, desert islands, the villain's lascivious attempts upon the fair heroine's virtue…'

'Perhaps she flees him and climbs into the rigging?' Alistair suggested. 'And he climbs after her and forces her down to the deck before pressing his foul attentions upon her in the cuddy.'

'It sounds highly improbable,' Dita said frigidly. 'Although the foul attentions sound…characteristic.'

'No, it's brilliant,' Callum contradicted. 'It will make a perfect cliffhanger. She hits him with the soup ladle and escapes to barricade herself in her cabin.'

'I was thinking of a carving knife,' Dita said with a tight smile at Alistair, who smiled back in a way that had the hair standing up on the back of her neck. *A hunting smile…*

'It sounds wonderful,' Averil said, breathless with laughter as she dabbed at her eyes with the napkin she was working on. 'You must write it, Lady Perdita.'

'In instalments,' Daniel added. 'And read one every evening. We will all contribute plot ideas as the story develops and take on roles. The hero is, of course, so perfect that none of us can approach him, but I see myself as the flawed, but ultimately noble first lieutenant of the ship, Trueheart. He loves the heroine from afar, knowing he is unworthy, but will redeem himself by the sacrifice of his life for her in about episode sixty-three.'

'Very well,' Dita agreed. 'I will do it. It will be a three-volume epic, I can see.'

The novel proved to be an absorbing occupation. Averil patiently embroidered the corners of innumerable handkerchiefs and table napkins and Dita wrote while they sat under their awning in the heat.

By the time they crossed the Equator Averil had moved on to pillow cases, the passengers, sustained by turtle soup, began to think hopefully of home and Dita had filled pages of her notebook.

Every afternoon after dinner the passengers retreated to their cabins out of the sun to recruit their strength before supper. Dita found that a difficult routine to settle to, despite having followed it for a year in India. Here, on the ship, she was too restless to lie dozing in her canvas box. And for some reason the restlessness increased the longer she was on board.

She was not afraid of her family's reaction when she got home, she decided—that was not what was disturbing her. Papa would still be angry with her—that was only to be expected, for he had taken her elopement hard—but Mama and her brothers and sisters would welcome her with open arms. Nor was it apprehension about her reception in society; she was ready to do battle over that.

No, something else was making her feel edgy and restless and faintly apprehensive in a not unpleasant kind of way, and she very much feared it was Alistair. The memory of their lovemaking on Christmas Eve should have served as a constant warning, she told herself. Instead it simply reminded her how much she wanted his kisses and his caresses. And Alistair, maddening man, had not tried to lay a finger on her, so she could not even make herself feel better by spurning him.

Had he turned over a new leaf and decided on celibacy? He was not flirting with anyone else; she knew that because she watched him covertly. Or was he deliberately tantalising her by apparent indifference? If so, he was most certainly succeeding.

Her only outlet had become the novel. The plot became more and more fantastical, the perils of Angelica, the fragile yet spirited heroine, became more extreme, the impossibly noble, handsome and courageous hero suffered countless trials to protect her and the saturnine villain became more sinister, more amorous, and, unfortunately, more exciting.

Three days after they crossed the Equator, with the Cape Verde Islands their next landfall, Dita found herself alone in the canvas shelter on deck. A sailor adjusted the sailcloth to create a shady cave and she settled back on the daybed the ship's carpenter had made and looked out between the wings of the shelter to the rail and then open, empty sea.

She lay for a while, lulled by the motion of the ship, the blue, unending water, the warmth on her body. Then, insidiously, the warmth became heat and the familiar ache and need and she shifted restlessly and reached for her notebook and pencil.

The roll of the ship sent the little book sliding away and she sat up and scrambled to the end of the daybed to reach for it. 'Bother the thing!'

A shadow fell over the book as Alistair appeared and stooped to pick it up. 'Ah, the *Adventures of Angelica.*' When she tried to twitch it from his fingers he sat down on the end of the daybed, held it just out of her reach and opened it.

'Give it back, if you please.' It was hard to sound dignified when she was curled up with her slippers kicked off, her petticoats rumpled about her calves and no hat on. Dita scrambled back towards the head of the daybed, pulled her skirts down and held out one hand.

'But I want to read it.' He flipped to the end and read while Dita pressed her lips together and folded her hands in her lap. She was not going to tussle for it. 'Now, let's see. So, Angelica has escaped on to the desert island and Baron Blackstone is pursuing her, so close that she can hear his panting breaths behind her as she flees across the sand towards the scanty shelter of the palm trees. How is she going to escape this time?'

'The gallant de Blancheville has sawn his way through the latest lot of shackles and is rushing to her rescue,' Dita said with as much dignity as the ludicrous plot would allow her.

'I cannot imagine why Blackstone hasn't thrown him overboard to the sharks,' Alistair commented. He leaned back, one hand on the far edge of the daybed, his body turned towards her, the picture of elegant indolence. 'I would have done so about ten chapters back. Think of the saving in shackles.'

'Villains never do the sensible thing,' Dita retorted. 'And if I kill off the hero, that's the end of the book. With you as captain of this ship the drama would be over on page three; de Blancheville would have walked the plank and poor Angelina would have thrown herself overboard in despair.'

He curled a lip. 'The man's prosy and disposable. Have her falling for Blackstone. Think of the fun they could have on a desert island.'

'I really wouldn't—Alistair! That is my ankle!'

'And a very pretty one it is, too. Has your chaperon never told you it is fast to shed your shoes in public?' He ran his hand over the arch of her foot, then curled his fingers round it and held tight when she jerked it back. 'Relax.'

'Relax—with your hand under my skirts?'

'Don't you like this?' His thumb was stroking the top of the arch of her foot while his fingers brushed tickling caresses underneath. It was disturbingly reminiscent of the way he had caressed her more intimately.

'I'll scream.'

'No, you won't.' He slid off the daybed, knelt beside it, bent and lifted her foot. 'Pretty toes, too.'

'You can't see my toes,' she said in a brisk, matter-of-fact tone, which became a muffled shriek when he began to suck them through her stocking. 'Stop it!'

In answer his hand slid up her leg to her knee, tweaked the garter and began to pull down her stocking.

'Alistair, stop that this minute…. Oh…' Her stocking was off, her toes were in his mouth and he was sucking and licking each one with intense concentration. It was wonderful. It was outrageous and she should stop him. But she couldn't, Dita thought as she flopped back inelegantly on to the pile of bolsters, not without creating the most dreadful scene by struggling.

Why having her toes sucked should be so inflammatory, she could not imagine. And Alistair must enjoy doing it, although she could not see his face, only his dark head bent over her foot as he sucked her big toe fully into his mouth. *'Aah...'*

He released her and went back to stroking her instep and ankle. 'Tell me the story.'

'How can I concentrate when you are—?'

'Do you want me to stop?' He glanced sideways, his eyes full of wicked mischief.

'Yes! No...no.'

'Go on then.' He closed his lips around her toes again, but did nothing more than nibble.

'Um...' She forced herself to concentrate. 'I think we need a sword fight. De Blancheville has been freed by—oh, that is wonderful, don't stop... Freed by Tom the cabin boy, who is really the lovely Maria in disguise. She has stowed away to follow Trueheart, whom she loves from afar, and thinks that if de Blancheville removes Angelina then Trueheart will stop wanting her and... ah, oh, *please*...be Maria's.'

'Please?' He lifted his head again, put down her foot and shifted up the daybed. 'Please what, Dita?'

'I don't know!' He was sitting on the edge now, his hip against hers. Her voice shook as he leaned in. 'That was my *toes*. Toes aren't—'

'Erotic? Oh, but they are. Every inch of your body, inside and out, is erotic, Dita. Think what fun we could have finding out about eyebrows, or earlobes or the back of your knees.' His hand slid up her leg as he leaned closer. 'And all the places my tongue wants to explore.'

'After Christmas Eve, I don't think it is wise,' she

managed to say. Eight years ago his lovemaking had not been so sophisticated. He had been practising, of course.

'Don't think.' His breath was on her lips now; his hand cupped her intimately. She closed her eyes on a shuddering sigh as something, distant, banged.

Alistair moved so fast that he was on his feet, tucking her stocking under her skirts, pulling them down round her feet, before she realised that it was the door of the cuddy banging to.

Dita sat up, pulled her feet under her and fanned her flushed face with both hands. Alistair, apparently engrossed in her notebook, was sitting on one of the chairs at the mouth of the canvas shelter as the approaching voices resolved themselves into the Chattertons and Averil.

'Oh, here you are, Dita,' Averil said, peeping into the shelter. 'What have you been up to?'

'Plotting,' Alistair said easily. 'We have just decided that the novel needs a duel.'

The others clustered round with exclamations of agreement. Dita made an effort. 'This swashbuckling is all very well, but someone will have to write the duel for me because I have never seen a sword fight.'

'We will choreograph it on the poop deck tomorrow,' Callum declared. 'And you can take notes. I've got my foils. Dan?'

His brother groaned. 'You know I'm useless with a rapier.'

'I'll fight you,' Alistair said. 'No reason why we can't do it after breakfast, is there? The chaperons aren't going to object to a harmless bout of fencing.'

'I would love to try it,' Dita said wistfully. Any kind of violent exercise appealed just at the moment. 'Would you show me, Mr Chatterton?'

'Of course!' Callum had loosened up considerably over the course of the voyage. He was not the only one, she thought, fanning herself. 'No reason why a lady cannot try a few of the moves with perfect propriety.'

'No.' Alistair still lounged in his chair, but his voice was definite. 'I will show you, if you insist.'

'Lady Perdita asked me,' Callum stated. The atmosphere became subtly charged.

'I will fight you for the privilege,' Alistair said.

Callum narrowed his eyes, his whole body tense, but Averil clapped her hands and laughed. 'How exciting! Shall we lay wagers? I will venture ten rupees on Lord Lyndon.'

'And I wager the same on my brother,' Daniel said. In the sunlight Alistair's amber eyes glinted like those of a big cat and she shivered.

'Will no one else back me? Lady Perdita?'

'Ten rupees on Mr Chatterton,' she said.

'Then if I win I will claim a forfeit from you,' Alistair said.

'Indeed?' Dita tried to sound dignified and knew she simply sounded flustered. 'I am sure you will choose something that is perfectly proper, my lord. *If* you win, that is. Gentlemen, perhaps you would excuse us? There is something I wish to discuss with Miss Heydon.'

The men took themselves off, Alistair with a sidelong smile. He made as if to slide the notebook into his pocket and then bent and put it on the end of the daybed. 'What is this? Someone must have dropped it. Is it yours?'

Her blue garter ribbon dangled from the tips of his fingers, the fingers that only moments before had been caressing her intimately.

'Certainly not.'

'Oh well, I had better keep it, then.' He put it in his pocket and strolled off while Dita seethed.

'That was a garter,' Averil whispered.

'I know. Mine. I have taken my shoes off, and a stocking. Very fast, I know, but it is so hot.' She retrieved her stocking from under her skirts and pulled it on. Perhaps Averil would assume her raised colour was due to the embarrassment of being almost caught shedding clothing.

'What was that about?' Averil asked, sitting down on the end of the daybed. 'One could cut the atmosphere with a knife, all of a sudden.'

'I expect the men are getting bored.'

'It wasn't that, I don't think. Lord Lyndon sounded as though he was challenging Mr Chatterton to a duel; his eyes positively made me shiver. I do wish you would not tease him so, Dita.'

'I do not tease him. I am going out of my way not to do so, but he is being extremely provoking.'

'May I ask? Have you and Callum Chatterton an understanding?'

'No!' Dita laughed. 'Of course not.'

'Why of course?' Averil put her feet up and curled her arms around her legs. With her chin resting on her knees she looked like a curious cat. 'He is intelligent and obviously destined for preferment. His brother is an earl, he is charming and good looking and he doesn't flirt like his brother. You like him, don't you?'

'Of course. I would be foolish not to. But I couldn't possibly *marry* him.' It occurred to her as she said it that she had looked at Callum, back in Calcutta, with interest. And close contact had only heightened her regard for him. So why couldn't she contemplate him as a husband?

'You would be a very good match for him and could only help his career.'

'You forget my reputation,' Dita pointed out.

'If you were the daughter of Mr Blank, with a dowry of five hundred pounds and freckles, then possibly that would be fatal. If he thought the worse of you for it, then he would not be so friendly, and if he had less honourable intentions, surely you have become aware of that by now?'

'True. But I do not love him.'

Averil was silent for just long enough for Dita to realise how tactless that was. They both spoke at once. 'I am sorry, I did not mean—'

'I am sure I will be very happy with Lord Bradon,' Averil said with stiff dignity.

'Of course you will,' Dita said. 'You are marrying with a strong sense of duty to your family and he is a most suitable choice and you have the type of character that will create happiness. I do not have a duty to wed and I do not have your amiable nature.'

Averil bit her lip. 'Is it Lord Lyndon? You and he seem to have so much in common.'

'Our only common ground is shared memories, and our only compatibility appears to be in the bedchamber,' Dita said, goaded. And not just the bedchamber. Here, in the open air, at the dinner table when he only had to look at her from under sensually drooping lids for her to ache with desire. Anywhere, it seemed.

Averil blushed and investigated the lace at her hem intently. After a moment she said, 'That is not enough, is it?'

'No, it is not.' Dita began to gather up her pencils. 'Alistair is not jealous, he is just territorial and I seem to have become part of that territory.'

'Oh dear,' Averil sighed. 'And I do love a romantic ending.'

'Never mind.' Dita conjured up a smile from somewhere. 'When you are married you can find me just the man.' *If he exists*, she thought as Averil, cheered by that idea, smiled.

Chapter Eleven

Alistair took one of the foils from Daniel Chatterton and tested the button on the point. It seemed secure and he brought the blade down through the air with a swish, pleased the weapon was light and well balanced in his hand. They were an expensive pair: Callum must take his fencing seriously.

Word of the bout had spread and most of the passengers were on deck to watch. One young lady had even brought her sketchbook and Dita was perched on a stool, notebook and pencil in hand, her face in shadow under a broad-brimmed hat.

Doctor Melchett had taken command of the wagers, which were growing prodigiously. As no one, except Daniel Chatterton, had any idea of the proficiency of either of them, it was hard to know on what basis people were staking their money.

'You are the favourite,' George Latham, one of the more senior Company clerks, remarked as he passed Alistair on his way to a place at the rail. 'Everyone's heard about the tiger, no doubt.' He glanced at Callum, who had discarded his coat and was rolling up his shirt sleeves. 'Chatterton looks competent though.'

'I am sure he'll give me a good bout,' Alistair said. He did not care if the man was the East India Company's foils champion, he was not teaching Dita to fence and getting his hands all over her in the process.

'How is the winner to be decided?' someone called.

'It is in the nature of a masquerade,' Daniel said. 'Lord Lyndon plays the villain, my brother the hero. They fight over the heroine, played by Mrs Bastable, who sits here.' He indicated a chair at the foot of the main mast where the lady dimpled and waved to her friends. 'She is the villain's captive. To win, one man must either disarm the other, or land a hit that in the opinion of our learned medical advisor—' Dr Melchett bowed '—is fatal or incapacitating, or must obtain the other's surrender.'

Callum picked up his foil, walked forwards and took his position. Alistair faced him and raised the foil for the salute. As Chatterton's blade came up Alistair saw the focus in the other man's eyes and blanked everything beyond his opponent from his mind; however this had started, it was not a game now.

'En garde!' Daniel called and the blades touched. Alistair stepped back sharply and Callum cut to his right. *So it begins*, he thought, watching the other man for balance and strengths, knowing he was being assessed in the same way as they cut and parried, shifting around their circle of deck.

He let his guard waver deliberately, took a touch to the arm that would have been a slash with an unguarded weapon and confirmed his suspicion that Chatterton was weaker on the left foot. But it was a damnably close match. Alistair pinked his opponent on the left shoulder, took another hit on the forearm and then, as Callum was extended from that lunge, shifted his weight and drove him back hard towards the hatch cover.

In a flurry of blows they were toe to toe, face to face, their hilts locked. On either side the spectators drew back, uncertain which way they might move.

'Just what are your intentions towards Lady Perdita?' Alistair asked between clenched teeth as they each thrust forwards against the weight of the other.

'My *what*?' Callum gave ground and recovered.

'You heard me.'

'Entirely honourable—if that's any of your damned business,' he retorted. 'What are yours?'

Alistair stepped back, lowered his weapon without warning and Callum stumbled, caught out by the sudden shift in weight. Alistair ducked under his guard, there was a sharp flurry of strokes and he had the button of his foil against Callum's jugular. *What the hell* are *my intentions?* 'Neighbourly,' he said, showing his teeth. *And that's a lie.*

For a long moment his opponent stared into his eyes as though trying to read his mind. Then Callum gave a half-smile, let his foil fall to the deck and spread his hands in surrender. 'You win,' he said, then dropped his voice, 'Just don't try and run me through if I smile at her, damn it. She's a delight—and I freely admit that it would take a stronger man than I to take her to wife.'

They went to get their coats, the antagonism between them vanishing as rapidly as it had built. Doctor Melchett was besieged by those who had laid wagers and the two duellists were buffeted from all sides by well-wishers.

When Alistair finally made it to the comparative peace of the poop deck, he found Dita sitting scribbling in her notebook. 'Was that helpful?'

'Yes, it was. And extremely exciting.' She closed the book and looked at him, her green eyes dark and troubled despite the steadiness of her gaze. 'You have a forfeit for me, I believe.'

'Yes.' He had been thinking about that, ever since he had thrown the challenge at her. 'You will allow me to show you how to defend yourself.'

'I am not likely to be carrying a sword if I find myself in trouble, Alistair!'

'No, but you have your teeth, your feet and your elbows and you will usually have a hat pin, or a glass of wine or your reticule.' He regarded her seriously. 'You are too attractive, Dita. That and the scrape you got into mean that men will try to take advantage of you when you get to London.'

She shifted uncomfortably. 'Surely not. I am not pretty—'

'I know that. And you know perfectly well how attractive you are, which is an entirely different thing—you didn't get that way without working at it.' Dita opened her mouth and closed it again. 'I will teach you a few fencing moves, as Chatterton could have done perfectly well, but I will teach you to fight dirty, too.'

'Where, might I ask?' She sounded outraged, but looked intrigued.

'In my cabin—if you dare.'

'You are teaching me how to repel unwanted advances—aren't you worried that you might find your own lessons turned on you?'

'Of course, you can try. You won't best me though. Besides, my advances are not unwelcome—are they?' he said with a deliberate arrogance designed to provoke.

Dita shook her head at him, but a smile she could not control twitched at the corner of her mouth. He felt something shift inside his chest, something almost like a twinge of fear. *Damn it, what am I getting myself into?* He gave himself a mental shake: she was not a virgin, he was not going to risk getting her with child, she was willing. What was there to worry about?

Dita stood up. She felt curiously shaken. It was probably the fight. Even though she knew there were buttons on the foils and that it was essentially a game, there was something primal and stirring about two men fighting with deadly skill and elegance. Especially, she had to admit, over her. Even more so when one of them was Alistair. She did not want to investigate that thought too deeply.

'Would you care to try the foils now? You do not mind an audience?'

She hardly had time to nod before he was gone, to return with the swords and Mrs Bastable, both Chatterton twins and Averil at his heels. Alistair placed one foil in her hand and she exclaimed at how light it was.

'The point is to impale your opponent, not bludgeon him to death,' he said, and she snorted with nervous laughter as he put his hand over hers to adjust her grip. 'Good, check the button is secure, you do not want to run Mr Chatterton through just yet.' Callum grinned, picked up the other foil and stood opposite her. 'Now stand sideways, with your feet like this...'

Alistair nudged her into position, his hands warm yet impersonal on her shoulder, at her elbow. She had thought he would need to hold her more closely and found herself oddly piqued that he did not. *'En garde,'* Callum said, bringing his foil up, and she imitated him.

'Now lunge.' Alistair moved behind her, his body suddenly as close as she could have wished, one arm bracketing her, his hand over her fingers. Their weight shifted together, Callum moved, his foil coming across to deflect her blade, and Alistair pulled her back. 'Bring up your foil; he is going to counter-attack.'

'Oh!' It was alarming, seeing that blade coming towards her, even slowly. Hers met it at right angles. 'Push,' Alistair said in her ear and she did, as he twisted her wrist, moved their balance and Callum, caught unawares, found his foil flicked out of his grasp.

'Now, in for the kill!' Instinctively she straightened the blade, let her body go with the thrust of his and Callum was standing there, the button of her foil pressed against his heart.

'I've killed you!' She jumped up and down in glee before she realised what she had said. 'Oh! I am so sorry, Mr Chatterton, I didn't mean—'

'You, Lady Perdita,' he said with a grin, 'are quite lethal, with or without a weapon. I think I will let my brother stand as your opponent in future—he has no reputation as a swordsman to lose.'

'I think that is quite enough,' Dita said. 'I know what it feels like to hold a sword now, and I would like to learn more—but I do not think that proper lessons would be quite—'

'Proper?' Alistair released her and reversed the foil over his arm for Callum to take before he went to retrieve the fallen one. 'Thank you,' he added, holding out his hand to shake the other's. 'That was good sport.' He nodded to Dita and strode off.

'What was that about?' Dita demanded when she found herself alone for a moment with Callum while Daniel wiped the blades with an oiled cloth and laid them back in their case. He looked at her blankly. 'Mr Chatterton, one minute you and Alistair are bristling at each other like two tom cats on a wall and the next you are shaking hands and appear to be friends for life.'

'Oh, that.' He took her arm and strolled to the rail where they could look down on the main deck. 'He thought my intentions towards you might be less than honourable, I suspect. Now he believes me when I tell him they are simply those of friendship and I believe *him* when he tells me that he is acting purely as a concerned neighbour.'

'A neighbour?' Dita stared at him. 'Lord Lyndon has been no neighbour of mine for the past eight years.'

'He obviously feels he still has a responsibility to look after you, Lady Perdita,' Callum said with a perfectly straight face and laughter in his eyes. 'If you will excuse me.' He bowed and left her a victim to considerable confusion.

Why on earth did Alistair feel he had to warn Callum off, and why did he want to teach her to defend herself? Was he a rake or a reformed man? Or a rake who was trying to lull her into a false sense of security? Whatever the answer, it was intriguing. Not that she should give in to her regrettable attraction to him again.

She was still leaning on the rail and brooding when Alistair came back. 'That empty cabin is still unoccupied and no one is around down there. Do you want to attempt to disarm me now?'

Dita followed him warily, but the space was brightly lit by three lanterns and there were an array of props on the unmade bunk. It seemed he really did have a self-defence lesson in mind.

After ten minutes he had her in fits of laughter as he demonstrated the best way to wield a hat pin to deter a pest sitting next to her in a pew at church, the easiest way to tip a glass of wine down a gentleman who was standing too close whilst making it seem like an accident, the most painful part of the foot to stand upon with a French heel and how to free one's hands if they had been seized. It was all fun and extremely useful.

'Girls ought to be taught this sort of thing instead of endless embroidery,' she remarked as Alistair rubbed a twisted thumb.

'That will deal with the pests,' he said. 'What I will show you now is how to deal with an over-amorous gentleman who completely oversteps the bounds of decency.'

'Indeed?' Dita raised an eyebrow. 'You intend to stop kissing me and…other things, do you?'

Alistair studied her without amusement. 'Tell me that anything I have done has been unwelcome and I will not speak to you, or approach you, for the remainder of this voyage.'

That was handing her her own with a vengeance. Dita searched her conscience, then shook her head. 'You have done many things that are shocking, unwise and outrageous, and I have not been unwilling.' It was difficult to meet his eyes, but when she did the tension had vanished from his face.

He nodded. 'After this, should you change your mind, you will be able to give me a very pointed hint. There are a number of places where a jab or a blow is extremely painful and will win you time to get away. If you will allow me to take you in my arms, like so—'

Dita knew she was still flushed, and it was hard to remember that she was supposed to be fighting and not yielding.

'Make your fingers stiff and jab here, then raise your knee…' Her hand and knee hardly made contact before he twisted away, eel-like. 'You have it to perfection. Now, let's try again.' Alistair took her in a firm embrace, turning so his broad shoulders were to the bunk. 'Try for the solar plexus.'

'You are holding me too tightly,' she protested. 'That isn't fair!' It was no longer a game, but she could not have said quite why not. She felt hot and bothered and far too close to him. Her nipples, she could feel, were peaking hard against her bodice, her breathing was all over the place and the wretched man was stroking his fingers down her spine.

'Rakes don't play fair, Dita,' he murmured, bending to nibble her ear. 'Stop palpitating and think about what I showed you. I have all the time in the world while you decide what to do.' His tongue traced hot and moist down to the lobe and she jumped as though he had pinched her.

'You…' *Think, Dita, your hands are free. He said something about ears… Oh my lord, he is sucking my earlobe…* She raised her hands, grabbed both Alistair's ears and twisted. The result was instant.

'Aagh!' They stood, a foot apart, glaring at each other, then Alistair began to laugh. 'Excellent.' He rubbed his ears with a grimace. 'You see, there is no point pussy-footing about. If you are serious, then act and put everything you have into it. What you should have done, the moment I released you, was to use your knee. If you had done it hard enough, I would be rolling about on the floor by now and you would be out of the door.'

'Thank you, ' Dita said. 'If I ever encounter a wolf, I will know what to do now.' She still felt unsettled and aroused and simmering beneath that there was anger with herself for feeling that way—and with him for manipulating her so. She turned and opened the door. 'A wolf, or any other kind of deceiver. Good day, Alistair.'

'Wait.' He took her arm and pulled her back into the cabin, pushing the door to with the flat of his other hand. 'What exactly do you mean by that? Who has been deceiving you?'

'Why, you, of course. You make love to me and then you lecture me on defending myself against rakes. Are you a lover or a seducer? A friend or is this just a game? You made love to me here before and you know full well you could have ravished me if you had wished it—I had no defences. You caressed me on deck until I was a trembling wreck and you held me in your arms just now and made me melt for a foolish second. You know how to make me react to you, you seem to understand me all too well, but I do not know who you are any more.'

'I am an awful warning, that is what I am,' he said with no humour whatsoever. 'I want, Dita my dear, to make love to you and because I know you are not a virgin I want to take advantage of that. So far, I have had enough self-control not to risk leaving you with child. So, yes, I am a rake and a seducer. And yes, I know I should not make love to you and I know I will try to kill any man who does, because part of me remembers that I grew up defending you. So that makes me a hypocrite as well.'

'You remember me as a child?'

'Yes, of course I do! We have discussed this—how could I forget the trouble you got me into, time and again?'

'I was sixteen when you left. Do you remember me then?'

'Not really.' He frowned. 'I'd been to Oxford and then I was away—London, travelling, staying with friends—

for much of the time after that. When I came back you were still too young for parties and balls, so I didn't see you at those. You had grown up, I can remember that: all eyes and hair and gawky long legs.'

'We kept bumping into each other, though,' she reminded him. 'Out riding and walking, in the grounds. You seemed happy. Excited even.'

His face became expressionless. 'Oh, yes, I was in wonderful spirits.'

He had been different, she had sensed that. Laughing, light-hearted, even, she could see in retrospect, just a little flirtatious. She had been falling in love with him, all unknowing that that happiness and flirtation had not been for her. Another woman?

'The last day. The day before you left,' she persisted. 'Do you remember…meeting me that day?'

He frowned, troubled. 'No. I was angry and I was devilish drunk by the evening, that I do know. I woke up with one hell of a hangover. It is all very fuzzy. You were there though, weren't you?'

'Yes,' she conceded. 'And, yes, you were angry and a little drunk.'

'I am sorry. You obviously went away and left me to it—very wise. I got a lot drunker.' Alistair turned and began to put the cabin to rights.

He did not remember. He did not recollect her finding him in the garden of Lyndonholt Castle with a bottle in his hand and another at his feet, distracted, both furious over something and desperate with grief. She had pulled him towards the house, worried that he would stumble into the moat, and somehow had towed him up the stairs to his bedchamber. As she had pushed him in through the door he had turned and the pain in his face had torn at her heart. Her friend was hurting. And so she had stood on tiptoe and kissed his cheek, for comfort. Only she had missed and found his mouth and feelings she had never known flooded through her and she had put her arms around his neck and he had pulled her to him and into the room and…

As she stood there now, all she wanted to do was walk into his arms and turn up her face to his again. He would kiss her, she was certain. She should leave, she knew that. He was no longer a desperate, drunken young man who did not care what he was doing. But there was a question she had to ask, even though she dreaded the answer and knew that if she asked it, things would never be the same again.

'If you want me so badly,' she said before she could lose her nerve, 'why not marry me?'

It rocked Alistair back on his heels. She saw him recoil and found she had bitten her lip. It hurt, but not as much as his reaction.

He recovered in the blink of an eyelid. 'Is that a proposal?' he drawled.

'No, it is a rhetorical question; there is no need to panic. When I marry—if I marry—it will be a love match. I do not have to settle for less.' She put up her chin and stared back into the cynical amber eyes that watched her. 'I want you, but I do not love you. Half of the time I do not even like you, as the child I was did.'

'And there you have it. You want love and emotion and devotion.' He shrugged. 'I do not. Love is a fantasy, overrated at best, poison at worst. Those giggling girls on board would tell me they loved me if I gave them the slightest encouragement, and they would convince themselves they meant it, any of them. What they *love* is my title and my money.

'Friendship and loyalty now, those are another matter.

I like you, Dita. I want you and I am doing my damndest to balance those two things because I owe you loyalty.'

'You call licking my ear—'

'I never said I was a saint,' he said with a grimace. 'I take my pleasures where I can. And you, my darling Dita, are certainly a pleasure.'

'Oh, you…you maddening man. Just keep out of my way from now on. No help, no defending me from other men, no teasing, no games. *Nothing.* Do you understand me?'

'But of course.' Alistair sketched a bow. 'Behold, your most indifferent servant—until you ask me to behave otherwise. May I hold the door for you, or is that too demonstrative?'

Dita glared, beyond any retaliation. Inside something hurt. She wanted the old Alistair back, the boy, her friend. Instead she had this man whom she desired beyond safety or reason and who she could not understand any more than she understood herself just at the moment.

'Far too demonstrative,' she snapped, opened the door and swept out.

Chapter Twelve

Alistair was as good as his word. His manner was polite, impeccable, indifferent and drove her wild with desire. The cynical part of her wondered if he knew that. However, he still attended the evening meetings of what Daniel Chatterton had christened the 'editorial committee'. As they left Madeira behind them the novel reached chapter thirty, enlivened now by the swordfight, pirates, the attempted keelhauling of the hero with a dramatic escape and the unfortunate Angelina still barely eluding the clutches of the evil Blackstone.

'Who is not exerting himself very hard in that direction,' Dita heard Alistair mutter to Daniel as they left the deck after a spirited discussion of the day's incidents.

Neither are you, thank goodness, she thought, attempting to be glad of it. But the fact that Alistair was behaving perfectly did not mean that her own treacherous feelings were as obedient. She still wanted him, still longed to touch him. And she wanted their old friendship back as well. She wanted, she was well aware, the moon.

The light was fading fast and Dita reminded herself

they were not yet halfway through March. It was chilly now they were in the Bay of Biscay, the ladies put heavy cloaks over their shawls before venturing out and Averil, brought up from childhood in India, shivered.

'How much longer, Captain?' she asked as they crowded into the cuddy, cheerful and warm with its lamps burning in their gimbals and the smell of the baked goods the cook had sent up with tea.

'Impatient, Miss Heydon?' He smiled. 'We have made good time, you know. Provided we do not run into any trouble with French warships, or privateers—and the captain of British navy brig we encountered two days ago thinks we should not—and the wind holds, then I expect to sight Land's End in two days and you should be on land in Plymouth the day after that.'

Most of the passengers, Dita included, would disembark at Plymouth and travel overland to their destinations, even those heading for London. After so long at sea the chance to be free of the ship more than made up for the trials of road travel.

'Are you London-bound, Lady Perdita?' Alistair asked her as she sipped her tea. He passed her the cakes, taking care not to touch her hand, she thought. Or perhaps she was being too sensitive. This distance was what she wanted, wasn't it?

'No. I shall go home to Combe,' she said, with a smile of pleasure at the thought. 'We will go up to London for the Season a little late, but Mama did not wish to make firm plans—the length of the voyage is so unpredictable.'

'I will escort you then. I am returning to Lyndonholt Castle.'

'There is no need,' Dita protested, then caught herself. Her alarm at the thought of being in a close carriage with

Alistair for a long day's journey must sound as though she did not trust him. It was herself she did not trust. 'Thank you, but I would not want to inconvenience you. Mr Bastable must get up to town immediately we land, but Mrs Bastable is going to stay with Averil and me until we are collected. My father will come for me and Averil's betrothed will presumably send a carriage and a maid for her.'

'But do you want to wait?' Alistair passed her a biscuit, but she shook her head, too undecided to think about food. 'Mrs Bastable can select a reliable maid that your parents would approve of. I will hire a chaise for you and a horse for myself.'

'Thank you. I must admit that when I have landed I am sure I will not want anything more than to be home.' She put her hand on his forearm and felt him stiffen. She lifted it away. 'You are very kind, Alistair.'

No,' he said, his smile thin. 'I am a selfish devil; you would do well to remember that, Dita.'

'Are you cold, too?' Averil asked. Dita jumped and stopped watching Alistair's back as he left the cabin. 'You are shivering as much as I am. Shall we change into something warmer before supper?'

Wednesday 15th March—off the Isles of Scilly

'We will put into Hugh Town on St Mary's tomorrow, Mrs Bastable,' the captain said as the steward cleared the cheese board from the supper table. 'That storm last night has taken us west, and it will be as well to check the ship in quiet waters before we enter the Channel, but it will not delay us long.'

Alistair stretched his legs under the table, bumped feet with Daniel who was discussing fox hunting with George

Latham, and grimaced. Oh, to be on land, stretching his legs. To run, to ride, to feel grass under his feet and a gentler sun on his skin. To have the freedom to be alone without the constant need to make conversation and allowances. Without the constant, aching, nearness of Dita Brooke. *Marriage.* Her question had both surprised him and made him wary. She wanted love, and that he could not give her. It was unfair to dally with her, to tease her into an unconsummated *affaire*, he kept reminding himself. So far that resolution had held.

'English soil at last,' the matron said with a sigh, dragging her shawl more tightly around her shoulders. 'An English spring. It is twelve years since I last saw one of those. Can we not go into harbour tonight, Captain Archibald?'

'No, ma'am, I'm afraid not. We must wait here at anchor until a pilot rows out to us at first light. The waters around the Isles are littered with reefs and rocks and sand bars and are not safe to be approached in the dark.'

'I had no idea spring in England would be so chilly,' Averil remarked. 'I thought the sun would shine and it would be warmer than this.'

'Not on a March night, Miss Heydon,' Callum said with a grin. '*Ne'er cast a clout til May be out*, is the saying. It will be a while before we have temperatures that you might consider even passably warm enough for you to break out your pretty muslins.'

She sent him a smile that froze as the ship gave a sudden lurch, sending the wine glasses sliding. Alistair saw Daniel's head snap round to met his brother's eyes and exchange a silent message. He put down his own wineglass and watched the captain.

Archibald was frowning. 'What the—?'

He was on his feet even as a sailor appeared in the doorway. 'Mr Henshaw's compliments, Captain, but the wind's got up and she's dragging the anchor and will you come at once?'

Several woman gave little shrieks, but not, Alistair noted as he got to his feet, Dita. She had gone a trifle pale, but she was calm.

'What should we do?' a man asked from further along the table, his voice rising in barely controlled alarm.

'Nothing,' Alistair said, thinking furiously. Through storms and wild seas the ship had never felt so strange under his feet as it did now. Something was very wrong, but panic would only make it worse. 'I expect it will be a trifle unsettled while they put out another anchor or shift position to find a better hold on the sea bed. Better not to retire to our bunks just yet, in case it becomes rough for a while.'

He exchanged a swift glance with the Chatterton twins. The three of them were the youngest, fittest men amongst the civilian passengers in the cuddy. If there was any danger, they would help the officers get the women to the boats.

'Should we go on deck?' Mr Crabtree, a middle-aged merchant, asked.

'Why, no,' Alistair said easily. 'Think how underfoot we would be. There are all the sailors rushing about doing whatever they do with yards and sheets and anchors. We should just settle down for a while until the captain comes back.'

He strolled across to where Callum was stooping to look out of the window. 'What can you see?' he murmured against the babble of conversation. Across the cabin Daniel was teasing the ladies about their plans for London shopping, but he had stayed on his feet and Alistair could sense his tense alertness.

'It is as black as the devil's waistcoat, except for that light over there.' Callum nodded at a spot on the port bow. 'And that's moving.'

'Wreckers?'

'No, it's us. We're going before the wind and closer to the light and the land. I don't like the feel of this.'

'Neither do I. We're all up here, aren't we?'

'Yes.' Callum cocked his head towards the door to the Great Cabin from where a babble of voices and the sound of a crying child could be heard. One of the lieutenants walked briskly through the cuddy and they heard his feet clattering down the companionway.

'He'll sort them out down there,' Alistair said. 'There are enough able-bodied men to help. Up here there's seventeen if you don't count the three of us.' He jerked his head towards Daniel. 'Just in case, we'll divide them up, five or six each. You have a word with your brother and we'll start to cut them out and get them into groups without them noticing, with any luck.'

Callum nodded and strolled over to speak to his twin under cover of a lively discussion about London hotels. Most of the other men knew what the danger was, Alistair was pretty certain, but they were staying outwardly calm. They were tough, experienced characters, all of them, even those who were older and fatter. Certainly he received slight nods of acknowledgment as the three younger men edged the ladies into little groups and the motion of the ship became stronger.

Dita made her way to his side and whispered, 'You think we are in danger, don't you?'

'Best to be careful,' he murmured back, 'and not to panic.'

'Of course,' she said. She had gone even paler, but she kept her chin up and a smile on her face as though they were discussing a trivial matter, and he felt a flash of pride in her courage. 'I'm sure there is nothing to be—'

The *Bengal Queen* shuddered to a stop as though she had run into a wall, sending Dita stumbling into his arms. For a moment there was silence, then one of the older women began to scream and was shushed by her husband.

'Up on deck now,' Alistair ordered, setting Dita on her feet. 'You all with me. That group there—*Mrs Bastable!*—with Daniel Chatterton. You five with Callum. Hold tight as you go. We'll get the ladies into the boats first.'

The cabin shifted, throwing them all into a heap, half on the deck, half sprawled across table and chairs. A lamp crashed down, burning oil spilled out, and Dita yanked the shawl from Mrs Bastable's shoulders and smothered the fire. Without a word the men began to get the fallen to their feet. Beside him Alistair was aware of Averil helping an older woman, her voice calm as she took her arm.

Dita had blood trickling from her forehead. 'Dita? Are you—?'

'It is nothing.' She brushed off his hand and went to get Dr Melchett upright.

'Hurry.' Daniel was at the door, braced against the worsening tilt of the deck, his hand stretched out to pull the others towards him until he had his little group of six, then he gave way for Alistair to get his charges on deck. At his side Callum hauled and pushed until everyone was huddled around the main mast.

It was dark, lit only by the moving light from the lanterns, and the wind that had come up so fast was cold and gusting. Hair and shawls flapped wildly, men's faces came in and out of focus as the sailors fought with the ropes to lower the boats. Passengers from the Great Cabin began to pour out, milling around, adding to the confusion.

While Alistair fought to keep people together and sort the women and children and the frail from the more able-bodied, the twins helped load the first boat, with four of the sailors to row and some of the older men to help the women down the ladder and into the wave-tossed boat. It pushed off from the side and vanished into the darkness.

'Now you.' Alistair pulled Dita towards the side as the second and third boats were lowered. Their feet slid on the tilting deck; water was coming over the side as waves hit the ship broadside. Then the moon came out from the clouds and he saw the rocks as its light lit the breaking surf.

'No, get the older women on this one.' Dita twisted from his grasp and went to help Mrs Bastable and a grey-haired lady who was sobbing wildly. It took longer this time—the angle of the ship was greater, the wind seemed to be gaining strength. Or perhaps, Alistair thought as he fought his way to Daniel's side, they were losing theirs.

At last the boat was loaded and away, and another lowered to be crammed with the Great Cabin passengers. Alistair found Lieutenant Henshaw at his side. 'All the rest of the passengers into the next one,' he ordered.

Alistair pulled Dita and Averil up the tilting deck to the rail. 'I'll go first,' he said, holding Dita's eyes with his. 'I'll keep you safe.'

'I know.' Her smile was shaky, but real, and he felt a stab of fear for her that was almost painful.

Alistair climbed down the ladder into the pitching boat with the sailors. He was cold and soaked; how the women were coping he had no idea. *Dita.* He blanked emotion from his mind and concentrated. The *Bengal Queen* was shifting on the rock that had snared her; he could hear the grinding sound, like a great beast in agony in a trap.

Daniel landed in the boat beside him, his face white as he stared up at his brother, still on deck. Callum began to help people over the rail, shouting encouragement over the crashing of the waves. Dita came sliding down the ladder into Alistair's arms; he pushed her back on to a seat. 'Hang on!'

Then Averil Heydon was clinging to his neck, gasping. 'I'm all right,' she shouted above the noise as she stumbled away to join Dita. The two girls wrapped their arms around each other as they huddled on the plank seat.

'Cal! Come on!' Daniel shouted, his hands cupped around his mouth.

Alistair saw Callum raise a hand in acknowledgment and put one hand on the gunwale, ready to climb over. Then he froze, staring out with a look of blank shock. Alistair swung round. Coming towards them was a foaming wall of water, black and white in the stark moonlight.

'Dita—' The wave hit, picking the boat up like a toy. They were falling, tossed up and over. Bodies crashed into him as they tumbled helplessly into the sea. He reached out as he fell, grabbed, almost blind, on nothing but instinct, and a hand fastened around his wrist. He saw Dita's face, stark with horror, and then they were in the water and all rational thought ceased.

Chapter Thirteen

'Dita! Dita, open your eyes.' She was dreaming about Alistair. She wished she could wake up because in her dream she was freezing cold, and her whole body ached and he was shouting at her. 'Dita, darling!' Now he was shaking her. She tried to protest, to push him away. It hurt and the blanket must have fallen off the bed which was why she was so cold…

'Dita, damn it, wake up or I am going to slap you!'

'No,' she managed and opened her eyes on to near-darkness. It was not a dream, she realised as fitful moon-light caught Alistair's face. His hair was plastered to his head, his shirt was in tatters. 'What?'

Water, even colder than she was, splashed over her feet. Her bare feet. It all came back: the ship and the fear and the great wave that had hurled them out of the boat into the sea.

'Thank God. Can you crawl up the beach?' Alistair asked. He was kneeling, she realised. 'We need to get away from the sea into some shelter. I don't think I can carry you, I'm sorry.' His voice sounded harsh and pain-

ful as he hauled her up into a sitting position against his
shoulder.

'Don't be,' Dita murmured against the chilled skin.
He must be exhausted, beyond exhausted, and he was
still asking more of himself. 'You saved me. I can crawl.
Oh—' She leaned over and was violently ill, retching
sea water until she was gasping. 'All right…now.' Her
throat hurt; she must sound as bad as he did, she thought,
aware of Alistair holding her, shielding her with his own
shivering body against the cold wind.

The beach was sand, thank heavens—she did not
think she could have managed if it had been rock or
shifting pebbles. As she struggled Alistair half-lifted,
half-dragged her, her arm around his shoulders, their
free hands clawing at the gentle slope until the texture
changed. 'Grass.'

'Yes.' He staggered to his feet and pulled her the rest
of the way until she lay on the short, salt-bitten turf.
'Hell, I can't see any lights.' He turned, peering into the
gloom. 'But there's something over there, a hut perhaps.
Can you stand now?'

She managed it, climbing up his body until he could
hold her against his side, and there, fifty feet beyond
where they stood, was the sharp edge of a roof line. With
an aim in sight they moved faster, stumbling across the
turf, stubbing bare feet on rocks.

'It's not locked, thank God.' Alistair pushed against
the door and it creaked open. 'Hold on here.' He placed
her hands on the door jamb and went inside. Dita heard
curses, a thump, then a rasping sound. A thread of light
became a candle, then another. 'There's a lamp,' she said
and he lit that, too.

'A fisherman's hut, perhaps,' Alistair said. 'Here,
come and lie down.' He came across the room to help

her to the rough cot and she saw him clearly for the first time. He was still wearing his evening breeches, but his shirt hung on in shreds and tatters, his stockings clinging to his calves. Dita looked down and found she only had her petticoats, much ripped, her stays and, under them, her chemise. Beneath that her questing fingers found a row of tiny globes. The necklace was safe.

'And get those clothes off,' Alistair added. 'They'll only make us colder. There are blankets. And, by St Anthony, the fire's laid and there is wood.'

Beyond modesty, Dita began to claw at the sodden fabric with shaking fingers. Alistair turned his back, knelt and set a candle to the fire. 'You, too,' she managed between chattering teeth as she furled a stiff and smelly blanket around herself. 'If we pull this cot to the fire, we can both get in and share the heat.'

Between them they dragged the rough-framed bed to the hearth. Alistair heaped the firewood close so he could reach out and throw it on, and then he stripped, the rags of his shirt disintegrating under his cold-clumsy fingers.

Dita stared as he stood there in the firelight. 'You are covered in marks.'

He glanced down, unselfconscious in his nakedness. 'The long boat hit me as we went in, I think. That's probably the ribs.' He prodded and winced. 'The rest is rocks. There was a bad patch just after we were thrown out.'

'Come to bed.'

To her astonishment he managed a wicked grin. 'I thought you would never ask, Dita.'

'Idiot,' she said and found she was near to tears. 'Come and hold me.'

He threw the other blanket over her and then slid in

under it so her back was to the fire. Dita pulled open the blanket she was wrapped in and wriggled close until she was tight against his long, cold, damp body.

'Mind you,' he said, as he reached out to drag the covering over them, 'this isn't how I imagined our first time in a bed would be.'

'We've been in a bed,' she mumbled against his chest. *Twice, if only he remembered.*

'Not naked and not in it.' Alistair wrapped his arms around her tightly. 'What's this?'

'Your pearls. I had them made into a necklace in Cape Town and I've been wearing them ever since.' She had put them under her clothes because she hadn't wanted to give him the satisfaction of seeing how she prized his gift. That seemed so petty now.

'Next to the skin?'

'It improves the lustre,' she said, daring him to comment.

But all he said was, 'Are you all right?'

It was an insane question, she thought, then smiled. The hair on his chest tickled her lips as they curved. 'Yes. Yes, I am.'

'So am I. Good being alive, isn't it? Sleep now, I've got you safe.'

He had kept her safe through that nightmare, her childhood terror made a thousand times worse, in darkness, in numbing cold. She pressed her lips to his skin in a kiss as she closed her eyes and tried to piece together her jumbled memories.

She had been thrown out of the boat, Averil's screams in her ears, and a hand had fastened around her wrist. She had known it was Alistair—those strong fingers, that implacable grip that did not loosen as they sank and then were thrown to the surface. How he had got her to shore she had no recollection. She must have passed out, but they could not have been in the water long or they would surely have died of the cold.

'The others,' she said, tensing in his arms. 'Averil, the Chattertons, Mrs Bastable…'

'We are safe, they may be too,' he said, tucking her head more firmly under his chin. 'And the other boats got clear of the rocks before that wave hit us. There are a lot of islands, it isn't as though we went down in mid-ocean.' His hand stroked down her back. 'Sleep, Dita. There is nothing you can do about it now.'

She slept and woke to find herself warm, with Alistair leaning over her on one elbow to toss another branch on the fire. There was a faint grey light in the room, coming through the thick salt-stained pane of glass in the window. The candles had gone out and the lamp burned pale in the dawn.

'Hello,' he said, looking down at her. 'How are you?'

'Alive,' she said and smiled up into his stubble-darkened face. 'You look a complete pirate.'

He grinned. 'You sound like one. Your voice is as hoarse as mine feels. I'll have a look round in a minute, see if there is anything to drink. Then I'll go and find if there is anyone living on this island. I don't know which one it is.'

Instinctively her arms tightened around him. 'Don't leave me.'

'It won't be for long—they are all small, I'll be back soon.'

'I'll come, too.'

'You need to rest, Dita.' He looked down at her as she lay back against the lumpy pillow. 'You've got a lion's heart, but not its strength.'

'I can manage. Alistair—I don't want to be alone.'

'Dita—oh lord, don't cry, sweetheart, not now we're safe.' He bent over her, his amber eyes soft with a concern she had never seen before, not in the adult man.

'I'm not.' She swallowed, looked up, lost herself in his gaze.

'No? What's this?' He bent and kissed the corner of her eye. 'Salt.'

'We're both salty,' she murmured and, as he moved, she lifted her head and kissed his mouth. 'You see?'

Alistair went still, his eyes watchful. 'Dita?' There was a wealth of meaning in that question and he did not have to explain any of it to her. She was warm now, and her blood ran hot and she was alive and she wanted him—because she was *alive* and because he had given her that gift. Against her body she felt him stir into arousal.

'Yes,' she said. 'Oh, yes, Alistair.'

He rolled, pinned her under him and she ignored the protests from battered, bruised muscles and wriggled until her hips cradled him and the wonderful hot threatening promise of his erection pressed intimately against her.

Alistair took his weight on his elbows, which rocked his hips tighter into hers, and she gasped at the pleasure of it. 'You are so lovely,' he murmured. 'You look like a mermaid, washed up at my feet.'

She almost protested. She was sticky with salt, her hair a tangled, still-damp, mess. She knew how she looked every day, scrubbed from the bath with no artifice of hairdressing or jewellery or the subtle use of cosmetics. The lack of balance in her face, her long nose, her wide mouth—he would see all that with complete clarity. But he appeared sincere; he appeared to see her,

at this moment, as *lovely* and she could not protest, not
when the man she loved was about to make her his.

'What is it?' She must have gasped. 'Did I hurt you?
Am I too heavy?'

'No. No.' Dita stared up at the face above her, the
man she had known virtually all her life. Her friend,
the man she had thought she simply lusted after. *I love
him? Oh my God, I love him.* And he would make love
to her now and this time it would be perfect, because it
was Alistair. He would heal that long-ago nightmare.

He smiled, that wicked smile that had drawn her after
him for all those years of her childhood, driving away
the other, so-familiar, expression from his boyhood, that
of concern for her. *He's saved me from every scrape I
have got myself into—except Stephen. And when he led
me into trouble, he got me out of that to, except that
once. He could have ravished me on the ship, but he
didn't...*

Alistair began to kiss her throat, one hand sliding
between their bodies, intent, she knew, on weaving
sensual delight that would make her mindless, blissful,
until she was his. *He is practiced, he won't hurt me,* she
thought as the first shiver of apprehension mixed with
the pleasure. It had been a long time.

*He will realise I am not a virgin, but then, he thinks
that I slept with Stephen.* Thank goodness she had fought
Stephen off, thank goodness the man she loved had been
the only one. She stiffened at the memory of Stephen's
groping hands.

'Dita? Don't worry, I won't risk a child.'

Alistair's lips closed around her right nipple and she
gasped as he sucked, her mind wiped blank for one
exquisite moment. Then she fought through the sensa-

tion. It was important, because she loved him, that he did not believe that she had given herself to Stephen

'I need to tell you something.'

'Now?'

'Yes, now, Alistair. You know that I am not a virgin.'

He lifted his head from her breast, intense, serious, his eyes dark and heavy with arousal. 'I know. The scandal—that character you eloped with.'

'Stephen Doyle. I never slept with him.'

Alistair sat up and she tried to see his expression in the gloom.

'Then why the hell didn't you say so and put a stop to all the gossip?'

'I suppose because I was too proud to explain that after an hour alone in the chaise I realised that I had been completely deceived in him. I spent two nights fending him off with the cutlery, but no one but my family would have believed me and I would have lost my dignity along with my reputation.'

'Dignity? But if you were still a virgin—' She saw the memory of her words come back to him. 'Who was it, then?'

'You.' She had not meant to blurt it out, but the word simply escaped.

'*What?* Don't be ridiculous, Dita. When, for heaven's sake? I would have remembered.'

'Not if you were drunk and angry and very upset about something else,' she said and watched his face change as he realised when she must mean.

'Are you saying that the night before I left home I took your virginity? And I don't remember it? Don't be ridiculous, Dita. You were a child—I wouldn't have done such a thing.' He sounded furious. Dita watched as he flung himself off the crude bed and went to light the lantern, her stomach a tight knot of hurt misery.

'I was sixteen,' she said flatly. 'I found you in the rose garden in the base of the ruined tower. I had never seen you like that—drunk and upset and so angry. You were almost incoherent and I couldn't make any sense of what you were saying. I didn't want any of the servants to see you like that, so I helped you inside and up the back stairs to your room.

'And then I pushed you inside and you turned around and—Alistair, you looked so unhappy, I kissed you. I just meant to comfort you, like I would if you had fallen off your horse or something. But I missed your cheek and found your mouth and then something happened. It didn't feel like comforting a friend any more. You were not the same. I was not the same. I didn't understand, but you seemed to and you pulled me inside and closed the door.'

'And ravished you? Is that what you are saying?' He stood there, naked, fists clenched, his body very visibly losing all interest in what they had been doing a minute before.

'No, of course not. I wanted it, too. I didn't really understand, but I wanted you.' She thought back to the excitement and the apprehension and the sheer delight of his caresses. There had been pain, but there had been the joy of being in his arms and realising that she was a woman and she loved him and he must love her, too. 'I don't think you knew who I was, not at first. Afterwards you just stared at me and said…something. So I left.'

'What did I say?'

Dita bit her lip. The words had haunted her for years; now she had to repeat them to the man who had used them on her like weapons. 'You said, "Of all the bloody stupid things to do. You. I must be mad. Get out." There were other things, I don't recall very well—I had my hands over my ears by then. You were so angry with me and the next day you had gone.'

'Oh dear God. I don't remember,' he said, his face pale in the lamp light. 'Dita, I swear I don't remember. I kept having dreams, but they were so confused I didn't believe them. I just thought they were fantasies. Hell, I might have got you with child.'

'Fortunately not,' she said with as much calm as she could muster. 'That never occurred to me until years later. I was very innocent, you see.'

'Innocent! You don't need to tell me that,' he said bitterly. 'You might have told me all this before I made love to you on board,' he said. 'Damn it, all that held me back was my fear of getting you with child. Now I know I should never have laid a finger on you at all.'

She stared at him. 'But you thought I had slept with Stephen. Why would this make any difference?'

'Because it makes you my responsibility. Don't you see that?'

'No, I do not. It was eight years ago, Alistair. And you were drunk.'

'That makes it worse. Why didn't you tell me straight away ?' He paced the small hut, ignoring his nakedness.

'In Calcutta? What would you suggest I should have said? Good evening, Lord Lyndon. Don't you recall the last time we met? You were kicking me out of your bedchamber after taking my virginity?'

'No! I mean before we made love.'

'I did not want to talk about it. I wanted, not to forget it exactly, but to put it behind me. And then it got rather out of hand,' she admitted. 'I was not expecting to feel like that: so overwhelmed. I hadn't got much experience, even now, remember?'

'Don't rub it in,' he said with a bitter laugh, as he turned away to pick up his breeches. 'Thanks to me, you have now.' He hauled the damp, clinging fabric over his hips, picked up the remnants of his shirt and tossed it away again. 'Get dressed, you are shivering.'

She was, Dita realised, and not just from cold. Why was he so angry with her? Was this her fault, too?

'Pass me my clothes, then,' she said, suddenly shy of her nudity. He gave them to her and she wriggled into the camisole and then the petticoats. They had fared better than Alistair's breeches; their thin cotton had dried in the warmth from the fire, although the salt made them feel unpleasant against her skin. The corset was still damp and she tossed it aside with a grimace of distaste.

'We must get married as soon as possible. It is fortunate your parents are down in Devon and not in London; we can organise something quietly.'

'Marry you?' She sat there in her damp undergarments and shivered at the tone of his voice. 'Why?'

He did not love her, for if he did, surely he would have said so. And when he had made love to her not one word of love or tenderness had passed his lips, only desire.

'I told you. I as good as raped you and that makes you my responsibility.' This was not what she needed to hear in his voice.

'So I must be yours because of one drunken incident eight years ago?'

'Exactly.' Alistair turned and began to rummage around the shelves and dark corners of the hut while she dressed. 'There's nothing to drink, but I've found a knife.' He took a blanket and cut a slit in the middle, then dropped it over her head. 'That's better than trying to walk with it wrapped round you,' he said, doing the same for himself. He opened the door. 'Come on.'

In the full daylight she could see his face clearly. Unshaven, bruised, grim. And, no doubt, he could see her very clearly, too, as she stood up. Did he realise that she was not shivering, but shaking with anger?

'I will not marry you,' she stated flatly. 'I cannot believe you would insult me by offering it.'

'Insult?' He stopped in the doorway, every muscle tense.

'Yes. I would not marry you, Alistair Lyndon, if you went down on your knees and begged me.'

'You will have no choice. I will tell your father what happened.'

'And I will say that you got a blow on the head in the shipwreck and are having delusions. They know the truth about Stephen, but they also know that no one else believes I did not sleep with him. I will tell them you are being gallant as an old friend, but that I do not want to marry you. They are going to believe me—what woman in her right mind would turn down Lord Lyndon, after all?'

'So when you made love with me on the ship, when you returned my kisses—what was that?'

'Desire and a curiosity to see if there was any difference in the way you make love sober and with some experience.' That was not the truth, of course. She must have been in love with him for weeks. But it was not *her* feelings that were at issue here. 'You don't think I was in love with you, do you? No, of course not—you'd have avoided me like the plague.'

He could have had no idea how she felt about him, she supposed, seeing his mouth tighten into a hard line and his head come up. But then, neither had she, until a short while ago.

'And do I make love better sober?' Alistair made himself drawl, made himself sound cynical and blasé when all he wanted was to shout and rage and shake her until her teeth rattled. How could she have kept that from him? Everything he believed about himself seemed to crumble. He had been capable of behaving like that and had not even remembered it.

By any objective standards Dita looked ghastly—pale, bruised, serious, her hair hanging in tangled, sticky clumps—but her dignity and her anger shone through. He would have been happier, he realised, if she had been weeping. That did not make him feel any better about himself either.

'Oh, considerably. It was very nice the first time, but this was better,' she said. 'I haven't any grounds for comparison, you understand, but the sobriety would have helped. And, of course, no doubt your technique has improved with age and experience.'

'You little cat.'

'Meow,' she said bitterly as she got to her feet with none of her usual grace. For a moment he glimpsed the ungainly child as she adjusted the grey blanket.

He hardened his heart. Dita, who valued love and emotion in marriage, had rejected him. Foolish, headstrong, romantic idiot of a woman. Did she think he *wanted* to be leg-shackled to a passionate, troublesome, headstrong female? *A narrow escape*, he told himself, feeling sick. But it wasn't. She had thrown his honour back in his face.

'Ready?' He made his voice as brisk as he could with his throat rasped raw by salt water and emotion. 'We will discuss this later.' She shot him a mutinous look. 'Now the sun is up I can at least tell which direction we're facing. Last night I couldn't make head nor tail of the stars—I have been away from northern Europe too long, I suppose.'

'Or possibly you were a trifle weary for some reason,' Dita suggested with some of the old spirit back in her voice as she came out of the hut to join him.

'Could be that,' he conceded. Now was no time to pursue this shattering argument; he needed to get her safe. 'Now, that's a good-sized island over there and that's east, so, if I recall the map correctly, it must be St Mary's, which is the biggest. Which makes this one Tresco, and if I'm right it has a fishing village at the northern end.' He glanced down at her, but her face was averted. 'It won't take me long; you should rest here.'

'I am coming,' Dita said with an edge to her voice that warned him that she was close to the end of her tether.

'All right,' he said and began to walk. It was hard now he was actually moving. Everything seemed to hurt, he was desperately thirsty and shaken to the core over what Dita had told him. But she kept up with the slow pace he set, doggedly putting one foot in front of the other, and he wondered whether any of the other women on the ship would have shown the same stoical courage. Averil Heydon, perhaps, but none of the other young women had the sheer guts. Probably they wouldn't need them; thanks to Averil and Dita, they had gone off in the first boats.

'I should have insisted you went off in an earlier boat,' he said, following his thoughts.

'How? By picking me up and throwing me into it?'

she asked in a valiant imitation of her best provocative voice. 'You must learn you cannot order me about, Alistair.'

'So you say,' he snapped. It was bite back or take her in his arms and kiss her until her voice lost that little quaver that cut straight through his anger and shame and frustration. And he knew where that would lead. 'Damn it, Dita, you must marry me.'

Her silence was almost more loaded with anger than a retort would have been. Then after a few more steps she said, 'I doubt I will ever marry. If a man asks me to marry him, despite the scandal, and I love him, then I will marry him. Otherwise, I will just have to stay a spinster. I am not going to marry you in order to ease your guilty conscience, Alistair.'

They plodded on for a few more painful steps along the turf above the high-water mark. The sea was grey and choppy after the storm and he kept his body between it and her as much as he could. 'So you propose a test if someone proposes—does he love you enough to marry you despite Doyle?'

'I suppose so. I had not given it much thought; I just know that is what I would do.'

Would he have passed her test? he had wondered. If, before this shattering revelation, he found he loved Dita Brooke and wanted to marry her, would the thought of one lover in her past make a difference? He thought of his one love, his past love. She'd had another lover, and that had broken his heart. But then, look who the man was—

Love was a fantasy and a trap. Dita must agree to marry him whether she liked it or not.

'I hear voices!' Dita looked up, alert. 'Over there, past those rocks.'

They stumbled forwards, his arm around her shoulders, and, as they reached the low tumbled headland three men in blue came over it. Sailors. 'They've set the navy to search,' he said as the men broke into a run. 'It is all right now, Dita, you're safe.'

'I was always safe with you,' she said, her voice thready, then, as he held her, she went limp and fainted dead away.

Chapter Fourteen

'...Several ships at anchor in St Mary's Pool, so the Governor ordered off crews to all the islands to check along the shorelines.' The confident West Country voice soothed Dita with the longed-for cadences of home.

'How many survivors?' Alistair's voice rumbled against her ear. He must be holding her, she realised, coming out of the hazy dream-state she had been in. *Hiding*, she reproved herself. *Coward*. But she did not move. He was warm now, and it was not blanket she was snuggled against, but good woollen cloth. *I love you, I hate you, I need you... Why couldn't you have told me you loved me and made it all right?*

'Can't say for sure, my lord. All the longboats that went off before yours got in to harbour—some to St Mary's, some to Old Grimsby on Tresco. But an elderly man on one of those had a heart seizure and a lady perished of the cold, so I hear. There are injuries as well—I don't know how serious. The crew all got off safe after your boat was swamped.'

'There was a passenger left with the crew—any news of him?'

'No, my lord, I'm sorry, I don't know. But they'll be picking people up all along the beaches, I'll be bound. You'll hear the news when we get you back to the Governor's house. Not long now, this is a good strong crew.'

The strange rocking motion made sense now, and the breeze on her face: she was in a boat. Dita opened her eyes and moved and Alistair's hand pressed her cheek tighter against his chest. 'Don't be afraid. We're nearly there.'

'I'm all right.' She shifted again and he relaxed his arms so that she could sit up straight on his knees. She wanted to move away from him, but there was nowhere to go. They were in a navy jolly boat with smartly dressed sailors at the oars, making good progress towards a rugged little jetty dead ahead. Opposite her a lieutenant with red hair and a crop of freckles looked at her with concern on his plain face. 'I am sorry to have been so feeble,' she apologised. 'I think it was relief.'

'It will be that, my lady,' he said. 'Lieutenant Marlow, ma'am. You probably don't recall, but we took you to Mrs Welling's cottage and she found you some clothes— not that they'll be what you are used to. You'll be wanting a nice hot cup of tea, I expect.'

'A nice cup of tea.' She quelled the urge to laugh; if she started she might not stop. Of course, a nice cup of tea would make everything all right. 'Yes, that will be very welcome.' It was an effort to speak sensibly—her frantic, circling thoughts kept pulling her away from the present. She wondered if she was going to faint again. *Why did I tell him about that night? But I have to be honest with him. I love him.*

'Have this now.' Alistair pressed a flask into her

hands and she made herself turn to look at him. Someone had lent him clothes, too, and he had shaved and washed and combed his hair. If it wasn't for a black eye and the scrapes and bruises, he might be any gentleman out for a pleasure trip. 'It is cold tea and you need the liquid,' he said prosaically, steadying her.

'Thank you,' she said, as politely as a duchess at a tea party, and took the flask. It was cold, without milk or sugar, and it slid down her throat like the finest champagne.

When the boat bumped against the fenders at the quayside Dita made herself stand up and picked her way over the rowing benches to the side, determined to put on a brave face and not make an exhibition of herself in front of all these strangers. But curiously her fear of being in a small boat had gone and she stepped on to the stone steps without a qualm or an anxious look at the water slopping against the jetty. Perhaps after that great wave anything else was trivial, or else it was the emotional impact of that confrontation in the hut.

There was a crowd at the harbour side: onlookers; small groups of sailors with their officers, apparently being briefed for the next part of the search; some harassed clerks with lists and men holding half-a-dozen donkeys.

'It's very steep up to the Garrison,' Lieutenant Marlow said. 'Best ride a donkey, my lady.'

'Very well.' She let Alistair take her arm as they walked to the animals. She knew she should be strong and not lean on him, not encourage him in his delusion that he was responsible for her, but his strong body so close was too comforting just now to resist. He boosted her up to sit sideways on the broad saddle. 'Alistair!

Look—there's another boat coming in with people in it. Who is it?'

'Stay here.' He walked to the edge of the jetty and stared down, then came back. 'Mrs Edwards, a merchant's wife whose name I don't recall, and one of the Chattertons. He looks in bad shape.' He hesitated. 'They all do. Best you go on up to the house; the Governor's people will look after you.'

'See whether it is Daniel or Callum,' Dita urged. 'Find out how he is.' It must look bad if Alistair was trying to get her away.

This time he took longer, waiting as the three were lifted out of the boat and carried up the steps. None of them could walk. She saw Alistair bend over the limp form of the man as they shifted him into a cart, then he went to speak to the clerks and walked back, his face sombre.

'It is Callum. He's unconscious now and very cold. He must have dived in when we were overturned. They found him clinging to the upturned boat with the two women—he was holding them on. No sign of Daniel or Averil yet. The Bastables are all right, although she broke her arm or her ankle—the man isn't sure—getting into the boat. And they found Dr Melchett clinging to an oar, alive and kicking. He's a tough old buzzard.'

'Oh, thank goodness for those, at least.' She bit her lip as the donkey was led away, Alistair walking by her side. 'How soon will the news reach the mainland? I must write and let my family know I am safe before they read of the wreck.'

'The Governor will have it all in hand, don't fret,' Alistair said as they wound up the narrowed cobbled street.

He must be exhausted, Dita thought. *He shouldn't*

have to keep soothing me. 'Of course, I should have thought of that.' The final turn took them to the bottom of a slope so steep that even the sure-footed little donkey struggled before they came out through the gate in the castle walls and on to the wide expanse of grass and workshops that surrounded the strange little Elizabethan castle on the top of the promontory.

The man leading the donkey turned left to follow the line of the battlements, past gun platforms, to a great wide-fronted house set back against the slope and commanding a view over Hugh Town straggling between its two bays.

Footmen ran out to meet them, helped Dita down and ushered them into the warmth and the shelter of the Governor's residence. It seemed bizarre to be walking on soft carpets, past works of art and gleaming furniture and to be surrounded by attentive servants after the cramped cabins of the *Bengal Queen* and the crude hut that had sheltered them last night.

The Governor's secretary was on hand to greet them, to note their names and who they wanted notified of their safe deliverance. 'We are sending a brig to Penzance every day,' he explained. 'Anyone who is fit to travel can go in it and we send news to the mainland as we get it.' He snapped his fingers at a footman. 'Take Lady Perdita to Mrs Bastable's room—I hope you do not object to sharing, ma'am, but I understand she is your chaperon? And Lord Iwerne to the Green Bedchamber—again, my lord, I trust you do not object to another gentleman in the same chamber? The house is large, but with so many to accommodate—'

'What did you call me?' Alistair demanded and the man paled.

'You did not know? My lord, I must apologise for

my tactlessness. The marquis passed away over a month ago.'

'Alistair.' Dita put her hand on his arm. His face was expressionless, but under her palm he was rigid. 'Why do you not go to your room now? You will need to be quiet, a little, perhaps.'

'Yes.' He smiled at her, a creditable effort, given the shock he had just received. 'Will you be all right now?'

'Of course. Mrs Bastable and I will look after each other.'

He nodded and she watched him walk away, his shoulders braced as though to shoulder the new burdens of responsibility that were about to descend on them. Even less, now, should he think of marrying her, she thought. He needed a wife he loved to support him in his new role.

Mrs Bastable, her bandaged arm in a sling, was tearful and shaken and Dita found relief that day and the next in helping her and attempting to boost her spirits. She had the happy idea of suggesting they nurse Callum Chatterton, who was confined to bed. He was almost silent, asleep—or pretending to sleep—for most of the time. But tucking him in, harassing the maids and bringing him possets kept the older woman's mind a little distracted from her worries about Averil.

By the next evening the Governor called together everyone who was able and read the list of those who were dead and those who were missing.

'Every beach has been walked and every rock that remains above high water inspected,' the Governor said, his voice sombre. 'We must give up hope now for those who have not been found.'

Dita sat quite still, the tears streaming down her face. They had not found Averil, but they had recovered Daniel's body just two hours before.

'I'll go and tell Callum,' Alistair said. He put out his hand as though to squeeze her shoulder, then dropped it without touching her and went to break the news. He had not touched her since she had mounted the donkey, she realised.

'There will be a service tomorrow in memory of those who have been lost,' the Governor continued.

'I will attend that,' Dita whispered to Mrs Bastable, who was mopping her eyes, her hand tight in that of her husband. 'And then, dear ma'am, we will take the ship to the mainland the day after, unless Mr Chatterton needs us.'

Callum, pale, limping, frozen, it seemed to Dita, in shock at the loss of his twin, still managed to attend the service at the church overlooking Old Town Bay. 'I'll take him home tomorrow,' he told Dita as she walked back with him, her arm through his, trying to lend him as much warmth and comfort as she could. 'Lyndon— Iwerne, I should say—has been like a brother, you know. No fuss, no prosing on, just good practical stuff, like finding a decent coffin and—I'm sorry, I shouldn't speak of such things to you.'

'Not at all,' Dita murmured, looking out over the sea and wondering where Averil was now. She had written to her friend's family in India and to her betrothed, but even now, it still seemed impossible that she would not hear her voice again. 'We cannot pretend it has not happened, and we need to speak of those we have lost. Daniel was betrothed, was he not?'

'Yes.' Callum sounded even grimmer. 'And Sophia

has waited a very long time for him. Now I must tell her that she has waited in vain.'

Dita had thought she would be afraid to go on a sailing vessel again, but there was too much else to think about to allow room for nerves: Mrs Bastable, frail and anxious on her husband's arm; Callum grimly determined to behave as though he was completely fit, to get his twin's coffin home and to comfort Daniel's betrothed; Alistair, who would not speak to her about his father and who was going home to a life utterly changed.

And Averil. 'I cannot believe she has gone,' Dita said when Alistair joined her in the stern to watch the islands vanish over the horizon. 'We were such good friends— surely I would know for sure if she was dead? It feels as though she is still *there*. Alive and there.' She gestured towards the islands.

'She'll always be there for you, in your memory,' he said. 'Come inside now, those borrowed clothes aren't warm enough for you.'

He was practical and kind and firm with all of them and as distant as a dream.

When they arrived in Penzance, Alistair took rooms at a good inn and then hired maids for both Dita and Mrs Bastable. He procured a chaise and outriders and sent the older couple on their way to their daughter's home in Dorset and found a carriage to carry Daniel's coffin and a chaise for Callum and dispatched that sad procession on its way to Hertfordshire.

Finally, at dawn the next day, Alistair helped Dita and Martha the maid into a chaise before swinging up on to horseback to ride alongside.

'Isn't his lordship going to sit inside?' Martha enquired. She stared wide-eyed at Alistair through the window. 'He's a marquis, isn't he, my lady? Surely he isn't going to ride all that way?'

'He has been shut up on board ship for three months,' Dita said. She, too, was watching Alistair; it was very easy to do. 'He wants the exercise.'

And doubtless he did not want, any more than she did, to be shut up together in the jolting chaise with all those things that must not be spoken off hanging in the air between them. He should be resting, of course, but telling Alistair to rest was like telling a river to stop flowing.

She let her fingers stray to the pearls and found some comfort in running the smooth globes between her fingers. She wore them outside her clothes now; he knew she had them, after all. *The only thing of his I possess*, she thought. *If things had been different I might have a child of his. An eight-year-old child to love.*

'Those are lovely pearls, my lady,' Martha remarked. She was proving talkative, Dita thought, not sure whether to be glad of the distraction or irritated. 'I thought you'd lost everything in the shipwreck, ma'am.'

'I was wearing them,' Dita said and went back to staring out of the window. Alistair had ridden ahead and there was nothing to distract her now, just the small fields, the windswept trees, the looming mass of the moorland. Home. She thought about her family. Mama, Papa and her youngest sister Evaline, who would be coming out this Season, rather late because they had to wait for Dita to come home. Then there was Patricia, two years younger and already married to Sir William Garnett. Perhaps Dita was going to be an aunt and did not know it yet.

And the boys, of course. Serious, tall George, the heir and a year older than her, and Dominic, sixteen now, and a perfect hellion when she had left. Had they changed? Were they well and happy?

She thought about them all fondly for a while, then let her memory explore Combe, the old sprawling house that had been extended by generations over the years. It snuggled into the protection of the wooded valley that surrounded it and shielded it from the winds from the coast to the north or from the moors to the south.

There were thick woods, meadows, small, tumbling streams and buzzards mewing overhead. She loved it, bone deep. Perhaps she could stay there until she could face life without Alistair.

But, no, that would be selfish. She could not keep her family from London and Evaline's Season, and she could not bear to be apart from all of them either. She must draw what strength she could from Combe and then she would go and face London and the gossip and the snide remarks and the men who would think she was fair game.

At least if anyone tried to take liberties she was prepared now. Dita thought about Alistair's lesson, the strength of his hands on her body, the feel of him, pressed so close to her, and sighed.

'He's ever so handsome, isn't he, my lady?' Martha, with her back to the horses, must be able to see Alistair riding behind the post chaise.

'Martha, if you have ambitions to become a lady's maid in a big house—*my* maid, for example—you must learn not to make personal remarks about gentlemen, or to gossip. Do you understand?'

'Yes, ma'am.' The girl bit her lip. 'Might you take me, my lady? If I'm quiet enough?'

'I'll give you a fortnight's trial and see how you manage my hair and clothes,' Dita said, yielding a trifle. Martha's references from the agency were good and at any other time the maid's pert observations would have amused her, but she was in no mood for chitchat about Alistair now.

It had been a long day's journey, broken only by the need to change horses and to snatch a bite to eat at two o'clock. Alistair must have been saddle-sore, but he rode on, attentive to her needs at each stop, but as impersonal as a hired courier. His eyes promised that this silence would not last.

'We are almost there,' Dita said as the light began to fade. 'Here are the gates.'

Her brothers appeared on the threshold as the party drew up, her parents and Evaline just behind them. Dita tumbled out of the chaise without waiting for the step to be let down and the family ran down to meet her, catching her up in a chaotic embrace. They had never been a family to stand on ceremony, or to hold back on displays of physical affection, and it was several minutes before she emerged, tear stained and laughing, from her father's arms. He had forgiven her a little, it seemed.

'Mama, Papa, here is Alistair Lyndon—Lord Iwerne, I should say. You must know that he saved my life not once, but twice—in the shipwreck and in India, from a mad dog.'

The Earl of Wycombe strode over to where Alistair stood at his horse's head, apart from the family reunion. 'My dear Lyndon!' He enveloped him in a bear hug that, after a moment, Alistair returned. 'We can never repay you for bringing us our Dita home safely.' Her father held the younger man by the shoulders and regarded him sombrely. 'You have been through a most terrible ordeal, and now to come home to the news of your father instead of the reunion you must have longed for so much—it is a bad business. You may rely upon me for any assistance I can give you.'

'Thank you, sir. I appreciate your generous offer.' He looked directly at Perdita and then, with reluctance, it seemed to her, came across and took her hands in his. 'Home safe, Dita. Your courage will see you the rest of the way. We will talk later.' He bent and kissed her cheek, bowed to her mother and walked back to his horse.

'But, Lord Iwerne,' Lady Wycombe called, starting across the gravel towards him, 'will you not stay tonight with us? I know it is only a matter of a few miles, but you must be so weary.'

It was one mile by the direct route: jumping the stream, scrambling up and down wooded slopes, cutting through the kitchen gardens. Dita had done it often enough as a child and she guessed that that was the way Alistair would take, not troubling to ride the six miles round by road, through the lodge gates and up the winding carriage drive to the castle.

'Ma'am, thank you, but I should go home.' It seemed to Dita that he hesitated on the last word, but perhaps it was her imagination. 'And, besides, you will want to be alone with your daughter now.'

He swung up into the saddle, touched his whip to his hat and cantered off down the drive. *Off into his new life*, Dita thought. *His English life. A new title, a new role and a new wife when I can persuade him that I am not his responsibility.*

'Oh, I am so glad to be home,' she said, turning and hugging George. 'Tell me absolutely everything!'

Chapter Fifteen

Alistair kept the tired horse to a slow canter across the Brookes' parkland, then slowed as they entered the woods. The ride had narrowed to a narrow track now, proof of the lack of recent contact between the two estates. He wound his way through, then cut off to send the horse plunging down to the boundary brook, up the other bank. On this side, his land, the track became a path that eventually led him to the high wall of the kitchen gardens.

Strange how it all came back, he thought, as he leaned down to hook up the catch on the gate with the handle of his whip. It creaked open as it always had and he ducked his head as they passed through. It was almost dark now and no one was working amidst the beds and cold frames, but there was a light in the head gardener's cottage.

The horse plodded along the grass paths to the opposite gate, patient as Alistair remembered the knack of flicking the catch open, then it was a short ride to the looming bulk of the stable block.

The grooms were just finishing for the night; most of the doors were closed, the yard almost deserted, although there was light spilling from the tack room door and the sound of someone whistling inside. A lad was filling buckets at the pump and looked up at the sound of hooves.

'Sir? Can I help you?'

Alistair rode closer, then dismounted where the light from the tack room caught his face. The boy gasped. 'My lord?' So, his resemblance to his father had strengthened as he had grown older. He had thought it himself, but it was interesting to see the confirmation in the lad's face.

'Yes, I am Alistair Lyndon,' he said. Best to be clear, just in case the lad thought he was seeing a ghost.

'And right welcome you are, my lord,' said a voice from the tack room door as a burly man came out. 'You won't remember me, my lord, but I'm—'

'Tregowan,' Alistair said, holding out his hand. 'Of course I remember you, you were a groom here when I left. Your father taught me to ride.'

'Aye, my lord.' The groom clasped his hand and gave it a firm shake. 'He died last November and I'm head groom now.'

'I'm sorry to hear he is gone, but he'd be proud to know there's still a Tregowan running the stables here.'

'Fourth generation, my lord. But you'll be wanting to get up to the house, not stand here listening to me. Jimmy, lad, you run ahead and let Mr Barstow know his lordship's home.' The boy took to his heels and Tregowan walked with Alistair towards the archway.

'I did hear that your letter arrived yesterday, my lord, all about the shipwreck. I'm powerful sorry to hear about that—you'll have lost friends, I've no doubt.' Alistair gave a grunt of acknowledgment. 'Her ladyship took a proper turn. As bad as she was when your father died, from what they say.' His rich Cornish burr held no shade of expression.

'Indeed. Well, I had better go and reassure her that I am safe and alive.' Alistair kept his own tone as bland. 'Goodnight, Tregowan; I look forward to seeing the stables tomorrow.'

As he rounded the corner the front of the castle came into view. In 1670 the Lyndon of the day had extended and fortified the old keep that had suffered so badly at the hands of Cromwell's forces. His grandson had added an imposing frontage in the taste of the early eighteenth-century and successive generations had added on, modernised and improved until any lover of Gothic tales would have been hard put to find a draughty corridor, a damp dungeon or a ruined turret in the place.

Alistair thought about Dita's sensation novel, lost now, and wondered whether she would try to rewrite it. He stopped to get the feelings that thinking about her evoked under control. How could he have done that—and how could she not have told him? What did it take to preserve a perfect social façade with a man who had so brutally taken your innocence?

The thought had come to him on today's interminable ride that perhaps she had gone to his arms on the ship in order to prove something to herself, to lay a ghost. Or perhaps, when his thoughts had been darkest, she intended him to fall in love with her so she could punish him by her refusal.

She was certainly punishing him now; his conscience and his honour demanded he marry her, but without her consent he was left with few options. He could tell her father, he could abduct her, he could seduce her and get her with child…

His face must have been grim as the massive front doors opened and he strode up the steps and into the Great Hall. The butler, who was a stranger to him, froze and then stammered, 'My lord. Welcome back to Lyndonholt Castle, my lord. I am Barstow.' He looked beyond Alistair, into the gloom. 'Your luggage, my lord? Your man?'

'I have neither. If there is one of the footmen suitable, I'll have him as valet for the moment; he can find me evening wear in my father's wardrobe, I have no doubt. My compliments to her ladyship and I will join her at dinner. I would like a fire lit in my room and hot water for a bath immediately.'

'My lord.' The butler stepped forwards as Alistair made for the stairs. 'Her ladyship gave no orders about his late lordship's bedchamber. It is exactly as he left it, the bed is not made up—'

'Then see that it is,' Alistair said, allowing his displeasure to show. He had no fear of ghosts and he had every intention of stamping his ownership on this house from the start.

'Her ladyship is still occupying the adjoining suite, my lord. And she has taken over his late lordship's—your—sitting room and the dressing room,' the butler said, looking wretched.

'I see.' Alistair put one booted foot on the bottom step. 'I have no wish to inconvenience her ladyship at this hour. I will take whichever of the guest chambers is easiest, Barstow.'

'My lord, of course. The Garden Suite would be most comfortable, I believe.' He began to gesture to footmen. 'Gregory, you will act as his lordship's valet for the time being. Fetch his lordship whatever he needs from the

Marquis's Suite. I will have the decanters sent up, my lord. Her ladyship dines at eight.'

Alistair began to climb past the lavish trophies of arms and armour on the wall. *So, she had won the first round, had she?* Even as he thought it there was a flurry of rustling silk and the patter of slippers on the stair. He looked up as he reached the first turn and saw the black-clad figure of his stepmother.

'Alistair!' She held out her hands and waited while he climbed the stairs to her side. It allowed him ample time to appreciate the picture she presented, as no doubt she intended.

'Stepmama,' he said, bowing over her hand. 'My condolences.'

'So cold, so formal,' she said, but there was something very like fear in the wide blue eyes. 'There was a time when you called me Imogen.'

'Indeed, but that was before you married my father,' he pointed out politely.

'I know I broke your heart,' she murmured. 'But are you still angry after all this time?'

'Do you really wish to discuss it here?' he asked. 'Allow me to walk you back to your retiring room. Or, should I say, mine?'

'Alistair, are you going to grudge me one tiny room?' The fear had gone, perhaps when she realised he was not going to treat her to some Cheltenham tragedy. Where had the affected wide-eyed manner come from? Eight years ago Imogen had been sweetly naïve—or so he had thought.

'Not at all,' he said with a smile as he opened the door for her. 'You will have the whole of the Dower House all to yourself.'

'What?' She turned like a cat as he closed the door behind them. 'You cannot throw me out of here!'

'I most certainly can require you to move to the Dower House,' Alistair said. 'I will have it overhauled for you immediately.'

God, but she is lovely, he thought, studying her dispassionately. For over a year the thought of her had torn his heart. Petite, vivid, with big blue eyes and glossy black hair, she had a certain something that transformed her piquant little face from merely pretty to a loveliness that took men's breath away. She had certainly deprived him of both breath and sense as an idealistic twenty-year-old.

'But how can you exile me? After all I have been to you!' The flounce was new as well, although it gave the most excellent opportunity for any onlooker to admire the curves of her figure.

'A stepmother?' he enquired, deliberately obtuse. 'Do sit down, Imogen, because, frankly, I would appreciate the chance to.'

'You loved me,' she declared in throbbing tones as she sank on to the *chaise*. 'I know I broke your heart, but—'

'I was infatuated with you eight years ago when you were nineteen,' Alistair said flatly. 'Young men are liable to be taken in by lovely faces and you are, my dear, very lovely.' She cast her eyes down as though he had made a passionate, but slightly improper, declaration. 'It was a shock to discover that you had been—shall we say, *flirting*?—with me when all the while you were in my father's bed. I had not thought myself so unobservant, I must confess.'

'Alistair! Must you be so crude?' Imogen lifted one hand as though to ward off a blow. 'I had no idea of the depth of your feelings and my lord was so…passionate and demanding.'

'Let us be frank, Imogen.' He found he had no patience with her games. 'You thought my father might not come up to scratch, so you strung me along as your insurance policy. Either that or you thought a marquis in the hand, even if he was old enough to be your father, was a more certain bet than the heir.'

Her guilty colour was proof enough. The daughter of the local squire three parishes away, Imogen Penwyth had been an acknowledged local belle and her parents were avid in their ambition for her. At the time he had been too angry and wounded to think this through, but he had had time since to realise just what had been going on.

'Mama was simply anxious to do the best for me,' she whispered. He wished he could believe she had not been as ambitious and unscrupulous as her parent.

Between them his father and this woman had made him deeply cynical about love, but he knew how gullible he had been. *An idealistic young idiot, in fact*, he thought with wry affection for his youthful self.

That young man had been serious, rather studious and puzzled about where his life was going to lead him, given that he had a vigorous, tough father who had shown no desire to hand over any part of running the estates to his only child. He knew then that he wanted to travel, to explore. His interest in botany was already leading him to read widely on the subject, but it never occurred to him that he could—or should—leave England.

His duty was to be at his father's side, he had assumed, aware that the other man despised him for not being the hard-drinking, wenching gambler he was himself. The marquis had been unable to condemn his son for being a milksop, however, not when Alistair was acknowledged to be the best shot in the county, rode hard and even, much to his father's loudly expressed relief, conducted a number of discreet *affaires*.

But he had paid off his current mistress when he had come face to face with Imogen Penwyth at a dance. She was too lovely, too pure for him to even look at another woman when he loved her.

'You don't understand,' Imogen said, petulant now.

'I understood perfectly well what was going on when I walked into the library and found my father with his breeches round his ankles and you spread all over the map table with your skirts up to your ears,' Alistair replied. He was too tired for this, but if he didn't make it quite clear to Imogen that he was no longer a slave to her charms life was going to get even more complicated. 'And don't try to tell me he forced you, or your parents forced you or you had no choice in the matter,' he added. 'Frankly, I don't care.'

'Oh!'

'Let us be clear,' he said, getting to his feet and wishing he could just fall into bed and sleep for a month. 'I will spend a week or so here to deal with the most pressing business and I will put the refurbishment of the Dower House in hand. I will then go up to town for the Season. When I get back I expect you to have moved out.'

She turned huge, imploring eyes on him and he noticed the sapphires, just the colour of those eyes, dangling from her ears and adorning her neck. 'And I expect to be able to account for every item of entailed jewellery when I get back,' he added. 'My wife will be requiring them.' Her mouth dropped open, probably the first genuine expression he had seen on her face that evening. 'I will see you at dinner, Stepmama.'

As he closed the door behind him something hit the other side—a dainty slipper, no doubt.

Gregory was bustling round the Garden Suite, looking nervous when Alistair reached it. 'Your bath is ready, my lord.' He gestured towards the dressing room door. 'Are these clothes acceptable, my lord? And shall I assist you to undress, my lord?'

'They look fine.' Alistair gave them a cursory glance. His father, he was sure, had kept his lean figure to the end and they had been much of a height. 'I am quite capable of undressing and dressing myself, thank you. And one *my lord* every twenty minutes will be adequate.' The footman bit his lip and Alistair smiled, getting a grin in response. 'I'll shave myself, too.'

He glanced at the clock. Half past seven. No time for dozing in the bath then. 'Get a jug of cold water, Gregory, in ten minutes.'

He sank into warm water, soaped himself lavishly and felt himself drift off. *Dita.* How would Imogen have coped with everything that Dita had been through over the past few months? He thought of her in that hut on the island, soaked, shivering, courageous and the most desirable woman he had ever seen.

And the most pig-headed and defiant and proud, too. She was his whether she wanted to be or not. Or whether he wanted it either. God, life would be hell with Dita, resentful and furious and intelligent enough to get up to any madcap scheme that took her fancy. Her face seemed to shimmer on the inside of his closed lids—

'Aagh!' The cold water was like a slap in the face. Alistair reared up out of the tub, spluttered and shook himself like a large dog as Gregory backed away, clutching the jug like a shield. 'Good man,' Alistair said as he climbed out and grabbed for a towel.

'My lord?' Gregory was staring at him.

Alistair glanced down. The bruises and abrasions were spectacular and the scars from the tiger's raking claws always went red in hot water. 'Shipwrecks tend to have that effect.'

'Arnica?'

'Does it do any good?' He began to towel himself dry.

'My old gran always swears by it, and there's some in the stillroom,' Gregory volunteered.

'We'll try it tomorrow,' Alistair said, amused at the thought of Gregory's 'old gran'. He was a pleasant young man with a sense of humour and might be worth keeping on as a valet. It was time to put the East behind him, at least for a few years, and concentrate on learning to be an English gentleman again.

Gregory made himself scarce while Alistair dressed, although the silence that was presumably him holding his breath while the neckcloth was being tied was almost as distracting as chatter would have been.

He reappeared with a box in his hands. 'Mr Barstow said I was to be sure to put these into your hands, my lord. He says to say they have been in the silver safe under his lock and key since his late lordship died.'

'Did he, indeed?' It sounded as though the butler had taken his mistress's measure and that his loyalties lay with the new marquis, not with her. Alistair opened the box and found tie pins, fobs and one old, heavy signet. He had never seen it off his father's hand before. It slid on to his with a cold rightness, the almost black stone heavy on a hand unused to rings. But it made a point: he was Iwerne now.

Just in case Imogen missed it, he lifted out the heavy

gold watch with its chain and fobs and put it in his waist-coat pocket, arranged the chain across to the buttonhole, then took a modern piece, a fine amber-topped pin, and set it in his neckcloth.

'Goes with your eyes, my lord,' Gregory said chattily as he locked the box and was thus spared Alistair's frown. 'There's an amber brocade waistcoat in the clothes press, that would suit you, too.' He offered Alistair the key. 'His late lordship used to put it on his watch chain.'

There was a certain sardonic amusement in contemplating what his father would say if he saw him in his clothes and jewellery. 'Dead men's shoes,' he said under his breath as he tried on the evening slippers and found they fitted.

There was a choked snort from Gregory, who looked appalled at his own reaction. Alistair raised an eyebrow at him and went down to deal with Imogen with a grim smile on his face.

* * *

Imogen sulked for the rest of the meal, treating Alistair to an exhibition of frigid disdain that would have amused him if he were not so tired. As soon as the dessert, which she merely picked at, was removed, she got to her feet.

'Goodnight, ma'am,' Alistair said, rising. 'I will see you at breakfast, perhaps?'

'I doubt it, I rarely rise before noon.' She swept out, quivering with affronted dignity.

Alistair stayed on his feet, poured himself a glass of port and carried it to the other door. 'Barstow, send Gregory to me in my chamber, if you please. I will take breakfast at eight.'

The footman bustled about, turning down the bed, shaking out a long silk robe, trimming the candle wicks as Alistair shed coat and neckcloth. 'Is there anything else, my lord? Goodnight then, my lord, your nightgown is on the bed.'

Alistair gave him a minute, then got up and turned the key in the lock, walked through to the dressing room and locked the outer door there, too. He sat for a while at the desk, savouring his port and making lists, one eye on the clock. As it struck midnight there was a light scratching on one panel, repeated when he made no move to open it. After a moment the handle turned. Silence, then he heard the handle in the dressing room rattle.

It was as well he had taken precautions. Perhaps, he thought, his smile thin, he should find himself a chaperon. Once he had thought he would die for that woman. What nonsense love was.

'We must call at the Castle,' Lady Wycombe said, two days after Dita's return, when the family had finally stopped talking. 'We should not be neglectful in welcoming Lord Iwerne formally to the neighbourhood again—and, of course, we must thank him once more for all he has done for us.' She smiled fondly at Dita.

'Must we, Mama?' Evaline wrinkled her nose. 'Lord Iwerne, by all means, but her *ladyship...*'

'Is she so very unpleasant?' Dita asked, curious. 'I met her, of course, now and again. She is beautiful.'

'And empty-headed and spiteful,' her sister retorted.

'Evaline! Oh dear. Yes, well, she is not a female I would wish my daughters to associate with, if I am to be honest,' Lady Wycombe admitted. 'As you are both grown up now and none of the men are here, I will not disguise the fact that I fear her morals are not all they should be either, even when the late marquis was alive.'

'Really? Surely he was not a man to stand for that sort of thing?'

'Sauce for the goose, my dear,' her mother said with startling frankness. 'Once it became clear she was barren, they appear to have agreed to find their pleasures where they chose. It was obvious the lack of children was not his fault, for, although Alistair's mother died before she could have more babies, there are enough bastards of his in the area to crew a brig.'

'Mama!' Dita said on a gasp of shocked laughter.

'While Alistair is in residence we must show every courtesy.' Lady Wycombe smiled. 'And, Evaline, lend Dita your new emerald-green afternoon gown and the villager hat with the velvet ribbons, I'll not have Imogen Lyndon sneering at how my daughters dress. Oh, yes, and the pearls.'

Elegantly gowned, and with Evaline in a delightful rose-pink ensemble beside her, Dita regarded her mother fondly as the carriage rattled over the drawbridge to the outer gatehouse of the castle. Her frankness and lack of prudery had made Mama easy to confide in during the aftermath of her ruinous elopement when her father was still coldly angry with her. She had assured her mother that she had not slept with Stephen, and that had tempered her father's ire somewhat, but even so, he had taken longer than her mother to come to terms with her foolishness.

Now she looked forward to seeing Mama deal with the widow. And she ached to see Alistair again, even though it was certain to be difficult. They had not been apart for three months, she realised—now two days seemed an eternity. Whatever else lay between them, she could not forget that she loved him. That emotion was not the product of the shock of the shipwreck, she knew that for certain now. She loved him, in spite of everything.

Lady Wycombe asked for his lordship, not her ladyship, when Barstow opened the door to them, an interesting breach of etiquette. His lordship was At Home and would be with them directly, the butler informed them as he ushered them through to the drawing room.

When Alistair came in Dita found she could not take her eyes off him as he shook hands with her mother. The space of those two days seemed to have sharpened her focus. He looked fine-drawn and there was a pallor under his eyes that spoke of late nights and worry; in the darkly formal clothes, he looked older, too. They must be his father's, she realised, and wondered if he minded very much having that intimate connection to a man from whom he had been estranged.

'Lady Perdita.' He took her hand and she looked into his eyes. Was he happy? Was he looking after himself?

Was her expression betraying how much she needed him? There was something in his face that warned her that he had not forgotten, or changed his mind. He was going to do something to force a marriage, whatever she had to say about it.

'Lord Iwerne. Have you settled in yet? I expect, like me, you are having to borrow everything from slippers to combs.'

He nodded and smiled. 'Yes—it feels very strange, does it not? Lady Evaline.' His eyebrows rose a trifle as he turned to her sister and Dita felt a sudden, quite shocking, pang of jealousy. Evaline looked lovely, and sweet, and the perfect image of the kind of young lady Alistair had been talking of marrying. The sort of young lady he *ought* to be marrying. 'May I say that you have grown up quite considerably since I last saw you? And very charmingly, too.'

Evaline blushed and lowered her lashes, but she did not simper or stammer. 'You are very kind, Lord Iwerne, but as it is eight years, I think a little change is to be expected.'

Alistair laughed and they settled around the tea table as the footmen brought in the urn and china. 'Before we say anything else, I must thank you for everything that you have done for my daughter,' her mother said with her usual directness. 'I know now that if was not for your courage and endurance Dita would have drowned—or met a horrible death if that dog had bitten her. My husband will be calling, of course, but I felt I had to say what I feel as a mother: I will never forget and if there is ever anything the family can do for you, you have only to ask.'

Alistair was silent, looking down at his clasped hands on the table. Dita saw the unfamiliar ring on his signet finger and how he rubbed it, absently, as though it helped him think.

After a moment he said, 'If I have been able to be of service to Lady Perdita, it is an honour. You should know, ma'am, that your daughter is a lady of courage and integrity. Great courage,' he added. 'She put herself at risk to save a child.' The silence grew uncomfortable. Evaline gave a little sob, Lady Wycombe cleared her throat. 'And talent,' Alistair added. 'Did you realise that Lady Perdita is a novelist?'

'Really?' Her sister turned, wide-eyed. 'You have written a book?'

'It is at the bottom of the sea, I fear,' Dita said. 'Although that is probably the best place for it.'

'Never say that!' Alistair began to tell the story of *Adventures of Angelica* and soon had Evaline and Lady Wycombe in a ripple of laughter while Dita buried her face in her hands and implored him to spare her.

'It sounds *wonderful*,' Evaline declared as the door opened and a lady walked it. She was quite, quite lovely, Dita thought, staring at her for a startled moment before she recognised her, *and* her mood. The marchioness was furiously angry.

'My dear Lady Wycombe!' She advanced with hands outstretched, a charming smile on her lips, ice in the big blue eyes. 'I am so sorry! My fool of a butler announced you to Alistair and not, as he should, to me. Really...' she turned her gaze on Alistair '...the man is incompetent—you must dismiss him.'

'You are labouring under a misapprehension, Lady Iwerne,' Lady Wycombe said. 'I asked for Lord Iwerne. We have come to welcome him home and to thank him for everything he has done for Perdita.'

'I see. I quite long to hear all about these adventures.

Will you walk with me in the garden, Lady Perdita? I am certain your mother and sister will not want to listen to the tale all over again.'

It was the last thing Dita wanted to do. She opened her mouth to invent a twisted ankle and was suddenly seized by curiosity. This self-centred female most certainly did not want to hear about her, so what *did* she want? 'I would love to see the gardens, Lady Iwerne,' she said, getting up. Her skirts brushed Alistair's knees as she passed and he looked up and frowned at her. So he did not want her walking alone with his youthful stepmother. That was interesting.

'I am glad you have come home,' Imogen began, the moment they were on the terrace. 'I so need a female friend of my own age to confide in.' She was a couple of years Dita's senior, but she was not going to correct her—this was too intriguing.

'How flattering,' she murmured, 'but I will be going up to town very soon with my parents and sister.'

'You will?' The prettily arched eyebrows rose. 'But—forgive me—I thought you were no longer in society… after the elopement.'

'That little affair?' Dita laughed. 'I am used to dealing with gossip; I will not regard it. And besides, I am not husband-hunting.'

'Oh? Perhaps that is wise, under the circumstances. But I am quite cast down, for I shall be so lonely, shut away in the Dower House.'

She made it sound like a prison. Dita was vividly reminded of *Adventures of Angelica*—how well Lady Iwerne would fit into such a melodrama. 'Shut away? Surely not. You are two months into your mourning; the first year will soon go. And besides, there is this lovely park, the gardens...'

'Ah, but you do not understand.' Imogen cast a hunted look around, as if expecting to see assassins appearing from behind every topiary bush. 'I must shut myself away for my own protection.'

Dita pinched herself. No, she was awake so she could not be dreaming that she had strayed into a Minerva Press novel. 'From what? Or whom?'

'Alistair,' Imogen declared, as she sank on to a bench and pulled Dita down beside her. 'May I confide in you?'

'I think you had better,' Dita said. 'You can hardly leave it there.'

'When I was a girl, he loved me, you see,' Imogen said. 'He adored me, worshipped the ground I walked upon. It was a pure love. A young man's love.'

'Er...quite,' Dita said, feeling vaguely nauseous. 'It would be if this was before Alistair left home.' At least, he was only twenty, so *young* was accurate, although whether his affections were entirely pure, she had her doubts—very few young men of that age had a pure thought in their heads in her experience. 'And you loved him? Encouraged him?'

'I was flattered, of course, although I had many admirers.' She simpered and Dita folded her hands together firmly—the urge to slap was tremendous. 'Perhaps I was too kind and he misunderstood.'

Dita said nothing, thinking back. She had no memory of Alistair mooning about, love-struck, but then she had only been sixteen and she never saw him at dances or parties. But he had seemed different, somehow. That fizzing excitement, the way he was almost flirtatious. Had that been it? He had been in love and she had sensed it. Perhaps that had awakened her own new feelings for him.

'Then another man declared himself and I was…' she sighed '…swept away. He was older, more sophisticated, titled.'

The realisation of what Imogen was saying hit Dita like a blow. 'You are saying that Lord Iwerne courted you at the *same time* as his son? It wasn't after Alistair left home that he paid his addresses?'

'No.' Imogen produced a scrap of lace and dabbed her eyes. 'It was dreadful. My lord found me alone and his passions overcame him. He held me to him, showered kisses on my face, declared his undying devotion—and Alistair walked in.' She went extremely pink.

'He was doing rather more than rain kisses on your face, was he not?' Dita said with sudden conviction. 'He was making love to you. Where?'

'In the library,' Imogen whispered.

So that was it. He found his father and the woman he loved in an act of betrayal and he walked out, furiously angry, and got drunk. And then I found him. And when she had given herself to him the disgust he must have felt with Imogen, with women in general and with himself, had swept over him. He had thrown her out of his room and the next day he had left.

Of course he had. How could he live in the same house as his father when he had seduced the woman Alistair loved? How could he accept Imogen as his stepmother after that betrayal? He had been in an impossible situation. Any other man he could have punched, or called out, but this was his father.

'So he left and made a new life for himself abroad,' Dita said, thinking out loud. 'And now he is back.' How hideously embarrassing for both of them. 'But I am sure with tact on both sides you can put it behind you.'

'But he still loves me,' Imogen said. Dita stared at her. Impossible. 'He desires me,' the young widow whispered. 'I am afraid to be in the house with him, that is why I must take refuge in the Dower House. I told him, it is wrong, sinful. I am his father's widow. But—'

'That,' Dita said with conviction, 'is nonsense. Of course he no longer loves you. Or desires you.' Her certainty wavered a little there—Imogen was very lovely. No, surely Alistair had better taste now he was an experienced man.

'Oh!' Imogen glared at her. 'I see what it is—you want him yourself and cannot face the fact that he is besotted with me. Well, you beware, Lady Perdita, he is dangerous.' She sprang to her feet and swept off along the terrace, silken skirts swishing.

Dita sat and stared after her. 'Dangerous? No, but you are,' she murmured. After a few minutes she got up and made her way back to the drawing room. 'Lady Iwerne was a little tired and went to lie down,' she said. Alistair looked at her, questions in his eyes, but she produced a bright smile, incapable of thinking what to do about this revelation.

Alistair was charming to all three of them, saw them to the door, waved them off, but Dita had the impression that his gaze rested on her with speculation.

'What on earth did that woman want with you?' her mother demanded, the moment the carriage door was closed.

'Oh, to poke at me and be catty,' Dita said. 'She is bored, I have no doubt—I do not grudge her the amusement.' She fiddled with the pearls for a while, then asked, 'Will she be moving into the Dower House?'

'I imagine so. Alistair said something about having it renovated,' Lady Wycombe said.

That sounded likely. A planned renovation for the Dowager to move into before Alistair came home with a bride was only to be expected. Surely, if Imogen felt threatened in any way, she would have fled there immediately. No, for some reason she was feeling the need to attack Alistair and he ought to know what she was saying.

Inwardly Dita quailed at the thought of discussing that day when he had made love to her, but if Imogen spread this vicious nonsense some of the mud might stick. How could she? she railed inwardly, more furious the more she thought about it. How she must have changed—or had Alistair been blinded by love, all those years ago? She would have to think how to tell him, but she must do it tomorrow. It would be a sleepless night.

Chapter Seventeen

Please meet me at the hollow oak by the pond, the note read in Dita's impatient black hand. *Ten o'clock this morning. It is* very *important. D.*

Alistair studied it while he drank coffee. That could only be the old tree that he and her brothers had used as a shelter when they fished in the horse pond as children. Dita would tag along, too, but it was one of the few occupations that would drive her away with boredom after half an hour.

What did she want that was so urgent and that could not be discussed in the house? Had she thought better of her situation—or realised how determined he was—and had decided to accept him?

He suspected not. Dita was stubborn. No doubt a frustrating encounter lay ahead, but it would get him out of the house with its increasingly poisonous atmosphere. Alistair found himself longing for the moment when he could, with a clear conscience, leave the estate and go up to London.

He strolled down to the stables and spent an hour

with Tregowan, looking over his father's horses, but he found he was too restless to concentrate.

Was Dita unhappy? He missed her, he found, more every day. There was no one to wake him up with tart observations over breakfast, no one to make him laugh or to freeze him with a sharp look from green eyes. No one to stir his blood as only Dita stirred it. *Green-eyed hornet*, he had thought her that evening in Calcutta. She would certainly sting when he finally had her trapped.

Alistair shifted restlessly, changed his position leaning against the mounting block, and considered how long it would be before he could go to London and set up a mistress. It would be a short-term arrangement until he took Dita as his wife; he despised men who took marriage vows and then immediately broke them.

'I'll take the grey hunter out now, Tregowan.' It was early, not half past nine, but he'd gallop the fidgets out before he met her.

Dita was already sitting under the oak when he got there, her back against the trunk, her knees drawn up with her arms around them as she'd been used to sit, watching the boys fish until her patience gave out. It made him smile despite everything, just to look at her. She turned her head at the sound of hooves, but did not move position. The long skirts of her riding habit pooled around her feet and his horse snickered a greeting to her mare, tied to a nearby willow.

'He's handsome,' she said in greeting as Alistair dismounted and threw the reins over a branch.

'Very,' he agreed and came to sit next to her on the turf. 'My father had an eye for horseflesh.' *And female flesh, too.* 'Are you all right?' She was silent and he turned his head against the rough bark for a better look at her face. 'You are not, are you? Couldn't you sleep?'

'No,' she agreed, 'I couldn't.'

'Nightmares? Or have you made up your mind to do the right thing and marry me?' He put his arm around her shoulders. She sighed and leaned in to him for a second and he felt himself relax.

'No. A dilemma.' After a moment she sat up straight, pushing herself away from his arm. 'Alistair, I am worried about Lady Iwerne.' When he did not reply, she added, 'She told me a very unpleasant story about you. If she is spiteful enough to spread it, she could do a lot of damage.'

'What is she saying?' he asked, surprised his voice was not shaking with the temper that flashed through him.

'That you were in love with her, eight years ago, and that you left home when you realised she was going to marry your father, which in itself is quite understandable,' Dita said flatly. 'But she told me that she is frightened of you now and feels she has to flee to the Dower House to be safe from you forcing your attentions on her.'

Alistair swore. 'Quite,' Dita said. 'The question is, what are you going to do about it?'

'You don't believe her?' He had to ask.

Dita made a scornful little noise. 'I believe you were in love with her, yes. She is quite extraordinarily lovely and I expect then she was prettily behaved and flirted with a sweet sort of innocence. You were in such a state when you realised the truth that your emotions must have been deeply involved.

'But now? I can imagine that she is distractingly beautiful to have around the house, but she is foolish and empty-headed and you have higher standards than that. I would guess that she irritates you greatly. Leaving aside the small matter of it being incest to lie with your father's widow.'

The relief that Dita so categorically believed in him distracted Alistair from how she had phrased it and it took a while for her words to sink in. 'Thank you for your faith in me.' He found her calm intelligence both bracing and refreshing after Imogen's tantrums. 'But how do you know how I reacted to the realisation that she and my father—'

'I saw you that day, don't forget.' She kept her voice carefully neutral, but Alistair winced. 'Imogen said that your father found her alone, his passions overcame him and he swept her into his arms and showered kisses on her face while declaring his undying devotion. It was rather more than that, I imagine.'

'I walked into the library and found him taking her on the map table,' Alistair said. 'I turned right round and walked out and didn't go back until I was sure I wouldn't do something stupid, such as hit him.'

'And so you went and got drunk.'

'Yes. And, unfortunately you know more about what happened next than I do.' He got to his feet and walked away from her. 'I must have sunk at least two more bottles after you left me.'

'I am so sorry. Look at me,' Dita said. 'It is all right,' she went on as he turned, and he saw she was studying him gravely. 'I told you after the shipwreck—it wasn't your fault. And it wasn't your fault that I realised that I was in love with you and that you broke my heart.'

'What?' He sat down with a thump on a tree stump.

'Along with every other impressionable girl for twenty miles around,' Dita explained with flattening calm. 'You were very handsome then, you know. You still are, of course, but so many of the boys and young men we knew had spots, or kept falling over their feet or were complete boors. I didn't see it because I was still thinking of you as my friend, you understand. Or like George. Only, when you kissed me like that I realised that you most certainly were not my brother and I didn't want you to be. That is why I came to you. Don't think you forced me.'

Alistair knew he was gaping and had no idea what to say. 'I was *sixteen*, Alistair. Girls that age are all emotions and drama and there is nothing they enjoy more than the agonies of exaggerated love. We grow out of it, you know. You broke my heart, of course, when you went away. I thought it was all my fault, because I didn't know about Imogen. But then I heard Mama and Papa talking about some row you had had with your father over land and I saw it was nothing to do with me. Girls that age fall in and out of love four times a month.'

'You were in love with me? Then why the hell won't you marry me?' he demanded. 'That's what you want in marriage, isn't it? Love?'

'I told you—I fell out of it soon enough. And I was rather hoping for a husband who loved me,' she said tartly. 'Mind you,' she added, 'it did make a lasting impression, making love with you. You know how if ducklings hatch and there is no duck around they become fixed on whatever they see first and think the cat or a bucket is their mother?' He nodded, bemused. 'Well, I think I must have become imprinted with the image of tall, dark, handsome men with interesting cheekbones— because Stephen looks a bit like you, I realise now. And I don't find blond men very attractive.'

He shook his head as though to dislodge an irritating

fly. 'Look, you know you have to marry me. You love me.' The thought filled him with terror.

'You were not listening,' she reproved. 'That was eight years ago. Calf-love. But that doesn't matter now. How are we going to neutralise Imogen before she spreads this tale round half the county?'

Alistair dragged his mind—and his body, which was taking an entirely inappropriate interest in the thought of how Dita might demonstrate love—back to the problem. 'I need a chaperon,' he said. 'In fact, half a dozen of them. I'll invite a houseful of men, sober professional men, to stay immediately. I'll get in my London man of business, an architect, someone to advise on landscaping the grounds, the steward here, my solicitor—they'll drop everything if I call. I'll have the vicar to stay, while I'm at it, tell him I want to discuss the parish and good works, or something. I've got the devil of a lot of business to see to—I'll do it here and now.'

'Of course!' She clapped her hands together. 'They won't be a houseparty of bucks or rakes but deadly dull businessmen of the utmost respectability. There is no way she can accuse you of harassing her with them in the house. And, I've just thought of another idea—why not bring her to call on us and ask Mama's advice on finding a suitable companion to live with her? Mama can tell everyone quite truthfully how thoughtful you are and how concerned that Imogen is looked after and how you are exerting yourself to make the Dower House comfortable for her.'

'Yes, that should put a stop to her nonsense. We make a good tactical team, you and I.' There it was again, the sense of connection that he so often felt with Dita stealing over him, as though their minds were touching. 'I don't understand her—she seems to be reacting with spite because I haven't fallen at her feet. But she must know perfectly well that any sort of relationship other than the obvious one is impossible—and scandalous.'

'She has a guilty conscience.' Dita rested her chin on her knees and tipped her head to one side, thinking. 'She knows she betrayed you and that both she and your father acted badly—it is much easier to attack the person you have wounded rather than beg forgiveness. I feel sorry for her. At least, I feel sorry for the girl she was, and it is sad that she did not have the character and intelligence to mature into a happy person now.'

'Sorry?' He stared at her. 'What is there to arouse your pity, pray?'

'It kept me awake last night, thinking about it,' she confessed. 'I was so angry with her, and so frightened at the damage I feared she could do you. But gradually I began to think about her all those years ago. She was very young and, I have no doubt, completely under the influence of her parents, as any well-bred girl would be. What they said was law. She fell for you and I am sure they encouraged it, for you were an exceptionally good match. And then someone—probably her mother— realised that your father's roving eye had fallen on her. Not the heir, but the marquis himself. They didn't care that he was old enough to be her father, or that she had a *tendre* for you. He was the better match and that is all there was to it.

'They would have told her to encourage him, she would have found herself alone with him when she might have expected to be chaperoned.' Dita shivered and looked up at him as he stared back at her, appalled. 'He had a reputation, did he not? This was not some kindly, fatherly figure. This was a mature rake and she was an innocent little lamb.'

'My God. She was unwilling?'

'She did as she was told, as was expected of her,' Dita said and he heard the anger quivering in her voice. 'I wonder if the fact that you look like him made it better or worse. But I doubt she ever thought she had a choice; young girls in our world do not, you see. They are raised to make a good match at all costs. That is what the Marriage Mart is, a market, and they are the lambs brought for sale.'

'All of them? What about you?' he asked and her fierce expression softened.

'I have exceptional parents.' She chuckled, 'And I am a disobedient and difficult daughter. Evaline is not like me,' she added, a frown creasing her forehead. 'She is the dutiful one, like Averil. I hope she will be all right; this is her first Season.'

'I won't be in London for another week at least, but I will keep an eye on her,' Alistair promised. 'And then you and I will talk and you will realise by then that marrying me is the right thing to do.'

Her face must have changed for the arrogant male certainty of his expression softened. 'Dita? Are you all right?'

'No. I am not,' she said. 'I am thinking about those young women like Imogen was. Like Evaline. All those hopes and expectations, all that duty and ignorance. A few months when they are the focus of attention, their virtue and their bloodlines and their dowries on display—and then a lifetime to live with the results of the bargains that are struck.'

'It is the way it has been done for people of our class for hundreds of years.'

'And it suits the men very well, does it not?' she flashed back. 'Listen to yourself: the complacent marquis. You will keep an eye on my sister and make sure she finds a suitable man, never mind her true feelings. You will satisfy your own pride and sense of honour by trying to force me to marry you. Not because you love me, or even because I am *suitable*, but because you took my virginity.'

Too angry now to sit at his feet, she scrambled up. 'Nothing else matters, does it? Such a little thing to make such a fuss about—a thrust, some pain. But that makes the woman your possession and you will duel and kill for that. Was that what it was with Imogen? Your father had her virginity and you did not even stop to think about her feelings? Damn you and your honour.'

'Honour and desire,' Alistair said, and closed the distance between them in two strides. He took her wrist and bent his head even as she reached to lash out at him. 'Let me show you.'

He had taught her well. She had him twisting to avoid her knee, grunting as her stiffened fingers found his stomach, cursing under his breath as her teeth found the back of his hand.

'So you will force me now?' she panted as he crushed her back against the tree.

'But you want me. Tell me you don't want me.' Almost eye to eye the amber gaze held hers, demanded the truth, made her knees tremble.

'Damn you.' But she stopped struggling. *I love you, you arrogant creature. Why can't you love me? I want you.*

'Tell me to stop,' he said. His body heated hers; the thrust of his erection felt as though it had the power to pierce their clothing. Her mind emptied of everything but need.

'Let go of my arms,' she managed to say and he did,

his eyes darkening at what he must think was her refusal. Dita curled her arms around his neck and brought her mouth, open, to his. There was a moment of stillness, then his tongue thrust in to take possession.

She expected urgency, roughness, anger. Instead, he stilled again, then began to lavish languid strokes into her mouth. She had time to taste him and savour every texture, the slide of her tongue across his teeth, the muscular agility of his tongue, the soft, wet interior of his mouth, the firmness of his lips. This was kissing as luxurious as the most decadent dessert and she surrendered to it with soft whimpers of delight.

His hands cupped her breasts, his fingers seeking her nipples, frustrated by the tight weave of her tailored habit. She slid her hands between them, fumbling with the buttons until the top opened and he could push aside the short habit-shirt and free her breasts from the constraint of the light corset she wore for riding.

In contrast to his mouth his fingers were not gentle as they found the peaking nipples, trapped them, rolled them until they became aching pebbles and the sensation lanced down through her belly to where she throbbed for him.

Dita found the fall of his breeches, opened it, clumsy with her haste, and sobbed with relief against Alistair's mouth as she closed her fingers round the hard silken shaft. He lifted his head as his hands left her breasts and took hold of her skirts, but the length and weight of the voluminous habit defeated him.

'Down,' he rasped, pulling her to the grass. 'Like this.' She found herself on hands and knees, her skirts up to her waist, her jacket hanging open as he bent over her. 'Dita.' He buried his face in the nape of her neck, biting softly as his hands cupped the weight of her breasts.

'You are mine.' She felt him nudge her legs apart and gasped. She wanted to look at him, to see his eyes, kiss his mouth, but the weight of him, the excitement of what he was doing was strange and arousing almost beyond measure.

He left her breasts, one hand braced on the ground as the other parted her. 'Such sweet honey.' She should be embarrassed that she was so wet for him, but she was beyond that now, pushing shamelessly against his probing hand. One finger slid into her, then another and she moaned as he caressed her deeply, withdrew, tormented the throbbing focus of her need, plunged in again. The exquisite feeling built and built to the point of pain and she gasped, wordless words that he seemed to understand.

Alistair shifted and she felt him against her, hard and implacable. '*Yes*, now!' And he surged into the heat and the tightness. There was discomfort, momentary; it had been a long time and he was a big man, but her body opened for him, sheathed him as he entered, and she shuddered with delight as he began to move, driving them both with his passion until the spiralling tension took her, shook her, threw all conscious thought from her as she felt him groan above her and pull away.

Dita came back to herself to find she was leaning back against Alistair's chest as he knelt, supporting her. 'I should have got you with child,' he said and his voice was not quite steady.

'You—' She did not know the words, could hardly speak.

'I withdrew,' he said, his arms tight when she would have twisted to look at him. 'It makes no difference. You must marry me now.'

So, that had not been a spontaneous expression of

passion, perhaps concealing feelings she longed for, but which he was unaware of. It had been a calculated move to force her. The hurt was almost as great as that first rejection had been.

'Nothing has changed,' she said, finding her voice was as harsh as his. 'I am not a virgin and I am not with child.'

'Damn it.' He stood, pulling her with him. 'Then I should finish the business and do it properly this time.'

'Then you would be forcing me.' She moved away and fumbled with her buttons. When she turned back he was stuffing his shirt into his fastened breeches, his face thunderous.

'How do you know I am not capable of that?'

'Because I know you,' she said. He made no move to stop her as she untied her mare and stood on a tree stump to mount. She did not turn back as she rode away into the woods.

She went back to Wycombe Combe by way of the ruined tower where she had found him that evening eight years ago. It was deserted, so she slid down and sat there amongst the flowerless rose bushes, out of sight of everyone and everything except the jackdaws, and got her weeping done, once and for all. There was a pool of rainwater, clear and fresh, on top of one of the tumbled walls, and she bathed her eyes afterwards and walked briskly home to plot with Mama against the spiteful, damaged woman who would try to ruin Alistair. The woman who had loved him once.

Chapter Eighteen

4th April—Grosvenor Street, London

'Lord Iwerne is in London.' Lady Wycombe spread the single sheet of notepaper open beside her breakfast place, not noticing Dita drop her bread and butter back on the plate.

A week apart had not made the separation any easier to bear, as she had hoped it would. Perhaps nothing ever would. 'Alone, I trust?' she said, making her voice light.

'Yes, this is a letter of thanks, I believe. He says that Lady Iwerne is settled in at the Dower House and is planning its redecoration with the assistance of Miss Cruickshank, whom he considers was an inspired choice of mine.'

What we need, Mama had said, *is a lady as apparently frivolous as Imogen, but with the sense to realise who is paying her very substantial wages and enough insight to hazard a guess as to why.* It appeared they had succeeded. 'It was a masterstroke of Alistair's to have expressed doubts about Miss Cruickshank,' Dita said.

'Lady Iwerne is quite content, thinking she has bested him in this.' Despite that earth-shattering incident in the woods he had still called with Imogen and Dita had done her best to help. It seemed they had succeeded.

'And is he at the Iwernes' town house in Bolton Street?'

'Yes, he writes it is in drastic need of redecoration and is tempted to send the entire contents to the Auction Mart. He also says that if we are attending Almack's this evening he will see us there and he hopes we will ease his initiation into the Sacred Halls, as he puts it.'

Evaline laughed. 'I do feel sorry for the poor gentlemen. They have to wear the stuffiest of evening dress, the food and drink is almost non-existent and they spend their entire time escaping from predatory mamas.'

'I hope that is not directed at me, my dear,' Lady Wycombe remarked with a chuckle. 'I cannot feel so sorry for them; they have every eligible young lady presented for their inspection—think of all the effort it saves them!'

Twelve hours later Dita overheard Evaline put this point of view to Alistair as they stood beneath the curving front edge of the orchestra balcony. Her sister had seemed rather subdued and thoughtful for the past few days, but teasing Alistair appeared to have revived her spirits.

'Rather it confuses the eye,' he retorted. 'All this beauty and vivacity dazzles the poor male brain.' He did not appear very dazzled to Dita, watching this exchange. If anything, his expression as he surveyed the dancing in the centre of the ballroom and the chattering groups around it was detached and judgemental. She put out a hand and steadied herself against a pillar. It was hard to believe that this man was the one with whom she had shared those passionate interludes. How could their experiences together not brand them as lovers for every eye to see?

'So may a sultan inspect his seraglio,' she murmured, recovering herself. She waved her fan languidly.

'I have no need of one of those,' he said, not turning his head. 'My choice is fixed.'

'It takes two to make a contract,' Dita retorted. 'Where has Evaline gone?'

'Over there with that fellow with the crimson waist-coat.' Alistair pointed.

'Oh, yes. I wonder who he is,' she mused, more out of an instinct to keep an eye on Evaline than from any real curiosity.

'No idea, but then, I hardly know a soul here. Dita, I will call on you tomorrow.'

And I will be out, she vowed. 'Come and let me introduce me to some of our acquaintances.' She slipped her hand through his arm.

'Are you having any problems with gossip?' he asked bluntly as they strolled along the edge of the dance floor. She could feel his muscles under her palm and sensed he was every bit as tense as she was, despite appearances.

'Some. There are snide remarks from the usual cats, some of the chaperons look at me a little sideways, but I can ignore that. The men—' She shrugged, making light of it in case he reacted badly. There had been things said, hinted, glances and touches and several outright offers that were most definitely not honourable. Somehow she had coped, although it hurt. Sooner or later they would realise she was not available, she hoped.

'Lady Cartwright,' she said as they came up to a lively group, 'may I make known to you the Marquis of

Iwerne, just returned from the East?' As she expected, Fiona Cartwright, a lively young matron, pounced on this promising-looking gentleman and promptly drew Alistair into her circle of friends. With that start he would soon know virtually everyone in the place and surely, once he did, he would see that there were many young women who took his fancy and this foolishness would cease.

A glance at the dancers showed that Evaline was partnered by the young man in the handsome waistcoat. With a mental note to find out who he was, just in case he should prove undesirable, Dita strolled on, in no mood to dance herself. She felt weary and out of sorts, her mood not helped when she saw Alistair walk on to the floor with the charming Lady Jane Franklin on his arm. It was just what she hoped for and the sight was like a knife in the stomach.

'Madam? May I assist you?'

Startled, she turned to find a gentleman at her side. He was slightly over average height, with light brown hair, hazel eyes and tanned skin. 'Sir?'

'I beg your pardon, but you sighed so heavily I thought perhaps…'

'Oh, no, I am quite all right. Just bored, if the truth be told.'

'Would you care to dance? I am sure I can find someone to introduce me.'

'I fear I am not in a dancing mood this evening, sir. But thank you for offering.' Impulsively she held out her hand. 'Shall we forget propriety for a moment and introduce ourselves? I am Perdita Brooke; my father is Lord Wycombe.'

'Lady Perdita.' He bowed over her hand. 'Francis Wynstanley. You may know my brother, Lord Percy

Wynstanley. I am quite a newcomer to Almack's myself; I have been in the West Indies for several years.'

'And I am just back from India, so I am equally out of touch,' Dita said.

A flash of crimson caught her eye and she saw it was the waistcoat of Evaline's partner—and he was dancing with her again.

'What makes you frown, if I may ask?'

'My sister, dancing a second time with a man I do not know. See, the blonde girl in the pale green and the man with the crimson waistcoat.'

'Oh, I can help you there. That is James Morgan, my brother's confidential secretary. Percy is much involved in politics, you know, and Morgan is his right-hand man. Good character and all that, nothing to be worried about.'

'No, indeed. If you can vouch for him I am quite reassured.' But she was not. Confidential secretaries, however well bred, were not what her parents were looking for.

A week later her friendship with Lord Percy's brother was pronounced enough for her mother to be asking questions. 'He seems a most pleasant gentleman,' she observed. 'And intelligent. I spoke to him for a while at Lady Longrigg's soirée last night. Has he any prospects?'

'I really have no idea,' Dita said, with truth.

'I trust he is not some idler hanging out for a rich wife.'

'Mama, we are friends, that is all.'

But she was provoked enough to probe a little as they sat in the supper room at the Millingtons' ball. Alistair, she noted with a pang, was partnering one of Lord Faversham's daughters and Evaline had her head together with James Morgan, which was worrying.

'Do you make your home in London, Mr Wynstanley?' Alistair was flirting, she could tell, just from the back of his head—and the way the Faversham chit was blushing.

'I am doing the Season and living with my brother for the duration, but I have an estate in Suffolk I inherited from my maternal grandfather and I shall be basing myself there and seeing what is to be done to bring it about.'

'How interesting. It needs much work?'

He was a nice, intelligent, apparently eligible man. It would be pleasant, but unwise, to continue their friendship. Was this whole Season to be like this, fearing to make any male friendships while she watched Alistair find his wife?

'Good evening, Lady Perdita.'

Dita jumped and then managed a smile of welcome as Francis got to his feet. 'Oh…' *Pull yourself together!* 'Lord Iwerne, Miss Faversham, may I introduce Mr Wynstanley? Mr Wynstanley: the Marquis of Iwerne, Miss Faversham.'

'Will you not join us?' Francis pulled out a chair for Miss Faversham and they all sat down again. Francis gestured to the waiter and wine and glasses were brought.

Dita met Alistair's eyes with what she hoped was tolerable composure, only to find he was at his coolest, one eyebrow slightly raised. She stared back defiantly and engaged Miss Faversham, who appeared very shy, in conversation. Beside her she was aware of Francis undergoing a skilful interrogation—damn Alistair, he would be warning the man off in a moment!

* * *

After what seemed like an hour, but was probably only fifteen minutes, Alistair rose. 'Might I beg the honour of a dance, Lady Perdita?'

'Why, yes.' Her instinct was to refuse, but that would show she cared. She consulted her card. 'The second set after supper?'

'Ma'am. Wynstanley.' He bowed and escorted Miss Faversham out of the supper room.

By the time Alistair came to claim her for the set she had lost her nerve. 'I have changed my mind,' she said, staying firmly in the seat where Francis had left her when he went to claim his own partner.

'Don't sulk, Dita, it isn't like you.'

'I am not sulking and you, Alistair Lyndon, are not my keeper; I'll thank you not to embarrass me by interrogating perfectly respectable gentlemen just because they are in my company.'

'I am going to marry you,' he said, taking the chair next to her without being asked. 'And besides, you should not toy with men's affections this way. Wynstanley seems a decent enough fellow and he is within an inch of falling for you, if I am any judge.'

'Well, we know you are not, don't we?' she countered, refusing to react to the declaration that he would marry her. 'You place no importance upon love.'

Alistair stretched his legs out in front of him, showing every sign of settling down for a long and intimate conversation. 'It is a chimera, a delusion. You will come to your senses soon enough and marry me, Dita.'

'What if I fall in love with someone else and want to marry them?' she demanded. 'Or are you so arrogant that you believe that would be a delusion that I must be saved from?'

It was not a possibility, of course. She had come to accept that she was not going to fall out of love with him and into love with some other man. Given that, marrying someone like Francis and settling down to a pleasant, if second-best, life might be possible if only she could square her conscience over hiding her feelings for Alistair from him. But to marry Alistair when she loved him and he did not love her would be misery. She would be constantly hoping that he would fall in love with her and every day she would be disappointed.

'If he is a decent man and if I was convinced you loved him, then perhaps.' He did not look happy about it. 'And if you gave me your word of honour that you did love him and were not simply trying to escape from me.'

'You trust my honour?'

'I thought I could trust it with my own,' he countered and there was no mistaking the bitterness now.

'So you place your honour above my happiness?' she asked. 'No, do not answer that, I do not think I want to hear it. 'Why not give some thought to your own happiness instead and then perhaps we can both sleep easy in our beds?'

Alistair sat down again as Dita swept off. Happiness. He had never thought of it as something to go out and seek. He had lived life as he wanted it and on his terms ever since he had left home and he supposed that for most of the time he had been happy. Certainly he had felt challenged, fulfilled, energised by the life he had lived.

Happiness, Dita appeared to be implying, required him to take a wife. He knew he needed one, but these little peahens were intolerable; he had observed them for two weeks and they bored him rigid. He studied the room, feeling like a punter assessing racehorse form. *Silly laugh, intolerable mother, rude to servants, never washes her neck...* None of them had Dita's class or intelligence. And she, with every reason in the world to marry him—except her fantasy of love—refused him.

He sat and watched the dancing until he caught sight of Lady Evaline Brooke waltzing, which he was fairly certain she shouldn't be, with that young man who only appeared to possess one waistcoat. He should extricate her from that flirtation before her mama saw her. Alistair waited until the music stopped and then walked across to cut into their conversation that was continuing as they left the floor.

'Lady Evaline.'

She jumped and looked guilty. 'Lord Iwerne.'

'Won't you introduce me?'

'Of course. Lord Iwerne, this is Mr Morgan, Lord Winstanley's confidential secretary. James, the Marquis of Iwerne.'

'My lord.' The young man made a neat bow. He was slightly stocky, dark—Welsh, perhaps, as his name might suggest—and met Alistair's cool regard with a expression that was polite but not cowed. *He's got some backbone, then.*

'Mr Morgan. Lady Evaline, I was hoping for a dance.'

'Oh. Well, my card is quite full, my lord.' She fiddled with it, nervous.

'How dashing of you, Lady Evaline.' He caught the dangling card and opened it. 'Are you sure you cannot spare me a single county dance?' Every remaining dance had JM pencilled against it. The uncomfortable silence dragged on. 'How did you expect to get away with that?' he asked.

'We were going to sit them out, my lord,' Morgan said. 'Over there.' He nodded towards a partly curtained alcove. 'Not outside, I assure you.'

'I suggest you have rather more of a care for the lady's reputation, Mr Morgan. Lady Evaline, you, I believe, will dance this set with me.' He swept her on to the floor, leaving Morgan white-faced on the sidelines. It was a country dance, not the best place for a delicate exchange, but he managed to ask, 'What would your mother say?'

'She'd be furious,' Evaline murmured. She was as white as her swain, but her chin came up and she fixed a bright social smile on her lips. 'You are quite right to chide me, my lord.'

'I am not chiding,' he said. 'I'm rescuing you.'

The steps swung them apart and they said no more until the set was finished and he walked her off to find her mother. 'Hide that card,' he suggested. 'Lady Brooke, here is your youngest daughter, who has danced me to a standstill.'

'Thank you,' Evaline said as he stood looking down at her. 'You are quite right, I know.'

'I wouldn't want to see you come to harm,' he rejoined as her mother's attention was claimed by a friend. 'You matter to me.' She would be his sister-in-law if he had his way; it behoved him to protect her. Besides, he owed her mother much for her help with Imogen. Evaline blushed and lowered her eyes, but he was not displeased. She had seen the folly of that silly flirtation. Enough of acting the big brother for one evening, he thought, and went in search of the card tables.

Chapter Nineteen

'Good morning.'

Dita started and dropped her reticule. Her footman dived for it and Alistair removed his hat with a suave politeness that made her want to hit him for making her react so revealingly.

'Good morning, Lord Iwerne. This is an early hour to meet you in Bond Street—I would have thought at ten o'clock you would still be contemplating breakfast. Thank you, Philips.' She took her reticule from the footman and tried for a bright smile as she gestured for him to retreat to a discreet distance.

'I had some shopping.' He was carrying nothing, nor did he have a man in attendance, but perhaps he was having whatever it was delivered. 'Will you be at the Cuthberts' masquerade this evening?'

'We all will. Or at least, Mama and Evaline and I. It would probably take wild horses to drag Papa to such a thing.' They began to stroll along the pavement.

'And what will you be going as?' Alistair raised his tall hat to Lady St John, who was observing them with interest from her barouche.

'A milkmaid,' Dita admitted with a sigh. 'Very pretty and conventional, but Mama thought it suitable.'

'You are still in trouble with the old tabbies?'

'Not really, but people are aware of me, I suppose. You saw Lady St John just now. Who am I with, what am I doing?' She shrugged. 'I don't care, but I should be cautious for Evaline's sake.'

'Then I cannot lure you off for a morning's delicious sin in Grillon's Hotel?' he suggested.

'No! Don't say such things, even in jest.' She eyed him sideways. 'That was in jest, wasn't it?'

'No. It was a perfectly serious invitation. And now you are blushing most delightfully. Come and look at the wigs in Trufitt and Hill's window while I make you go even pinker.'

'Certainly not. I have no desire to look at horrid wigs, or to have you put me any more out of countenance than I already am. I wish you would go away, Alistair, and stop tempting me.'

'Am I?' He sounded very pleased at the thought.

'Yes, and you know it and there is no need to be smug about it.'

'Very well, but not before I make you another, quite unexceptional, offer. I have sent for Indian silks and jewels from my house in south Devon. It is where I have my plant collection and where I shipped goods back to while I was away. Would you like a costume for the masquerade? I am going to wear Indian dress myself.'

'Oh, yes!' The thought of fine silks and fluttering veils made her heart race. To see Alistair dressed in Indian fashion, to partner her... 'Oh, no. It would look as though we were a couple.'

'Not at all. Everyone knows we have been in India—

what more natural that we should both chose to dress like that. We will arrive separately, after all.'

It was rash, possibly even reckless. She knew how she would feel when she put on those sensual, sensuous clothes, how she would feel when she saw him, a peacock in all his magnificence. Dita took a deep breath to say *no*.

'Yes, please, Alistair.'

'Mama.' Both Dita and her mother looked round at the tone of Evaline's voice. 'I am very well dowered, am I not? I mean, I do not have to hang out for a rich husband?'

The Wycombes' town coach, driving along Piccadilly, seemed a strange location for such a question. 'Yes, you are, my dear.' Lady Wycombe put down the book she had just bought and turned her full attention on her daughter. Dita twisted on the seat, puzzled. 'And it is important that you marry a man of equal status and at least the same resources as yourself.'

'But why, Mama? What if I met a young man of prospects?'

Oh dear, Mr Morgan, Dita thought. She had done some investigating and James Morgan was about as well paid as the average curate, was the second son of a country squire, had an excellent degree from Oxford and ambitions to enter government service. Papa would never countenance such an unequal match.

'It would depend on his connections and pedigree, my dear. Have you met such a man? I am trying to think to whom you might be referring.'

'It was a rhetorical question,' Evaline said with a bright smile that to Dita was patently false.

'Dear Alistair Lyndon is quite another matter,'

Lady Wycombe continued. 'Now he might well take an interest, I believe. He would be eminently suitable, a most superior catch. Your father would be delighted.'

'Yes, Mama,' Evaline said and Dita closed her open mouth with a snap.

Oh my lord, she thought. No, he wouldn't, surely? That morning in Bond Street he had given no sign of having changed his fixed intention of bending her to his will—the very opposite, in fact.

'I hope he will be at Lady Cuthbert's masquerade tonight,' Lady Wycombe said. 'Your shepherdess costume is charming, Evaline, but I wonder what Lord Iwerne will be wearing.'

'He is going as an India maharajah,' Dita said without thinking. 'I saw him in Bond Street this morning and he told me he has sent for a trunk full of silks and jewellery and so forth that he shipped home to England last year. He promised to send me a selection of Indian female garments and jewels so I could wear Indian dress tonight.' She prattled on, convinced her confused and jealous thoughts must be visible on her face. 'He's got a small house in south Devon he bought because it had a garden suitable for the plants he has been collecting. Whenever he sent things back they went there and not to the castle.'

'How interesting.' Her mother looked thoughtful. 'If Evaline wears the Indian garments it will be subtle, but it will put the idea of a pairing into his head. You can go as the milkmaid as we originally planned.'

She did not appear to notice Evaline's look of dismay. Dita only hoped her own expression was not as unguarded. 'Yes, Mama,' she said obediently. It was providential, it would save her from more temptation. She wanted to refuse and sulk and disobey. Instead she closed her eyes and made herself accept her mother's instructions.

Alistair swept into the ballroom at the Cuthberts' hired mansion with a considerable flourish, resplendent in brocades and silk, a turban with a large moonstone and an aigrette of feathers at the front, a curving sword thrust through his sash and hung about with enough jewellery to stock a small, if exotic, jewellers. All around him masked faces turned and a ripple of appreciation ran through the ladies. He looked the part, he knew, because everything was authentic, just as the silks and gems he had sent to Dita were those of a Mogul princess.

And there she was. He recognised the costume although her hair, flowing freely down her back, had been dyed black and her eyes were hidden by her mask, her lower face by her veil.

When he had met her that morning it had not been by accident, although he was certain she had no idea he had been following her with the aim of giving her the clothes for this evening. The masquerade was an opportunity to recall the sultry heat, the sensual pleasures, of India. Dressed in exotic silks, surrounded by the licence of a masked ball, reminded of the East and its delights, she would be more receptive to the seduction that tonight he was set on.

What had happened in Devon had not shifted her intransigence; his patience since had not caused her to yield, but she was not immune to him—her blushes this morning had shown him that. And this time he would not be careful; if he got her with child, then she would surrender.

Dita was beginning to fill his thoughts, obsess him.
The truth of what had happened that night seemed worse
the more he brooded on it. What if she had become
pregnant? He had left the country—she would have
been alone, ruined. He had prided himself on meeting
his responsibilities and now he knew he had defaulted
on something as fundamental as a lady's honour. No
wonder his dreams had been haunted by her face, by
erotic images that had left him ashamed of his imagination. But it was not imagination.

Alistair narrowed his eyes on the slim figure and felt
his breathing quicken. He wanted her, and he would have
her. It was like following a fish through a pond full of
weed. Every time he almost reached her she slipped away
and he was stopped over and over by ladies exclaiming
at his costume and men asking questions about the curving scimitar. Finally he saw a flash of golden silk as she
went through a doorway and followed. What the devil
was she up to? Or did she know he was behind her? Was
she leading him here?

Soft-footed in his doeskin boots, Alistair padded
along a passageway that opened up suddenly into a conservatory. Dita was nowhere to be seen. He scanned the
crowded palms and ferns as though expecting a tiger to
emerge from them, but all he heard was a sob, and then
another.

He eased closer, parted some greenery and found
himself looking into a little arbour with a fountain and
Dita locked in the arms of a shepherd. *What the hell—?*

'I'm sorry,' she said, still sobbing, 'it is impossible.
You were right: I must marry someone with money and
a title. Mama and Papa expect me to encourage Lord
Iwerne and they believe he will offer for me.'

Evaline? And then the man embracing her straightened up and Alistair recognised James Morgan. 'They cannot force you,' Morgan said. 'He is years older than you—'

'Ten, I suppose,' Evaline said drearily, making it sound like fifty. 'But he is kind, I think. He isn't like his father, after all. I wouldn't mind so much if it was not for you. I love you so much, James.'

'And I love you.' He bent his head and Alistair let the greenery drop, trying not to listen. 'But I must do what is right for you,' Morgan said after a moment, his voice stronger. 'I cannot allow you to be estranged from your family. It will be years, if ever, before I can support you in the style you are used to. I was wrong ever to let it get this far.'

Alistair sat down on a stone bench and realised that the churning sensation inside was nausea. *He isn't like his father*, Evaline had said of him. No, please God, he wasn't. What had he done to make the Brookes believe he would offer for Evaline? Perhaps his shadowing of Dita had appeared as something else in her parents' eyes.

Whatever the reason, he had come within an inch of sundering a young couple and breaking two hearts. It was only temporary, that illusion of love, but Evaline was a sweet girl and Morgan was apparently an honourable and likeable young man and they would make a good marriage if they got the chance.

He thought of Dita when she was talking about Imogen and his own youthful heartbreak and found that now he could understand what might force a young and dutiful girl into the marriage bed of a man she did not want. He stood up and took off his mask as he walked round the edge of the potted plants and into the grotto.

Evaline gave a small scream of alarm, but Morgan

stood his ground, only shifting to put out an arm and draw her behind him. He put his chin up as he faced Alistair. 'My lord, I hope you will believe me when I assure you that I am entirely to blame for what must appear to be a compromising situation, but—'

Alistair waved a hand dismissively. 'Six of one and half a dozen of the other, I imagine, if she's anything like her sister. Evaline, put your mask on and get back to your mama or Dita. Do not say anything about this and try not to look as though you have been misbehaving in the conservatory.'

Evaline gave a little gasp and ran. Morgan confronted him. 'My lord! If you wish for satisfaction—'

'Mr Morgan, I am not a suitor for Evaline's hand, just a friend of the family. If you want a wife at the end of this, please control your desire to shoot me dead, sit down here and listen.'

'Evaline, what is the matter with you?' Dita murmured under cover of Lady Wycombe giving instructions to the housekeeper. 'I know this is boring, but we did promise to help Mama write the invitations for the dinner party; if you sigh like that once more, I am going to scream.'

'I'm sorry, girls, can you manage without me?' Lady Wycombe left the room, still discussing missing table linen.

Dita looked closely at her sister. 'You don't look as though you slept a wink. Whatever is the matter?'

'I am in love with James Morgan,' Evaline blurted out. 'And Lord Iwerne caught us in the conservatory last night and I keep expecting there to be the most awful row.'

'Oh, Evaline, I didn't realise you truly loved him.

Are you sure?' Her sister's face was pale and miserable and Dita hated herself for the ruthless way she had been thinking about James Morgan. How could she have wanted to blight her sister's happiness when she knew all too well what it was like to love hopelessly?

'Yes. I know it is impossible. We both know it. And James is so honourable and…and then Lord Iwerne was *horrible*.'

'I'm not surprised, if he caught you in the conservatory unchaperoned! What happened?'

'He looked all cold and distant. And he sent me back to Mama and I don't know what happened with James, because I didn't see him again and perhaps he's called him out and he'll kill him and—'

'Stop it!' Dita gave her a little shake. 'You'll make yourself ill. I will write to Alistair and ask him to call on me and find out what he means to do. He won't challenge James, I am sure. You weren't… I mean, he wasn't doing anything very—'

'He was kissing me,' Evaline said. 'That was all.'

'Oh goodness, that was the knocker. I'll say we aren't at home.' They both stared at the door, waiting for the butler to open it, but nothing happened. After a few minutes Dita rang the bell. 'Pearson, who was that at the door?'

'Lord Iwerne, my lady, for his lordship.'

'Thank you, Pearson. That will be all.'

The next half-hour crawled by. A footman came to say that Lady Wycombe had been detained in the kitchen, discussing the dinner party menu with Cook, and would they please finish the invitations without her. Evaline, apparently beyond tears, sat tying her handkerchief in knots, Dita made a mess of three invitation cards and gave up. What on earth was Alistair doing? Telling their father about Evaline's shocking behaviour? Surely not offering for Evaline's hand? The nightmare idea that perhaps he had decided to tell her father what had happened eight years ago gripped her and she tried to stay calm. There would have been an explosion from the study by now, surely?

The door knocker sounded again and this time, after a few moments, Pearson came in without them having to ring. 'That was a Mr Morgan for his lordship, my lady.'

Evaline fell back on the chaise with a gasp. Dita asked, 'Is Lord Iwerne still with my father?'

'Yes, my lady. Both the gentlemen are now in the study with his lordship.'

'I am going to have hysterics,' Evaline announced after another twenty minutes of sitting staring at each other. 'I am definitely going to—'

The door opened and Lady Wycombe came in. 'Evaline, please come to the study.'

'Dita—'

'No, you do not need your sister,' her mother said as she took her arm. She left the door open and after a moment Alistair strolled through, shut it behind him and collapsed on the *chaise* where Evaline had been sitting.

'My God, I need a brandy.'

Dita splashed the liquor in a glass and handed it to him. 'Are you going to tell me what is going on?'

'Come and sit down beside me and tell me how wonderful I am,' he said with a grin. 'I have just convinced your father that Mr James Morgan is an eligible suitor for your sister's hand. Now, do I not deserve a reward?'

'No! How?' Dita shook her head, 'But he *isn't* eligible. No money, no prospects, no connections...'

'Oh, yes, he has. As of him giving a month's notice to Lord Percy Wynstanley, he is my confidential agent and secretary on a most respectable salary and with a very nice little house on the south Devon estate, which I am giving them as a wedding present, and the use of the third floor of my London house, which I am finding is approximately four times bigger than any reasonable man would want.

'And the young idiot did not realise, until I did some research and pointed it out, that his second cousin is the Earl of Bladings and his mother is a connection of the Duke of Fletton. Apparently his parents like to rusticate and never bothered to mention the family tree.'

'And Papa said *yes*?' Dita flopped down on the cushions beside him and grabbed both his hands.

'That's better. He did. And your mother. I must admit, I gave them to understand my friendship with Mr Morgan is somewhat more long-standing than it is, but I think Evaline is a good judge of character and all my enquiries, and a very long conversation with him, convince me he is an honourable and hard-working young man who will look after her. And he's just the man I need to have beside me—the amount of work with the estates is significant and then if I am going to take my seat in the House of Lords—'

'Alistair, I do love you!' Dita threw her arms around his neck and kissed him on the mouth before she realised what she was doing and what she had said.

He kissed her back, hard, then lifted his head and stared at her. 'If I realised I got that sort of response every time I employ someone, I would do it daily,' he said slowly with the air of a man working something through.

'Well, I could kiss you for a month, I love you so

much for making Evaline happy,' she said, hoping the qualification would blur her true meaning.

'Ah. And there I was thinking you had decided to accept my marriage offer.' There was an edge to his voice that told her he was not as light-hearted as he would have her believe.

'Of course not. Nothing has changed.' She sat up straight, away from him. 'It is so good of you—why did you do it when you have no belief in love? I would have expected you to say they were both deluded.'

For a moment the thick dark lashes veiled the amber glow of his eyes and then he laughed, a dry chuckle that sounded as though he was laughing at himself, not at what she had said.

'I remembered what you had said about Imogen and how she would have done what her parents expected of her. Those two in the conservatory renouncing each other out of a sense of duty—it made me feel about eighty.'

It had affected him more than that, she could tell. There was something behind the light words and the laughter. Sadness, self-reproach and perhaps something that would help heal that old wound.

'Never mind, it all came out well in the end.' What Alistair was thinking about, she had no idea, but the thought of Evaline's happiness warmed her right through.

'Your little sister is marrying before you,' Alistair said, moving along the chaise and closing the distance between them until she could feel the warmth of his thigh pressing against hers. 'Why not make your parents doubly happy and give in? You know you will eventually.'

'Why is what I want not enough for you?' she demanded. 'Why do you not believe that I think this would be very wrong? Are you so arrogant that you believe that women should have no opinions of their own?'

'No!' He flung himself to his feet and paced away from her. 'You must know that I value your intelligence and your courage and your wit. But this is not a matter of choice, this is a matter of right and wrong. I did something unforgivable and it can only be righted by marrying you.'

'I forgive you,' she said starkly.

'If you marry anyone else, he will not.'

'You wanted to make love to me on the ship, even though you believed I had lost my virginity with Stephen. You didn't appear to mind that!'

'I wasn't thinking of marrying you then,' he shot back.

His words told her nothing that she did not already know. Why then did it feel as though he had slapped her? Because it came from his own mouth, she realised, the confirmation that he did not love her, despite the pitiful fantasies that came in the early hours, the dream that really, he did care with his heart and not just with his head and his honour.

She felt the prickling heat behind her eyes and knew, horrified, that she was about to cry.

Then the door opened and her parents came in with Evaline and James Morgan. Alistair stood up. 'You will want to be alone. We'll meet tomorrow, Morgan, as we agreed.'

'My lord.' The young man looked faintly stunned, Dita thought as she sat digging her nails into her palms in an effort to control the tears.

'Lyndon, I insist,' Alistair said, shaking hands all round as he made his way to the door. When he got to

Evaline he stopped and kissed her. 'You be happy now, even in ten years' time when he is old.'

Evaline blushed and laughed and came to sit next to Dita. Dita squeezed her hand and whispered, 'What was that about?'

'He overheard me saying he was old,' Evaline hissed back. 'Wasn't that awful? I could have died, but he did this for us!' They hugged tightly, then Evaline disentangled herself. 'Dita, this is James.'

'Congratulations,' Dita said, kissing him on the cheek. Her own cheeks felt as though they were cracking with the effort to smile. 'I know you will make my sister very happy.'

'I swear I will, Lady Perdita. I confess, I am stunned by my good fortune. You know Lord Iwerne well, I believe? I heard how he saved you in the shipwreck. Is he always this generous?'

'Call me Dita. I believe that he will always want to reward the deserving if it is in his power. You obviously impressed him, he is fond of Evaline and you seem to be the sort of man he needs to assist him. But he will not be an easy employer, I imagine—he sets his standards high and expects a lot.'

'He'll get it from me,' Morgan vowed, his eyes full of passionate devotion as he looked at Evaline. 'And I will never let Evaline down.'

For two nights running she saw Alistair at the social events they both attended: a soirée followed by a ball one night, a full dress dinner the next. Dita noticed that he paid a great deal of attention to attractive widows in their late twenties and early thirties, of whom there were half a dozen in society this Season. She tried to tell herself that this was a good thing: well-bred, worldly-wise women who knew how to go on in society and who presumably knew enough to keep him faithful for more than a few months. The fact that she wanted to scratch their eyes out, especially the very lovely Mrs Somerton, was neither here nor there.

Watching him made her feel restless and reckless. Perhaps, she wondered, eyeing the rakish-looking stranger who had been seated almost opposite her at Lady Pershaw's dinner party, she should flirt a little herself. She always had flirted, and enjoyed it, but since she had been back in England, she realised she had lost the taste for it. It might take her mind off a certain amber-eyed gentleman who was watching Eliza Somerton with lazy appreciation.

The stranger was a little taller than Francis Wynstanley, although of much the same colouring, and he had well-defined cheekbones, a square chin and deep blue eyes which, just now, were staring back at her. Their eyes locked and Dita let hers widen a little, just enough to show interest, before she looked away and began to discuss church politics with the nice, and very dull, rural dean who sat on her left. Was that enough to pique his interest? Well, time would tell.

Chapter Twenty

The gentlemen rejoined the ladies less than an hour after the covers were drawn, for Lady Pershaw liked a lively party and had given her husband strict instructions not to dally over the port.

Alistair, Dita noticed, went straight to Mrs Somerton, who was looking particularly lovely in golden brown silk with cream lace accentuating white shoulders and an adventurous degree of décolletage. She was making him laugh.

Out of patience with her own inability to forget, and wishing she did not care about either him, or his *amours*, Dita looked for the blue-eyed stranger and found he was watching her.

She looked sideways and caught the full force of a very blatant stare. 'Who is that?' she asked Maria Pershaw, a young lady who could be relied upon to know all the gentlemen. 'By the music stand.'

'Sir Rafe Langham,' Maria said. 'Delicious, is he not? He is said to be highly dangerous and Mama has strictly forbidden me to flirt with him, which is so provoking of her.' She laughed and moved on and Perdita deliberately turned her back and drifted over to the long windows that were ajar on to the terrace to let in some fresh air.

'Lost, my lady?' a deep voice enquired.

'You know Latin or perhaps you are a Shakespearian scholar?' Dita responded, turning slightly to find Sir Rafe beside her.

'Both. Perdita, the lost princess of *The Winter's Tale*, cast adrift upon the coast. Apt, I thought, in view of the shipwreck.'

'Wrong coast, however.' She kept her shoulder a little turned and her voice cool. It would not do to seem over-eager.

'Indeed. It is warm in here, is it not?'

Ah, a very fast worker! 'I do not believe we have been introduced, sir.'

'Sir Rafe Langham. I have been out of town for some time otherwise…' He let his voice trail off. 'I knew who you were, of course—your beauty had been described to me.'

Nonsense, you heard I have a shady past and you thought you would try your luck, Dita thought. But it was so tempting to play with fire, just a little. 'You make me blush, Sir Rafe. Or perhaps it is the heat in here.'

He needed no further encouragement. He opened the window wide and Dita stepped through and into the cool night air. 'How refreshing,' she said. The edge of the terrace was not far. It was well lit by the spill of light from the uncurtained windows, and should be quite safe, even with a gazetted rake such as this one.

'And what a delightful fragrance in the air. I wonder if it is this shrub.' Before Dita could get her balance she was swept off to the side, out of the light and into the shadows of a little gazebo.

'Ah, no. It is your perfume and not a flower at all.' He gathered her to him with alarming competence.

'Sir Rafe! Stop it—'

He kissed her and his right hand fastened on her breast while the left, spread over her behind, trapped her intimately close to his body. Dita tried to raise her knee, but he had her too close. Alistair's lesson came back to her vividly: ears are very sensitive. She reached up, seized an earlobe and twisted, hard.

He released her mouth with an oath, grabbed her wrist and yanked her deeper into the shadows. 'You little hell-cat! So you like to play it rough, do you?'

I am going to castrate you with blunt scissors, Dita thought as she fought him. *If I can just get my fingers round this loose stone…* But she knew, with a sinking heart, that the only way she was going to get out of this was at the cost of another, possibly ruinous, scandal.

Where the devil was Dita going? Alistair removed his gaze from Mrs Somerton's face, which was lovely enough to compensate a trifle for her frivolous conversation, and saw Dita slip through the window on to the terrace with a man. The mouse-brown hair looked like Winstanley's. The devil! He thought she had stopped encouraging that milksop.

It would only be flirtation, the man was to be trusted, surely, and Dita could look after herself. He himself had been flirting, blatantly, hoping that he could provoke a reaction from her. It seemed he had succeeded rather too well.

Alistair shifted, uneasy for some reason. The thought of her in another man's arms, another man's bed, made his stomach churn. He swore softly under his breath.

'My lord?' Mrs Somerton must have been chattering on for minutes while he brooded.

'I beg your—' Francis Wynstanley strolled out from behind a large plant on a stand. Whoever Dita was outside with, it was not her lukewarm admirer. 'Excuse me.'

He crossed the room as unobtrusively as he could, stepped out on to the terrace and closed the window behind him.

There. Alistair strode across the flags towards the gazebo and the flutter of pale fabric he could just see in the darkness.

'Take your hands off me, you reptile, before I hit you again.' Dita's furious voice had him grinning despite his anxiety. The *again* sounded promising. He should have trusted her to fight back.

'I warn you, drop that stone or I'll make such a scandal out of this—'

Alistair didn't recognise the voice, but his night vision had recovered enough to make out the two joined figures clearly. He sent a crashing right over Dita's left shoulder. The man slumped back, Dita staggered into Alistair's arms and dropped something painfully on his toes.

'Alistair! Oh—thank you!'

Alistair hauled the fallen man to his feet. 'You, sir, will meet me for this. Name your seconds.'

'No, he will *not* meet you,' Dita said, all the gratitude gone from her voice. 'I can do without the scandal, thank you very much. And I have hit him with that rock, wherever it has gone, and I twisted his ears as you showed me, Alistair.'

'It is not enough.' Alistair said through his anger. He wanted to kill this lout. 'What is his name?'

'Rafe Langham,' Dita said. Langham had one hand

clamped to his bleeding nose and was in no fit state to say anything.

'Langham,' Alistair gave the man a shake. 'Apologise to the lady, now.'

'Sorry. Carried away.' It sounded as though he had teeth loose as well as a broken nose.

'You will certainly be carried away, if you so much as whisper a word to this lady's detriment,' Alistair said, twisting his hand into Langham's neckcloth. 'Do you know who I am?'

'Iwerne,' Langham choked out.

'Indeed. If you are not out of London by this time tomorrow I will find a reason to challenge you and then, I swear, I will kill you. Is that quite clear?' There was a nod. 'In fact, I find you so unpleasant that I think that if I ever see you again I will have to challenge you anyway. Clear?' Another nod. 'Then go now, and if there is the slightest rumour about this evening I will find you.'

Langham stumbled off into the darkness, leaving them alone in the gazebo. 'Thank you,' Dita said, putting out both hands to him. 'I really thought only to take the air and enjoy a mild flirtation—and it got quite out of hand.'

Alistair clasped her hands in his. 'You are cold, you are not used to these temperatures.' She shook her head, not meeting his eyes. 'Dita, if you want to flirt, flirt with me.'

'I should join the queue, you mean?' she asked. He should have felt triumph; she had seen him flirting with other women and she was jealous, but something of her unhappiness reached him. This was not petty, she really was distressed.

'Dita?' he put his arm around her shoulders, not amorously, but gently, His palm rested on the soft skin of her shoulder; as he pressed he felt the slender bones, the beat of her pulse. 'What is it?'

'I cannot play these games any more, Alistair. I will not marry you, do you not understand? If you care for me at all, even the slightest bit, you will stop asking me.' She sounded bitterly in earnest, a woman at the end of her tether.

'Why?' he asked. 'I know you talk of love, but you enjoy *making* love with me, you cannot deceive me about that. We share so much history, we are old friends. We could have a good marriage. What is it, Dita?' He tipped her face up and the light from the reception room flooded across it, unsparing on the tears glittering unshed in her eyes. He had seen her cry with grief over Averil, but never like this. 'Dita, is there someone you love?'

'Yes. Now let me go.'

'Does he love you?' Who the devil could it be? Who had she met that he had not noticed?

'No. Now, are you satisfied?'

'Not if you are unhappy. Never, then.' He felt sick and shaken. 'Dita, what can I do?' He would bring her the man on his knees if it would wipe that bleakness from her eyes.

'Leave me. Stop asking me to marry you.'

For a long moment he could find no words. He was not used to defeat and he had not expected it here, or to find it so crushing. But a gentleman did not rant or complain; he had asked her what she wanted and she had told him with a sincerity that was utterly convincing.

'Your scarf, Dita.' He picked up the gauze strip and put it around her shoulders, his fingers brushing the soft skin. That was probably the last time he could legitimately allow them to linger like that, he realised, and gave himself one more indulgence, as he touched the back of his hand to her cheek.

The party was still animated and the room crowded as he let himself back into it. No one appeared to be looking for Dita so he stood there feeling lost and wondering at himself while he massaged the bruised knuckles of his right hand.

She was out there thinking about the man she loved. The bastard who obviously did not care for her, or he would be with her, protecting her from rakes. Protecting her from Alistair Lyndon.

His vision clouded and it took him a moment to realise it was with tears. Appalled, Alistair strode from the room, into the hall, snapped his fingers for his hat, cane and cloak. 'Tell my coachman to drive home, I'll walk,' he said.

When he reached the street he strode out, uncaring where he was going. Damn it, she was his. He loved her—what was she doing, wanting another man? *He loved her.* Alistair stopped dead in the middle of the pavement.

So that was what this was, this restlessness, this feeling of peace when he was with her, the mingling of thoughts and the shared laughter. The passion. The need to protect her. Love, the emotion he did not believe that mature, clear-headed men felt.

'Want to be friendly, ducky?' He glanced down to find a sharp-faced girl looking up at him, her right arm crooked in the time-honoured invitation to take it and walk with her to some dark alley.

'No,' he said as he fished in his pocket and found her a coin. 'No, I am not inclined to be friendly at all.'

The street-walker bit it and walked off, casting a

coquettish look over her shoulder, her skinny figure swaying in her tawdry finery.

On the ship Dita had asked him why he didn't marry her and then, without waiting for his answer, had told him why she wouldn't take him, even if he offered. *I want you, but I do not love you. I do not even like you, half of the time*, she had said.

And he had pressed her to marry him, over and over so that the passages between them when the old, uncomplicated friendship had seemed to return were marred by his insistence, her resistance. And for him that lingering friendship, the passion, the sense of duty, had changed into something more, so slowly, so naturally he hadn't even been aware of it. Perhaps that love had always been there, waiting to emerge.

Could he convince her? Woo her? But if she had given her heart to another man she would not settle for anything—anyone—less.

'Hell, I have made a mull of this,' he said to the empty street. How was he going to live without Dita?

He had gone, without protest, and left the field to some unknown man, Dita thought bleakly. Of course, he didn't even know there *was* a field. He didn't know she loved him, didn't know she longed for him to love her, too. Like the honourable man he was, he had rescued her from Langham, made sure she was safe and then walked away, finally accepting her refusal because she was in love. The perfect gentleman.

But that touch, that lingering, gentle caress… Had that been a farewell or a blessing? Both, perhaps. She stared, unseeing, into the darkness. It had always been Alistair, all her life. Now, she had lost him for ever.

She shuddered, but it was not the cold that made her

shiver, it was the thought that there was nowhere in London to get away from Alistair, and the knowledge that she could not bear to see him find someone else to marry and to live his life with.

In the end she was too cold to think properly. She went inside to where her mother was deep in conversation with two friends. 'I thought St George's, Hanover Square, and the wedding breakfast at Grosvenor Street. They'll be going down to the house in south Devon, I expect, and then— Ah, Dita dear, I was wondering where you had got to.'

'Mama, I'm sorry, but I am not feeling very well. I think I might have caught cold. May I take the carriage and send it back?'

'You do look very pale, dear. I will come with you.'

Her mother swept her out with punctilious farewells to their hosts. 'I do hope you have not got anything more than a slight chill,' she said, tucking rugs around Dita in the carriage. 'At this stage in the Season it would be such a pity to miss anything.'

'I would like to go home, Mama. At once. To Combe.'

'Home now? But why?'

'I don't want to talk about it, Mama.' Her mother opened her mouth, but Dita pressed on. If she was asked any more questions or talked at, she felt she could not bear it. 'Now Evaline is betrothed there is no reason for me to stay in town, is there? There is no one I am going to marry, Mama. I am sorry, but I am certain of it. I need time to decide what I want to do and I cannot think in London.'

Nor can I bear to dance and flirt and smile and watch Alistair make his choice. Much better to hear about it at a distance. When he brings his new bride home I can come back to town or go to Brighton or something.

Anything. Her hand crept to her cheek where his had touched. *Goodbye.*

Dita straightened her shoulders and made herself sit up. She was not going to run away and mope for the rest of her life. She had money, she had contacts, there was a new life out there if she only had the strength to find it. Widows managed it when they had lost the men they loved and so could she. She just needed some peace to plan, that was all.

Chapter Twenty-One

Alistair left it until eleven before he called. He had to tell her how he felt. It was hopeless, of course, if she was in love and not just telling him that to stop him insisting on their marriage. That it might be a ruse was the only thing that supported his spirits—until he remembered the tears on her cheeks. They had been so very real.

It was still far too early for a morning call, which properly, if illogically, should take place in the afternoon, but there was a limit to how much suspense he could take. Pearson answered the door. 'Good morning, my lord. I regret that none of the family is at home this morning.'

'None of them? I will return this afternoon.'

'I believe it unlikely that they will be receiving today at all, my lord.'

What the devil was going on? The only thing he could think of was that Dita had announced that she wanted to marry whoever it was, her father had objected and a major family upset was in progress. The fact that she must be holding out would indicate that she was serious, he thought, striding down St James's and into his club. It was going to be a long twenty-four hours.

The second day produced almost exactly the same result. 'His lordship is at the House and is expected back very late. Her ladyship and Lady Evaline are, I believe, shopping, my lord, and will be going on to afternoon appointments. Lady Perdita is not receiving.'

Frustrated, Alistair reviewed his options, other than breaking and entering. He did have, if not a spy in the camp, a source of intelligence, he realised.

The note he had written to James Morgan brought the young man himself around to White's in the early evening. 'How may I be of service?' he asked as they settled into chairs in a quiet corner of the library.

'I need to know what is going on in the Brookes' house,' Alistair said. No point in beating around the bush. 'Is Lady Perdita betrothed to someone, or is there a problem over some man?'

'I don't think so.' James frowned. 'But then, I haven't seen Lady Evaline today as she had various obligations. I can ask her tomorrow though—I am hiring a curricle and taking her driving in the park. Of course, if it is very delicate, she might not be able to say anything.' He hesitated. 'You could ask Lady Perdita, perhaps?'

'I would if she was receiving,' Alistair said, almost amused by the way James struggled to keep the speculation off his face. 'Never mind, I will call again tomorrow.' And this time, if he was still refused, he was going to go in through the tradesmen's entrance and find out, one way or another. But he had betrayed more than enough to his new secretary. 'Do you enjoy the play?' he asked. 'We could go to the Theatre Royal and then on to some supper.'

Pearson looked decidedly uncomfortable to find Alistair on the doorstep at ten the next morning. 'I am sorry, my lord, Lady Perdita is indisposed.'

'Seriously?' Alistair's blood ran cold. Had Langham hurt her and she had said nothing at the time?

'I could not say, my lord.'

The man was hiding something. Alistair smiled. 'Please tell her I called.' As soon as the door closed he went along the pavement to the area gate, down the steps into the narrow paved space and tried the handle of the staff door. It was unlocked.

'Here, you can't come through here! Oh. My lord…' One of the footmen stared in confusion as Alistair nodded pleasantly to him and took the back stairs, up past the ground floor, on up to the first where the ladies had their sitting room.

The door was ajar and he walked in to find Evaline trimming a bonnet at the table. 'Alistair!'

'I need to talk to Dita,' he said without preamble.

'You can't. She's not… I mean, she isn't well.' Evaline appeared decidedly flustered.

'Not here?' She bit her lip and then nodded. 'Where?'

'She left for Combe yesterday morning, first thing,' Evaline admitted.

'Why?' Evaline just shrugged, her pretty face showing as much bafflement as he felt. 'Is she betrothed to someone?'

'Oh, no.' She seemed glad to have something she could answer. 'Although it something about marriage,

I am certain. I heard Papa and Mama… I should not repeat it.'

Alistair sat down without waiting to be invited, finding, for the first time in his life, that his legs were none too steady. As he realised it Person opened the door. 'Do you wish refreshments to be served, Lady Evaline? Good morning, my lord.' It was as close to a rebuke as he was going to deliver. Alistair smiled at him. Even disapproving butlers were to be tolerated now he knew that Dita was still not promised to another man.

'Not on my account, thank you.' He got to his feet and bent to kiss Evaline's cheek. 'I'll go and see she is all right.'

'Oh, good.' She beamed back at him. 'And tell her to come back to town soon—I need her help for all the shopping I have to do!'

The temptation to take his curricle was almost overwhelming, but Alistair controlled it. He had no idea how Dita would react when he arrived on her doorstep and he wanted his wits about him. Speculation about what was going on kept running round and round in his head, but he could make no sense of what was happening.

He ordered Gregory to pack for at least a week away, ordered a chaise and four and set out at midday with one terse instruction to the postillions. 'Make the best time you can and there's money in it for you.'

It took them fifteen hours to Bridgewater, and another five on the narrower, twisting roads, and then lanes, that led to the Castle.

By the time the chaise pulled up in front of the great doors it was eight in the morning, Alistair had taught his valet to play a variety of card games, they had snatched dinner in Bristol and had slept in moderate discomfort for the past five hours.

Two hours later, with breakfast inside him, bathed, shaved and dressed in buckskins and boots, Alistair rode up to the front door of Wycombe Combe. At least he had got inside the door this time before he was refused, he thought, confronting the Brookes' butler.

'Is Lady Perdita not receiving me, or is she not at home to anyone?' he demanded.

'Lady Perdita has given orders that she is not to be disturbed, my lord. She's shut herself up in the Library Suite in the tower, my lord. And she hasn't come down. We take her meals up to her and I have to knock; the door at the foot of the tower is locked, my lord.' Gilbert had known Alistair since he was a boy and seemed grateful for the prospect of some guidance.

The butler would have a master key, Alistair reflected, but he did not want to put him in a difficult position; besides, he was experiencing a strong urge to do something flamboyant to make his point to Dita. She wanted romance? Well, if she locked herself up in a tower like Rapunzel, romance was what she was going to get.

Her grandfather had added an incongruous tower at one end of the house in a fit of enthusiasm for the Gothic, inspired by his friend Hugh Walpole. It overlooked the miniature gorge that the river made and created the impression that one of the turrets of his own castle had taken flight and landed there. Dita's father had moved the library into the second floor and Alistair recalled from childhood games of hide and seek that there was a guest suite above that.

He wondered why had she abandoned her own rooms as he made his way along the frontage of the house, round the curve of the tower wall and along to a point where a mass of ivy clung to the stonework. Forty foot up a window was open. Alistair shed his coat and hat, gave the ivy an experimental shake and began to climb.

He had made harder climbs, and more dangerous ones, although the result of falling on to the slabs below would be terminally unpleasant, but the ivy was old and thick and made a serviceable ladder. He was within six feet of the window when a wren erupted out of the foliage, shrieking with alarm, a tiny brown bundle of aggression.

The ivy tore under his hands as he swung out reflexively, swearing, then he grabbed hold above the weak spot and threw his weight more securely across.

'What the devil are you doing?' Dita's voice, immediately overhead, almost had him losing his grip again.

'Climbing this ivy,' Alistair said, while his heart returned to its proper place.

'That is such a male answer!' He looked up and found her glaring down at him, her arms folded on the sill. 'The question, as you very well know, Alistair Lyndon, is *why* are you climbing the ivy?'

'To get to you. I want to talk to you—I am worried about you, Dita.'

'Well, I don't want to talk to you.' She straightened up and the window began to swing closed.

'I can't get down,' he called.

'Nonsense.' But she poked her head out again.

'Let down your hair, Rapunzel,' he wheedled.

'This is not so much a fairy tale, more a bad dream,' she retorted, vanishing again.

Oh well, if she was not to be teased into a good humour he would just have to climb up and hope she didn't slam the window in his face. Alistair climbed another four feet before it opened wide again. This time a cloud of brown silk billowed out, settled, and revealed itself as Dita's hair. His fingers clenched into the ivy as a wave of erotic heat swept through him. He had seen it down wet, sticky with sea salt, tangled into knots, and it had affected him deeply then. But now it was clean, glossy and smelled of rosemary.

Alistair fisted one hand into it and tugged gently. 'Don't you dare,' she said, and swept it back and over one shoulder out of his reach. 'I always wanted to do that as a little girl, but I never realised how painful the weight of a grown man on the end of it would be.'

'May I come in?' he asked.

'Yes.' Dita vanished, leaving the window wide, but as he breasted the sill she held out her hands to help him climb through. 'Of all the idiotic things to do! You might have been killed.'

'Easier than climbing rigging.' It was interesting that that made her blush. 'Dita, why are you here?'

It seemed, as she turned and walked back to the big table in the centre of the room, that she would not answer him. Alistair did not push her, but looked around. They were in the library, the walls lined with curving book-shelves to fit within the circle of the tower. On the table there were piles of books, maps weighted at their curling corners and pen and paper.

'I am not going to marry,' Dita said, her back still turned. 'I realise I cannot compromise on what I need: marriage is too permanent, too important to settle for a lifetime of second best. And I don't want to hurt someone by not being able to offer them everything that I have to give. So I came here to think about what I want to do and I decided that I will travel. I will find a congenial older woman as a companion and I will discover this country first. Then, perhaps, the war will be over and I can go abroad.

'I enjoyed writing. I might well rewrite our novel, and I will write about my travels.'

'You may hurt someone else, by deciding not to marry,' Alistair said.

'Who?' She turned, puzzled.

'Me.' He said nothing more, but let her work it out for herself.

'You? You would be hurt by my not marrying? You are saying that you care for me?'

'You know that I care.' His voice was rough, and he knew he was not gentle as he closed the distance between them and jerked her into his arms. 'I am telling you that I love you.'

'But you don't *want* to fall in love,' she wailed. 'You don't believe in it. Don't do this to me, Alistair. Don't pretend and say this just because you think you must marry me.'

He looked furious and more nearly out of control than she had ever seen him. 'I will be all right, Alistair. I don't have to marry—'

'I. Love. You,' he repeated. 'Love: not like a friend, not like a neighbour—like a lover. I had no idea until I walked out of that garden knowing you were in love with someone else, and then I found I was shaking and sick and I realised that I had lost you because I'd had no idea that what I felt for you was love.'

Dita felt as though the tower floor was shifting under her feet, but Alistair was holding her. She would not fall while he was there. Alistair, who was telling her he loved her.

'Then Evaline said you were not betrothed to anyone, so I guessed he either does not love you or is totally ineligible. Take me, Dita,' he urged. 'We'll travel and I'll take you wherever you want. We'll write together—you can help me reconstruct my notes and I'll help with the novel. We'll make love. You like me, I know that. Desire me, too. I think you trust me. One day I'll make that enough for you. I'll make you forget him.'

'You don't know, do you?' she said, looking into his eyes and reading the truth and an utterly uncharacteristic uncertainty in them. 'When I saw you on the ivy I thought you must have guessed.' He shook his head, not understanding. 'It is you. I love *you*, Alistair. I've loved you all the time, even when I told myself I hated you, when I told myself it was just desire, when I knew it was hopeless.' Dita smiled at him, trying, failing, to conjure an answering smile.

'But you said you grew out of it.'

'I lied. Do you think I could bear you knowing and not feeling the same? I would have sunk with mortification.'

And then he did laugh, his whole body convulsing with it. 'I believe you—I can imagine how that would feel.'

'But you were prepared to risk it,' she said, sobering as rapidly as he relaxed. 'You were prepared to risk your pride by coming here and telling me you loved me.'

'Because I realise my task in life, Perdita my darling, is to cherish you and protect you and love you and if that means carving out my heart and my pride and my honour and laying them at your feet, that's what I will do.'

'Oh.' Her voice broke as the tears welled in her eyes. 'That is so lovely.'

'Don't cry, sweetheart, not before I tell you your duties. You are fated to give me purpose, make me smile and restore my faith in the world as a good place.'

'I won't stop you being an adventurer,' she promise as she swallowed the tears. 'I'll never close the window and leave you to climb alone again or tell you to stay at home and be safe. But you'll take me with you, always, won't you?'

'I promise,' Alistair said. 'Do you want to get married at the same time as Evaline?'

'I don't know. I didn't know I was getting married until five minutes ago! Why?'

'Well, she is not marrying for about three months and I have every intention of taking you to bed as soon as I can find one—and I really don't want to be careful.'

'Careful? Oh, you mean children.' She had tried not to think about babies, the ones she would never have because she was not going to wed. And now she would have Alistair's children. 'No, I don't want to be careful either. We'll tell everyone we want to let Evaline have her day to herself and we'll be married as soon as we can, if you want.'

'I want.' Alistair swept her up off her feet. 'Now, where's this bed?'

'Upstairs.' Half-breathless, half-inclined to giggle, Dita let herself be carried. Alistair shouldered open the door and laid her on the bed. 'This is very romantic, my lord.'

'Something from our novel writing obviously rubbed off,' Alistair said as he sat on the end of the bed and pulled off his boots. He turned back to her, shrugging off his waistcoat. 'I'll take it slowly, Dita, don't worry. By the pond—I should have been gentler, more careful.'

'I have been waiting a very long time for you to love me,' she said, kneeling up to untie his neckcloth and undo the buttons of his shirt. 'Could we be fast first and *then* slow, do you think?'

'I won't tease you,' he promised, dragging his shirt over his head. Dita reached out to run her hands over his skin, raking her nails lightly through the dark hair on his chest. She saw the way he tensed as she brushed his nipples, heard the intake of breath as she hooked her fingers into the waistband of his trousers and the arrogant swell of his erection and closed her eyes for a moment to let the wave of pleasure and power sweep through her.

Alistair took her mouth, his hands swift and sure on the fastenings of her gown, and she opened her eyes on his closed lids, the sweep of his lashes sooty against his tan, and shivered in delight at the sensation of skin against skin as the simple cotton gown fell around her hips along with her petticoats.

'Better than in the hut on the beach,' she murmured as she pulled back to look into his face. 'Dry and warm and not sticky.'

'Sticky can be good,' he said as he pressed her back on the bed, pulled off her chemise and began to lave her nipples with long, wet, lavish strokes of his tongue.

Dita surrendered to his skill and to the sensation. She made no attempt to stifle the moans of pleasure as he began to suck and tease and nibble at the hard, aching knots, his hands cupping and caressing her breasts, lifting them to his hungry mouth. They were alone at the top of her fairytale tower and nothing, now, was going to stop the full consummation of their love.

It seemed the most natural thing in the world to be here, naked, with Alistair, all pretence and misunderstanding stripped away. She felt no shyness when he lifted himself on his braced arms to gaze down at her, nor alarm when he lay back beside her and began to caress her breasts again, then her belly, then the sensitive mound with its tangle of dark curls.

'Let me look at you,' he said. 'We have made love and every time, it seems, there has been no time, or our emotions were getting in the way of knowing each other.' He slid down the bed and parted her thighs. She opened to him, blushing a little as he touched her there, opening her with gentle fingers. 'So soft and plump and wet.'

Dita closed her eyes as one finger slid between the folds, exploring intimately. She tightened around him as he eased a second finger into the aching heat, but it was not enough—she wanted him, *needed* him, there. She tried to say so, twisting, lifting her hips, and he chuckled, a wicked, affectionate sound, and did that thing with his thumb that made her gasp with pleasure.

'Now, Dita?'

'Yes.' He moved up her body, covering her and she wriggled to cradle him, relishing his weight and the sensation of leashed power in the muscles she could feel tense under her spread palms. 'Now,' she urged as she felt him nudge against her, large and hard and potent. 'Oh, now, Alistair.'

'I love you,' he said as he moved and she gasped at the sensation, still not used to lovemaking. But the pressure, the fullness, were exciting and she arched against him, wanting more, wanting all of him. He lowered his head to take her mouth and surged and they were one again and she laughed against his lips and felt his smile curve in response.

He was right; there had been so many things wrong when they had made love before—guilt and secrets and anger. Now she could think of nothing but Alistair's body, hot and strong and relentless, driving into her with a rhythm that was as elemental as the sea and as dangerously exciting. Her nostrils were filled with the scent of his body and the tang of their mutual arousal and her ears were filled with the sound of their breathing, the roar of her blood.

She felt him lift away, his arms braced. It pressed his pelvis tighter into hers, drove him impossibly deep within her and she opened her eyes to see he was watching her, his tiger eyes burning gold with passion. She was so tense it was painful, so tight that she felt she would die of it. *'Now,'* he said. 'Let go, Dita', and everything peaked and then untangled in an explosion of pleasure and she lost herself in it, in him—drowning, yet safe.

Dita woke and found herself hot and sticky and entangled in Alistair's arms, pressed as tightly against his body as she could be. 'Mmm,' she said, eyes closed, kissing damp, smooth skin and working out that it was his shoulder.

'Awake?' He lifted the hair away from her face and she wriggled round to smile up at him. 'I love you.'

'I love you, too. Which is,' she added thoughtfully, 'an extremely satisfactory coincidence.'

'I think satisfactory may be an understatement,' Alistair said. He rolled her gently on to her stomach and began to lick his way down her spine. 'What a very lovely back you have,' he mumbled, his voice indistinct as he kissed the sensitive dip right at the base. 'Let us try something very, very slow.' He slid one hand under her, found the place that gave such exquisite pleasure and began to tease it, his other hand holding her down.

'Oh, peaches,' he said, nipping the swell of one buttock with his teeth while she whimpered and writhed. 'Do you want me to stop?'

'Yes! No... Oh...no.'

* * *

'Are you hungry?' Dita said. She had no idea what the time was, but the shadows were lying long across the floor and the breeze from the open window was cooler now.

'Ravenous,' Alistair said. He was lying sprawled on his back, one arm flung across his eyes. 'You have exhausted me, you witch.'

'I don't think so.' Dita rolled over, propped herself up on one elbow and cupped her fingers around the weight of his testicles. 'Look—you have woken up.'

'Food, you bad woman,' Alistair said, and sat up to swing off the bed before she could tease any more. 'Is there water?'

'Cold, but I expect that's no bad thing.' Dita got off the bed, too, conscious of stiff muscles and a not-unpleasant awareness of her insides. 'Here, in the dressing room.'

Half an hour later they returned to the library. 'We'll go down, shall we?' Alistair said 'It isn't fair to ask them to haul a big dinner for two up all these stairs.'

She was feeling far too happy to mind the studious way the footmen ignored the fact that Alistair had appeared, apparently out of nowhere, and the smooth way in which Gilbert announced that a dinner for two was even now in its final stages of preparation.

Alistair's valet came in as they were settling in the salon to wait for the meal to be served. 'A package has arrived for you, my lord. It seem to have been delivered after your departure from London and they had it sent down, post haste, in case it was urgent.'

Alistair turned the small parcel over in his hands. 'A London post office stamp and no seal impressed in the wax. I wasn't expecting anything.' He opened it, shedding several layers of brown paper and stared at what was revealed. 'Dita, look at this.'

It was the small oval box that she had given him. 'Open it,' she urged and he slid back the lid to reveal the Noah's Ark animals still packed tight inside. 'Is it the same one?'

In answer he turned the lid over and showed her the initials, AL. 'I marked it.' He took out the little carvings and shook the box. A few grains of sand fell out. 'It has been wet—see the stains on the wood?'

'But how?'

'I left it on the table in the cuddy. I had been showing it to Mr Bastable before dinner. It could have escaped the wreck and been washed out and on to a beach somewhere. But who would know to send it to me? And why anonymously?'

They eliminated everyone they could think of by the time dinner was announced. 'All the survivors took ship back to the mainland and no one on the islands would know it was mine.'

Dita twisted the miniature figure of Noah in her fingers. 'Averil?' They stared at each other, silent with the weight of speculation. 'I felt that she was still alive,' Dita murmured at last.

'A mystery.' Alistair took the scrap of wood from her and put it back safe in the box. 'We have had our miracle—perhaps, after all, against all the odds, Averil has experienced one, too. We can only wait and see.'

They were sitting at a small oval table, close enough to touch. Dita looked up and caught the butler's eye. 'Gregory, would you all kindly leave us for a few minutes?' They filed out, expressionless, and she got up, walked around and placed her hands on Alistair's shoulders from behind, bending down to rest her cheek against his.

'It *is* a miracle, isn't it?'

He put up his hands to capture hers. 'A miracle that we're alive, that we're together, that we love each other. Every day from now on is going to hold that magic for us.'

'And every night,' she whispered in his ear.

'Oh, yes, my love. Believe it. Every night.'

* * * * *

*Seduced by
the Scoundrel*

LOUISE ALLEN

Chapter One

March 16th, 1809—Isles of Scilly

It was a dream, the kind you have when you are almost awake. She was cold, wet… The cabin window must have opened in the night…she was so uncomfortable…

'Look 'ere, Jack, it's a mermaid.'

'Nah. Got legs, ain't she? No tail. Never got that. How do you swive a mermaid if she ain't got legs?'

Not a dream…nightmare. Wake up. Eyes won't open. So cold. Hurt. Afraid, so afraid.

'Is she dead, do yer reckon?'

Uncomprehending terror ran through her veins in the dream. *Am I dead? Is this hell? They sound like demons. Lie still.*

'Looks fresh enough. She'll do, even if she ain't too lively. I 'aven't had a woman in five weeks.'

'None of us 'ave, stupid.' The coarse voice came closer.

No! Had she screamed it aloud? Averil became fully conscious and with consciousness came memory and realisation and true terror: shipwreck and a great wave and then cold and churning water and the knowledge that she was going to die.

But she wasn't dead. Under her was sand, cold, wet sand, and the wind blew across her skin and wavelets lapped at her ankles and her eyes were mercifully gummed shut with salt against this nightmare and everything hurt as though she'd been rolled in a barrel. Wind... skin... She was naked and those voices belonged to real men and they were coming closer and they wanted to... *Lie still.*

Something nudged her hard in the ribs and she flinched away, convulsed with fear, her body reacting while her mind screamed at it to be still.

'She's alive! Well, there's a bit of luck.' It was the first speaker, his voice gloating. She curled into a shivering ball, like a hedgehog stripped of its prickles. 'You reckon we can get 'er up behind those rocks before the others see 'er? Don't want to share, not 'til we've had our fill.'

'No!' She jerked herself upright so she was sitting on the sand, her arms wrapped around her nakedness. It was worse now, not to be able to see. She dragged her eyes open against the sticky sting of the salt.

Her tormentors stood about two yards away, regarding her with identical expressions of lustful greed. Averil's stomach churned as her instincts recognised the look. One man was big, with a gut that spoke of too much beer and muscles that bulged on his bare arms and calves like tree trunks. The one who had kicked her must be the skinny runt closer to her.

'You come along with us, darlin',' the smaller one said and the wheedling tone had the sodden hairs on her neck rising. 'We'll get you nice and warm, won't we, 'Arry?'

'I'd rather die,' she managed to say. She dug her fingers into the wet sand and raked up two handfuls, but it flowed out of her grasp. There was nothing to use as a weapon, not even a pebble, and her hands were numb with cold.

'Yer, well, what you want don't come into it, darlin'.' That must be Jack. Would it help if she used their names, tried to get them to see her as a human being and not just a thing for their use? She struggled to get her terrified brain to work. Could she run? No, her legs were numb, too, she would never be able to stand up.

'Listen—my name is Averil. Jack, Harry—don't you have sisters—?'

The big one swore foully and she heard the voices at the same time. 'The others. Damn it, now we'll 'ave to share the bloss.'

Averil focused her stinging eyes along the beach. She sat on the rim of sand that fringed the sea. Above her a pebble beach merged into low rock outcrops and beyond that short turf sloped up to a hill. The voices belonged to a group of half-a-dozen men, sailors by the look of them, all in similar dark working clothes to the two who had found her.

At the sight of her they broke into a run and she found herself facing a semicircle of grinning, leering figures. Their laughter, their voices as they called coarse comments she could barely understand, their questions to Jack and Harry, beat on her ears and the scene began to blur as she closed her eyes. She was going to faint and when she fainted they would—

'What the hell have you got there?' The voice was educated, authoritative and rock hard. Averil sensed the men's attention turn from her like iron filings attracted to a magnet and hope made her gasp with relief.

'Mermaid, Cap'n.' Harry sniggered. 'Lost 'er tail.'

'Very nice, too,' the voice said, very close now. 'And you were about to bring her to me, I suppose?'

'Why'd we do that, Cap'n?'

'Captain's prize.' There was no pity in the dispassionate tone, only the clinical assessment of a piece of flotsam. The warm flood of hope receded like a retreating wave.

'That's not fair!'

'Tough. This is not a democracy, Tubbs. She's mine and that's an order.' Boots crunched over pebbles as the sound of furious muttering rose.

None of this was going to go away. Averil opened her eyes again and looked up. And up. He was big: rangy, with dark hair, a dominant nose. The uncompromising grey eyes, like the sea in winter, looked at her as a man studies a woman, not as a rescuer looks at a victim. There was straightforward masculine desire there, and, strangely, anger. 'No,' she whispered.

'No, leave you to freeze to death, or, no, don't take you away from your new friends?' he asked. He was like a dark reflection of the men she had come to know over the past three months on the ship. Tough, intelligent men who had no need to swagger because they radiated confidence and authority. Alistair Lyndon, the twins Callum and Daniel Chatterton. Were they all dead now?

His voice was hard, his face showed no sympathy, but for all that he was better than the rabble on the beach. The big man had his hand on the hilt of a knife and her rescuer had his back to him. 'Behind you,' she said, ignoring the mockery.

'Dawkins, leave that alone unless you want to end up like Nye.' The dark man spoke without turning and she saw his hand rested on the butt of a pistol thrust in his belt. 'There's no money if you're dead of a bullet in your fat gut. More for the others, though.' He raised an eyebrow at Averil and she nodded, lured into complicity. No one else was touching a weapon. He shrugged out of his coat and dropped it over her shoulders. 'Can you stand?'

'No. T-t-t-too cold.' Her teeth chattered and she tightened her jaw against the weakness.

He leaned down, caught her wrists and hauled her to her feet as she groped with clumsy fingers for the edges of the coat. It reached the curve of her buttocks, she could feel it chafing the skin there. 'I'll carry you,' he said as he turned from raking a stare over the watching men.

'No!' She stumbled, grabbed at his arm. If he lifted her the coat would ride up, she'd be exposed.

'They've seen everything there is to see already,' he said. 'Tubbs, give me your coat.'

'It'll get all wet,' the man grumbled as he pulled it off and shambled down the beach to hand it over. His eyes were avid on her bare legs.

'And you'll get it back smelling of wet woman. Won't that be nice?' Her rescuer took it, wrapped it round her waist and then slung her over his shoulder. Averil gave a gasp of outrage, then realised: like this he had one hand free for his pistol.

Head down, she stared at the shifting ground. The coats did nothing against the cold, only emphasised her essential nakedness and shame. Averil fought against the faintness that threatened to sweep over her: she had to stay conscious. The man she had hoped would be her rescuer was nothing of the sort. At best he was going to rape her, at worst that gang of ruffians would attack him and they would all have her.

Last night—it must have been last night, or she'd be

dead of the cold by now—she had known she was about to die. Now she wished she had.

The sound of crunching stones stopped, the angle at which she was hanging levelled off and she saw grass below. Then her captor stopped, ducked, and they were inside some kind of building. 'Here.' He dropped her like a sack of potatoes on to a lumpy surface. 'Don't go to sleep yet, you're too cold.'

The door banged closed behind him and Averil hauled herself up. She was on a bed in a large stone-built hut with five other empty bed frames ranged along the walls. The rough straw in the mattress-bag crackled under her as she shifted to look round. There was a hearth with the ashes of a dead fire at one end, a wooden chair, a table with some crockery on it, a trunk. The hut had a window with threadbare sacking hanging over it, a few shelves, the plank door and a rough stone slab floor without so much as a rag rug.

Rather be dead... The self-pity brought tears to her eyes. The room steadied and her head stopped swimming. *No, I wouldn't.* Averil knuckled the moisture out of her eyes and winced at the sting of the salt. The pain steadied her. She was not a coward and life—until a few hours ago—had been sweet and worth fighting for.

An upbringing as the pampered daughter of a wealthy family was no preparation for this, but she had fought off all the illnesses life in India could throw at her for twenty of her twenty-two years, she had coped with three months at sea in an East Indiaman and she'd survived a shipwreck. *I am not going to die now, not like this, not without a struggle.*

She must get up, now, and find a way out, a weapon before he came back. Averil dragged herself off the bed. There was a strange roaring in her ears and the room seemed to be moving. The floor was shifting, surely? Or was it her? Everything was growing very dark...

'Hell and damnation.' Luc slammed the door closed behind him. The sprawled naked figure on the floor did not so much as twitch. He picked up the pitcher from the table, knelt beside her and splashed water on her face. That did produce some reaction: she licked her lips.

'Back to bed.' He scooped her on to the lumpy mattress and pulled the blanket over her. The feel of her in his arms had been good. Too good to dwell on. As it was, the memory of her sitting like a mermaid on the beach with the surf creaming around her long, pale legs was enough to keep a man restless at night with the ache of desire.

He poured water into a beaker and went back to the bed. 'Come on, wake up. You need water—drink.' He knelt and put an arm behind her shoulders to lift her so he could put the beaker to her lips. To his relief she drank thirstily, blindly. Tangled dark blond hair stuck to his coat, bruises blossomed on lightly tanned skin. Long lashes flickered open to reveal dazed hazel-green eyes and then closed as though weighted with lead.

Then her head lolled to one side against his shoulder, she sighed and went limp.

'Nom d'un nom d'un nom...' This was the last thing he had planned for, an unconscious woman who needed to be cared for. If he put her into the skiff and sailed her across to St Mary's and said he had found her on the beach, just one more survivor of the shipwreck last night, then she would be safe. But what if she remembered? Her seeing him did not matter: he had a cover story accepted by the Governor. But he had been with the men and was obviously their leader.

Luc looked down at the wet, matted tangle of hair that was all he could see of her now. She sighed and snuggled closer and he adjusted her so she fitted more comfortably against him while he thought. She was young, but not a girl. In her early twenties, perhaps. She had not been addled by her experience; her reaction when she warned him about Dawkins told him that she had her wits about her. In fact, she seemed both courageous and intelligent. What were the chances that she would forget all about this or would dismiss it as a nightmare?

Not good, he decided after a few more moments holding her. She might blurt out what she had seen to anyone when she regained consciousness and he had no idea who he had to be on his guard against, even in the Governor's own household. Even the Governor himself.

His prudent choices were to leave her here with some food and water, lock the door and walk away—which would probably be as close to murder as rowing her out to sea and dropping her overboard would be—or to nurse her until she was strong enough to look after herself.

What did he know about nursing women? Nothing— but how different could it be from looking after a man? Luc looked at the slender figure huddled in the coarse blankets and admitted to himself that he was daunted. And when she woke, if she did, then she was not going to be best pleased to discover who had been looking after her. He could always point out the alternatives.

She had drunk something, at least. He would tell Potts to cook broth at dinner time and see if he could get that down her. And he supposed he had better wash the worst of the salt off her and check her for any injuries. Broken bones were more than likely.

Then he could get her into one of his shirts, make the bed more comfortable and leave her for a while. That would be good. He found he was sweating at the thought of touching her. *Damn.* He had to get out of here.

Luc stood on the threshold for a moment to get his breathing steady. He was in a bad way if a half-drowned woman aroused such desire in him. Her defiance and the intelligence in those bruised hazel eyes kept coming back to him and made him feel even worse for lusting after her in this state. Better he thought about the problem she would pose alive, conscious and aware of their presence here.

To distract himself he eyed the ships in St Helen's Pool, the sheltered stretch of water bounded by St Helen's where he stood, uninhabited Teän and St Martin's to the east, and Tresco to the south.

That damned shipwreck on the reefs to the west had stirred up the navy like a stick thrust into an anthill. Even the smoke from the endless chain of kelp-burning pits around the shores of all the inhabited islands seemed less dense today. They must have searchers out everywhere looking for bodies and survivors. In fact, there was a jolly boat rowing towards him now. If she had been dead, or unconscious from the start, he could have off-loaded her on them. But then, if his luck was good, he would never have been here in the first place.

He glanced round, made certain the men were out of sight and strolled down to the beach to meet the boat, moving the pistol to the small of his back. Eccentric poets seeking solitude to write epic works did not, he guessed, walk around armed.

A midshipman stood up in the bows, his freckled face serious. How old was this brat? Seventeen? 'Mr Dornay, sir?' he hailed from the boat.

'Yes. You're enquiring about survivors from the wreck, I imagine? I heard the shouting and saw the lights last night, guessed what had happened. I walked right round the island at first light and I didn't find anyone, dead or alive.' No lie—*he* had not found her.

'Thank you, sir. It was an East Indiaman that went down—big ship and a lot of souls on board. It will save us time not to have to search this island.' The midshipman hesitated, frowning as he kept his balance in the swaying boat. 'They said on St Martin that they saw a group of men out here yesterday and the Governor had only told us about you, sir, so we wondered. Writing poetry, he said.' The young man obviously thought this was strange behaviour.

'Yes,' Luc agreed, cursing inwardly. The damn fools were supposed to stay out of sight of the inhabited islands. 'A boat did land. A rough crew who said they were looking for locations for new kelp pits. I thought they were probably smugglers so I didn't challenge them. They've gone now.'

'Very wise, and you're more than likely right, sir. Thank you. We'll call again tomorrow.'

'Don't trouble, you've got enough on your plate. I've got a skiff, I'll sail over if I find anything.'

The midshipman saluted as the sailors lifted their oars and propelled the jolly boat towards the southern edge of Teän to find a landing place. Luc wandered back up the beach until they were out of sight, then strode over the low shoulder to the left, behind the old isolation hospital he was using as his shelter and where the woman now lay.

He did a rapid headcount. They were all there, all twelve of the evil little crew he'd been saddled with. There had been thirteen of them at the start, but he'd had to shoot Nye when the man decided that sticking a knife in the captain's ribs was easier than the mission they had been sent on. Luc's unhesitating reaction had sharpened up the rest of them.

'That was the navy,' he said as they shifted from their comfortable circle around a small, almost smokeless, fire to look at him. 'Someone on St Martin saw you yesterday. Stay round this side, don't go farther east along the north shore than Didley's Point.'

'Or the nasty navy'll get us?' Tubbs sneered. 'Then who'll be in trouble, Cap'n?'

'I'll be deep in the dunghill,' Luc agreed. 'From where I can watch you all be hanged. Think on it.'

'Yer. We'll think on it while you're prigging that mermaid we found you. Or 'ave you come round for a bit of advice on technique, like? Sir,' a lanky redhead asked, as he shifted a wad of chewing tobacco from one cheek to the other.

'Generous of you to offer, Harris, but I'm letting her sleep. I prefer my women conscious.' He leaned one hip against a boulder. Instinct told him not to reveal how ill she seemed to be. 'It could be four or five more days before we get word. I don't want you lot getting rusty. Check the pilot gig over this afternoon and we'll exercise with it some more tomorrow.'

'It's fine,' the redhead grumbled and spat a stream of brown liquid into the fire. 'Looked at it yesterday. Just a skinny jolly boat, that's all.'

'Your expert opinion will be a consolation as we sink in the middle of the bloody ocean,' Luc drawled. 'Dinner going to cook itself is it, Potts? My guest fancies broth. Can you manage that? And, Patch, bring me a bucket of cold water and a bucket of warm, as soon as you can get some heated. I don't want her to taste of salt.'

He did not bother to wait for a response, nor did he look back as he walked down to the little hospital building, although his spine crawled. At the moment they thought their best interests were served by obeying him and they were frightened enough of him not to push it, not after what had happened to Nye. That could change if the arrival of the woman proved to be the catalyst that tipped the fragile balance.

He needed them to believe her conscious and his property, not vulnerable and meaning nothing to him. He didn't want to have to kill any more of them, gallows'-bait though they were: he needed twelve to carry out this mission and they were good seamen, even if they were scum.

Chapter Two

The light was coming from an odd angle. Averil blinked and rubbed her eyes and came fully awake with a jolt. She was not in her cabin on the *Bengal Queen,* but in some hut. She had seen it before—or had that been part of the nightmare, the one that never seemed to stop but just kept ebbing and flowing through her head? Sometimes it had become a pleasant dream of being held, of something soft and wet on her aching, stiff limbs, of strong hands holding her, of hot, savoury broth or cool water slipping between her lips.

Then the nightmare had come back again: the wave, the huge wave, that turned into a leering hulk of a man; of being stared at by a dozen pairs of hungry eyes. Sometimes it became a dream of embarrassment, of needing to relieve herself and someone helping her, of being lifted and placed on an uncomfortable bucket and wanting to cry, but not being able to wake up.

She lay quite still like a fawn in its nest of bracken, only her eyes daring to move and explore this strange place. Under the covers her hands strayed, and found coarse sheeting above and below, the prickle of a straw-filled mattress, then the finer touch of the linen garment that she was wearing.

There was no one else there. The room felt empty to her straining senses, she could hear nothing but the sea beyond the walls. Averil sat up with an involuntary whimper of pain. Everything hurt. Her muscles ached, there were sore patches on her legs, her back. When she got her arms above the covers and pushed back the flopping sleeves to look at them they were a mass of bruises and scratches and grazes.

She was wearing a man's shirt. Memory began to come back, like pages torn at random from a picture book or sounds heard through a half-open door. A man's voice had told her to drink, to eat. A man's big hands had touched her body, held her, shifted her. Washed her, helped her to that bucket.

What else had he done? How long had she been unconscious and defenceless? Would she know if he had used her body as she lay there? She ached so much, would one more pain be felt?

Averil looked around and saw male clothing everywhere. A pair of boots stood by the window, a heap of creased linen spilled from a corner, a heavy coat hung from a nail. This was his space and he filled it, even in his absence. She twisted and looked at the pillow and saw a dark hair curling on it. This was his bed. She drew a deep, shuddering breath. For how long had he kept her here?

Water. A drink would make it easier to think. Then find a weapon. It was a plan of sorts, and even that made her feel a little stronger. She fumbled with fingers that were clumsy and stiff and threw back the covers. His shirt came part way down her thighs, but she was sitting on a creased sheet. Averil got to her feet, wrapped it around her waist, then staggered to the table. She made it as far as the chair before she collapsed on to it.

There was a jug beside a plate and a beaker on the table and she dragged it towards her with both hands. She spilled more than she poured, but it was clear and fresh and helped a little. Averil drank two beakers, then leaned her elbows on the table and dropped her head into her hands.

Think. It wasn't only him, there were those other men. They had been reality, not a nightmare. Had he let them in here, too? Had he let them…? No, there was only the memory of the dark-haired man they had called *Cap'n*. *Think.* The rough wooden planks held no inspiration, but the knife next to the plate did. She picked it up, hefted it in her hand. He'd be coming back, and she might only have that one chance to kill him when he was off guard. When he was in bed. Kill? Could she? Yes, if it was that or… Her eyes swivelled to the bed. Under the pillow. She had to get back there. Somehow.

Her legs kept betraying her as she tottered to the bed, but she made it, just in time as the door opened.

He swept the hut with a look that seemed to take in everything. Averil clenched her hand around the knife under cover of the sheet, but it had been on the far side of the plate, out of sight from this angle. Surely he wouldn't notice?

'You are awake.' He came right in, frowning, and looked at her as she sat on the edge of the bed. 'You found the water?'

'Yes.' *Come closer, turn those broad shoulders of yours, I'll do it now, I only need a second.* Where do you stab someone who is bigger and stronger than you? How do you stop them shouting, turning on you? High, that was it, on the left side above the heart. Strike downwards with both hands—

'Where is the knife?' He swivelled to look at her, a cold appraisal like a man sighting down the barrel of a weapon.

'Knife?'

'The one you are planning to cut my throat with. The one that was on the table.'

'I was not planning to cut your throat.' She threw it on the floor. Better that than have him search her for it. 'I was going to stab you in the back.'

He picked it up and went to drop it back beside the plate. 'It is like being threatened by a half-drowned kitten,' he drawled. 'I was beginning to think you would never wake up.' Averil stared at him. Her face, she hoped, was expressionless. This was the man who had slept with her, washed her, fed her, probably ravished her. Before the wreck she would have watched him from under her lids, attracted by the strength of his face, the way he moved, the tough male elegance of him. Now that masculinity made her heart race for all the wrong reasons: fear, anxiety, confusion.

'How long have I been here?' she demanded. 'A day? A night?'

'This is the fourth day since we found you.'

'Four days?' Three nights. Her guts twisted painfully. 'Who looked after me? I remember being washed and—' her face flamed '—a bucket. And soup.'

'I did.'

'You slept in this bed? Don't deny it!'

'I have no intention of denying it. That is my bed. Ah, I see. You think I would ravish an unconscious woman.' It was not a soft face, even when he was not frowning; now he looked as hard as granite and about as abrasive.

'What am I expected to think?' she demanded. Did he expect her to apologise?

'Are you a nun that you would prefer that I left you, helpless and unconscious, to live or die untouched by contaminating male hands?'

'No.'

'Do I look like a man who needs to use an unconscious woman?'

That had touched his pride, she realised. Most men were arrogant about their sexual prowess and she had just insulted his. She was at his mercy, it was best to be a little conciliatory.

'No. I was alarmed. And confused. I… Thank you for looking after me.' Embarrassed, she fiddled with her hair and her fingers snagged in tangles. 'Ow!'

'I washed it, after a fashion, but I couldn't get the knots out.' He rummaged on a shelf and tossed a comb on to the bed by her hand. 'You can try, just don't cry if you can't get the tangles out.'

'I don't cry.' She was on the edge of it though; the tears had almost come. But she was not in the habit of crying: what need had she had for tears before? And she was not going to weep in front of him. It was the one small humiliation she could prevent.

'No, you don't cry, do you?' Was that approval? He put his hand on the latch. 'I'll lock this, so don't waste your effort trying to get out.'

'What is your name?' His anonymity was a weapon he held against her, another brick in the wall of ignorance and powerlessness that was trapping her here, in his control.

For the first time she saw him hesitate. 'Luke.'

'The men called you *Captain*.'

'I was.' He smiled. It was not until she felt the stone

wall press against her shoulders that Averil realised she had recoiled from the look in his eyes. *Don't ask any more,* her instincts screamed at her. 'And you?'

'Averil Heydon.' As soon as she said her surname she wished it back. Her father was a wealthy man, he would pay any ransom for her, and now they could find out who her family was. 'Why are you keeping me a prisoner?'

But Luke said nothing more and the key turned in the lock the moment the door was shut.

At about two in the afternoon Luc opened the door with a degree of caution. His half-drowned mermaid had more guts than he'd expected from a woman who had been through what she had, let alone the well-bred lady she obviously was from her accent. She must be desperate now. The table knife was in his pocket, but he'd left his razor on the high shelf, which was careless.

She was embarrassed as well as frightened, but she would feel better after a proper meal. He needed her rational and she was, most certainly, sharing his bed tonight. 'Dinner time,' he announced and brought in the platters and the pot of stew.

Averil turned from the stool by the window where she had sat for the long hours since he had left her, thinking about this man, Luke, whose bed she had been sharing. The one who sounded like a gentleman and who was as bad as the rest of that crew on the beach. What was he? Pirate, smuggler, freebooter? The men were scum—their leader would be no better, only more powerful. She had dreamed about him, and in her dream he had held her and protected her. Fantasy was cruelly deceptive.

'Here,' he said as he dumped things on the table. 'Dinner. Potts is a surprisingly good cook.'

The smell reached her then and her empty stomach knotted. It was stew of some kind and the aroma was savoury and delicious. Luke had put the platter on the table so she would have to go over there to reach it, dressed only in his shirt and the trailing sheet. He was tormenting her, or perhaps training her as one did an animal. Perhaps both.

'I want to eat it here, not with you.'

'And I want you to use your limbs or you'll be as stiff as a board.' He leaned one shoulder against the wall by the hearth. 'Are you warm enough? I can light a fire.'

'How considerate, but I will not put you to the trouble.' The worn skim of sacking over the window let in enough light to see him clearly and she stared, with no attempt at concealment. If he had any conscience at all he would find her scrutiny uncomfortable, but he merely lifted one brow in acknowledgement and stared back.

He was tall, with hair so dark a brown as to seem almost black. He was tanned, and by the shade she guessed he was naturally more olive-skinned than fair. She had seen so many Europeans arrive in India and burn in the sun that she knew exactly how every shade of complexion would turn. His eyes were dark grey, and his brows were dark, too, tilted a little in a way that gave his face a sardonic look.

His nose was large, narrow-bridged and arrogant; it would have been too big if it had not been balanced by a determined jaw. No, it *was* too big, despite that. He was not handsome, she told herself. If she had liked him, she would have thought his face strong, even interesting perhaps. He looked intelligent. As it was, he was just a dark, brooding man she could not ignore. Her eyes slid lower. He was lean, narrow-hipped…

'Well?' he enquired. 'Am I more interesting than your dinner, which is getting cold?'

'Not at all. You are, however, in the way of me eating it.' She was not used to snubbing people or being cold or capricious. Miss Heydon, they said, was open and warm and charming. Sweet. She no longer felt sweet—perhaps she never would again. She tipped up her chin and regarded him down her nose.

'My dear girl, if you are shy of showing your legs, allow me to remind you that I have seen your entire delightful body.' He sounded as though he was recalling every detail as he spoke, but was not much impressed by what he had recalled.

'Then you do not have to view any of it again,' Averil snapped. Where the courage to stand up to him and answer back was coming from, she had no idea. She was only too well aware that she was regarded as a biddable, modest Nice Young Lady who did not say *boo* to geese, let alone bandy words with some pirate or whatever Luke was. But her back was literally against the wall and there was no one to rescue her because no one knew she was alive. It was up to her and that was curiously strengthening, despite the fear.

He shrugged and pulled out the chair. 'I want to see you eat. Get over here—or do you want me to carry you?'

She had the unpleasant suspicion that if she refused he really would simply pick her up and dump her on the seat. Averil fumbled for the sheet and stood up with it as a trailing skirt around her. She gave it an instinctive twitch and the memory that action brought back surprised a gasp of laughter out of her, despite the aches and pains that walking produced and the situation she found herself in.

'What is amusing?' Luke enquired as she sat down opposite him. 'I trust you are not about to have hysterics.'

It might be worth it to see how he reacted, but he would probably simply slap her or throw cold water in her face—the man had no sensibility. 'I have been practising managing the train on a court presentation gown,' she explained, as she reached for the fork and imagined plunging it into his hard heart. 'This seems an unlikely place to put that into practice.'

The stew consisted of large lumps of meat, roughly hewn vegetables and a gravy that owed a great deal to alcohol. She demolished it and mopped up the gravy with a hunk of bread, beyond good manners. Luke pushed a tumbler towards her. 'Water. There's a good clean well.'

'How are you so well provisioned?' she asked and tore another piece off the loaf. 'There are how many of you? Ten? And you aren't here legitimately, are you?'

'*I* am,' Luke said. He returned to his position by the hearth. 'Mr Dornay—so far as the Governor is concerned—is a poet in search of solitude and inspiration for an epic work. I told him that I am nervous of being isolated from the inhabited islands by storms or fog, so I keep my stock of provisions high, even if that means stockpiling far more than one man could possibly need. And there are thirteen of us and we are most certainly here in secret.'

She stowed away the surname. When it came to a court of law, when she testified against the men who had imprisoned and assaulted her, she would remember every name, every face. If he left her alive. She swallowed the fear until it lay like a cold stone in her stomach. 'A poet? *You?*' He smiled, that cold, unamused smile, but did not answer. 'When are you going to let me go?'

'When we are done here.' Luke pushed himself upright

and went to the door. 'I will leave you before the men eat all of my dinner. I'll see you at supper time.'

His hand was on the latch when Averil realised she couldn't deal with the uncertainty any longer. 'Are you going to kill me?'

Luke turned. 'If I wanted you dead all I had to do was throw you back or leave you here to die. I don't kill women.'

'You rape them, though. You are going to make me share your bed tonight, aren't you?' she flung back and then quailed at the anger that showed in every taut line of his face, his clenched fist as it rested on the door jamb. *He is going to hit me.*

'You have shared my bed for three nights. Rest,' he said, his even tone at variance with his expression. 'And stop panicking.' The door slammed behind him.

Luc stalked back to the fire. He wouldn't be on this damn island with this crew of criminal rabble in the first place if it was not for the attempted rape of a woman. Averil Heydon was frightened and that showed sense: she'd had every reason to be terrified until he took her away from the men. He could admire the fierce way she had stood up to him, but it only made her more of a damn nuisance and a dangerous liability. Thank God he no longer had to nurse her; intimacy with her body was disturbing and he had felt himself becoming interested in her more than was safe or comfortable. Now she was no longer sick and needing him, that weakness would vanish. He did not want to care for anyone ever again.

The crew looked up with wary interest from their food as he approached. Luc dropped down on to the flat rock they had accepted as the captain's chair and took a platter from the cook's hand. 'Good stew, Potts. You all bored?' They looked it: bored and dangerous. On a ship he would exercise them too hard for them to even think about getting into trouble: gun drill, small arms drill, repairs, sail drill—anything to tire them out. Here they could do nothing that would make a noise and nothing that could be seen from the south or east.

Luc lifted his face to the breeze. 'Still blowing from the nor'west. That was a rich East Indiaman by all accounts—it'll be worth beachcombing.' They watched him sideways, shifting uneasily at the amiable tone of voice, like dogs who expect a kick and get their ears scratched instead. 'And you get to keep anything you find, so long as you don't fight over it and you bring me any mermaids.'

Greed and a joke—simple tools, but they worked. The mood lifted and the men began to brag of past finds and speculate on what could be washed up.

'Ferret, have you got any spare trousers?'

Ferris—known to all as Ferret from his remarkable resemblance to the animal—hoisted his skinny frame up from the horizontal. 'I 'ave, Cap'n. Me Sunday best, they are. Brought 'em along in case we went to church.'

'Where you would steal the communion plate, no doubt. Are they clean?'

'They are,' he said, affronted, his nose twitching. And it might be the truth—there was a rumour that Ferret had been known to take a bath on occasion.

'Then you'll lend them to Miss Heydon.'

That provoked a chorus of whistles and guffaws. 'Miss Heydon, eh! Cor, a mermaid with a name!'

'Wot she want trousers for, Cap'n?' Ferret demanded. 'Don't need trousers in bed.'

'When I don't want her in bed she can get up and make herself useful. She's had enough time lying about getting over her ducking,' Luc said. He had not given the men any reason to suppose Averil was unconscious and vulnerable. They had believed he was spending time in her bed, not that he was nursing her. His frequent absences seemed to have increased their admiration for him—or for his stamina. 'I'll have that leather waistcoat of yours while you're at it.'

Ferret got to his feet and scurried off to the motley collection of canvas shelters under the lea of the hill that filled the centre of the island. St Helen's was less than three-quarters of a mile across at its widest and rough stone structures littered the north-western slopes. Luc supposed they must have been the habitations of some ancient peoples, but he was no antiquarian. Now he was just glad of the shelter they gave to the men on the only flank of St Helen's that could not be overlooked from Tresco or St Martin's.

Stew finished, Luc got to his feet, took a small telescope from the pocket of his coat and turned to climb the hill. It took little effort, and he reckoned it was only about a hundred and thirty feet above the sea, but from here he commanded a wide panorama of the waters around the Scillies as well as being able to watch the men without them being aware of it. Beachcombing would keep them busy, but he did not want a knifing over some disputed treasure.

He put his notebook on a flat rock and set himself to log the patterns of movement between the islands, particularly the location of the brigs and the pilot gigs, the thirty-two-foot rowing boats that cut through the water at a speed that left the navy jolly-boat crews gasping. The calculations kept his mind off the woman in the hut below.

With six men on the oars the pilot gigs were said to

venture as far afield as Roscoff smuggling, although the Revenue cutters did their best to stop them. They got their name from their legitimate purpose, to row out to incoming ships and drop off the pilots who were essential in this nightmare of rocks and reefs.

The gig he'd been given for this mission lay on the beach below, waiting for the word to launch with six men on the oars and the other seven of them crammed into the remaining space as best they could. Beside it was his own small skiff that he used to give verisimilitude to the story of his lone existence here.

For the men hunting amongst the rocks below him what happened next would bring either death or a pardon for their crimes. For him, if he survived and succeeded in carrying out his orders, it might restore the honour he had lost in following his conscience. Luc shied a pebble down the slope, sending a stonechat fluttering away with a furious alarm call.

Scolding loudly, the little bird resumed its perch on top of a gorse bush. 'Easy for you to say, *mon cher*,' Luc told it, as he narrowed his eyes against the sunlight on the waves. 'All you have to worry about is the kestrel and his claws.' Life and death—that was easy. Right and wrong, honour and expediency—now those were harder choices.

Chapter Three

❧

Averil sat by the window with the old sack hooked back and studied what she could see through the thick, salt-stained glass. Sloping grass, a band of large pebbles that would be impossible to run on—or even cross quietly—then a fringe of sand that was disappearing under the rising tide.

Beyond, out in the sheltered sound, ships bobbed at anchor. Navy ships. Rescue, if only they were not too far away to hail. She could light a fire—but they knew Luke was here, so they would see nothing out of the ordinary in that. Set fire to the hut? But it was a sturdy stone building, so that wouldn't work. Signal from the window with a sheet? But first she would have to break the thick glass, then think of something that would attract their attention without alerting her captors.

With a sigh she went back to searching the room. Luke had left his razor on a high shelf, but after the episode with the knife she did not think he would give her a chance to use it and she was beginning to doubt whether she had it in her to kill a man. That was her conscience, she told herself, distracted for a moment by wondering why. It was nothing to do with the fact that she kept wondering if he could really be as bad as he appeared.

Intense grey eyes mean nothing, you fool, she chided herself. When darkness came he would come back here and then he would ravish her. His protestations about not taking an unconscious woman surely meant nothing, not now she was awake.

Averil thought about the 'little talk' her aunt had had with her just before she sailed for England and an arranged marriage. There would be no female relative there to explain things to her before her marriage to the man she had never met, so the process had been outlined in all its embarrassing improbability, leaving her far too much time, in her opinion, to think about it on the three-month voyage.

Her friend Lady Perdita Brooke, who had been sent to India in disgrace after an unwise elopement, had intimated that it was rather a pleasurable experience with the right man. Dita had not considered what it would be like being forced by some ruffian in a stone hut on an island, surrounded by a pack of even worse villains. But then, Dita would have had no qualms about using that knife.

The light began to fail. Soon he would be here and she had no plan. To fight, or not to fight? He could overpower her easily, she realised that. She knew a few simple tricks to repel importunate males, thanks to her brothers, but none of them would be much use in a situation like this where there was no one to hear her screams and nowhere to run to.

If she fought him, he would probably hurt her even more badly than she feared. Best to simply lie there like a corpse, to treat him with disdain and show no fear, only that she despised him.

That was more easily resolved than done she found when the door opened again and Luke came in followed by two of the men. One carried what looked like a bundle of clothes, the other balanced platters and had a bottle stuck under his arm.

Averil turned her head away, chin up, so that she did not have to look at them and read the avid imaginings in their eyes. She was not the only one thinking about what would happen here tonight.

'Come and eat.' Luke pushed the key into his pocket and moved away from the door when they had gone. 'I have found clothes for you. They will be too large, but they are clean.' He watched her as she trailed her sheet skirts to the chair. 'I'll light the fire, you are shivering.'

'I am not cold.' She was, but she did not want to turn this into a travesty of cosy domesticity, with a fire crackling in the grate, candles set around and food and wine.

'Of course you are. Don't try to lie to me. You are cold and frightened.' He stated it as a fact, not with any sympathy or compassion in his voice that she could detect. Perhaps he knew that kind words might make her cry and that this brisk practicality would brace her. He lit a candle, then knelt and built the fire with a practised economy of movement.

Who is he? His accent was impeccable, his hands, although scarred and calloused, were clean with carefully trimmed nails. Half an hour with a barber, then put him in evening clothes and he could stroll into any society gathering without attracting a glance.

No, that was not true. He would attract the glances of any woman there. It made her angrier with him, the fact that she found him physically attractive even as he repelled her for what he was, what he intended to do. How could she? It was humiliating and baffling. She had not even the excuse of being dazzled by a classically hand-some face or charm or skilful flirtation. What she felt was a very basic feminine desire. Lust, she told herself, was a sin.

'Eat.' The fire blazed up, shadows flickered in the corners and the room became instantly warmer, more intimate, just as she had feared. Luke poured wine and pushed the beaker towards her. 'And drink. It will make things easier.'

'For whom?' Averil enquired and the corner of his mouth moved in what might have been a half smile. But she drank and felt the insidious warmth relax her. Weaken her, just as he intended, she was sure. 'Who are you? What are you doing here?'

'Writing bad poetry, beachcombing.' He shrugged and cut a hunk of cheese.

'Don't play with me,' she snapped. 'Are you wreckers? Smugglers?'

'Neither.' He spared the cheese a disapproving frown, but ate it anyway.

'You were Navy once, weren't you?' she asked, on sudden impulse. 'Are you deserters?'

'We were Navy,' he agreed and cut her a slice of bread as though they were discussing the weather. 'And if we were to return now I dare say most of us would hang.'

Averil made herself eat while she digested that. They must be deserters, then. It took a lot of thinking about and she drank a full beaker of wine before she realised it had gone. Perhaps it would help with what was to come... She pushed the thought into a dark cupboard in the back of her mind and tried to eat. She needed her strength to endure, if not to fight.

Luke meanwhile ate solidly, like a man without a care

in the world. 'Are you running to the French?' she asked when the cheese and the cold boiled bacon were all gone.

'The French would kill us as readily as the British,' he said, with a thin smile for a joke she did not understand.

The meal was finished at last. Luke pushed back his chair and sat, long legs out in front of him, as relaxed as a big cat. Averil contemplated the table with its empty platters, bread crumbs and the heel of the loaf. 'Do you expect me to act as your housemaid as well as your whore?' she asked.

The response was immediate, lightning-swift. The man who had seemed so relaxed was on his feet and brought her with him with one hand tight around her wrist. Luke held her there so they stood toe to toe, breast to breast. His eyes were iron-dark and intense on her face; there was no ice there now and she shivered at the anger in them.

'Listen to me and think,' he said, his voice soft in chilling contrast to the violence of his reaction. 'Those men out there are a wolf pack, with as much conscience and mercy as wolves. I lead them, not because they are sworn to me or like me, not because we share a cause we believe in, but because, just now, they fear me more than they fear the alternatives.

'If I show them any weakness—anything at all—they will turn on me. And while I can fight, I cannot defeat twelve men. You are like a lighted match in a powder store. They want you—all of them do—and they have no scruples about sharing, so they'll operate as a gang. If they believe you are my woman and that I will kill for you, then that gives them pause—do they want you so much they will risk death? They know I would kill at least half of them before they got to you.'

He released her and Averil stumbled back against the

table. Her nostrils were full of the scent of angry male and her heart was pattering out of rhythm with fear and a primitive reaction to his strength. 'They won't know if I am your woman or not,' she stammered.

'You really are a little innocent.' His smile was grim and she thought distractedly that although he seemed to smile readily enough she had never seen any true amusement on his face. 'What do they think we've been doing every time I come down here? And they will know when they see you, just as wolves would know. You will share my bed again tonight and you will come out of this place in the morning with my scent on your body, as yours has been on mine these past days. Or would you like to shorten things by walking out there now and getting us both killed?'

'I would prefer to live,' Averil said and closed her fingers tight on the edge of the table to hold herself up. 'And I have no doubt that you are the lesser of the two evils.' She was proud of the way she kept her chin up and that there was hardly a quiver in her voice. 'Doubtless a fate worse than death is an exaggeration. You intend to let me out of here tomorrow, then?'

'They need to get used to you being around. Locked up in here you are an interesting mystery, out there, dressed like a boy, working, you will be less of a provocation.'

'Why not simply let me go? Why not signal a boat and say you have found me on the beach?'

'Because you have seen the men. You know too much,' he said and reached for the open clasp knife that lay on the table. Averil watched as the heavy blade clicked back into place.

'I could promise not to tell anyone,' she ventured.

'Yes?' Again that cold smile. 'You would connive at

whatever you suspect we are about for the sake of your own safety?'

'I…' No, she could not and she knew it showed on her face.

'No, I thought not.' Luke pocketed the knife and turned from the table. 'I will be back in half an hour—be in bed.'

Averil stacked the plates, swept the crumbs up, wrapped the heel of the loaf in a cloth and stoppered the wine flask. She supposed it would be a gesture if she refused to clean and tidy, but it gave her something to do; if she was going to be a prisoner here, she would not live in a slum.

It was cool now. That was why she was shivering, of course, she told herself as she swept the hearth with the crude brush made of twigs and added driftwood to the embers. The salty wood flared up, blue and gold, as she fiddled with the sacking over the window. What was going to happen was going to be private, at least. She wiped away one tear with the back of her hand.

I am a Heydon. I will not show fear, I will not beg and plead and weep, she vowed as she turned to face the crude bed. Nor would she be tumbled in a rats' nest. Averil shook out the blankets, batted at the lumpy mattress until it lay smooth, spread the sheet that had been tied around her waist and plumped up the pillow as best she could.

She stood there in Luke's shirt, her hair loose around her shoulders, and looked at the bed for a long moment. Then she threw back the blanket and climbed in, lay down, pulled it back over her and waited.

Luke spent some time by the shielded camp fire listening to the game of dice in one tent, the snores from another, and adding the odd comment to the discussion Harris and Ferret were having about the best wine shops in Lisbon. Some of the tension had ebbed out of the men with their efforts all day hunting along the shoreline for wreckage from the ship. Nothing of any great value had been found, but a small cask of spirits had contained just enough to mellow their mood.

He was putting off going back down to the little hospital, he was aware of that, just as he was aware of trying not to think too closely about Averil. He wanted her to stay an abstraction, a problem to be dealt with, not become a person. None of them wanted to be there, most of them were probably going to die; he had no emotion to spare to feel pity for some chit of a girl who, with any luck, was going to come out of this alive, although rather less innocent than she had begun.

'Good night,' he said without preamble and strode off down towards the hut. Ferret and Harris were on guard for the first two hours; they were reliable enough and had no need of him reminding them what they were looking out for or what to do under every possible circumstance. There was a lewd chuckle behind him, but he chose to ignore it; he could hardly control their thoughts.

The hut was tidy when he unlocked the door and stepped inside. There was a lamp still alight and the fire had been made up; Luc inhaled the tang of wood smoke and thought the place was as nearly cosy as it would ever be. But one look at the bed dispelled any thought that Averil had decided to welcome him and had set out to create an appropriate ambiance. She was lying under the blanket as stiff and straight as a corpse, her toes making a hillock at one end, her nose just visible above the edge of the covering at the other. He did not look at the swells and dips in between.

'Averil?' He moved soft-footed to the middle of the room and sat down to pull off his shoes.

'I am awake.' Her voice was as rigid as her body and he saw the reflected light glint on her eyes as she turned her head to watch him.

Luc dropped his coat and shirt over the back of the chair. As his hands went to the buckle of his belt he heard her draw a deep, shuddering breath. Well, he wasn't going to undress in the dark; she was going to have to get used to him—or close her eyes.

'Have you never seen a naked man before?' he asked, slipping the leather from the clasp.

'No. I mean, yes.' Averil found it was difficult to articulate. She cleared her throat and tried again. 'I was brought up in India—*saddhus* and other holy men often go naked.' And there were carvings in the temples, although she had always assumed they were wildly exaggerated. 'They smear themselves with ash,' she added. Now she had started talking it was hard to stop.

Luke said nothing, simply turned towards the chair, stepped out of his trousers and draped them over the back with his other clothes. Averil shut her mouth with a snap, but her eyes would not close. This was not an ash-smeared emaciated holy man sitting under a peepul tree with his begging bowl, watching the world with wild, dark eyes. Luke was… She searched for a word and came up with *impressive,* which seemed inadequate for golden skin and long muscles and broad shoulders tapering into a strong back, down to narrow hips and—

He turned round and her mouth dropped open again, although all that came out was a strangled gasp. 'You see what effect you have on me,' he said, coming towards the bed with, apparently, no shame whatsoever.

'Well, stop it,' she snapped, then realised immediately how ridiculous it was. Obviously *that* was necessary for the humiliating and painful business that was about to occur. 'Stop flaunting it,' she amended in the tone of voice her aunt used for rebuking the servants.

Luke gave a snort of laughter, the first genuine amusement she had heard from him. 'That part of the male body does what it wants. You could close your eyes,' he suggested.

'Is that supposed to make me feel any better? It will still be there.'

He shrugged, which produced interesting undulations in those beautiful muscles and made *that* bob in a most disconcerting way. She could well believe that it had a life of its own. She wanted to look away, but her neck seemed paralysed, as rigid as the rest of her.

Luke reached out and turned back the blanket. Averil forced herself not to grab it back. *Don't struggle, don't react. Don't give him the satisfaction.*

'Could you move over?'

'Wh…what?' She had been expecting something quite different, not this polite enquiry. He just had to get on top of her, didn't he?

'Shift across.' Luke stopped, one knee on the bed. Averil found she could move her eyes after all; she fixed them on the cobwebbed rafters. 'You aren't expecting me to leap on you, are you?' He sounded impatient and irritated, not crazed with lust. Perhaps he did this sort of thing all the time.

'I have no idea what to expect,' she flashed back. The

anger and humiliation freed her locked muscles and she twisted round to sit up and confront him. 'I am a virgin. How would I know how to go about being ravished?'

Chapter Four

He closed his eyes for a moment. 'I am going to sleep in this bed with you, that is all. Did you not realise? Did you still think I was going to force you, for heaven's sake?'

'Of course I did! I am not a mind reader!' Fury flashed through her, obliterating the relief. She had been so frightened all day, she had tried so hard to be brave and now...now he was implying that she ought to have realised? That it was her fault she had been so scared?

'Oh, you—you infuriating man!' She lashed out, her hand hitting him across the chest with a dull thud. His skin was warm, the dark curls of hair surprisingly springy.

'You *want* me to make love to you?' He caught her wrists as she tried to hit him again. His hands were hard and calloused against her pampered skin and this close she could smell him—fresh sweat over traces of some plain soap and what must be the natural scent of his skin.

'Make love? Is that what you call it? No, I don't want you to *make love* or ravish me or anything else. I've been terrified all day and *now* you tell me you never had any intention—' She ran out of words and sat there in the tangle of blankets glaring at him, holding on to her temper because if she did not the alternative was to give way to tears.

'I do not ravish women,' Luke said flatly and released her hands. 'Unconscious or awake.' She had insulted him, it appeared. Good. She had not thought it possible.

'Then what are you doing with that?' Averil made a wild gesture at his groin and he recoiled before her flailing hand made contact.

'I told you, it has a life of its own. I don't have to take any notice of it.' Luc sounded torn between exasperation and anger. 'I am sorry you were frightened unnecessarily,' he added, with as much contrition as if he was apologising for jostling her elbow at a party. 'I thought you realised I had no intention of hurting you in any way. If you can just move over so I can get in, we can go to sleep.'

'Just like that? You expect me to be able to close my eyes and sleep with you in the bed?' She heard the rising note of hysteria and bit her lower lip until the pain steadied her. The relief of realising he was not going to take her had cracked her self-control; now it was hard to hang on to some semblance of calm. 'Why can't you put some clothes on?'

'I have no spare clean shirts to wear—you are wearing the last one. And one more layer of linen between us will make no difference to anything.'

She wondered what the grinding noise was and then realised it was her own teeth. At least if Luke was in the bed with the covers over him she couldn't see his naked body. It was an effort not to flounce, but she turned on her side with her back to him and lay against the far edge of the bed, her face to the wall.

The ropes supporting the mattress creaked, the blankets flapped. 'There is no need to rub your nose against the stones like that,' Luke said. 'Come here.' He put an arm around her waist and pulled her backwards until she fitted tight against the curve of his body. 'Stop wriggling, for heaven's sake!'

'We are *touching*,' Averil said with what calm she could muster, which was not much. He was warm and hard and her buttocks were pressed against the part of his anatomy that he said had a mind of its own—and was still very interested by the situation by the feel of it—and one linen shirt was absolutely no barrier whatsoever. Below the edge of the shirt her thighs were bare and she could feel the hairs on his legs.

'I am certainly aware of your cold feet,' he said and she thought he was gritting his teeth. 'Will you stop moaning, woman? You're alive, aren't you? And warm and dry and fed and still a virgin. Now lie still, count your blessings and let me sleep and you might stay one.' She thought she heard a muttered *If I can* but she was not certain.

Woman? Moaning? *You lout,* she fulminated, as she tried to hold her body a rigid half-inch away from his. But that only pushed her buttocks closer into his groin. The heavy arm across her waist tightened and she gave up and let her muscles relax a little.

Count my blessings. It was a distraction from the heat and solidity behind her and the movement of his chest and the way his breath was warm on her neck. She was alive and so many people were not, she was certain. She had kept their faces and the sound of their voices out of her mind all day; now she could not manage it any longer. Her friends, so close after three months, and her numerous acquaintances, even the people she glimpsed every day but had never spoken to, were like the inhabitants of some small hamlet, swallowed up entire by the sea.

Averil composed herself and prayed for them, her lips moving with the unspoken words. She felt better for that, the grief and worry a little assuaged. The long body curled around hers had relaxed, too; he was sleeping, or at least, on the cusp of sleep. *I am alive, and he is protecting me. For now I am safe.* But the dark thoughts fluttered like bats against the defences she tried to erect in her mind. These men were deserters, traitors perhaps, and she knew too much about them already. What might she have to do to maintain even the precarious safety she had now?

Luc felt Averil's body go limp as she slid into sleep. He let himself relax against her as her breathing changed and allowed himself to enjoy the sensation of having a woman so close in his arms. The softness and the curves were a delicious torment; the female scent of her, not obscured by any soap or perfume, was dangerously arousing. It was over two months since he had lain with a woman, he realised, thinking back over the turbulent past weeks. And then they had been making love, not lying together like this, almost innocently.

The tight knot in his gut reminded him that he was still angry that Averil had supposed he would take her by force. Luc thought back over the words they had exchanged—they hardly qualified as conversations— and tried to work out why she had thought him capable of rape. He had never once said he would make use of her body, he was certain of that, and he had explained why he needed to share her bed.

She had been tired and frightened by all she had gone through; obviously she had not been thinking clearly, he told himself. He supposed stripping off had not been tactful—but she could have shut her eyes, Luc thought with a stirring of resentment. If she wanted him to wear a nightshirt, then she could do some washing tomorrow; he had too much else to think about without worrying about Averil's affronted sensibilities.

It did occur to him as he began to drift off to sleep that he was not used to being with well-bred young women on an intimate level. He had been at sea, more or less permanently, since he had been eighteen; he had no sisters at home, no young sisters-in-law. No one, thank heaven, to have to care about. Not any more.

But this wasn't some society drawing room or Almack's. To hell with it, she was in his territory now and she would just have to listen to what he said and follow orders. His aching groin reminded him that something else was refusing to follow orders. It would be interesting to seduce her, he thought, toying with the fantasy as he let sleep take him. Just how difficult would it be?

Averil woke with an absolute awareness of where she was and who she was with. In the night she had turned over and now she half lay on Luke's chest with her naked legs entangled with his. One moment she had been relaxed in deep sleep, the next her eyes snapped open on a view of naked skin, a tangle of dark curls and an uncompromising chin furred with stubble. He smelled warmly of sweat and salt and sleep. She should have recoiled in disgust, but she had the urge to snuggle closer, let her hands explore.

Every one of her muscles tensed to fight the desire.

'You're awake,' he said, his voice a deep rumble under her ear, and moved, rolling her on to her back so his weight was half over her. 'Good morning.'

'Get off me!' Averil shoved, which had no effect whatsoever. 'You said you don't ravish women, you lying swine.'

'I don't. But I do kiss them.' He was too close to focus on properly, too close to hit, but ears were easy to get hold of and sensitive to pain. She reached up a hand, got a firm grip and twisted. 'Yow!' Luke had her wrist in his grasp in seconds. 'You little cat.'

'At least I am not a liar.' She lay flat on her back, her hands trapped above her head, her senses full of the smell and feel of him, her heart pounding. She had hurt him, but he had not retaliated and there was amusement, not lust or anger, in his eyes, as though he was inviting her to share in a game.

But she was not going to play—that was outrageous. Luke was too big even to buck against, although she tried. And then stopped as her pelvis met his and that rebellious part of his body twitched eagerly against her belly. Something within her stirred in response, a low, intimate tingling. She blushed. Her body wanted to join in with whatever wickedness his was proposing.

'Since when has kissing amounted to ravishment? I need us to go out there looking as though we have just been making love.' There was exasperation under the patience and somehow that was reassuring. If he was bent on ravishing her he would not be discussing it. Still, it was wrong to simply succumb so easily.

'Making love?' She snorted at the word and he narrowed his eyes at her.

'Do you prefer *having sex?* It will make life easier for both of us if you can give the impression that you have been seduced by my superior technique and are now happy to be with me.'

Averil was about to tell him what her opinion of his

technique was when his words the previous evening came back to her. *A pack of wolves.* 'I see,' she conceded. 'I am safer if I do not seem like a victim. If I am happy to be with you, then it is convincing that I would be confident. And they will think I am unlikely to try to escape and put you all in danger.'

'Exactly.' Luke breathed out like a man who had been braced for a long argument. 'Now—' He bent his head.

This was not how it was supposed to be, the first time. This was the antithesis of romance. *And I wanted romance, tenderness...*

'You don't have to kiss me. I can pretend,' Averil said as she tried to move her head away. She only succeeded in clashing noses. Luke had a lot of nose to clash with. But she did not want to pretend. She realised that it was herself and her own desires that were the danger, not him.

'You *are* an innocent, aren't you?' That was not a compliment. 'Never been thoroughly kissed?'

'Certainly not!' She had never been kissed at all, but she was not going to tell him that.

'You'll see,' Luke said, releasing her wrists and capturing her mouth.

It was outrageous! He opened his mouth over hers, pushed his tongue inside and...and... Averil gave up trying to think about what was going on so she could fight him. But she did not seem to have any strength; her muscles wouldn't obey her and the rest of her body was in outright mutiny.

Her arms were round his neck, her fingers were raking through his hair, her breasts were pushing against his chest—which had to be why they ached so—and her lips...

Her lips moved against Luke's, answering his caress, and it was, some stunned part of her mind that was still working realised, a caress and not an assault. His mouth was firm and dominant, but that dominance was curiously arousing. The heat and the moistness were arousing too and the thrust of his tongue was so indecent…and yet she wanted to echo it, move her own tongue, although she did not dare.

Against her stomach she felt his flesh pulsing and lengthening and sensed the restraint he was imposing on himself. Her legs wanted to open, to cradle him, and her aunt's words came back and made sense now of what had seemed embarrassingly ludicrous before. He only had to move a little, to thrust… Suddenly she was frightened again and he sensed it.

'Averil?' They looked at each other, noses almost touching. 'Have you *ever* been kissed before?'

Mute, she shook her head.

'I thought not.' He threw back the covers and got out of bed, the sudden cool rush of air as effective in cutting through her sensual daze as his abrupt words had been. This time she had the sense to turn her head away from his nudity and to stare at the wall. After a few minutes he came back. 'Averil?'

'Yes?' She kept her head averted.

'Look.' She risked a quick look. He was holding out a small mirror. 'You see?'

A wanton creature stared back at her in the scrap of glass. Its hair was a wild tangle, its eyes were wide and dark and its mouth—*her* mouth—was swollen and pouting.

'Oh,' she breathed. 'Oh, my. Does it last?'

Luke had moved away and was lifting some things down off the shelf, but at that he turned his head and studied her. 'For a bit. Then I have to do it again.' She felt the crimson flood up from breast to forehead and his lips quirked. He looked thoughtful. He had, thank goodness, put on his clothes. 'I'll get you some hot water. When you come out don't forget that you have been conscious these past four days.'

Averil sat up as the door banged behind Luke. One kiss and she felt like this—and she didn't even like the man, or want him. He thought it was amusing, the wretch. It was not amusing, it was outrageous and shameful, those were the only possible words for it. Her breasts still tingled, her stomach felt very strange—almost as though she was apprehensive, but not quite the same—and lower down there was the most embarrassing awareness and that strange little pulse stirring. He had made her feel like this—and he must have realised—and then he had stopped.

The door opened, Luc dumped a bucket inside and then closed it again. Whatever his morning *toilette* consisted of, he was performing it elsewhere. Averil climbed out of the tangled bedding and went to fetch the hot water. *Then I have to do it again,* Luke had said.

'Oh, my heavens,' she murmured. 'I had no idea.'

Luc stood on the shore, pocket watch in hand, as half-a-dozen of the crew fitted the oars in the rowlocks and pulled away towards the bulk of Round Island to the north. There were no other ships or boats out in the area and it seemed a good opportunity to work the excess energy out of the men.

Behind him the others lounged on the short grass, jeering at the rowers. 'You reckon you'll do better?' Luc asked. 'You drew the short straw—you'll be rowing with breakfast in your bellies to weigh you down and they're pushing to get back to eat.'

'Wot about the mermaid—Miss Heydon, I mean,

Cap'n? I'll take her breakfast down to her, shall I?'
Harris's tone could have served as a definition of the
verb *to leer*.

'I—' Luc broke off as a figure walked over the shoulder of the hill. 'No need, Harris, Miss Heydon has come
to eat with us.'

He had to admire her. From the set of her shoulders
and the frown between her brows she was as tense as
any sensible woman would be under the circumstances,
but her back was straight, her chin was up and she had
scraped back her hair into a plait down her back in a
way that must have been intended to diminish her attractiveness. The fact that it simply showed off her bruised
cheekbones and her wide hazel eyes was not her fault,
Luc pondered appreciatively as she got closer.

He saw with satisfaction and a sharp pang of arousal
that her mouth was still lush and swollen from his kisses.
He had never kissed a complete innocent before and it had
been…interesting. He wanted her. Was he going to have
her? It was a stimulating fantasy, that and the thought that
by the time he took her she would want it just as much
as he did.

'Good morning,' she said, her voice as coolly polite
as if they were all in a drawing room. 'Is that breakfast?
You are Mr Potts—the one who cooks?'

Potts gawped, displaying his few remaining teeth,
then, to Luc's amazement, touched a finger to his forehead. Goodness knew how long it had been since someone had addressed him as *Mister,* if they ever had. 'Aye,
er…ma'am, I am and 'tis that. Got mackerel or bacon,
unless you fancy porridge, but it's wot you might call
lumpy.'

'I would like bacon and some bread please, Mr Potts.'
Averil sat down on the flat rock Luc usually took for him-

self. He wondered if anyone else noticed the automatic gesture to sweep her non-existent skirts out of the way. 'And is there tea?'

'Aye, ma'am. No milk, though.'

'Really? Never mind.' She turned and looked directly at Luc for the first time, as haughty as a duchess at a tea party. 'Couldn't you have stolen a goat?' She was overdoing the confidence and completely forgetting that she was supposed to have just passed a night of bliss in his arms.

'We did not plan on company,' he said with an inimical glance at the cook. Potts might well decide that a raid on the neighbouring islands to steal some livestock would be amusing. 'And we will not be drawing attention to ourselves by stirring up the islanders and lifting their goats either.'

Potts grunted; he knew a warning when he heard it. Luc studied Averil and was rewarded by the colour staining her cheeks. So, she was still agitated by that kiss; it was strangely satisfying to know that he had unsettled her like that—and it would be a pleasure to do so again. He was not used to virgins and Averil's untutored responsiveness was unexpected. It was doubtful whether she realised she had responded—it was all very new to her and she had been too shocked to think.

The other men had been down by the water's edge, catcalling at their rapidly vanishing comrades. Now they turned and began to walk back to the fire, their focus on the woman in the badly fitting clothes. He saw her eyes widen and darken as the haughty young lady vanished, leaving a girl who looked ready to run. His hand rested on the hilt of his knife as he watched the men's reaction. Would they react as he intended or would they turn as a pack and attack to get at the girl?

Chapter Five

Luc saw Averil's eyes dart from one man to the other and the almost imperceptible relaxation when she realised that Tubbs and Dawkins, the two who had found her, were not there. He had sent them off with the first crew so they would be too winded for an immediate reaction when they encountered Averil again. In their turn the men stared at her with interest, but the mood was different from when they had found her on the beach. He took his hand from his knife and shifted his weight off the balls of his feet.

Time to mark his territory. Luc took two platters from Potts and went to the rock where Averil sat, legs primly together, hands clasped in her lap. 'You're in my seat,' he said and got a cool stare in return. In the depth of her hazel eyes fear flickered, but she tipped up her chin and stared him out. *'We're lovers, remember,'* he mouthed and she blushed harder and shifted to make room for him next to her, hip to hip.

Luc handed her a plate and touched her cheek with the back of his free hand. 'Hungry, sweetheart?'

'Ravenous,' she admitted dulcetly, her eyes darting daggers at him. She folded the bread around the slices of bacon and bit into it. 'This is good, Mr Potts.'

'Thank you, ma'am,' the cook said, then spoiled it by adding slyly, 'nothing like a bit of exercise to give you an appetite, I always say.'

'Quite,' Averil retorted. 'That hut was in a shocking state—it took a lot of work to tidy it up.'

Thwarted, Potts returned to his frying pan, glowering at the grins of the other men. They were good-humoured smiles, Luc noticed, neither jeering nor directed at the young woman on the rock. 'Well done,' he murmured. She narrowed her eyes at him, so he added more loudly, 'I've a pile of washing needs doing.'

'I am sure you have, Luke darling,' Averil said, then softened her tone with an effort he could see. 'I will need hot water, please.'

'See to it after breakfast, Potts.'

'Is she doing all our washing, Cap'n?' Ferret asked through a mouthful of herring.

'*Miss Heydon* is not doing anything for you, Ferret.'

'Are you the man who lent me these clothes?' Averil asked as Potts handed her a mug of black tea.

'Aye, ma'm.'

'Is Ferret your real name? Surely not.' She took a sip of tea and gasped audibly at the strength of it.

'Er…it's Ferris, ma'am.'

'Thank you, Mr Ferris.'

The man grinned. 'Pleasure to help the Cap'n's lady, ma'am.'

The others said nothing, but Luc sensed, with the acute awareness of his men any captain learns to acquire, that something in their mood had changed. They had stopped thinking of Averil as a nameless creature for their careless pleasure and started regarding her, not just as his property, but as a person. She was frightened of them still, wisely so—they had not forgotten that she was a woman and they had been celibate for weeks. He could feel the apprehension coming off her like heat from a fire, but she had the intelligence and the guts to engage with them.

Miss Averil Heydon was a darned nuisance and enough to keep any man awake half the night with lustful thoughts and an aching groin, but he was beginning to admire the chit. Admiration did nothing to dampen desire, he discovered.

'They're coming,' Tom the Patch said, his one eye screwed up against the sun dazzle on the waves.

Luc pulled out his watch. 'They need to do better than that.'

'Nasty cross-current just there,' Sam Bull observed with the air of a man determined to be fair at all costs.

'These waters are one big cross-current,' Luc said. 'You reckon you can do better?'

'Yeah,' Bull said, and nodded his curly head. 'Easy.'

They are training for something, Averil thought, watching the men as she sipped the disgusting tea. Her teeth, if they had any enamel left, would be black, she was sure.

The men were a crew, a real ship's crew, not a motley group of fugitives. They weren't hiding here because they were deserters, or waiting for someone to come and take them off. It was incredible how much more she was noticing now her terror had abated a little. Instinct had told her to try to treat the men as individuals and, strangely, that had been easier to do over the shared food than it had been to pretend an intimacy with Luke that she did not feel.

Or, at least, she corrected herself as she felt the warmth of his thigh through the thickness of their trousers, she felt an intimacy, just not one involving any sort of affection or trust.

He was a good officer though, albeit a rogue commanding rogues. She had seen enough army officers in her time in India, and she had watched how the *Bengal Queen* was run; she could recognise authority when she saw it.

The men were focused on the approaching boat while Luke ate his bacon, his eyes on the pilot gig, too. 'Why are you here?' she asked, low voiced.

He shook his head without looking at her.

'Deserters have no need to train for speed,' she carried on, speculating. 'And why steal one of those big rowing boats, why not a sailing ship? A brig—you have enough men to crew a brig, haven't you?'

'You ask too many questions,' Luke said, his eyes still trained on the sea. 'That is dangerous, be quiet.'

A threat—or a warning? Averil put down her empty plate and mug and studied his profile. She could believe he was a man of violence, one who would kill if he had to and do it with trained efficiency, but she could not believe now that he would kill her. If he had been capable of that, he would have been capable of raping her last night.

'It is less dangerous to tell me the truth.'

'For whom?' he asked. But there was the slightest curve to the corner of his mouth and Averil relaxed a little. 'Perhaps later.'

The rowers were close now and she could see Tubbs at the tiller and Hawkins heaving on an oar. Some sound must have escaped her lips for Luke turned towards her.

'They won't hurt you—you are mine now.' He dipped his head and the shock of his mouth on hers, here, where the men could see them, froze her into immobility. It was a rapid, hard kiss on the lips, nothing more, but it felt startlingly possessive and so did the way his hand stayed on her shoulder when he stood to watch the men land, his pocket watch in the other palm. That big hand would curl into a formidable fist in her defence. She could feel the pressure of each finger and shivered—how would it feel if he caressed her?

'Not bad,' he called down to the rowers as they splashed through the shallow surf and up the beach. 'You could do better. The rest of you, get going. On my mark—now!'

There was a scramble as the others heaved themselves aboard and began to back-water away from the shore. The first crew, without a backward glance, made for the fire and the food Potts had left for them. Then they saw Averil on her rock and they slowed like a pack of dogs sighting a cat, their eyes narrowing.

Luke left his hand where it was for a moment longer, then strolled down to meet them. 'Close your mouth, Tubbs, or something will fly in,' he said mildly. The man muttered and a snigger went round the group as their eyes shifted between Luke and Averil.

She wanted to run. Instead she got to her feet, picked up Luke's plate and walked down to the fire. 'More bacon, darling?' Somehow she produced the purr that her friend Dita had managed to get into the most innocuous sentence when she wanted to flirt. Dita, who was probably drowned. Averil blinked back the prickle of tears: Dita would have both charmed and intimidated this rabble.

Close now, they gawped at her and Averil remembered

what Luke had said about the wolf pack. These men eyed Luke as much as they ogled her, on the watch for his reaction, edgy as if they waited for him to snarl and lash out if they encroached on his property.

'Will the others beat your time, do you think?' she asked, direct to Tubbs.

He blinked, startled, as if the frying pan had addressed him. 'I reckon we're better by a length,' he said when Luke did not react.

'The boat looks very manoeuvrable. At least it seems so to me. I have been on an East Indiaman for three months, so any small boat looks fast.' She sat on the grass by Luke who had hunkered down, apparently intent on the gig. Without looking at her he put out his arm and tugged her closer and the men's eyes shifted uneasily. Now what? Instinct told her to keep talking to them, make them acknowledge her as a person, not a commodity, but she dared say nothing that would seem as if she was probing into their purpose here.

'Had a lot of treasure on it, did it?' Dawkins said.

'Not bullion, I'm sure. But there would have been silks, spices, gem stones, ivory, rare woods—those sorts of things.' There could be no harm in telling them; the cargo would have gone down or been ruined by the water.

'You come from India, then?' one of the men asked. Luke began to stroke the side of her neck languidly, as a man pulls the ears of his gun dog while they sit and wait for the ducks to rise to the guns.

Averil found she was leaning in to him, her lids were drooping… She made herself focus. 'Yes, India. I lived there almost all my life.'

'Ever see a tiger?'

'Lots of them. And elephants and huge snakes and crocodiles and monkeys.'

'Cor. I'd like to see those. Did you ride on the elephants?'

They asked questions, and she answered, for almost twenty minutes. She felt better, safer in their presence now. Almost safe enough to be alone with them, she thought and then caught Dawkins's eye and almost recoiled. What the big man was thinking about was plain to see and her whole body cringed against Luke.

His hand stilled. 'What?' he murmured.

'Nothing.'

He stood, pulling her to her feet. 'Just time to show you that washing I want doing. Timmins, bring a bucket of hot water and one of cold from the well.'

'I suppose you realise I have never washed a garment in my life, let alone a male one,' Averil said as they walked back to the old hospital.

'Men's clothing ought to be easier,' Luke said. 'No frills, no lace, stronger fabric.'

'Sweatier, dirtier, larger,' Averil retorted. She lifted one hand and touched her neck where he had been stroking it. The skin felt warm and soft, and her own touch sent a shiver of awareness through her that was disconcerting. She had not wanted him to stop, she realised, shamed by her reaction. What was the matter with her? Was she naturally a complete wanton, or was it shock, or perhaps simply instinct to try to please the man who could protect her?

'You are a belligerent little thing, aren't you?' Luke said as they stepped into the hut.

'You would be belligerent under the circumstances,' she snapped. 'And I am not little. I am more than medium height.'

'Hmm,' he said, and turned, trapping her between the wall and his body. 'No, not little at all.'

'Take your hands off my...my breasts.'

'But they are so delightful.' He was cupping them in his big hands, the slight movement of his thumbs perceptible through the linen of the shirt.

'Don't,' she pleaded, as much to her own treacherous body as to him.

'But you like it. Look.'

Shamed, she looked down. Her nipples thrust against the fabric, aching, tight little points, demanding attention.

'I cannot help that reaction, any more than you can help *that,* apparently.' The bulge straining against his breeches was very obvious. Luke moved back a little and she remembered another of her brothers' lessons. But his reactions were faster than hers. No sooner had she begun to raise her knee that she was flat against the stones, his weight pinning her.

'Little witch,' he said and bent his head.

The kiss was different standing up. Even though she was trapped Averil felt she had more control, or perhaps she was just more used to the sensations now. She found she no longer wanted to fight him, which was disconcerting. She moved her head to the side and licked into the corner of Luke's mouth, then nipped at his lower lip, almost, but not quite hard enough to draw blood. He growled and thrust his pelvis against her, blatantly making her feel what she was doing to him.

Averil let him take her mouth again, aching, wanting, despite the part of her mind that was screaming *Stop!* She was going to have to sleep with this man again tonight—was he going to be able to control himself after this?

'Damn it,' Luke said. He lifted his head and looked down at her, his eyes dark, his breath short. 'I think you've been sent to try my will-power to the limit—'

The door banged open behind them, and he turned

away so abruptly that she almost fell. 'Over there by the table, Timmins.'

The man put down the buckets and walked out while Averil hung back in the shadows behind the door. He must have guessed what they had been doing, she thought, her face aflame.

'I can't do this any more,' she said the moment they were alone. 'I cannot. I don't understand how it makes me feel. I am *not* wanton, I am not a flirt. I don't even *like* you! You are big and ugly and violent and—'

'Ugly?' Luke stopped sorting through the heap of linen in the corner and raised an eyebrow. Nothing else she had said appeared to have made the slightest impression on him.

'Your nose is too big.'

'It balances my jaw. I inherited it from my father.' He tossed the tangle of clothing on to the table. 'There is some soap on the shelf.'

'Did you not hear a word I said just now?' Averil demanded, standing in his path, hands on hips.

'I heard,' Luke said as he dragged her back into his arms and kissed her with such ruthless efficiency that she tottered backwards and sat down on the bed with a thump when he released her. 'I just do not intend to take any notice of you losing your nerve.

'You'll get over it. Make sure the collars and cuffs are well scrubbed. You can dry them on the bushes on the far side of the rise. Just make certain you keep the hut between you and the line of sight from the sea.'

Averil stared at the unresponsive door as it closed behind him and wished she had listened and taken note when she had overheard the sailors swearing on board the *Bengal Queen*. It would be very satisfying to let rip with a stream of oaths, she was quite certain.

Castration, disembowelling and the application of hot tar to parts of a certain gentleman—if he deserved the name—would be even more satisfying. She visualised it for a moment. Then, seized with the need to do something physical, if throttling Luke was not an option, Averil shrugged out of the leather waistcoat, rolled up her sleeves and went to find the soap. It was just a pity there was no starch or she would make sure he couldn't sit down for a week, his drawers would be so rigid.

She began to sort the clothing, muttering vengefully as she did so. None of it was very dirty—the captain was obviously fastidious about his linen. It also smelled of him, which was disconcerting. Was it normal to feel so flustered by a man that even his shirts made one think of the body that had worn them?

Averil searched for marks, rubbed them with the soap, then dropped those garments in the hot water. How long did they have to soak? She wished she had paid more attention to the women doing their washing in the rivers in India; they seemed to get everything spotless even when the water was muddy. And it was cold, of course…

She was scrubbing briskly at the wristbands of one shirt before she caught herself. What was she doing, offering comfort to the enemy like this? Let him launder his own linen—or do whatever he would have done if she hadn't been conveniently washed up to do it for him. But then, she was clad in his shirt and he said he had no clean ones, so if she did not do it, goodness knew when she would get a change of linen herself.

Her fingers were as wrinkled as they had been when she had come out of the sea, and she had rubbed a sore spot on two knuckles, but the clothes were clean and rinsed at last. Wringing them dry was a task beyond her strength, she found, so she dumped the dirty water outside on the shingle, filled the buckets with the wet clothes and trudged up the slope towards the camp fire.

The buckets were heavy and she was panting by the time she could put them down. 'Would someone who has clean hands help me to—?' Luke was nowhere in sight and she was facing eight men, with Dawkins in the middle.

'Aye, darlin', I can help you,' he drawled, getting to his feet.

'Leave it out, Harry.' Potts looked up from a half-skinned rabbit. 'She's the Cap'n's woman and we can do without you getting the man riled up. He's got a nasty temper when he's not happy and then he'll shoot you and *then* we'll have more work to do with one man less. Besides...' he winked at Averil who was measuring the distance to his cooking knives and trying not to panic '...the lady likes my cooking.' He lifted one knife, the long blade sharpened to a lethal degree, and examined it with studious care.

'Just joking, Potts.' Dawkins sat down again, his brown eyes sliding round to the knife. The cook stuck it into the turf close to his hand and went back to pulling the skin off the rabbit as the whole group relaxed. Averil began to breathe again.

'I'll wring 'em, ma'm.' A big man with an eyepatch got to his feet and shambled over. 'I'm Tom the Patch, ma'am, and me 'ands are clean.' He held up his great calloused paws for inspection like a child. 'Where do you want 'em?'

'I'll drape them over those bushes.' Averil let out the breath she had been holding and pointed halfway up the slope.

'Not there,' Potts said. 'They'll see you.'

'Who will?'

'Anyone in a ship looking this way. Or on Tresco. Put 'em there.' He waved a bloody hand at the thinner bushes close to the fire. Potts, she was beginning to realise, had either more intelligence, or more sense of responsibility, than the other men. Perhaps he had been a petty officer of some kind once.

'Why don't you want anyone to know you are here?' Averil asked as Tom twisted the shirts and the water poured out.

'Hasn't the Cap'n said?' He dropped one shirt into the bucket and picked up another.

'We haven't had much time to talk,' she said and then blushed as the whole group burst into guffaws of laughter.

'Why not share the joke?' Luke strolled out from behind one of the tumbledown stone walls. He had his coat hooked over one finger and hanging down his back, his shirt collar was open, his neckcloth was loose and he gave every indication of just coming back from a relaxing stroll around the island. Averil suspected that he had been behind the wall ever since she had approached the men, waiting to see what happened, testing their mood.

'I said that we had not talked much.' She hefted the bucket with the wrung linen and walked towards the bushes. Any gentleman would have taken the heavy pail from her, but Luke let her walk right past him.

'No, we have not,' he said to her back as she shook out each item with a snap and spread it on the prickly gorse. 'I'll tell you over dinner.'

'Tell 'er *all* about it, will you, Frenchy?' Dawkins said and the whole group went quiet.

Frenchy? Averil spun round. He was French? And that made the men…what? Not just deserters—turncoats and traitors.

'You call me Captain, Dawkins,' Luke said and she saw he had the pistol in his hand, loose by his side. 'Or the next time I will shoot your bloody ear off. Nothing to stop you rowing, you understand, just enough to make sure you spend what is left of your miserable life maimed. *Comprends-tu?*'

The man might not have understood the insult in the way he had just been addressed, but Averil did. And her French was good enough to recognise in those two words not the pure accent of someone carefully taught as she had been, but a touch of originality, a hint of a regional inflection. The man was French. *But we are at war with France,* she thought, stupid with shock.

'Aye, Cap'n,' Dawkins said, his face sullen. 'Just me little joke.'

'Go back to the hut, Miss Heydon,' Luke said over his shoulder. 'I will join you at dinner time.'

'I do not want to go to the hut. I want an explanation. Now.' It was madness to challenge him in front of the men; she realised it as soon as she spoke. If he would not take insubordination from Dawkins, he was most certainly not going to tolerate it from a woman.

'You get what I choose to give you, when I choose,' Luke said, his back still turned. 'Go, now, unless you wish to be turned over my knee and taught to obey orders in front of the men.'

Her dignity was all she had left. Somehow she kept her chin up and her lips tight on the angry words as she walked past him, past the silent sailors and down the slope towards the hut. *Bastard. Beast. Traitor...*

No, she realised as she got into the hut and flung herself down on a chair, Luke was not a traitor. If he was French, he was an enemy. *The* enemy. And she was sitting here, an obedient little captive who shuddered under his hands and wanted his kisses and washed his shirts and trailed back here when she was told. She was an Englishwoman—she had a duty to fight as much as any man had.

Averil jumped to her feet, sending the chair crashing to the floor, and twitched back the crude curtain. There was a navy ship at anchor out there—too far to hail, and probably, unless someone had a glass trained on the island, too far to signal with anything she had to hand. But she could swim. Why hadn't she thought of that before? If she ran down to the sea, plunged in and swam, surely they would see her? And if Luke gave chase then that would create even more of a stir. Someone would come to investigate and, even if he shot her, he would have to explain the commotion.

She was out of the door and running before she could think of any objections, any qualms to slow her with fear. The big pebbles hindered her, but she was clear of them, up to her knees in the water, before she heard anything behind her.

'Get back here!'

Luke! She did not turn or reply, only ploughed doggedly on, fighting through the thigh-high waves.

'Stop or I will shoot!'

He wouldn't. He wouldn't shoot a woman in the back. Even a French agent wouldn't—

She didn't hear the shot, only felt the impact, a thumping blow below her left shoulder, behind her heart. It pitched her forwards into the sea and everything clouded and went dark. Her last thought as she felt the water closing over her head was of shocked anger. *He said he would not kill me... Liar.*

Chapter Six

'Wake up.'

It seemed that the voice had been nagging at her for hours. Days, perhaps. She did not want to wake up. She did not think she was dead and this obviously was not heaven unless angels habitually sounded angry and impatient. But even if she was alive, Luke had shot her. Why should she have to wake up and face that? It would hurt.

'Why should I?' Averil asked.

'So I can strangle you?' the voice enquired and became identifiable as Luke.

'You shot me.' She opened her eyes, surprised to find she was not frightened or in great pain. Perhaps she was in shock. Best to lie very still—she was badly wounded, surely she must have lost a great deal of blood?

'I did not shoot you.' He was looming over the bed, tight-lipped and furious. 'I threw a stone at you and you seem to have fainted.'

'Oh.' Averil sat up and yelped in pain. 'It hurts! You could have killed me if you had hit my head.'

'I hit what I aim at,' Luke said. 'It is just a bruise. You might want to cover yourself up.'

Averil glanced down and found she was naked. Again. Her borrowed clothes were draped, steaming, over chairs in front of the fire. She grabbed the edge of the blanket, pulled it up to her chin and sat there glowering back at him.

'What the hell were you doing?' He turned on his heel and walked away as though he was having trouble keeping his hands off her. Averil was not deceived into thinking he was restraining lustful urges.

'I intended to swim to the nearest ship,' she said. 'It was one thing not to try to escape when I believed you were just deserters, but when I realised you are a French spy I had to do something.'

Luke folded his arms and looked at her without emotion or denials. 'Why do you assume I am a French spy?'

'Because you are French, because you have lied to the Governor about why you are here and because you are hiding those men and training them for some nefarious exercise.'

'That is almost entirely correct on all points, Miss Heydon, and you have drawn entirely the wrong conclusion from it.'

'What is not correct?' she demanded, wishing she had her clothes. Defiance was much easier when one was not naked, she had discovered.

'I am half-French.' Luke's shoulders lost their angry rigidity and he sat on the edge of the table and regarded her with what looked like exasperated resignation. 'I am going to have to trust you.'

'Well, you cannot. Not if you are my enemy.'

'I may be that—you seem determined that I am—but

I am not England's enemy. I am an English naval officer and I am also *le comte* Lucien Mallory d'Aunay.'

'A French count? A Royalist?'

That produced a bark of laughter. 'Shall we say, a constitutional monarchist? That, at least, was what my father was until Madame Guillotine took his head off and ended his political philosophising.'

He rubbed both hands over his face and through his hair and emerged rumpled and with no sign of the anger of a few moments before, only a weary patience. 'Averil, will you take my word of honour that what I tell you is the truth? Because if you will not, then I fear we are at an *impasse*. I cannot prove any of it, not here and now.'

'I don't know,' she said with total honesty. He shrugged and suddenly seemed very foreign. 'I wish I had some clothes on,' she added, half to herself.

'Why on earth would that make any difference?'

'I want to look into your eyes.'

'I will come to you then.' He knelt by the bedside and looked steadily at her. 'What can you see?'

'My own reflection. Your cynicism. Weariness.' She made herself relax, let herself sink into the wide grey gaze. 'Truth. Truth and anger.'

'Ah.' He sat back on his heels. 'I will tell you then, but you must swear to keep it secret.'

'Who am I likely to be able to tell?' she demanded.

'You never know.' He got to his feet and went back to the table. 'My mother was Lady Isabelle Mallory and she married my father in 1775. In 1791, when the king was forced to accept the written constitution, I was fifteen. My father was strongly in favour of the new order and believed that bloodshed and revolution would be averted by the more democratic form of government.

'*Maman* insisted that it would be a disaster and said

she would return to her parents in England. I wanted to stay in France, but my father told me my duty was to look after my mother and that he would send for us when France became the stable land of freedom and prosperity that he predicted.' He paused and Averil found she was holding her breath. 'She was right, he was wrong and he paid for it with his head during the Terror in '94. Our loyal family servants followed him to the guillotine.'

'Oh, I am sorry. Your poor mother.' He spoke so flatly that she could only guess at the emotions under the words, what he must have felt when the news reached England. 'You speak very good English. I would never have guessed you were French.'

'I have thought in it for years. I was already in the English navy when my father died. I went from being Comte Luc d'Aunay to Midshipman Mr Luke d'Aunay— or Dornay—and I did my level best to be an Englishman. But they called me Frenchy and it stuck—the name and the whispers and the lack of acceptance. I was never *one of us,* never quite English. But I worked and I was lucky and my mother lived long enough to see me gain post rank.'

'She must have been very proud of you,' Averil said. Poor, tragic woman, her husband executed, an exile in her own home country, her son far away and in danger.

Luke—no, she supposed she should say *Luc*— shrugged again, but it was not modesty, she could see that. He knew what he had achieved and against what odds and he was not going to discuss his feeling about his mother's death with her.

'What went wrong?' she asked. She wrapped her arms around her knees, wincing a little as the movement stretched the bruise on her shoulder where the stone had hit.

'Admiral Porthington was what went wrong,' Luc said. He took the knife from his pocket and began to throw it into the tabletop, pull it out, rethrow. 'I was seconded to assess intelligence and I found a pattern of events that pointed to leaks originating from here. The islands are used a lot by navy shipping, and by supply vessels, and they are conveniently close to France. I dug deeper and found that it all appeared to lead back to a certain gentleman who has interests here. I presented my evidence and it was set aside.'

'But why would it not be accepted and the man investigated?'

'He is Porthington's second cousin. I had not dug deeply enough.'

'Oh.'

'Oh, indeed. I was not permitted to investigate any further. Porthington ridiculed the work I had done and refused to countenance any action being taken. I lost my temper.' Averil could imagine, but she bit her lip, unwilling to provoke him now by saying as much. 'I brooded on things, drank rather too much and decided to confront him in his quarters—this was at Portsmouth. I would give him an ultimatum—do something or I would go to the Admiralty and lay it before them.

'I barged in and found he had company—very unwilling company. A young woman who he was about to force.'

'What did you do?'

'Asked him to stop. He laughed in my face and told me to get out. I hit him.'

'Oh, my goodness.' Averil knew what would have happened to an East India Company naval officer if he had done such a thing. 'What happened?'

'Porthington demanded a court-martial, but someone

in the Admiralty seems to have had his suspicions, too. I was called in and given one chance—two months to prove my theory right or I would face a court-martial, which, if it chose, could sentence me to death for striking a superior officer. I could not deny I had done it.'

To face death as it stared you in the face at sword point or, as she had experienced, in the form of a towering wave, was one thing. To live with a potential death sentence hanging over you for weeks was a refined form of torture.

'That is terrible,' Averil burst out.

'It was more than I deserved for striking him. I have shot men for less.'

'You were doing your duty by pressing for him to listen to you and you were acting as any gentleman should by defending that woman—surely they saw that?'

'Porthington denied that he had forbidden me to proceed and said I had been told merely to exercise caution while he considered tactics. He portrayed me as headstrong and likely to blunder in and blow the entire investigation. Losing my temper did not help prove him wrong! And as for the woman, she was a servant, not a lady. They seemed to think it made a difference.' He raised one of those slanting eyebrows. 'Don't make me a saint.'

'I am very well aware you are no such thing,' Averil retorted. 'I might dislike you personally—' he raised the other brow '—but I hate injustice. Where did the crew come from?'

'The condemned cells. If I am correct and we track down the source of the leaks, then they are pardoned. If I am wrong, or we fail, they die.'

'They do not have very much to lose by killing you

and escaping, have they?' And if they killed Luc, then they would not hesitate to do their worst with her.

'No, they do not. Leadership with men like these is a confidence trick. It is much the same as the way a rider needs to convince a horse that is infinitely stronger and heavier than he that it must obey his commands and bear his weight.'

'But you use brute force when leadership and personality will not work?'

'Oh, yes. And, Averil, do not think I would have hesitated to turn you over my knee up there if you had persisted in questioning me.'

'You would beat a woman?' she bristled at him, outraged. 'I cannot believe any gentleman would!'

'I would if it was necessary, but you had the sense to yield.' Was that the hint of smugness on his face? 'It would have hurt you far less than that stone I was forced to throw at you.'

'It would have been undignified to brangle about it.'

'Certainly undignified, but the more I think about it, the more the idea interests me.' His eyelids drooped, hooding his eyes, and she felt the change in the atmosphere like a shift in the wind. 'You do have a most delightful posterior, my dear. It would be a pleasure to warm it, just a little.'

'You promised…'

'I promised I would not ravish you, Averil, but I said nothing about seduction. You are a serious temptation to a man who has few pleasures in his life just now. A challenge.'

'Well, I am not going to become one of your few pleasures,' she retorted, hauling the blanket tight around her chin. 'Stop teasing me and finish telling me what you are doing over here on this island.' The trouble was, she did not think he was teasing. She must face him down, behave as though such a thing was unthinkable. 'What can you do from here?'

'Wait for a signal. The source who first aroused my suspicions tells me that when the informant—let us not name names yet—has papers for his masters he sends out a brig from Hugh Town which meets a French naval brig beyond the Western Rocks. We take the Scillonian vessel, then we make the rendezvous. The thought of two prizes is a help in motivating the men.'

'I see. I believe you.' He bowed—an ironic gesture, she was sure. 'So now I know the truth you can let me go. Obviously I will not betray you, you have my word.'

'Let you go? My dear Averil, you must see that is impossible.'

'Impossible? By why? Do you not trust me?' Indignant, Averil swung her legs out of bed and stood up. She hauled the blanket around her, ignoring the pain in her shoulder. Luc's eyes widened as she stormed up to him, blanket flapping, and she stopped to yank it tight. 'Stop ogling!'

'There is so much to ogle at when you do that,' he said as he lifted his eyes, full of appreciative amusement, to meet hers. 'You are an intelligent woman—think. Where are you supposed to have been since the ship went down?'

Luc moved around the table and sat on the far side as though to put a safe distance between them before he went on. 'It is four days since the wreck. The navy and the local sailors have scoured the islands, checked every rock that stays above high tide. The population of the Isles is about three hundred souls—there is nowhere you could have been undiscovered and yet in as good a condition as you are now. So, what story do you tell?'

'I—I do not know,' she admitted. 'Can't I tell the

Governor?' He shook his head. 'You think he might be implicated? Then I must stay here, I suppose. For how long?'

'I expect to get the signal within the day, tomorrow at most. There is plenty for the traitor to report on, I imagine, and it would fit the timing of the leaks we could trace.'

'And what now?' She moved to shake out the clothes that hung in front of the fire. 'These are almost wearable.' The thought of being able to dress, to get out of this hut and away from the nearness of him led to another question. 'Do the men know I tried to escape?'

'No, and it would be dangerous for you if they did. Now, we wait and you and I will emerge looking as though we have been working up an appetite for dinner.'

'I do not want you to kiss me again.' Averil edged backwards, realised it was taking her straight to the bed and stopped, holding on to the other chair back.

'Liar.'

Luc got up and stretched and she found she could not take her eyes off him. She had seen him naked—wasn't that enough? Did she have to do what she accused him of doing and ogle him, just because he was a man? A big, virile, exciting… *Oh, stop it!*

'Tell me why not,' he said.

'Because you are a hypocrite. You condemn the admiral for forcing that girl and yet you expect me to kiss you.'

'Am I forcing you?' He came round the table and sat on the edge of it, perhaps two feet from her. It felt far too close for comfort.

'I have no experience of men. I do not know how to deal with the way you make me feel,' she admitted. 'I want to say no and somehow, when you touch me, I cannot. I must be very wanton,' she said, looking away while she fought the blush that was heating her cheeks.

'Not wanton, just sensual,' Luc said. 'Do you not like how it feels when we kiss?'

'Yes, I do. And it is *wrong.*'

'It is perfectly right,' he countered and reached out to turn her face to look at him. 'Natural.'

'I am betrothed,' she said, shocking herself with the way she had lost sight of why she had ended up here. 'I have hardly given that fact a thought since we hit the rocks. I have not thought of Viscount Bradon himself *once* until just now. The reason I was coming back from India was to marry him and I just did not think of him, even when you kissed me.' How on earth could she have ignored something as important as that? How on earth could she have enjoyed another man's caresses as she had? She stared at Luc, appalled at herself. 'That is the most shocking thing of all.'

Luc dropped his hand from where it cupped her cheek. Averil was betrothed? That should change nothing—and yet, subtly, it did. It made him want her more. He had never been competitive with Englishmen for their women. When he married it would be to a French *émigrée,* one of good birth and title. He would not ask for money—he had invested his prize money with care and had few expenses—nor for land—he would be the one providing that once Bonaparte was defeated and he could reclaim what was rightfully his. What he wanted was good French blood to breed back into the d'Aunay line.

Once this episode was over he would either be dead or in a position to court a bride seriously. Bonaparte could not hold out much longer, he felt it in his bones; in three or four years he must be ready to return to France and fight to regain what was his by right.

The woman in front of him knotted her hands into that ridiculous blanket, her face a picture of guilt and confusion. 'Shocking that you should forget?' Given the natural sensuality of her responses he found Averil's expression amusing. 'I do not think so. Surprising, perhaps. I suppose I could find it flattering.' She sent him a withering look. 'But I fancy that being caught up in a shipwreck and almost drowned may account for a little forgetfulness. Do you love him?' Surely not, if she could forget, even when she was being kissed by another man—she might be sensual, but she was not wanton. But then, she had never been kissed before, he remembered.

'Love? Why, no, but then I would not expect to. Love has nothing to do with marriage in aristocratic families, of course.'

'Ah, so you think as I do. Marriage is a matter of dynasty and land. Your father has found you a good match?' It must be if the girl had been sent all the way from India.

'I have never met him, nor had a letter from him, but Papa arranged it all, so there was no need. It is an excellent match,' she added. '*Everyone* says so.'

There was defiance in that statement and under it he sensed doubts. Any woman would have them, he supposed, sent so far from home and family to an unknown husband.

'His father is the Earl of Kingsbury,' Averil added as though playing a trump card.

Yes, on paper a very good match indeed. Luc nodded. 'You know him?'

'I have come across him.' Luc kept his voice carefully neutral. 'I do not know the son.' If Bradon was a spendthrift gamester like his father, then Miss Heydon was in for a most unpleasant shock. What was her own father thinking of? 'Your family are distant relatives of Kingsbury, perhaps?'

'Oh, no.' She smiled brightly. *On the defensive,* Luc thought, wondering what was coming next. 'My father, Sir Joshua Heydon, is a merchant.'

So this was becoming clearer. Kingsbury was doubtless securing a substantial dowry with his new daughter-in-law, money he could well do with. What, he wondered, was Sir Joshua gaining? Influence at court, perhaps, for the earl was one of Prinny's cronies. It was a trade deal, in effect. Luc revised his prejudices a trifle. He had not admired those daughters of cits he had come across so far, not that he had paid them any attention. A d'Aunay did not marry trade. Averil, however, seemed mercifully free of vulgarity.

'Lord Bradon will be anxious when the news reaches him that the ship has gone down,' she said with a frown. It did not seem to occur to her that he was going to be more than *anxious* when he got her back and discovered that his betrothed had been missing, unchaperoned, for several days. Miss Heydon could well have made a long sea voyage, survived a shipwreck and yet find herself rejected and unwed.

But that was not his problem. *She* was not his problem. He had to capture two brigs, against unknown odds, with the crew from hell, and then pray that with the ships he secured the evidence to expose a traitor and to restore his own career.

Chaperoning an innocent young lady under those circumstances was impossible—from the moment that he had made the decision to take her into the hut and not signal for a navy boat she was as near ruined as made no difference. Averil Heydon was no longer an innocent in the eyes of the world and, if he did not keep a tight rein on his desires and instincts, she would not be one in fact either for much longer. After all, once she was ruined in theory, that was it. She might as well be hanged for a sheep as a lamb.

He looked at her, thinking about it, his body becoming hard and heavy. She was temptation personified and he was in no mood for self-sacrifice.

Chapter Seven

'What are you frowning about?' Averil asked. Lord, but he had to get her dressed again—that blanket was driving him insane. Last night he had been too tired and too distracted to take much notice, although his body had been sending him frantic signals. Now, with it sliding off one shoulder and her hair clean and dry and waving from its tight braid and her face flushed with colour, she was beginning to exude a powerful femininity that he was convinced she had no conscious control over.

'Frowning about? Life,' he said, with perfect honesty. He wondered how much of a bastard he was. Enough of one to ruin this girl in reality? 'And, yes, I have no doubt that your betrothed will be anxious. He will doubtless give you up for dead. Managing your resurrection is going to need some care.' Her expression changed, lost some of its determination, and she caught her lower lip between her teeth as though to force some control over her emotions. Perhaps she could sense his desires—his thoughts were clamorous enough.

'What is it?' He knew he spoke abruptly, and disregarded it; he could not afford to involve himself too deeply with the problems of a young woman who had nothing at all to do with his mission, he told himself. If she thought she had been rescued by a man who was forming some sort of attachment to her, she was mistaken. He had learned not to care the hard way. Averil was a casualty of war and lucky to be alive. 'This can all get sorted out later,' he added. 'A few days is not going to make any difference now.'

'It isn't that. I try not to think about my friends on the *Bengal Queen*,' Averil said. 'But you speaking of resurrection made me think of the burial service at sea. A sailor died during the voyage and the words are different from the words they say on land. But of course you know that...' Her voice trailed away and he saw she was looking back into nightmare.

'When the sea shall give up her dead,' Luc quoted. He had said it more times than he cared to remember as the weighted canvas shrouds were tipped overboard.

'Yes, that is it. And I wonder how many from the *Bengal Queen* died, and how many of those the sea will give up so that families will have the comfort of being able to bury their loved ones.'

'Thinking about it cannot help,' Luc said. 'It will only weaken you. Time enough to mourn when you are safe.'

'And I am not safe now. I understand that,' she said, her voice cool. 'I will try not to bother you with my inconvenient emotions.'

Luc experienced a sudden and quite inexplicable urge to put his arms around her and hold her. Just hold her tenderly to give her comfort. He tried to recall the last time he had comforted a woman and realised it must have been when he had come home on leave after his father had been executed and his mother had finally given up the battle to be strong and had wept in his arms.

Maman had not lived long after that and so he had lost everyone who had mattered: his father, his mother, the loyal servants—they had all died because, in their way, they had done their duty. It was safer not to care, not to form new attachments because they would only lead to pain and distract him from his own duty, to the navy, to his inheritance. Sometimes he thought that if he had allowed himself to form new attachments he would at least have some anchor, some sense of where he truly belonged.

Averil shifted uneasily and he was pulled back to the present. This was not his mother and he had no idea how to console Averil. He did not get involved with women who needed comforting or hugging or cheering up. His relationships were functional and businesslike and, he hoped, involved a degree of mutual pleasure. The women who had been his mistresses had not sat in front of him bravely biting on a trembling lip and making him feel their distress was all his fault.

Damn it, he had not conjured up the storm that sank the East Indiaman and she was not going to make him feel guilty about it. Miss Heydon would have to take him as she found him. He damn well wanted to take her.

'Good,' he retorted. 'Emotions are dangerously distracting under these circumstances.' He got up and felt the clothes hanging in front of the fire. 'These are definitely dry enough now. Get dressed, the men will be wondering why we have not turned up for dinner.'

'I should think their dirty little minds will supply them with an explanation.' Averil did not stir from her chair. 'I am not getting dressed with you here.'

Luc shrugged and got to his feet. It was a reasonable

request and he had no need to heat his blood any more than it already was by being in the same room with Averil naked. Even with his eyes closed his recollection was too vivid. 'Try to see, a trifle more affectionate when you appear,' he said over his shoulder, halfway to the door.

'I don't think so.' Averil stood up in a swirl of blanket that somehow managed to be simultaneously provoking and haughty. It was made worse by the fact that he was certain she had no idea of the effect she was creating. 'I think a lovers' quarrel will be far easier to sustain.'

Luc did not bother to answer her. He closed the door behind him, taking care not to slam it, then leaned back against the wind-weathered planks while he got his temper under control. One belligerent, emotional, virginal young lady was not going to get the better of him, he resolved. The trouble was, she had disregarded just about everything he had told her to do, or not to do, and he could not help a sneaking admiration for her courage.

Even if she could swim, to launch herself into the sea, so soon after being almost drowned, took guts and she hadn't complained about the bruise on her back from the stone he had thrown either. It was the first time in his life he had raised his hand to a woman, let alone used a weapon against one, and it had made his stomach churn to do it. Which was another thing not helping his temper, he supposed.

Luc gazed at the horizon and focused his mind on the job in hand. He was a professional naval officer, despite everything, and he was going to overcome this, all of it, just as he had overcome the prejudice and the suspicion and the jibes that had followed him since he had come to England. The *émigré* community was wary because of his father's political views, the English saw him as

French and he had a suspicion that his father's marriage had contributed to his troubles in France.

He was a half-breed and he was not going to tolerate it any longer. He would force the damn English navy to exonerate him, he would find a wife befitting a d'Aunay from the *émigré* community and when this war was over, he was going to take back what was his.

A flicker of movement broke his concentration. A brown sail on a small boat that tacked across the Pool as it headed for the narrows between St Helen's and Teän. Now why, with the prevailing wind, was the skipper taking it that way to get to the open sea when the passage to the south, between St Helen's and Tresco, would be so much easier?

Because it was coming to call on him, he realised. It was the expected messenger and that way round took it as far as possible from the navy ships. He felt his mood lift with the prospect of action at last as he strode away from the hut and up the slope, Averil forgotten.

Averil hardly waited for the door to close before she scrambled into the slightly damp, salt-sticky, breeches and shirt. Her shoulder protested with twinges before it settled down to a throbbing ache around the bruise, but she ignored it as she ignored her painful bare feet. She felt strong, she realised, despite the battering her body had taken over the past few days and the misery at the back of her mind that threatened to creep out and ambush her, as it had just now with Luc.

He thought her an emotional female. Well, there was nothing to be ashamed of in that. But she felt resilient and independent as well, and that was new. Always she had had people to tell her what to do: her father, her aunt, her governess, her chaperones. She had been good and obedient and she had been rewarded by the opportunity to become a countess and to advance her family's fortunes.

And now, through no fault of her own, she was in the power of another man who expected her to do what she as told, and this time she was not inclined to obey him, not in everything—and that was liberating. In some things—kissing, for example—she was far too ready to give in to him and, of course, it was her patriotic duty to comply with Luc's orders in everything relating to the reason he and his men were on the island.

But all in all, Averil thought as she whipped her hair into a firm braid, she was coping. And changing. Whatever happened, the Averil Heydon who left this island was not going to be the same woman who had been washed up on its sands.

She took care to slip out of the door and round to the back of the hut when she left, but there was no sign of interest from the ships riding at anchor in the sunshine. Her frantic dash for freedom and Luc's swift recapture of her must have gone unnoticed.

But there was a strange boat drawn up on the beach below the camp and a stranger stood by the fire, a steaming mug in his hand as he talked. The men were clustered round and they were listening intently, but they were watching their captain. For all their apparent hostility it was clear they looked to him to deal with whatever was happening now. Averil felt an unexpected warmth, almost pride, as though he really was her lover.

She gave herself a brisk mental shake as she walked towards them. Luc d'Aunay was neither her lover nor her love, he was merely doing his job and if he happened to look confident and commanding and intelligent while he was about it, so much the better for the Royal Navy. There was no excuse for her to get in a flutter.

'Who's this? No one said anything about women.' The stranger spoke with an accent that she guessed must be local. He looked like a fisherman, there were nets and crab pots in the stern of his little boat, and he seemed uneasy with her presence.

'My woman,' Luc said, with a glance in her direction. 'Never mind her—are you certain of the times?'

'I am.' The man grinned. 'Stupid beggar didn't check the sail loft. Still can't work out who he is, mind you. I can't find out where he's coming from and he wears a cloak and his hat pulled tugged low. He keeps his voice low, too—a gentleman, I can hear that much, but if it wasn't for Trethowan not keeping *his* voice down I wouldn't have worked it out.

'He looked to see if he was being followed all right, but it didn't occur to him that someone knew where he was going from last time and got up there first. It's the same brig as before—the *Gannet*—but they've changed the sails, so someone's had some sense. The patch has gone and they've a new set of brown canvas.'

He took a gulp from the mug. 'They'll be slipping anchor at eleven tonight so you'll need to be in position off Annet. The tide'll be right for you to get in behind the Haycocks rocks. I'll signal from the Garrison when I see them leave. It'll be clear tonight.'

'How do we know we can trust 'im?' Harris said and the other men shifted uneasily.

'Because I say so,' Luc replied. 'I know him and he's good reason to hate the French.'

'Aye.' The man scowled at Harris. 'Killed my brother Johnnie they did. And I don't hold with them that'll sell out their country to foreigners.'

'Foreigners like Frenchy here?' a voice from the back muttered.

'Don't be more of a bloody fool than you can help, Bull,' Luc said.

'Sorry, Cap'n, I was only—'

'Don't you go insulting the captain.' The fisherman turned, furious. 'My Johnnie was serving with him when he was killed and he wouldn't have a word said against him. He'd come home and he'd say—'

'Yes, well, spare my blushes, Yestin. You get out fishing now. We'll look out for your lights, six bells on the first watch.'

The man grunted. 'You navy men and your bells. It'll be eleven by the clock on Garrison Gate.' He put down his mug, gave Averil another long stare, then marched down the beach and pushed off his boat. 'You kill the lot of them,' he called back as the wind caught the sail. 'And I'll have lobsters for all of you.'

'Good news,' Luc remarked. 'After dinner, Tom Patch, I want all the dirks and the cutlasses sharpened. Harris, double check the boat. Timmins, come with me and we'll sort out the ammunition and the handguns. The rest of you can take it easy—I need everyone alert and ready to go at two bells on the first watch.'

'Two hours to do that distance?' one of the men queried.

'I want you in good condition when we get there,' Luc said with a grin. 'You'll have some fast rowing and then some brisk fighting—no need to be blown before you start.'

They ate, all of them more cheerful than Averil had seen before. Even Dawkins found discussing the best way to cut a French throat more interesting that ogling her. When they had finished the men with tasks to do went off, leaving nine of them fidgeting around the fire.

'Oh, get away and look for wreckage,' Potts said, exasperated. 'I'm trying to clear up and cook supper and you lot are under my feet. Unless you want to help?'

That sent them off down to the shoreline. Averil watched who went where and then followed, taking the opposite end to Dawkins and Tubbs. There were splintered timbers and cask staves sticking up between ridges of rock, some torn canvas, tangled ropes. Averil picked her way along the shore, gripped by a horrid fascination, half dreading seeing something that she recognised, half as infected by the same treasure-hunting enthusiasm as the men.

Time passed; the sand was warm under her bare feet and the foam at the water's edge tickled her toes. If the cause was not so grim, this would be a delightful way to spend a spring day.

'You found anything?' It was Tubbs.

She straightened up, wary. 'Only shells and rubbish.'

'Aye,' he agreed, sounding almost amiable. 'You found anything, 'Arry?'

'Nah.' The big man was balanced precariously on a low ridge of rock sticking up a couple of feet from the sand. 'I'm for a kip in the tent.' He turned, awkward on the sharp edge. 'Wot's that?'

Tubbs darted forwards and picked something up. Averil saw it as it lay in his calloused palm, a dark oval, smooth and polished, a hinge on one side. 'I know what that is. Give it to me, please—'

'I saw it first,' Dawkins said and made a grab at Tubbs. It all happened so fast Averil did not even have time to step back. Dawkins slipped, fell, crashed into Tubbs, the box shot up in the air, she caught it and was drenched as the two men landed in the shallows. There was a bellow of agony and she saw that Dawkins was not getting up. The water around him was red.

She stuffed the box into the waistcoat pocket and splashed to his side. He was lying awkwardly, cursing with pain; his leg, where all the blood was flowing from, was jammed into a crack in the rock.

'Tubbs, get hold of him, try to get him straight while I hold his ankle!'

The man went to his mate's shoulders and started to heave as Averil got her hands around the trapped foot. 'It'll be 'opeless,' Tubbs remarked gloomily as Dawkins swore, a torrent of obscenity. 'Potts! Get a knife, we'll 'ave to cut it off.'

'Nonsense,' Averil said, hoping it was, as the cook ran down to her side. 'Look, if enough of you can lift him and stop his weight dragging on the leg, I might be able to work it free.'

It involved considerable splashing, cursing and heaving and more blood than Averil ever wanted to see again, but minutes later Dawkins was lying on the beach like a porpoise out of water, moaning and groaning while Averil sent men running for clean water and something to tear up for a bandage.

'I don't think it is broken,' she said when she had got the sand and broken shell washed out of the deep cuts and grazes. The others hauled Dawkins up and he balanced on one foot in front of her, white to the lips. He tried to put his foot down and swayed, gasping with pain. Averil grabbed hold, too, before he crashed down again. 'But I think you've damaged the tendons. You won't be able to walk for a—'

'What the hell?' It was Luc, at the run. 'What have you done? Dawkins, you bastard, get your hands off her!'

Chapter Eight

Averil glanced down at herself and realised what Luc was seeing—Dawkins with his hands on her shoulders, her shirt red with blood. 'It is all right, he has hurt his foot. It is *his* blood,' she said urgently as Luc reached them, murder in his eyes.

'His?' He stared at her, then turned and hit Dawkins square on the jaw, felling the big man.

'I never touched 'er!' the sailor protested, flat on his back on the sand, one meaty hand clamped to his face.

'Why did you hit him?' Averil protested. 'He's the one who is injured. It was an accident.'

Luc pulled her towards him, none too gently, and held her by her shoulders as he scanned her face as though looking for the truth. 'For scaring the living daylights out of me,' he said too softly for the men to hear, then raised his voice. 'The damn fool has probably hurt himself too badly to be any use tonight.'

'I can row,' Dawkins said. The others had hauled him to his feet again and he stood propped between Tubbs and Tom Patch, his slab of a face creased with anxiety.

'I can reload and guard the boat when you're boarding. I can shoot from the brig. Gawd, Cap'n, I've got to go or they'll say I haven't earned me pardon!'

'You haven't,' Luc said. 'You know damn well that the most dangerous part, the part I need the men for, is boarding the brigs and you go and fool around and have an accident—if it is an accident.'

'Tell 'im, Miss!' Dawkins turned to Averil, all trace of the blustering bully gone. 'Tell 'im it was an accident. Could 'ave 'appened to anyone!'

'It *was* an accident,' Averil confirmed. 'Honestly it was, Captain d'Aunay. He wasn't doing anything that the others weren't.'

There was a stinging silence while Luc contemplated Dawkins's sweaty face and the men seemed to hold their breath. 'Miss Heydon is remarkably forgiving, considering the disrespectful way you have behaved to her,' he said at last.

'Yes, Cap'n. She's a real lady and I'm sorry, miss.'

Watching him, Averil thought he probably was genuinely regretful. He was a bully who was used to being kept at a distance; her unforced help seemed to have shocked him.

'Very well. I accept that. If we are successful, then you will get your pardon like the rest. Now go and lie down and stop hopping about like a damned rabbit.'

'Er…miss?' Tubbs was eyeing her like a hopeful jackdaw after a scrap of meat. 'You've got the thing we found, miss. Rightfully mine, that is. Finder's keepers.'

'Yes, it would be, Tubbs,' Averil said. 'But it belongs to me.' It was a lie, but she wasn't allowing the only thing she had left of her friends to fall into Tubb's greasy fingers. 'Look, I'll prove it to you. What do you think is inside?'

'Dunno, miss.' He was looking more intrigued than resentful. Some of the others who were not helping Dawkins back to his shelter stopped to listen. 'Snuff? Money?'

'Tiny carved animals,' Averil said, slipping the box out of her pocket. 'A Noah's Ark. I couldn't have guessed that, could I? If you can find a flat rock out of the wind, I'll show you.'

She opened the lid and there they all were, the minute ivory animals, the ark, Noah himself—the gift Lady Perdita Brooke had bought for Alistair, Viscount Lyndon, in Cape Town. Her hand shook a little as she set them out on the rock with the men crouched down beside her or hanging over her shoulder to look. Where had it been when the ship struck—in Alistair's cabin or on his person? Was it a good omen or a sign that he and Dita were gone?

Averil took herself to task for superstition. It was chance, no more, no less, that this small object should have been washed up on this beach for her to recognise.

'Lovely workmanship,' Luc said behind her as he reached over her shoulder to pick up one of the camels, as small as his little fingernail. 'But very fragile for a child's toy.'

'It isn't a toy,' she said, as she blew grains of sand out of the box before she packed the pieces in again. The men drifted away, back to the beach or the fire, leaving them alone. 'It was a gift. A birthday gift from someone very special to me.' Dita had been her closest female friend and she had loved her like a sister. *I do love her,* she corrected herself. *She is alive, I know she is alive.* 'They bought it in Cape Town,' she added, thinking to explain the craftsmanship.

'I see,' Luc said. 'Lord Bradon would be interested to hear about that, I imagine.'

'You think I had a lover on board? Someone I met on the voyage?' she demanded, shocked and yet curiously gratified. Was he jealous? Not that she wanted him to be, of course, that would presuppose she actually had any feelings for the man, other than a grudging admiration for his leadership and sympathy for the fate that had brought him here.

'I know you did not,' he said. 'At least, if you did, he hadn't kissed you.'

Averil glared. 'It was a gift from a woman, my best friend. Just because you appear to place little importance on fidelity there is no need to assume everyone else is the same.'

'I am always faithful,' Luc protested, all injured innocence, she thought resentfully as he cocked a hip on the rock and made himself comfortable to watch her fiddle the pieces back into place.

'Serial fidelity to a succession of mistresses, I presume?' She could imagine Luc selecting a mistress, negotiating—he would be reasonably generous, she guessed—then… Enjoying her, she supposed, was the phrase. She would not let her imagination go there.

'Exactly.'

'Disgraceful!' She secured the lid of the box and stood up.

'How so? I am generous, I provide well for the woman when the liaison is over, she appears satisfied with the arrangement.'

'There is no need to be smug about your sins,' Averil snapped. Even to her own ears she sounded irritable and stuffy. 'I hope you are not going to tell me you are married *and* keeping a string of mistresses.'

'A succession, not a string,' he said. He appeared to find it mildly amusing, curse the man. 'And, no, I am not married. If I get my head out of this noose then I shall devote myself to finding a well bred, virtuous young lady of an *émigré* family.'

'Really?' Distracted from her anxieties, Averil turned back. 'Not an Englishwoman? You intend to go back to France one day?'

'Of course.' He stared at her as if she had suggested he go to New South Wales instead. 'I have responsibilities in France—that is where my title comes from, where my lands are. Obviously I need a wife who understands that. Once the war is over there will be nothing for me here.'

'Oh. I see. It is just that…you seem so English.' But he did not, somehow. Despite the completely perfect pronunciation there was something under the veneer of the English gentleman and officer, something foreign and unsettling and different.

She pulled herself together. Luc's marriage plans were no affair of hers. 'What will happen to me tonight?'

'You stay here, of course.' He was frowning again. Perhaps it was tactless of her to have mentioned his marriage when he must have feared all that was lost to him. 'There is ample food and water. I will collect you tomorrow. I don't think you need worry about Dawkins. With that foot you can outrun him easily. And I think he knows he is in your debt, although I would lock the door at night, if I were you. Reform is likely to last only so long.'

'And if you do not come back?'

'I always come back.'

'You are not immortal, even if you are arrogant,' she retorted. 'Don't tempt fate by saying such things.'

'I hadn't realised you cared.' Luc stood up and caught her in his arms. His eyes were dark and warm and his mouth was curving and he was just about to kiss her, she was certain.

Averil let herself sway closer, let herself absorb, just for a moment, the intensity of his gaze, the heat of his body, the tempting lines of his mouth that gave such wicked pleasure. 'I do not. Naturally I wish the mission well and that you all return safely, but I am worried about what happens to me if you get yourself killed,' she said, stepping back out of range.

'You wish the mission well?' he mocked, mimicking her starchy tone. 'That is enough to send us all off with a patriotic glow in our breasts, I am sure.' The satirical light in his eyes died and he became serious. 'If I do not come back by nightfall tomorrow, then light a fire on the beach outside the hut and discharge the pistol I will leave with you. I'll show you how to fire and load it now. That will be enough to attract interest from the nearest frigate.'

'A gun?' She had never touched one before and was not at all sure she wanted to start now.

'Here.' Luc pulled the pistol from his belt. 'This is loaded. Hold it.' Reluctantly she curled her fingers round the butt. 'You cock it—go on, it won't bite you— that's half cock, now fully back. Keep it pointing at the ground—no, not at your foot!—until you are ready to fire, then point it out to sea and pull the trigger.'

'Ow!' The bang made her jump, the recoil hurt her wrist. 'Won't that have been heard?'

'The wind is to us.' Luc produced a box from his pocket. 'Here's how to reload—you may need more than one shot.'

He showed her how to reload several times, more patient with her initial clumsiness than she would have expected. When he was satisfied at last he walked with her back to the hut and saw the pistol and ammunition safely stowed on the shelf.

'But you have no handgun now,' Averil realised. 'You will need one.'

Luc was already removing a stone in one wall. 'I have two.' He stuck the spare pistol in his belt and pushed the stone back.

'You would have taken two if it was not for me,' she said, worry fretting at her conscience. 'Here, take this one back, you'll need it. I can attract attention without it, I am sure.'

'I would feel more comfortable if you were armed.'

'Couldn't Dawkins sail your little skiff across to St Mary's? Oh, no, I suppose if you do not come back then he needs to be able to disappear and never to have been here. I see.'

Luc stood frowning at her, thinking about something else and not, she thought, listening to her work it all out aloud. 'There are papers in that cache. You just need to prise the stone out with a knife. If you have to leave without me, take them to the Admiralty when you reach London. Don't give them to the Governor, I am not certain about his loyalties yet.'

'But you will come back.' It mattered, *he* mattered, she realised. Half the time Luc was autocratic and cold as though he was not prepared to let another human being touch his feelings, yet he was fiercely protective. Was that simply the male need to dominate, to fight for possession of anything in his territory?

He could make her so angry—and she was never angry usually. And when he touched her, she wanted him. He had made her want him in a shameful, physical way. And that was not like her either; she had never had any trouble at all being perfectly well behaved and not flirting, not allowing stolen kisses.

'Ah! You care, *chérie*.' He grinned at her, an infuriating, cocky smile that took years off his apparent age and made him look completely French.

Yes, I care, she wanted to say. 'Do you want me to?' she countered. *I am betrothed. You seek a French wife. I am not thinking about friendship. This is impossible...or sinful.* What on earth was the matter with her? Averil found she had stopped breathing, waiting for his answer.

'I want—yes, what is it?' The bang on the door made him turn, the teasing young man gone, the captain back again.

Harris's head appeared round the door. 'Potts says, do we need to take any provisions with us?'

'Water, some ship's biscuit and cheese. I'll come and sort out final positions.' As the door closed behind Harris, Luc turned back to her. 'I'll be with the men now, up until it is time to go. I don't want to leave them on their own and they need to keep busy. Will you be all right?'

What kind of question was that? Averil thought with a spurt of resentment. All right? No, she was not all right, and she wondered if she ever would be again. The wretched man had made her care about him, so she would worry—and she would worry about that rabble of a crew of his. He had made her think about her marriage in a whole new light and to worry about a lot more than whether Lord Bradon would have a sense of humour, or whether she would remember all her lessons in the duties to be expected of her. Now she was thinking about kissing her betrothed and comparing him with this man who should never have touched her, let alone have lain naked with her in his bed.

But she could say none of that. 'Of course I will,' she said with a smile that was supposed to be confident and which obviously did not deceive Luc for a moment.

'Oh, hell.' He dragged her into his arms. 'One last time, damn it. The Fates owe me that, at least.

'I don't underst—' she began and he kissed her. It was not gentle or considerate or teasing. It was uncompromising, and so was the hard thrust of his body against her and the way he pulled her shirt clean out of her trousers and ran his hand up, over her bare skin, to take her breast and mould it with strong, calloused fingers.

Her flesh seemed to swell as though eager to fill his hand and she moaned into the heat of his mouth, wanting and aching, and both his hands were on her body now and she understood, finally, what her clamouring senses were telling her to do and dragged his shirt out, too, frustrated because his coat stopped her pulling it over his head.

Luc's skin was hot and smooth and she could feel those lovely muscles she had watched with such scandalised fascination. Her hands slipped lower, under the waistband of his trousers and his hands that had been doing indecently wonderful things to her breasts stilled.

'Luc?' His whole body was rigid, then she felt him relax as he stepped back.

'That very nearly got out of control,' he said, passing his hand across his mouth while his eyes held hers. 'I am sorry. It is a good thing you will be sleeping alone tonight, I think.'

Averil found she could, after all, articulate. 'It was my fault, too.'

'No. You are an innocent—you don't understand.'

'I am beginning to get the hang of it, a little,' she ventured, shocking herself.

'Lucky Bradon,' Luc said with a flash of the grin that made her smile back, a trifle uncertainly. 'I'll see you at supper.'

* * *

When he had gone she sat quite still for a while on the edge of the bed and tried to think. Luc said she was not wanton, only sensual. Was that true? He took the blame for that kiss becoming so much more, and yet she wasn't ignorant, or unobservant. She should have stopped him the moment his fingers slid under her shirt. But she had not; she had wanted to undress him and to touch him intimately and—and then what?

Averil got up and let herself out, walked over the rise behind the hut and, once she was out of sight of the ships at anchor, began to climb towards the island's little summit until she was at the top and looking out westward over open ocean. There was nothing between her and America, she realised, thinking of the endless ocean the *Bengal Queen* had ploughed across to bring her here, to this tiny speck on the edge of the Atlantic.

The breeze was brisk and cool, and the sea spread out like crumpled silk with tiny white wavelets all over it and sudden, sinister, patches of foam and disturbed water to mark submerged rocks. She had thought perhaps she would see the wreck of the *Bengal Queen* from this height, but she could not. Was it out of sight behind that big island—Tresco, she thought they had called it—or had it sunk to the bottom?

How could anyone navigate at night through this maze of islands and islets and reefs? She pulled her braid over her shoulder and began to play with the end while she watched the sea. Only a few days since the wreck and so much had happened. She was a different woman. *I have suffered a sea change,* she thought. *I thought I knew who I was and what I wanted. Who I wanted.*

'But it doesn't matter what I want,' she said out loud, as though arguing with someone else. Or, perhaps, just with her conscience. 'There is a contract, an agreement. Papa has said that I will marry Lord Bradon.'

There really was no option, after all. Whatever it was that was happening between her and the man she had met only days before, the man who had saved her life, it was not about the prospect of marriage. And marriage was her purpose in life: to marry well to help her family, then to be a good wife and support her husband and to raise happy, healthy children to carry on his line.

I have had a shock, Averil thought, sitting down, then lying back so she was watching the sky and not the troubling, shifting, sea. *I am not quite steady in my mind.* Almost killed, mourning for her friends… Of course she felt more for Luc d'Aunay than she would have under any other circumstances, she reasoned.

The bright sky hurt her eyes. Averil rolled over and lay on her stomach, propped herself up on her elbows and frowned at the short grass between them. It was starred with tiny flowers she did not know the names of and a minute black beetle was making its way through what must seem a jungle to it.

And what were those feelings when she came right down to it? Luc made her cross a lot of the time. He most certainly aroused wickedly sensual sensations that she was doing her best not to think about. He was attractive, although not handsome—she would not allow him that accolade. He was brave and strong and commanding and ruthless and even if he rescued women from admirals bent on rape he seemed to have no scruples over almost seducing her.

The world was full of strong, confident men like that, she told herself: Alistair Lyndon, the Chatterton twins, to name but three. She bit her lip—they were all right, they had to be. If she could reach land alive, then those men could.

Yes, there were thousands of attractive, courageous, dashing men and she was probably about to marry one. But in the meantime this one, the one she owed her life to, was going into danger. And behind his strength there was a darkness. His family tragedy and his isolation because of his birth would account for some of it. The injustice of the situation he now found himself in would be enough to make any man cynical and angry. She wondered if he would be in this position if he had been fully English or whether prejudice had told against him. Did he really know what he wanted? Did he secretly yearn for acceptance as an Englishman as well as for his French identity and title back again?

Averil sat up and looked down the slope to where the men were gathered round Luc as he stood in the pilot gig on the beach and realised what she had been meaning to do ever since he had pulled her into his arms in the hut.

She was going with them.

Chapter Nine

'Ferris.'

'Yes, miss?' As Averil reached the bottom of the slope the skinny little man looked up from the knife he was sharpening with loving care on a whetstone. She sat down beside him with a momentary thought about how convenient trousers were and how restricting skirts would seem when—if—she ever got back to them.

'With Dawkins injured you are one man down for tonight.'

'Aye, we are that.' He spat on the stone and drew the knife down it again with a sinister hiss. 'Clumsy lummock.'

'Is it all boarding and fighting or does someone have to stay in the pilot gig?' She had been trying to work out the tactics for boarding a brig from a much smaller boat and it seemed to her that they could not just all swarm on board and leave the gig to float away.

'Someone has to stay, miss. If Dawkins wasn't such a big lump, perhaps the cap'n would have taken 'im anyway, but he can't row with that bad foot—you can't get the strength behind the stroke, see—and we can't haul 'im on board, not and fight at the same time, and he's a great hulk of a man.' He tried the edge of his knife with the ball of his thumb and grunted with satisfaction. 'In the gig Dawkins is just that much more weight if he can't fight or row. We've got the extra weapons and the charts and stuff as well—you can't climb up the side carrying that lot *and* fight, so the man in the gig 'as to look after those.'

'So whose job is it to stay on the gig?' That would make them two fighting men down.

'Mine, miss.' He sighed. 'I'm the smallest and the fastest. Pity. I'd like to 'ave a go at them treacherous bastards. I gets to fight when we board the French brig, though. We'll come alongside, tie on and then jump 'em.' He held the knife up to catch the light and grinned with blood-curdling anticipation.

'Ferris, can you get me on board the pilot gig without the captain seeing?' His mouth dropped open, revealing a snaggle of stained teeth. 'I can stay in the gig and then you can go up and fight—you'd prefer that, wouldn't you? I've got a pistol and I can fire it if someone tries to climb down.'

Ferris looked thoughtful, and very much like his nickname. She could almost see his pointed little nose twitching as he scrubbed a hand over his whiskery chin. One benefit of dealing with a cunning, unscrupulous, wicked man like this was that he had no concerns about doing something against orders, if it suited him. And, apparently, the opportunity to kill and be killed tempted him more than any fear of the consequences deterred him.

'Aye, I'll do it. You'll need something dark and warm on your top, and a hat.' He squinted down the beach at the gig. 'I'll be in the prow so I can catch hold and tie us off. Cap'n will be in the stern on the tiller. This is what we'll do...'

'You will be all right.' Luc said it firmly, as though giving an order. He had come back to the hut after all. It was a good thing she had not changed into the dark clothing Ferris had given her yet.

'Of course I will. I know exactly what to do.' Averil smiled up at him with cheerful reassurance, then made her face more serious. It would not do to let the relief that she felt because she was going with him make him suspicious. And it was foolish to think that her presence could keep him safe. But it would give him one more fighting man in Ferris, and one more pistol.

They stood in the hut in front of the fire, suddenly as stiff and awkward with each other as two strangers at a social function. *Kiss me,* she urged him silently, as he stood, bare-headed, his hair disordered from the breeze that was getting up, his body indistinct in the dark clothing he wore, with no trace of white at cuff or throat. Luc showed no sign of wanting to even touch her hand in farewell.

'Will you kiss me goodbye?' She blushed to ask it and he looked, as far as she could see in the flickering light, less than enthusiastic. *How very flattening. I thought men about to embark upon danger welcomed kisses.*

'There is no excuse for a kiss now. We are beyond the need to deceive the men. I wish you well, Averil, and I am sorry if my actions have sullied the innocence you had every right to take to your husband.' He sounded deadly serious and his voice held, for the first time, the faint trace of an accent as he made the stilted speech. He was probably translating from the French in his head, she thought. Was that a sign that his emotions were engaged?

'I have to admit that I enjoyed what we did together,' she confessed. It was hard to resist the temptation to touch his face, caress his cheek, dark with evening stubble. 'I would like you to kiss me again.' *Must I beg?* She was beginning to feel angry with him, and she did not want to feel that, not now.

'I will kiss you when I get back,' he said and smiled suddenly and her heart thumped with an emotion she did not understand, although fear was a large part of it. Her stomach felt hollow with apprehension. Was it fear for his life, or her own? Or for what would happen when they left this tiny island behind them?

'Very well.' She stood on tiptoe and kissed his cheek, the stubble prickling her lips. 'Good luck and fair winds.'

He nodded, abrupt and withdrawn again, and she knew his focus was back with the mission, not this inconvenient female who had complicated his life for five days. 'Goodbye, Averil.' And then he was gone. She waited for ten heartbeats, then dragged the heavy navy wool Guernsey Ferris had given her over her head, making sure her collar and cuffs were tucked well inside. She stuffed her braid down inside it, then wrapped her head in the brown bandana he had found and blew out the lamp.

She knew the way over the slope of the hill now and she ran, higher than the route Luc would have taken moments before. There was jarring pain in her foot when she stubbed her toe on a rock and she swallowed a yelp, hopped a few steps, then fell into a gorse bush, its thick prickly arms enveloping her in a wicked embrace. She hissed curses between her teeth until she was free and then stumbled along, picking tiny spears out of her hands and arms, until she found herself above the small group on the beach.

They were intent on loading the pilot gig and Ferris was where he had said he would be, in the water, holding the nose of the boat steady. Averil walked into the surf beyond the circle of light and crept back to him until he was between her and the beach.

'In you get,' he hissed as the group turned to pick up the weapons that had not yet been loaded. He boosted her up, over the side, and she fell on to the bottom boards. Her ribs found the rowing benches on the way and she clenched her teeth to stop herself crying out. She was going to have a fine set of bruises in the morning.

'Hold it still, Ferret, for Gawd's sake,' someone called as the gig rocked. Averil caught her breath and curled into as small a ball as she could, right up in the prow.

'Crab got me toe,' the man called back. 'Come on then, mates, I've got it and I'm ruddy freezing me wedding tackle off, standing 'ere.'

The boat swayed and rocked as the crew climbed in, muttering and pushing as they got themselves into their rowing positions, the men not at the oars wedged down at the rowers' feet. Ferris heaved himself on board and sat down, his dripping wet legs draped over Averil's back. With the rest of the crew facing away from them no one could see her; unless she moved or spoke, she was safe.

What she was not, was comfortable. It was necessary to remind herself whose idea this was, because she found it was all too easy to blame Luc for the discomforts of his pilot gig. The trip seemed interminable; her position was cramped, her feet were stuck in the cold water that washed over splintery boards and the little boat seemed dangerously low in the water as it powered through the waves. Every now and again water slapped over the side, drenching her.

What was worse was the waiting once they had got into position. She wriggled so hard that Ferris let her sit up and peer around, but his horny hand pushed down on her head the moment the men began to settle themselves for the wait, turning on the rowing benches to get more comfortable.

They seemed to be in the shelter of some rocks that rose like a jagged crest from the sea, but despite the natural breakwater the pilot gig rocked with the swell, and Averil told herself, over and over, that she did not suffer from seasickness. Not one little bit.

The men were quiet, for sound travelled great distances over water. But Luc was talking, his voice a murmur, barely discernible over the noise of the waves hitting the rocks. Averil could not hear what he was saying, but she felt soothed by it, encouraged. He was calm, so she was, too. *A little touch of Harry in the night,* she thought, recalling her Shakespeare—King Henry walking amongst the camp fires as his troops waited for dawn and the great battle against the French.

She must have dozed as she huddled at Ferris's feet because the whisper from the men took her by surprise. 'The light! He's signalling.' She wriggled round and peered over the edge of the gig and there to the north-east a pinprick of light flashed on and off, on and off, then swung back and forth. Then it was gone for the space of perhaps ten seconds before the pattern was repeated. The men shuffled and bent down, she saw the flash of starlight on metal as weapons were handed around and heard the click as pistols were primed.

Then all there was to do was wait, and now the anticipation in the pilot gig was tangible and her mouth was dry and her heart pounded so much that she did not hear when the order was given. The men fitted the oars back into the rowlocks and began to propel the boat out from the shelter of the rocks.

As they slid into open water she saw the brig, sails dark against the slightly lighter sky, the bow wave a froth of white showing its speed. '*Go!*' Luc said and the gig shot forwards, turned and angled in on the other vessel. She thought they would be rammed, then that they would plough into the side of the ship, but Luc brought her round so they slid alongside with scarcely a thump. Ferris flung himself up, his feet trampling on her as he lashed the ropes to the brig. All along the side other arms were working, heaving ropes, making fast. The pilot gig was tethered, riding alongside as the brig forged onwards. And no voice shouted from on deck. They had achieved surprise, Averil realised and started breathing again.

Luc stood up and she saw him clearly for the first time: a silhouette reaching for the ropes. *Leading from the front,* she thought with a surge of pride that killed the fear for a moment. The men scrambled after him in ferocious silence and then she and Ferris were alone on the tossing gig.

'Check all the ropes,' he whispered. 'And keep checking. Get everything together and bundle it into that net, ready to swing up. You got the pistol?'

There was a shout from on deck, the sound of gunfire, a scream, shouted orders. Chaos. *Luc*... 'Yes,' she said and pulled it from her waistband. 'But you take it. Someone might need it. Watch his back, Ferris, please.'

'You call me Ferret, miss. You're one of us. Yeah, I'll watch your man's back for ye.'

He was gone, swarming up the side like his namesake

after a rabbit, and Averil was left in the tossing boat with no idea what was happening above. She got to her feet, was thrown down, crawled, flinched as shots rang out above and voices yelled. Her hands groped until she had collected up everything that was left. A long tube made of some hard material must contain the charts, she supposed. She stuffed it all into the net and tied the neck tight.

A man screamed, there was a splash. More yelling. Her foot found something sharp that she had missed: a cutlass. With it tight in her left hand she worked along the gig, testing each rope, each knot, as though they tethered Luc and his men to life.

A pistol cracked, the brig lost way and they were wallowing, so suddenly that for a moment it was like the awful, endless second when the *Bengal Queen* hit the rocks. The fighting had stopped. Averil shifted the cutlass into her right hand and stared up. Who was she going to see, looking down from the rail?

Then a voice roared, 'Ferris, what the hell are you doing up here?' and she sagged on to a rowing bench in relief. There was the sound of Ferret's voice, making excuses, she supposed, and then the wiry little man came scrambling down the ropes.

'All's well. Nobbut a few scratches all round and a hole in Tom Patch's shoulder and that's just an in-and-out,' he said, as a rope came over the side and he lashed the net to it. 'You better hold on tight to this, miss, and get pulled up with it. And keep yer 'ead down when you get on deck—Cap'n's fit to be tied. 'E says you're to stick with me and keep out of the way or he'll leave you in the gig and cut the lines.'

'He doesn't mean it,' Averil said and saw the glint of white as Ferret rolled his eyes.

'Ha! Most likely drop me over instead. Up you go.'

It was worse than being swung on board the *Bengal Queen* in the bo'sun's chair. Averil clung like a monkey and landed on the deck in a jumble of netting and sharp objects, rolled clear and stood up as Ferret came over the side to attack the bundle and free the weapons.

'Where is he?' she panted, looking round. They had lit a couple of lanterns and in the swaying light she could see that the deck of the brig was crowded. The original crew was huddled around the foremast with three of Luc's men systematically tying their hands and feet and removing hidden weapons. The rest of the men were moving about the small ship with a purposeful air of getting themselves familiar with its workings and she could see Potts at the wheel, feet braced, face calm, transformed from cook to helmsman.

'Cap'n's below in the cabin getting them papers safe.' Ferret dug the chart roll out. 'Be calling for this any minute, I expect—you want to take that down to 'im, miss?'

'Not in the slightest,' Averil said with complete truth, 'but I might as well get it over with.'

'Bark's worse than 'is bite,' Ferret said as he tidied the net away.

'He shot the last person who upset him, I hear,' she muttered as she made her way along the sloping deck and down the steep ladder.

Luc was scribbling on a piece of paper, his head bent over a table spread with charts. In the corner a red-headed man sat scowling in the light of the swaying lantern, his hands tied to the arms of the chair. 'Take this up to Potts,' Luc said, and pushed the note across the table without looking up. 'Tell him to hold that heading until told otherwise.'

'Aye, aye, Captain,' Averil said as she snatched the paper, dumped the chart roll on the table and beat a hasty retreat.

'Then get back down here!' he roared after her.

She had to face the music sooner or later, she thought, as she climbed down the ladder again. Better down there and not on deck in full view, and hearing, of the crew.

But Luc's attention was elsewhere when she peered round the cabin door again, so she slid in and perched in a corner.

'We're smuggling, that's all,' the red-haired man protested. It sounded like a continuing argument. 'Picking up lace and brandy.'

'I am sure you were.' A cupboard door in the bulkhead swung open on its hinges to reveal an empty interior. Luc studied an oilskin package in his hand, then slit the seals. 'Paid with by this, presumably.'

'Don't know anything about that,' the man said, shifting in his bonds. 'Private letters, those. Mr—er, the gentleman who hires us said they were letters to relatives in France. Personal stuff. I wouldn't dream of looking,' he added with unconvincing righteousness.

'Indeed?' Averil shivered at the cold disbelief in Luc's voice as he spread the papers open on top of the charts. 'They are certainly in French. What an interest his Continental relatives must have in naval affairs. Ship movements, provisioning, rates of sickness, armaments, prizes taken...' He read on. 'Rumours of plans for changes at Plymouth. Interesting—I hadn't heard about those.'

He looked up. That wolf's smile had the same effect on the other man as it had on Averil the first time he had used it on her. 'Treason, Mr Trethowan, that is what this is. You'll hang for it, along with your anonymous gentleman. Unless you cooperate, of course. I might be able to do something for you if I had names to bargain with, otherwise...' He spread his hands in a gesture of helplessness and smiled that smile again.

'He'll kill me. He's got influence, a tame admiral.'

'So have I—and the First Lord of the Admiralty trumps your man's cousin any day. It *is* his cousin, isn't it?'

'If you know it all, why ask me?' The red-haired man hunched a resentful shoulder, then winced as it made the cord dig into his wrist.

'Who else on the islands is involved in this?'

'No one, I swear. That interfering Governor is suspicious—had the brig searched last week, arrested my bo'sun on some trumped-up charge the day before yesterday—and his men are asking questions.'

So, the Governor is in the clear, Averil thought. That would make things easier for Luc.

'Any more papers on board? I'll have the vessel stripped down in any case, but it'll go better for you if you hand it all over now.'

'Nothing. I've got stuff in my house, though.' The man seemed eager to talk now. Averil eyed him with distaste—he had known exactly what he was carrying to pay for those French luxury goods. 'I'll give it all to you, if you'll save my neck.'

'I'm sure you will. And when we come alongside the Frenchman, you'll act as though nothing is wrong or you'll get a knife in the ribs and won't have to worry about the hangman at all.' Luc got to his feet, went out to the foot of the steps and shouted up, 'Two men, down here, now!'

When Trethowan was bundled out Luc turned, finally, to look at Averil. His expression did not soften in the slightest from the way he had looked at the traitor. 'And your excuse for being here is what, exactly?'

'You were a man down.' She wanted to wriggle back against the bulkhead and vanish, but it was solid against her shoulders. Luc neither raised his voice nor came any closer, but her mouth had gone dry and her pulse was pattering as though he had shouted threats at her. 'If I took Ferret's place in the gig then he could come up on deck and fight. I gave him the pistol as well, so you had one more weapon.'

'Very noble,' Luc said.

'There is no need to be sarcastic,' Averil snapped. 'I couldn't bear being stuck back there, not knowing what was happening. But I wouldn't have come if I hadn't been able to do something helpful.'

'Helpful!' The change from cool sarcasm to a roar of fury had her jerking back so violently that her head banged on the wood behind her. 'Do you call shredding my nerves helpful? I saw Ferret, asked him what the devil he was doing on deck and he said you were in that damned gig and I nearly throttled the little rodent. We still have a French brig to capture. You will stay down here. You will not so much as put your nose above deck until I send for you. Is that clear?'

Chapter Ten

What did I expect? To be welcomed with open arms and to be told I am a heroine? 'Yes.' Averil nodded. 'Yes, I promise to stay below deck. Is anyone wounded? Ferret said something about Tom Patch's shoulder. I could dress that if there are any medical supplies.'

'Have a look round,' Luc said as he stuffed the papers into the breast of his coat and strode out. 'And if you find anything incriminating, let me know.'

'How am I supposed to do that without putting my head out?' Averil enquired of the unresponsive door panels. Oh, well, it could have been a lot worse, she supposed. At least no one was seriously hurt and Luc could have been even more angry. It occurred to her after a moment's thought that he was probably more furious than he appeared, but was controlling it well. She could only hope that the fight to capture the French brig would take the edge off his temper.

She began to search the cabin systematically and found several cupboards built into the woodwork. None of them contained any sinister papers, which was a disappointment, but she did find a workmanlike medical kit rolled up in waxed cloth.

'You all right, miss?' Ferret poked his nose round the door, then sidled in. 'Thought I'd keep out of sight a bit.'

'Could you tell the captain that I have found a medical case and if someone could bring me some water and send anyone who is hurt down I will see what I can do for them?'

'I'll do that, if 'e don't throw me overboard on sight.' He vanished and a few minutes later Tom Patch arrived with a bucket in one hand and the other thrust into his bloodstained shirt.

Averil had been brought up to deal with far nastier injuries amongst the servants or sustained by her father or brothers on hunting expeditions, although Tom was reluctant to take off his shirt and show his wound to a lady.

'Don't make a fuss,' she said as she poured water into a bowl. 'I had to dig a bullet out of my brother once when the doctor couldn't be found.' Actually it was buckshot in the buttocks, the result of drunken horseplay. Still, bathing and bandaging a simple bullet hole was easy enough, and it kept her mind off Luc's scathing tongue.

'That's better, miss, thank you.' Tom got to his feet. 'Better get back up top, we'll be up with them at any moment, I reckon.'

Averil discovered that she could obey Luc's instructions and still catch a glimpse of what was going on by sitting on the second step down. It was frustrating, for all she could see was legs, but she could hear orders being given and listen to Luc's voice.

When it happened, it all happened at once. The brig slowed and came around. There was a hail, the red-headed man answered in poor French, then there was a shouted exchange and the brig lost more way. She almost tumbled down the steps with the bump as the small ships came together with a grinding of fenders and, suddenly Luc shouted, 'Board them!'

Gunfire, the clash of steel on steel, shouts in French and English. Averil gripped the steps in an effort to stop herself bobbing up to see. But if Luc saw her he would be distracted, or think he had to protect her; it was her duty to stay here, she told herself. Once being dutiful had been second nature, now it was something she had to struggle to achieve. Averil held on and prayed.

She did not have long to wait. The gunfire ceased and the voice she could hear clearly was Luc's, in French and then English, giving orders. Averil unclenched her reluctant fingers and went down to the cabin. She was seated at the table, rewinding bandages with mechanical precision when the door opened.

'There you are.' Luc came in and closed the door behind him, then leaned back against it like a man falling on to a soft feather bed, eyes closed. 'Come here.'

So now he was going to shout at her. Averil put down the gauze and went to stand in front of him. 'Is everything all right? Did you get what you needed?'

'Everything.' He kept his eyes closed. 'We got their orders, before they had a chance to throw them overboard, we took the captain and the officers unharmed. *Je te...* I have the proofs.' His educated English accent had changed. He had been speaking and thinking in French, she realised.

'*Très bon,*' she ventured and his lips quirked. Her accent was probably laughable. 'What happens now?'

'This.' He opened his eyes and looked at her and she saw the fire in them, the life, the fierce energy. The desire.

'Luc?' It came out as a quaver.

'Are you afraid of me?' He came upright with a speed that took her unawares, caught her in his arms, turned her and had her pressed against the door before she could say another word. Her nostrils were filled with the scent of man and fresh sweat and black powder smoke; her body quivered with an anticipation she could not control. 'Because you should be. I want to take you here, up against this door. Tell me *no*. Tell me no, *now.*'

One hand was in her hair, the other palmed her breast with possessive urgency. His mouth on her neck was hot, fierce, and her blood responded, all the tension and fear and triumph of the night merging into a fire that consumed the last shreds of restraint.

This is what I want: this, him, now. Nothing else was real, nothing else mattered except the moment, and the next few moments, in Luc's arms. *My hero, my man.*

Her hands were in his hair, trying to bring his mouth to hers, but he was intent on dragging her clothing off and she vanished, blinded and struggling, into the thick wool to emerge, naked from the waist up. She blinked in the lantern's light as she pushed her hair from her face so she could see Luc, reach for him. But he dropped his hands and stepped back, pale under his tan.

'Oh, my God.' He stared at her as if he was seeing her naked body for the first time, then lifted both hands and cupped her breasts, moving close so he could look down at them, as though they were treasures he had found and could not quite believe. Her flesh felt heavy and swollen in his palms, but he did not move more than his thumbs, caressing slowly across the hard, aching points of her nipples.

'Luc.' It was a whisper, but it brought that deep grey gaze to meet her eyes. 'What…what do I do?' Her aunt's lecture on Marital Duties had not included this quivering in her belly, the ache between her legs, the desire and the need. It had included nothing that did not involve lying on her back in the dark and submitting to embarrassing and probably painful intimacies.

His eyes went dark and his hands still and then he released her, turned, slowly, and dropped his hands to the chart table, bent over it like a man in pain.

'Nothing. You do nothing,' Luc said and heard his voice harsh with barely suppressed fury that was directed at himself, not at her. She was probably ruined. Probably. He could not take her until he had tried, and failed, to rescue her from the consequences of all this. He had made her his responsibility, fool that he was.

Behind him Averil was silent for the time it took her to draw in two, very audible, breaths. Then she said, 'Why are you angry? You do not expect a virgin to know what to do, do you?'

She was always thinking—when he allowed her to and was not addling her senses with lovemaking—always, always, courageous. 'I am angry at myself,' he said, wrenching his voice back under control. 'Get dressed before I lose my mind again and forget that you are an innocent.'

'My friend Dita says that men become amorous after danger or excitement. It seemed rather strange to me, when she said it.' Averil's voice faded, then strengthened, and he guessed she had pulled her clothes back over her head. 'Is that what it is?'

'My inability to control myself?' Luc asked. The lines on the chart under his spread hands came back into focus. He was supposed to be sailing this damn brig, and getting it and the French prize and the captured papers back safely, not ravishing virgins in the cabin.

'You seem quite capable of controlling yourself,' Averil said as she came round on his right side and sat down on the edge of the bunk. Her voice was steady, but one look at her white face and the slashes of colour on her cheeks told him that she had sat down because her legs were about to give way. 'Eventually,' she added. For a hideous moment he thought she was going to cry and his stomach, already knotted with guilt and lust, gave a stab of pain.

'You give me an opportunity to excuse myself?' Suddenly it felt as though speaking in French would be easier, for him, but from her accent it seemed unlikely that she would be fluent enough to follow what he was struggling to understand himself. 'I was fired up. I had been fighting and we had won. And, yes, some primitive creature inside me needed to take a woman—*my* woman—in triumph.' *My woman. She is* not *my woman. I do not have a woman. I will not think of her like that. I will not care.*

She was silent and he wanted to drop his eyes from that clear, troubled gaze, but that would be cowardice. 'I had been frightened for you, and angry because you had put me in a position where I might not have been able to protect you. I required, I suppose, to assert mastery and that is one step from forcing you.' *Which is no doubt why I feel sick. That and aching frustration.*

'*Your* woman?' Averil said as though he had not spoken those last sentences.

He could not unsay them. Nor, he realised, did he want to. He wanted her, wanted to be the man who took her virginity. He wanted to keep her and teach her…everything. 'You are not anyone's,' he said at last, making the effort to behave like an English gentleman. 'You are your own woman.'

'Not according to the law,' she pointed out with painful clarity. 'An unmarried woman belongs to her father in every practical way.'

'You are of age.' What was he arguing for? He wanted to make her his.

'I have an obligation,' Averil said. 'A duty. And I have been forgetting that.' And this time a tear did roll down her cheek. Appalled, unable to move, to touch her, Luc watched her dash it away with an impatient hand. No others followed it. 'I don't know—is this, whatever *this* is—' she waved a hand vaguely, encompassing him, the cabin, her own disordered clothing '—is it usual? Is this why unmarried girls are chaperoned so fiercely?'

'I do not know, I have never experienced this before,' he snapped and saw her shock at his tone. 'I have never dallied with an innocent.'

'Oh. Dalliance.' She gave a light laugh and turned her head. He could no longer read her face. 'A pretty word. If that is all it is, then there is nothing to worry about, is there? I must just learn to flirt and not take this all so seriously. Why did you come down here, just now?'

'Why—? Don't you want to discuss this?'

He wanted to, even if she did not. He needed to understand what she felt for him and what it meant.

Averil shrugged, an elegant turn of her shoulder reminding him that she was a lady, despite her seaman's clothing and her tangled hair. 'There is nothing to discuss, is there? We have controlled ourselves, you have remembered that you have a ship to navigate, I that I am betrothed. Don't you recall why you came down?'

'I came to look at the charts,' he said through gritted teeth. How was this little innocent tying him in knots? It was like being outwitted by a kitten, only to discover it was a well-disguised panther.

'Hadn't you better do so?' she asked. 'I don't want

to hit the rocks again.' She said it lightly, but he saw the shadows of controlled fear behind her eyes. Despite what had happened the last time she had been on board a ship she had stowed away on the frail pilot gig and then thrown herself into a sea fight. There was nothing wrong with her courage, that was certain.

'We're in deep water now and well clear here of any rocks. I was expecting to sail for the mainland, but now I know I can trust the Governor I can go to him on St Mary's—which will mean we can lay hands on our man without fear of him getting wind of this and escaping. I need to find somewhere for the brigs to hover while I'm rowed into Hugh Town in the pilot gig.'

He smoothed the rolled sheets under his hands and tried to focus. 'I will take you in, too, and leave you with the Governor's wife.' Yes, there was the best place to leave the brigs, in the channel between St Mary's and Gugh. It was a short row into Porthcressa beach and he could send the men back to man the brigs and guard the prisoners until the Governor could get the navy out to them.

'What will you tell her?' Averil swung round, her expression tense.

'That I found you on the beach and locked you in the old isolation hospital away from the men. I am sure she will want to help you. As far as the outside world is concerned there is no need to tell even that. I imagine that there has been enough confusion for us to conveniently gloss over the fact that you were not picked up the morning after the wreck.'

'You mean I should lie?'

'Yes, of course you should lie! At least, I suggest most strongly that you edit the truth. Do you want to be ruined?' *Say yes,* he thought. *Say the world and your virtue are well lost in my arms.*

'No,' she said, looking at him quizzically. 'No, of course not. May I go up on deck now?'

'I don't see why not. The prisoners are all down in the hold.' He turned his back and reached for a rule, pleased to find his hand quite steady. Out of the corner of his eye he saw Averil get to her feet and go to the door. For a moment he wondered if she would speak, but it closed behind her, leaving him alone with the memory of her silence.

Averil climbed up to the deck, found herself a corner out of the way of the crew and watched the French ship, a ghostly shadow that kept station beside them, while she waited for her body to stop trembling and the ache of desire to subside. Lord, how she wanted him—beyond all reason and certainly beyond all decency.

She made herself focus on the ships and what they were doing. The brigs did not seem to need many hands, which was fortunate, with prisoners to guard and allowance to be made for men wounded.

'You all right, miss?' Tom Patch appeared beside her, an unnerving sight with his bloodstained shirt.

'Yes, thank you. Are you? Was anyone else hurt?'

'I'm fine now, thanks to you, miss. And there's nothing much wrong, just the few of 'em with the odd scratch and bang. Cap'n knows what he's about, I'll say that for him, for all that he's a hard devil.'

'Is he? Hard, I mean? I thought all naval officers would be like that.'

'Yeah.' Patch leaned against the mast and sucked his teeth in thought. 'They're all for discipline, but he don't rely just on that, see?' She shook her head, not understanding. 'He can relax, let out the rope, like, because he knows, and we knows, that if we don't come to heel when he tugs it then there's hell to pay. And I gets the feeling that he didn't much care what happened to him, just so long as he could prove himself right and get the bug—um, get the traitors.'

'It was a bit more than that, surely? They had taken his career away. His honour. They could have had him shot. He had a lot to lose and to prove.'

'Aye,' Patch agreed. 'Dead men walking, the lot of us.'

'Not any more,' she said. 'Thanks to the captain.'

'You going to marry him, miss?'

'What? No! I am betrothed to someone else.'

'Oo-er,' Patch said and she could hear he was grinning from his voice. 'He's going to be pleased about all this then, your gentleman.'

'I was not the captain's mistress, that was just a pretence to…to keep me safe.'

That provoked a muffled snort. 'Pull the other one, miss, it's got bells on. I've seen him kiss you. And I've seen him look at you.'

'Captain d'Aunay is a very good actor,' she said stiffly and had to listen to Patch chuckling to himself as he walked away.

At least this motley crew were not going to be acquainted with Lord Bradon! Could she get away with this editing of the truth? Would her future husband guess that she had kissed another man with passion, that he had caressed her, pushed her to the point of reckless surrender? He would know that she had been kissed; Luc had been very confident that he was the first and she supposed she had been getting better at it. That could be explained as the result of flirtations, not anything more serious, she supposed, and frowned into the darkness as the lights of Hugh Town on St Mary's, the largest of the islands, came closer.

But it was not right to deceive the man she was contracted to, the man who would be the father of her children. The man she would spend the remainder of her life with. Should she confess to Andrew Bradon? The thought made her feel sick. She did not think she had even the words to describe what had happened, had *not* happened, let alone the will-power to speak of it to a complete stranger who was not going to be pleased about it, however tolerant he was.

Luc's deep voice behind her made her start. He had come up on deck without her hearing him and was giving the orders to bring them in closer to the beach below the Garrison, high above the town, the place where Yestin the fisherman had signalled to them. That seemed like days ago, not hours.

The men were working the sails, Luc hailed the French brig and it altered course with them. The wind sent her hair whipping across her face.

'There you are.' He leaned against the mast as Tom Patch had done. 'Are you cold?'

'No.' It was not the stiff breeze that made her shiver.

'Tired, then? You can go below and lie down and rest for half an hour. I won't disturb you.'

'I want to watch. I want to see this brought to an end now I have come so far with it.'

'Yes, for you this will be the end of the matter,' he agreed, not looking at her.

'I am sorry I was such a nuisance. It must have been a distraction you could have ill afforded,' she said. It was like speaking to a stranger. She kept her voice polite and formal.

'A distraction, yes, indeed. A nuisance? Never. This

will soon become part of a bad dream, part of the nightmare of the shipwreck, and then you will gradually forget.'

'I don't think I could forget Ferret,' she said with an attempt at a joke.

'No, probably not,' Luc agreed with a chuckle. He put his arm around her shoulder and gave her a quick, uncharacteristic, hug. 'Almost there now, Miss Heydon.'

Averil let herself go with the tug of his arm, let her head rest on his chest for an instant and breathed in salt and black powder smoke and damp wool and, under it, the essence of Luc. Her fingers lay on his sleeve and ached with the effort not to close and hold on. *Don't leave me.*

He moved away after a moment, the urgency of her feelings obviously invisible to him, and she clutched the mast for support. What was she thinking of to be clinging to this man, lusting after him? He had no interest in her beyond physical desire—and he would probably have felt that for any reasonably young and attractive female under these circumstances.

I am betrothed. If she repeated that over and over she might, somehow, convince herself it was real, that the shadowy, faceless man she was going to in London was the one she would spend the rest of her life tied to, not this brave, angry, half-Frenchman.

Chapter Eleven

The men swore under their breath as they took the pilot gig into the long sweep of Porthcressa beach. Averil held on to the sides of the pilot gig and stored the colourful language away. It was the early hours of the morning now, no one was about, so there were virtually no lights to guide them in.

Hugh Town was built straggling along a narrow strip of land between two great bites that the sea had taken out of the island, Luc had explained to her. The Garrison, the high mass of land to the east with the Elizabethan Star Fort planted on top and the encircling walls bristling with cannon, grew from one end of the town and the body of the island from the other.

The far side of the strip of town was where the harbour was, but he would not risk going in there and attracting the attention of the traitor. Who knew what watchers he had who would recognise Trethowan being brought back, a prisoner? Or someone might even know the French captain by sight.

But the shallow water and the lack of lights made

the men twitchy and their mood infected Averil. She was almost jumping out of her skin by the time the keel ground on sand.

'In you go.' Luc dumped her unceremoniously over the side into water that came halfway up her thighs. A wave sloshed with a cold slap at the base of her belly and she bit back the yelp of discomfort. Luc followed her over, then Ferret, his long knife in one hand. The remaining crew pushed the prisoners out, jeering quietly as they floundered in the surf with their hands tied behind them.

'Go back to the brigs,' she heard Luc tell the crew as Ferret prodded the two men up the beach to join her on the dry sand. 'I'll send Yestin out with orders. And, Potts, they are both very nice little brigs and if they are not where I expect them to be I will hunt them, and you, down and there will be no prize money, no pardons and either you will hang or I will disembowel you. Or possibly both. Clear?'

'Aye, aye, Cap'n.' Potts sounded as though he was grinning. The pilot gig vanished into the pre-dawn gloom with a faint splash of oars and Luc urged the two captives towards the dark huddle of the town. 'Up there, to the left. The sally port—Trethowan, you'll know it, I have no doubt.'

The man grunted. Beside him the French captain muttered something, low and fast.

'*Capitaine, je parle français,*' Luc remarked. 'I speak also the dialect of Languedoc,' he added, still in French. 'And any further insult to the lady will result in the removal of your ears. You understand me?'

'*Parfaitement. En effet,* you are a traitor to France.' The man reverted to standard French.

'*Mais non,* your France betrayed my family, murdered my father. I will be a loyal Frenchman still when she returns to sanity.' Luc prodded the captain round a corner beside a looming chapel and the road steepened.

'Ah! Un aristo.' The Frenchman spat.

'Absolutement.' Luc sounded amiable in the face of the insults. Averil trudged up the hill behind him, her wet trousers glued to her legs. They chafed the soft skin of her inner thighs, she was sweating in the heavy Guernsey, the cobbles hurt her bare feet and Luc had forgotten about her with the stimulus of trading insults. She cleared her throat.

'Keep up,' he said over his shoulder. 'It gets darker and steeper here.'

'Good,' she muttered mutinously. 'I needed some exercise.' Just in front of her Ferret gave a snort of laughter, then all four men seemed to vanish into darkness. She baulked at the entrance to the cave, then saw it was simply a narrow way through rocks that lead to the base of a high defensive bank. When she tipped her head back she could see ramparts above her.

'How do we get in?' she asked.

'Quietly.' Luc placed one hand over her mouth. 'There are sentries patrolling the top.'

'How do we get in then?' she repeated, resisting the temptation to either bite or kiss his palm.

'I have a key. Here, Ferret, take it and go first.' The little man vanished into the darkness at the foot of the wall. Luc followed, pushing the prisoners in front of him and Averil, reluctant, brought up the rear.

They were in a narrow twisting stone stairway climbing up through the bank and out by an iron gate that Ferret was holding open, on to a roadway wide enough for a horse and carriage. 'Sentries down there.' He nodded to the left where trees grew thick. And then gestured to the right. 'And I can hear some that way, too.'

'That'll be the guard on the Governor's house. This is where it gets interesting. Don't try to be quiet now or we'll get shot first and questioned afterwards. Just walk along the road so they have plenty of notice we are coming.'

They strode out towards the sounds of voices. Stones crunched underfoot and Ferret began to whistle. Averil smelled wood smoke and bacon. Breakfast. Someone was beginning to cook breakfast. She could eat a horse.

'Who goes there?' The challenge was a shout, then there was the sound of boots approaching at the run.

'Captain Luke d'Aunay of His Majesty's Navy to see the Governor,' Luc said loudly, his accent once more impeccably English. 'With escort and two prisoners.'

'Halt!' A new voice. An officer by the sound of it. A lamp appeared, illuminating black boots, white breeches and a scarlet coat. 'Identify yourself. How the blazes did you get in here?'

'With a key,' Luc stopped and held up a hand to halt them all. 'I have my papers here, if you will permit me?' He reached into his coat, pulled out a slim oilskin package and proffered it. 'Can we discuss this inside? These two are prisoners—one French captain, one English traitor. Their capture needs to be kept quiet.'

The officer looked up from the papers. 'These appear to be in order. Why aren't you in uniform?'

'Clandestine mission, Lieutenant.' There was an edge to his voice that would remind the army man who was the more senior officer.

He doesn't trust us, Averil thought, standing on one leg and rubbing the other dirty, aching foot against the calf while she watched the officer's face. *I don't blame him.*

'Titmuss, Jenkins! Bring them inside under guard until

the Governor has seen these.' They were marched forwards, across a sweep of grass and in through the wide front doors of a house.

Civilisation. Averil looked round at polished wainscots, pictures on the walls, heavy silk curtains drawn against the night, and felt weariness sweep over her. Her filthy bare feet sank blissfully into the deep pile of the rugs.

'Keep them here. Sir George is not going to be pleased, being woken at this hour.'

The silvery chime of a clock struck five. Averil looked with longing at the chairs that lined the walls, then set her feet apart, locked her knees to stop herself swaying and resigned herself to wait. Luc caught her eye and tipped his head slightly towards the guards. He did not want them to realise she was a woman, Averil realised. So, it seemed, did Ferret.

'You lean on me, mate,' he said, standing next to her. 'You're in no state to be standing about.' Averil swayed against him until their shoulders were touching. He slipped one arm surreptitiously around her waist and held on. With a sigh of gratitude she let his wiry, malodorous body support her.

'Wake up.' It was Ferret, an elbow in her ribs. 'Here's 'is nibs.'

A big man in a splendid brocade robe, his grey curls still tousled from removing his nightcap, spoke to the officer in the hallway, then took Luc's papers and scrutinised them.

'Mr Dornay, the poet. I see I have been entertaining you on one of my islands under false pretences, Captain.'

'Sir.' Luc was unapologetic. 'I need to speak to you alone as a matter of urgency.'

'Very well. My study. What are we to do with these four, might I ask?' He studied with disfavour the human flotsam dripping sand and seawater on his rugs.

'The two with their hands tied need securing somewhere apart from each other and where there is absolutely no risk of them communicating with anyone in the town. He—' he pointed at Ferret '—needs breakfast and somewhere to rest while he waits for me. That one...' He leaned towards the Governor and murmured in his ear.

'What? Well, I'll be damned. Very well. Better stay in here then. Foster, close the door, let no one in to disturb this, er...person.'

Luc added something else. 'Yes, yes. Foster, fetch a rug so he...er, they can sit down without ruining the upholstery. Now, let's hear the whole of this.'

The officer went out and reappeared with a rug which he threw over a *chaise,* then Averil found herself alone. The room swayed a little as she stood there, but she found if she went with the motion it took her down on to the *chaise* and that was soft and solid and held a faint trace of perfume. With a sigh she let herself drift. It would all be fine now, she thought. She was safe, Luc knew what to do. Safe...

'A female? George, really, you drag me out of bed and some ungodly hour to ask me to look after some disreputable female—'

'Olivia, please! I beg you to keep your voice down.' The door opened as Averil struggled upright and the Governor came in followed by a tall woman, fully dressed and with an expression that, Averil thought hazily, would stun wasps. Luc brought up the rear and closed the door.

'This is Miss Heydon, Lady Olivia. She was washed up on St Helen's after the shipwreck and, because of the extreme secrecy of my mission, I was unable to bring her over here at once. However, as you may know, there is the old isolation hospital there and Miss Heydon was able to sleep there behind locked doors…'

'To which you hold the key, no doubt, Captain.'

'Madam, Miss Heydon is betrothed to Lord Bradon—'

'But not for much longer, I'll be bound. Look at her!'

Averil struggled to her feet. 'Lady Olivia, I am aware that I must present a most disreputable appearance, but—'

The older woman fixed her with a withering look. 'Have you, or have you not, spent five nights in the company of this man, Miss Heydon?'

'Well, yes, but nothing… I mean, it was all perfectly—'

'Your blushes say it all! George, for you to expect me to lend countenance to Captain Dornay's *amours* is outside of enough. Must I remind you that you have two daughters of an impressionable age? They have already seen and heard things that they should not with the house full of half-drowned persons for days on end and whatever is going on up at the Star Fort with Lavinia's friend—'

'Oh, of course! You will know about Dita!' Averil interrupted her. 'Please, can you tell me who was saved?'

Lady Olivia looked down her nose. 'Dita?'

'Lady Perdita Brooke. She is a particular friend of mine.'

'You know Lady Perdita?' The Governor's wife relaxed a trifle.

Old snob, Averil thought. 'Yes, very well. Please—'

'Lady Perdita was heroically rescued by Viscount Lyndon.' From her expression Lady Olivia obviously approved of Alistair. 'They both left for the mainland yesterday along with most of the other survivors.'

'Thank goodness.' Averil sat down again with a thump.

'And Mrs Bastable, my chaperon? And the Chatterton twins? Daniel and Callum?'

The room went very quiet. 'Mr Daniel Chatterton was drowned. His body was recovered and his brother has taken it back to the mainland for burial,' the Governor said. 'I will have my secretary give you a list of those saved, those known to be dead and those still missing.'

'Thank you,' she said, the schooled politeness forming the words for her while her chest ached with the need to weep. Daniel dead? All that fun and intelligence and personality, gone in an instant. Poor, poor Callum. What a tragic homecoming for him. And Daniel was betrothed—Callum would have that awful news to break to a woman who had been waiting years for her lover to return to her.

'Miss Heydon should rest,' Luc said. 'She has received bad news and she is exhausted. We have been at sea all night.'

'And why it was necessary for her to accompany you out to sea, I really cannot understand,' Lady Olivia interjected.

'And why should you?' Luc said with a smile that would have frozen water. 'All this can wait, surely? Miss Heydon should retire. She will need a bath, some food—'

'Kindly allow me to know what is required for female guests in this house, Captain Dornay or d'Aunay or whatever your name is. Miss Heydon, if you will accompany me, please.' It was an order. Averil did not miss the point that she was a *female,* not a *lady,* in Lady Olivia's eyes. Friendship with Dita might save her from a room in the garrets with the servants, but the Governor's wife had not forgotten the scandalous circumstances of her rescue.

It was an effort not to seek out Luc's eyes, not to send a message—*help me, take me back to our island and make love to me*—but pride stiffened her spine and allowed her to stand, smile at her reluctant hostess and bid the gentlemen good-night as though she was a house party guest.

'Good night, Sir George. Good night, Captain d'Aunay.' She pronounced his surname with care, not that the older woman seemed to notice the implied reproof. She wanted to ask when she would see Luc again, but that would raise Lady Olivia's suspicions even higher. 'Thank you, Lady Olivia.' If a curtsy had not been ridiculous in damp cotton trousers and a smelly Guernsey she would have produced one before she followed her hostess out.

'I will send a maid to you.' Lady Olivia seemed to unbend a trifle now they were away from the men. 'Goodness knows what we can do about clothing. We have had the house full of survivors for days, none of them with so much as a pocket handkerchief to their names, of course.'

A blonde lady in her mid-thirties appeared round the corner, a list in one hand. 'Oh, there you are, Olivia.' She peered at Averil, then raised her eyebrows. 'Another survivor from the *Bengal Queen*?'

'Indeed, Sister. Miss Heydon has fallen into most undesirable company—'

'But at least she is alive,' the other woman said, her warmth reaching Averil like a comforting touch. 'I am so glad for you, my dear.' She held out her hand. 'I am Lavinia Gordon, Sir George's sister.'

'I was just saying that I have no idea what to do about suitable clothing,' her sister-in-law interjected.

'I am sure I have something I can spare—we are much of a size, I suspect. If you tell the maid to come and see me, Sister, I will put out some clothes for Miss Heydon.'

She glanced down at the shocking trousers. 'Do tell me, are those as comfortable as they look?'

'They chafe rather when wet, but the freedom is a revelation, Miss Gordon. Thank you so much for offering to lend me clothing.' Beside her, Lady Olivia tutted under her breath and urged her along the corridor.

'The next door on the left, Miss Heydon. I will send the maid along.' Averil found herself in a medium-sized bedchamber. Not a garret then. Perhaps Lady Olivia would unbend still further when she saw Averil properly dressed.

Lord, but she was tired. And hungry. And thoroughly uncomfortable with damp clothes and dirty, tangled hair. As she thought it there was a tap at the door and a maid came in.

'Good morning, miss. I am Waters, miss. There's hot water and a bath on its way up. Would you like some breakfast afterwards? Miss Gordon said you probably would, before you go to sleep. Her woman's bringing a nightgown and fresh linen and a gown.' She ran out of words and stood, mouth slightly open, staring at Averil.

'Thank you, Waters. I would like some breakfast very much. I expect you have been very busy with all the survivors brought here.'

'Yes, miss. None of the ladies had trousers though, miss.'

'Er, no, probably not. But I had to wear something, you see.' There was a knock at the door and Averil made a hasty retreat behind the screens in the corner while thumps and the sound of pouring water heralded the arrival of the bath.

When she looked out there was another maid spreading a nightgown on the bed while Waters tucked items away in the dresser. 'Here you are, miss. You'll need some help with your hair, I expect.'

Averil shed her damp, sandy clothing with a sigh of relief. 'Can these be washed and returned to Captain d'Aunay's man, Ferris? He was sent to the kitchens for some food, but I don't know where he'll be now.'

'Oh, yes, miss.' Waters waited while Averil settled with a sigh of blissful relief in the warm water, then produced soap and a sponge and left Averil to wash herself while she poured water over her hair and knelt to try to rinse out sand, salt and tangles.

It was pure bliss, despite the frequent tugs and tweaks at her hair. Averil lathered up the sponge and washed her hands and arms slowly, luxuriously, as she relaxed. And then she reached her body. The scented bubbles slid down the curves of her bosom and she looked at them as they crested the rosy nipples that peaked at the touch of the suds, ran over the slight swell of her belly, down to the point where the water veiled the dark curls. Her thighs rose above the surface, smooth and pink, marred with bruises and abrasions, and the innocent pleasure she was taking in the bath turned into something else entirely.

While she had been unconscious Luc had washed her naked body. His hands had lathered the strong soap that she had smelt on her skin, his eyes had rested on her breasts as his fingers had washed away the salt and the sand and cleaned her cuts. When she had woken she had felt clean—all over, so his attentions had not stopped with limbs and breasts—and yet, somehow, everything else that had happened, the shock and the grief and the fear, had stopped her thinking about the intimacy of the way he had cared for her.

She could feel the blush colouring her face and hoped the maid patiently working on her hair had not noticed.

The realisation should have been mortifying, yet it was not, and she wondered why. Because she had come to trust him? Because she knew with a deep certainty that he had nursed her with integrity and not to gain gratification from her helpless body?

It was more than that, Averil realised as she started to stroke the sponge over her legs. It was erotic, and just thinking about Luc's hands on her body, slick with soap, was arousing her. It had never occurred to her that bathing might be part of lovemaking, but the thought of him kneeling here, beside the tub, produced a soft moan.

'Oh, I am sorry, Miss Heydon! It is such a tangle I don't know that I can do it without pulling a bit.'

'Don't worry, Waters, it was not you. I have so many bruises, I knocked one, that is all.' *I must stop thinking about him bathing me,* she thought as the maid, reassured, went back to tugging the comb thorough her hair. She made an effort and the phantom touch of Luc's hands ceased. *What would it be like to bathe him? Oh, my goodness!* Averil made a grab for her toes and washed them with quite unnecessary vigour. It did not diminish the image of his naked body under her hands, slick with water and soap.

What would it feel like to run her hands into the dark hair on his chest, to follow it down as it arrowed into the water? Would he like it if she touched him there? Of course he would, he was a man. Very much a man.

And I am straying into very dangerous waters. Averil dropped the sponge and wriggled her toes to rinse them. Luc d'Aunay was not for her and Andrew, Lord Bradon, was waiting for her in London. Or, more accurately, he was mourning her; she must send a message as soon as possible

'There, miss. All clean and no tangles. We'd better be getting you dry and into bed before the food arrives.'

'Yes, of course.' Averil got to her feet, dripping, and reached for the towel the maid held out. She had washed Luc from her life as she had rinsed the last traces of soap from her skin. She was going to be Lady Bradon and she was going to start thinking like a viscountess from this moment on. Her throat tightened. It was not going to be as easy as arriving on his doorstep to universal relief that she was not drowned.

Chapter Twelve

'If you feel sufficiently revived, perhaps we should discuss our tactics, Miss Heydon.' The Governor put down his tea cup and the atmosphere in the drawing room changed subtly.

She had slept until woken in the early evening, dressed in her borrowed gown of dusky pink, had her hair coiffed and had walked in Miss Gordon's silk slippers down to join the party for dinner.

Her reception had been gratifying. Lady Olivia nodded approval, Miss Gordon beamed at her and Sir George enquired kindly if she had slept well and felt rested. Luc had looked at her, expressionless, then bowed over her hand with what she could not help but feel was excessive politeness for a small family dinner. She had been entertaining the fantasy that he would be bowled over by the sight of her, elegantly gowned, her hair up, her femininity restored.

But of course, he needed no prompting to think of her as female. He knew, none better, that she was a woman. But it was galling, despite her resolution, to be treated to such comprehensive indifference. Obviously, dressed and respectable, she was no longer attractive to him.

Now she felt them all looking at her. 'Tactics, Sir George?'

'For mitigating the consequences of your belated rescue,' he said.

'I have been thinking about it,' she said with perfect truth. She had thought of nothing else since she had woken and very uncomfortable her reflections had been.

'Indeed,' he said before she could continue. 'And Lady Olivia and I think the best thing would be for us to say nothing publicly about the time you have been…missing. I can write to Lord Bradon regretting that the fact that I was unaware of your betrothal. We will tell him that you have been unconscious for several days being cared for in a house elsewhere in the Isles. Both those statements are perfectly true and will give the impression that you have been with some respectable family all the time. What do you say to that?'

He was so obviously pleased with his solution, and so positive about it, that Averil found herself nodding her head before she realised what she was doing. Then her conscience caught up with her.

'No! I am sorry, Sir George, but I cannot lie by omission and I cannot involve you and others in your household in a deception.'

'Well, in that case,' Lady Olivia said, 'there is only one thing to be done. Captain d'Aunay must marry you.'

Luc's *'Non'* beat her own emphatic 'No!' by a breath. The other three stared at them.

Averil made herself breathe slowly in the long, difficult silence that followed. She felt as though she had been punched in the chest. Of course she did not want him to marry her, but he might at least have hesitated before repudiating the idea with such humiliating vigour! It was incredible how much that sharp negative hurt.

'I have matrimonial plans,' Luc said when it was obvious that she was not going to speak. His eyes were dark and hard and there was colour on his cheekbones under the tanned skin.

'You are betrothed, Captain? Oh, dear, that does complicate matters.'

'I am not betrothed, Sir George. But I am intending to marry a lady of the *émigré* community. A Frenchwoman. I see no reason why Miss Heydon cannot adopt your most sensible solution.'

'Because it is a lie, as I said.' She lifted her chin a notch and managed not to glare at him. That would have revealed too much of her feelings. 'I am contracted to marry Lord Bradon and I intend to honour that contract. I shall go to him and tell him all.'

'All what?' Lady Olivia demanded.

'That I was washed ashore, found by a group of men on a covert naval mission, protected by their officer and returned safely to your care, ma'am.'

'Safely?' There was no mistaking what the Governor's wife meant.

Averil hung on to the ragged edge of her temper with an effort. 'If you are enquiring if I am a virgin, Lady Olivia, the answer is, yes, I am.' She managed, somehow, to say it in a chilly, but polite, tone of voice.

Miss Gordon gave a gasp and Sir George went red. Luc merely tightened his lips and breathed out, hard. 'I am glad to hear it,' Lady Olivia retorted. 'One only hopes that your betrothed believes you.'

'Of course he will. He is, after all, a gentleman.'

The Governor's wife inclined her head. 'He is certainly that and will have expectations of his wife-to-be.'

'I will call on Lord Bradon,' Luc said. 'He will wish to assure himself of Miss Heydon's treatment.'

'I do not think that would be wise,' Averil said. 'It would make it appear that there was something that needed explanation.'

Luc stared at her profile. He could not read this new Averil. The half-drowned sea nymph, the innocently passionate woman, the boy-girl in her borrowed clothes had all gone and in their place was this elegant young lady. The intelligence was there still, of course, and the courage and downright inconvenient honesty. But those attributes lived in the body of this elegant, angry, beautiful creature he did not know how to reach.

And what had possessed him to snap out that one word? In French, too, which somehow made it worse. A few seconds and he could have been politely supporting Averil. As it was, his reaction had been one of deeply unflattering rejection. He, the last of the d'Aunays, was not going to marry an English merchant's daughter, however well brought up and however elegant her manners, but he could have managed the thing more tactfully.

'I think it would be helpful if I were to speak to Miss Heydon alone.' He had to explain, he could not leave it like this. He no longer had any responsibility for her, he could stop being concerned for her—thank the heavens—but even so, this must be ended properly.

'I hardly think—'

'If they were to stroll in the gardens, Sister?' Miss Gordon intervened. 'I could stay on the terrace as chaperone. The evening is balmy and the fresh air would be pleasant.'

'Very well,' Lady Olivia conceded.

Luc did not wait for her approval. He was on his feet, extending a hand to Averil, even as he said, 'Thank you,

Miss Gordon. Miss Heydon? It seems a very clement evening. It would be best if we could agree a mutually satisfactory approach to this, after all.'

'Of course.' Averil got up with grace, as though he had asked her to dance at a ball. 'Thank you, Miss Gordon.'

It was not until they had walked in silence down the length of the path that bisected the long garden that he realised just how angry she was. She turned, slipped her hand from his forearm where it had been resting, and faced him. In the distance, well out of earshot, Miss Gordon strolled up and down the terrace.

'How dare you!'

'Averil, I have explained. You know who I am, what I am. I cannot marry—'

'A merchant's daughter,' she spat.

'An Englishwoman.' Even as he equivocated he felt guilt at not matching her burning honesty.

'That is not what I meant. Of *course* I don't want you to marry me any more than you want to marry me, but could you not have trusted me to refuse? Did you think I want to trap you into marriage?'

'No, I did not think that.' Was that the truth? Why had he been so vehement? It had felt, for a second, almost like fear. Fear of something he did not understand, something that would turn his world on its head. He tried to focus on the important thing, protecting her from the consequences of all this. 'Lord Bradon may not understand. He does not know you as I do.'

'That is most certainly true—no man does!'

'Exactly. Averil, listen to me. He does not need to know about any of this.'

'Yes,' she said slowly. 'Yes, he does. This is the man I have promised to marry. I intend to spend the rest of my life with him and I will, God willing, bear his children. I cannot be anything less than honest with him just because I do not know him.'

He took her by the shoulders and pulled her round so he could see her face in the moonlight. 'You will tell him that I found you naked, that I nursed you for days, that you slept with me in my bed?'

'Certainly.' If he did not know her so well he would have missed the slight shake in her voice. 'It is only right that he knows that I am not quite what he expects me to be. But I am contracted. My father gave his word—'

'You are not a shipload of tea that has been bought and paid for, damn it!' He shook the rigid shoulders under his hands. 'Forget this merchant's obsession with contracts and use some sense. He will reject you out of hand if you tell him all this.'

'I doubt it,' she said, cool as spring water. 'I have a very large dowry and I hope he is able to see beyond his male prejudices and recognise the truth when he hears it. Will you let go of me, please?'

He kept his hands right where they were. 'You know he wants you for your money and yet you will humiliate yourself by confessing all this to him? You talk about a lifetime together, children—do you think *he* thinks about these things?'

'I am sure he thinks about children. This is, whatever you say, a business deal, a partnership with the succession a major factor. Don't tell me that the marriage you are considering will be anything else—a love match, perhaps? You will buy a French bloodline to ally with yours. Would you want your wife to come to you with lies on her tongue?'

She shifted in his grip but he held tight to the slender shoulders. 'Of course I would, if there was nothing serious to confess and if by speaking she ruined everything! Every marriage must contain secrets—and that way lies peace and coexistence. An arranged marriage is not some emotional entanglement.' That was what he wanted. That was safe. No one could hurt your heart and your soul when neither of you cared deeply. He took another deep breath and tried to convince her.

'You are a virgin, you are not carrying my child, I am never going to see you again once you leave this island. It is over, finished. Why ruin the rest of your life for nothing?'

'Honour?' Her tone made him flinch.

'A woman's honour lies in her chastity. You are a virgin.' She gave a little sob that was not grief. Anger, perhaps, or frustration. 'If you insist on this course then I must come with you. Bradon will want to call me out. *That* is a matter of honour.'

He must have jerked her closer without realising. His senses were flooded with the scent of her, the familiar Averil-scent of her skin mingling with the soap she had bathed with and the musk of excited, angry female. His body stirred into instant arousal.

'I have no intention of telling him who you are. This mission will remain secret, I assume? I cannot imagine that they will want it trumpeted that an admiral's cousin has been involved in treason and was thwarted by a Frenchman. Do you think I want you swaggering in, provoking a duel? What if you are killed?'

'I would not be the one killed. And I do not swagger.'

'Ha!' She tossed her head. 'And if you kill my betrothed? Do you think that a duel could be kept secret? You will ruin me—for what? Your honour. Not mine.'

'Damn it, Averil.' What she said was the truth. If she insisted on doing this insane thing then he must stand aside and allow her to do it, at whatever cost to his own honour. 'What will you do if he rejects you?'

'I do not know.' She stared at him, her face black and white and silver in the moonlight. He saw her bite her lip and a tremor ran through her, a vibration of fear under his hands. Then she collected herself. 'He won't. He wouldn't.'

'He might, he very well might. And then you *will* be ruined. Think of the scandal. Where will you go?'

'I don't know.' There was that shiver again. Her brave front was just that—underneath she knew the dangers of what she was intending to do. 'I suppose...I could always go home again.'

'Or you could become my mistress.' Even as he said it, Luc knew it was what he was hoping for. He wanted her and if Bradon rejected her the choices before her were few.

She could travel back to India, a perilous three-month voyage with the shame of her story following her; she could seek, without support, to find herself a less fastidious husband or she could join the *demi-reps*.

'Your mistress?' For a moment she did not seem to understand, then her whole body went rigid with indignation. 'Why, you...you bastard! You don't think I am good enough to marry, but you would keep me for your pleasure!' She wrenched round, fighting his grip. 'Let me go—'

Luc shifted his grip, afraid of hurting her, too aroused to release her. She thudded against his chest and he held her with one hand splayed on her back, the other in her hair, and kissed her.

He told himself it was to stop her creating a scene and bringing the others out into the garden. That degree of rational thought lasted long enough for him to open his mouth over hers and thrust his tongue between her tight lips as though he thrust himself into her virgin body. It was wrong, it was gloriously right, it was heaven. She tasted of wine and fruit and woman and he lost himself, drowning in her, until she twisted, jerking her knee up. If it were not for her hampering skirts she would have had him, square in the groin. As it was, her knee hit him with painful force on the thigh and he tore his mouth free.

'How could you?' she said, her voice as shaky as his legs had become. Luc took an unobtrusive grip on the statue base beside him and opened his mouth to apologise. Then he saw her face in the moonlight. Her eyes were wide, her lips parted, but it was not the face of a fearful woman, a woman who had been assaulted. It was the face of a woman in the throes of passion and uncertainty. There was longing and fear and excitement; she was as affected by that kiss as he was.

'You value honesty and truth,' Luc said, ignoring her question. If he was right her words had been aimed as much at herself as at him. 'Tell me that you did not want me to kiss you. Tell me that you do not want to be my lover. Make me believe you.'

'You arrogant devil,' she whispered.

'Go on, tell me. Surely that is much easier than confessing what happened on St Martin's to Bradon?'

'It would be wrong. Sinful, if I felt like that.'

'I asked for facts, not a moral judgement,' he said and saw her flinch at his harshness.

'Yes,' she threw back at him. 'Yes, I want to be your lover. Yes, I want to give my virginity to you. There—does that make you feel better? Because it makes me feel wretched.' And that time her sob was one of grief as well as anger.

'Averil.' The lust drained from him as rapidly as it had come, leaving him empty. 'Averil,' and he lifted his hand to touch her cheek. He could not take her virginity, he knew that. If she had a faint chance of making this marriage happen, then he had to leave it to her. Somehow he had let himself care that much.

The tendrils of hair that curled around her ears brushed his fingers as she made a little sound that might have been a shocked gasp, that might have been *Yes,* and feeling came back in a rush. A reluctant tenderness and desire and the realisation that she was his for the asking, here, now.

'You will go to London and you will be brave and honest and if Bradon does not take you with open arms, then the man is a fool,' he said. He could not entrap her in the coils of her innocent passion, but he could plan for the inevitable.

'I would rather not marry a fool,' she said, a shaky laugh in her voice. 'I hope he is a good, compassionate man who will forgive all this and makes a kind husband. I hope he makes me feel like this when he touches me.' Luc pulled her into his arms and bent his head. 'No,' she whispered.

'Let me make love to you, Averil. This once. I swear you will go to him as much a virgin as you are now.' And then, when Bradon showed her the door, she would know who to turn to—her desire and her passion would bring her to him.

She tipped up her head, her expression in the silver light eager, all the anger gone. 'You can do that?'

'I can give you pleasure and not harm you if you will trust me.' It was not harm, he told his conscience. The choices were all with the other man.

'Here? But—'

'Here.' He guided her into the arbour that faced away from the house towards the shelter of the slope. 'Here, now.'

She trusted him. Why, she did not know, for this was her virtue she was risking, not her life, which she knew he would protect at the cost of his. Luc had asked her to be his mistress, he had kissed her until she was dizzy with desire, he was the last man she should yield herself to. And yet she had no will to deny him. Or was it herself that would not be denied?

He pulled her down with him on to the broad-planked seat and kissed her, slowly, druggingly, until analysis was impossible and all that was left was the heat and strength of him and the caress of his mouth and the drift of his hands.

The neckline of the simple gown was no barrier to long fingers sliding under the lace trim to catch and tease her nipples. He rolled them between finger and thumb until she squirmed against him, panting with shocked pleasure. It was as though the wicked play of his fingers pulled on hot wires that led straight to the pulse that beat with urgent insistence between her legs. Averil moaned against his mouth and he stroked his tongue into hers as though to soothe, yet the caress was like pouring oil on to the flames of desire.

'Please,' she gasped against his lips. 'Please...'

She did not know what she was asking for, what to expect. The night air on her legs as Luc's hand lifted the full silken skirts made her stiffen, but his mouth and his other hand on her breast held her in thrall. Her hands were clasping his head, her fingers laced into the dark hair, his skull hard and shapely under her palms.

'Relax,' he said and she almost laughed because she was quivering with tension like an over-tightened violin string and surely she must snap. Luc had her sprawled in utter abandon across his thighs. The hand on her breast held her to him, the other smoothed back the rustling silken skirts until her legs and the paleness of her belly were exposed. In the semi-darkness the dark triangle at the top of her thighs showed stark against the white skin.

'Luc,' she whispered. It was shameful and shameless, but he was looking at her with utter concentration, his palm smoothing down over the quivering skin, and under her she felt the heat and thrust of his erection. He found her desirable, and that was infinitely exciting. But he had promised he would not take her virginity, so what happened now? Surely he would not leave her in this state—aching and needing and so taut that she was trembling?

His big, calloused hand cupped her mound under its sheltering curls as his mouth caught her whimper of protest. One finger slid between the hot, wet folds and began to rub in time to the thrust of his tongue and Averil arched into his palm, pressing against it, instinctively trying to intensify the pleasure.

He had found that tiny knot of sensation where the strange, aching pulse quivered into life every time he touched her and he teased it until he found the rhythm that had her sobbing into his mouth. 'More,' she said, her tongue tangling the word into a groan. 'Oh, more, Luc. More.'

Somehow he must have understood. He lifted his mouth from hers and she saw the glint of moonlight on his teeth as he smiled. 'More like this?' he asked and slid a finger deep into her.

She clenched around him, tight, desperate, as the tension swept through her, an irresistible wave, and she lost all hold on reality and screamed as his kiss swallowed the betraying sound.

Chapter Thirteen

'We had better go in.'

In where? Averil wondered, as she drifted back to reality. Or perhaps it was a dream. She was warm and safe and Luc was holding her and little ripples of pleasure kept running through her body. If they went in, wherever that was, the pleasure would stop.

'No,' she mumbled against his shirt front and heard the laugh rumble in his chest.

'Yes. Come on. Can you stand up?'

'No.' But he stood up anyway and she found her feet were on the ground, even though she had to hold tight to Luc's lapels. Her legs had no more substance than a rag doll's, her pulse was beating wildly and she wanted to do it all over again. Everything, and in a bed this time. But, of course, she could not. This had been once, and never again.

Averil stumbled as Luc helped her outside, his hand under her elbow. 'That was good?' he asked. Somehow she could not resent the thread of amusement in his voice.

'Amazing,' she said honestly. 'What was it?'

'An orgasm,' he explained, still managing to stay serious, although she guessed her ignorance was a novelty for him.

'Don't you need one, too?' Thank goodness it was dark so her crimson cheeks were not visible.

'Don't worry about it,' Luc said. 'It will be all right.'

'Oh.' Presumably that meant he would seek out whatever women in Hugh Town made their living seeing to the needs of the gentlemen of the island. At least they would not ask him foolishly naïve questions.

'You are naturally very passionate,' Luc said, his voice low. They were walking up and down a path parallel to the house; some sense of reality was returning to her. She could make out the shape of Miss Gordon strolling on the terrace, out of earshot: their tactful, ineffectual, chaperone. Was that deliberate on her part?

'You don't really want me to be your mistress,' Averil murmured back. 'I am ignorant and inexperienced.'

'And sensual and natural and very lovely. Of course I want you.' He began to make his way back to the house. Averil dragged her feet—what if the others knew what they had been doing? He seemed to guess at her reluctance. 'Don't worry, it will not be branded on your forehead *I had an orgasm in the summerhouse.*'

'Don't say such things!' she whispered, agitated.

'Pretend to be angry with me,' Luc said. 'That will convince Lady Olivia that we have been discussing the question of marriage and are set against each other and it will explain any colour in your cheeks. If you are determined to go through with this madness, then go to Bradon. I will give you an address. If you need me— *when* you do—send me word.'

'You really expect me to turn up on your doorstep

asking to become your mistress, don't you?' she said, reaction turning into something very like anger in reality.

'Yes,' he said. 'I look forward to it.'

Averil whirled out of his light grip and half ran down the path to Miss Gordon. 'It is quite impossible, ma'am, we should never suit, even if it was right that I should break my contract with Lord Bradon. I beg you, please help me to make my way to London.'

'Of course.' The other woman looked past Averil to where Luc stood on the path. 'My brother will advance the money for a chaise from Penzance and your lodgings on the way. You had better take Waters with you as your maid. We will give you instructions to my brother's agent in the port—he will find you respectable lodgings and then hire a chaise and reliable postilions. You must spend at least two nights on the road, I fear, for it is over three hundred miles. Do you think you can manage by yourself?'

'Thank you,' Averil said with real gratitude. The thought of dealing with the practicalities of travel sounded blissfully straightforward after the emotional turmoil of the past week. 'I am used to long journeys in India and a chaise with postilions sounds much easier to deal with than ox carts and elephants!'

Miss Gordon laughed and urged her inside and towards the stairs. There were footsteps on the terrace behind her, but Averil did not turn around.

'Good morning, miss.' The curtains swished back with a rattle of rings.

'Good morning, Waters. Hot chocolate? How delightful.' To wake in a soft bed with light streaming through a wide, clean window: luxury. Lonely luxury. Averil curled her fingers around the cup and inhaled with a shiver of delight as the aroma banished the lingering memory of Pott's evil tea.

'Miss Gordon says, will you come down for breakfast, miss, or would you like to take it in bed?'

'I will come down, thank you.' She slid out of bed, still cradling the chocolate cup, and went to the wash stand. 'Miss Gordon said you might be willing to come with me to London, Waters.'

'Yes, please, miss. I'm a London girl myself, you see, and I came down here because my young man got a job as a footman, but we fell out and I miss my mam and the young ones something awful. And I miss London, too.'

Averil dipped the toothbrush in the pot of powder. 'I can't promise there will be a permanent position for you—that depends on what Lord Bradon, my betrothed, says.'

'That's all right, miss. I can always stay with Mam in Aldgate until I get a new post. Miss Gordon's given me a good character.'

Averil paused at the landing window and looked out over a view of rooftops, then sea and scattered islands with white sand beaches glittering in the sun. Shifting sands. If the *Bengal Queen*'s anchor had not dragged on the sandy seabed, if she had not hit the rocks before the crew could get her back under control, Averil would have landed in Penzance, would have waited patiently until Lord Bradon sent an escort for her and would, even now, be preparing for her marriage.

She would not have met Luc, she would never have discovered the delights of physical love in his arms, she would not have had to make difficult choices. *No, I would still be the nice, well-behaved, dutiful young lady I always was.*

She smiled absently at the servants who met her at the foot of the stairs and directed her to the breakfast room. *Was I always so dutiful? Because if I was, where did this wanton creature come from who only desires to be in Luc's arms and in his bed? Would she have stayed buried for ever if he had not summoned her?*

Her smile was conscious and bright as she entered the cheerful small room and her stomach lurched—relief or disappointment?—when she saw the only occupant was Miss Gordon applying herself to a pile of toast with a book propped up before her on the cruet.

'Good morning, Miss Heydon.' She flipped the volume closed and rang the small bell by her place. 'We are alone, as you see. My brother and Captain d'Aunay breakfasted over an hour since and my sister-in-law prefers the solitude of her bedchamber before facing the hurly-burly of the day. Did you sleep well?'

'Thank you, I was most comfortable.' A footman poured coffee and indicated with a gesture the buffet and its covered dishes.

Miss Gordon nodded to the man and waited until the door closed behind him and Averil returned to her seat with a slice of omelette before speaking again. 'I gather that my brother spent half the night with the captain. The prisoners—although we are not supposed to know of them, of course!—are on their way to Plymouth already.' She took a folded paper from her pocket and handed it to Averil. 'From Captain d'Aunay.'

'Thank you.' Averil eyed the red wax with its impress of a unicorn's head. His seal ring, she supposed, although she had never seen him wearing it. She laid the letter down unopened and picked up her fork.

'Please, do not mind me.' Miss Gordon gave an airy wave of her toast and reopened her book.

Averil put a forkful of egg in her mouth, chewed it for a minute without tasting it, buttered some toast, sipped her coffee. The letter lay there looking as innocent as a snake under a stone.

Impatient with herself, Averil broke the seal and spread the single sheet open.

It goes well, so far, the letter began without salutation. Luc's handwriting was smaller than she imagined it would be, clear and somehow the style was different from the educated hands she was used to. He had been taught to write in France, she reminded herself. *Sir George is convinced, having had his own suspicions, and will tidy things up at his end. I will take the brigs to Plymouth this morning.*

When you need me, send to me at Albany, off Piccadilly.

God's speed on your journey.

L.M. d'A.

When you need me, not *if.* Arrogant man. His certainty that her meeting with Lord Bradon would be a disaster was not encouraging, nor was her complete panic about what she should do if her betrothed rejected her. *Andrew,* she reminded herself. She must begin to think of him as a real person, not an abstraction.

She folded the letter and pushed it into the pocket in the skirts of her borrowed gown. Miss Gordon looked up, closed her book again and cocked her head on one side like an inquisitive bird, but she asked no questions.

'I suggest you rest here another night to recover. It will take the best part of the day to sail to Penzance. I have written out some notes on the road journey for you, and my brother has a letter for his Penzance agent and some money. There is a letter for Lord Bradon as well. It contains no details other than to say that we are sorry we did not know of your connection with him and therefore did not know to contact him after the wreck. That leaves the explanations entirely up to you.' Averil murmured her thanks. 'I have given Waters some changes of linen for you and a cloak and bonnet.'

'You are very kind. I will have everything returned as soon as possible, of course. And Lord Bradon will recompense Sir George.' At least, she sincerely hoped he would. If he showed her the door, he might well forget all about the logistics of her arrival. She must note the amounts so, if the worst happened, Papa could repay her debts.

'Of course. I quite envy you going to London. I miss it sadly, but perhaps we will meet again there later this year. I hope to visit a friend of mine there. She is staying at the Star Fort at the moment, away from the chaos this household has been in this past week, reacquainting herself with a certain gentleman,' she added with a wicked twinkle in her eye.

That must have been what Lady Olivia had been so snappy about, Averil guessed. Miss Gordon appeared to have a *penchant* for assisting lovers. Perhaps she had been disappointed in love herself, or was merely a romantic.

'I should be very glad to see you there,' she said, and meant it.

By the sixth day of her journey from the Isles of Scilly Averil would have been glad to see London, with or without a friendly face. She was travelling in considerable comfort, although Sir George's agent had been so particular and painstaking that it had taken two days before he was satisfied with all the arrangements and she could convince him that she was well rested enough to undertake the journey, by which time it was Saturday and Averil did not feel she should travel on the Sunday.

Her courses had started on the ship between the islands and Penzance, just to add to the awkwardness of travel, and she confided to Waters that she was not sorry to have the excuse of an extra day in the comfort of a good inn.

But the travelling was comfortable enough once they had set out. The postilions were courteous and steady and both the inn in Penzance and the one she had stayed in the night before at Okehampton had been respectable and clean. Waters was proving sensible, competent and reasonably quiet.

All of which provided not the slightest stimulus, challenge or impediment to her thoughts about what was awaiting her and what had happened in that week with Luc. Her meeting with Andrew Bradon loomed ahead and, like a prisoner awaiting execution, she just wanted to get it over with.

Even the green rolling countryside, so utterly different from India, passed like stage scenery against which the phantoms of her imagination acted out one disastrous encounter after another. There was plenty of time for lurid imaginings. On the first day they had been almost twelve hours on the road; today, it seemed, would be eleven hours.

The chaise slowed for a moment, drew over and another vehicle went past, its bright painted body rocking and swaying. 'Another yellow bounder, and in a hurry,' Averil remarked to Waters, who was pulling up the window against the cloud of dust the other post-chaise left in its wake. 'The passenger must be immune to seasickness!'

'There'll be a lot of navy men on this road, I'll be bound,' Waters remarked.

'Of course, yes.' That would explain the impression she had received of navy blue and the flash of gold braid. 'I shall be glad to stop for the night, I must confess.' Journeys in India took weeks, ponderous affairs requiring much planning, the assembling of trains of creaking ox carts, the hiring of armed outriders, the organisation of the household to shift from the heat of the plains up to the cool of the hills for the summer and back again for the winter. The Europeans moved like the flocks, herding themselves, not for fresh grass, but for relief from heat and dust and disease.

This rapid travel, the ability of a lady to undertake a journey almost at a whim, was novel and rather alarming. As she thought it the chaise slowed to a trot, and she saw they were entering a town. It swerved, passed through the arch into the inn yard and came to a clattering halt.

'Here we are, ma'am.' One of the postilions opened the door. 'The Talbot at Mere. We were told this was the place for you to stop.'

Averil climbed down, stumbling a little, her legs stiff. 'It seems very busy.' As she spoke another carriage clattered into the yard, ostlers ran out with a change of horses and several people walked in from the street. 'Perhaps I had better check they have accommodation before you unharness the horses in case we must try another inn.'

He touched his forelock and she started to cross the yard. From the door a big man with an apron stretched across his belly bowed to her. The landlord, no doubt. On the far side men lounged, talking, several of them in navy-blue uniforms. She kept walking towards the landlord, ignoring them as a lady should, Waters at her heels.

'Good evening, ma'am. Would you be requiring a room?'

'Indeed, and with a private parlour if you have one available.'

'I'm sorry, ma'am. There's just the one bedchamber left—quiet, though on the small side. But all the parlours are taken.'

That would mean dining in the common room. Averil bit her lip—was it better to stay here where the host seemed respectable and she was sure of a room at least, or carry on and risk another inn?

'The lady may have my rooms,' a voice said. 'I have no pressing need for a parlour.'

She was tired and imagining things. Averil turned. A tall naval officer, his cocked hat under his arm exposing his neatly barbered black head, bowed. 'Your servant, ma'am. Landlord, please have my traps shifted at once. The bed—' the amused grey eyes lifted to Averil's face '—has not been slept in.'

'Captain d'Aunay.' There was no breath left in her lungs for questions.

'My pleasure, ma'am.' He bowed again and walked away without a second glance. The perfect gentleman.

'Well, that's all right then,' the landlord said, his delight at being able to satisfy both customers apparent. 'I'll show you up at once, ma'am.'

My pleasure... The bed has not been slept in. Yet.

'This was fortunate, miss, the captain being here.' Waters looked with approval at the meal the servant had set out on the round table in the parlour. 'Nice rooms, and quiet, too.'

'Yes, indeed.' They were ideal, Averil told herself. A trundle bed for Waters to sleep on in the same chamber as herself and no way to the bedchamber except through the parlour door, which had a stout lock on the inside.

What did she think was going to happen? That Luc would stroll in, evict her maid and ravish her? Or that she would lose all self-control and go and seek him out? Either was unthinkable.

Averil eyed the door again, wishing she could lock it now, but the servant would be in and out while they were eating and afterwards to clear the table. She would think Averil had run mad if she had to have the door unlocked every time.

'I didn't recognise Captain d'Aunay for a moment, miss. Scrubs up well, doesn't he?' Waters chatted away. 'Not that he'll ever be handsome, exactly, not with that nose and that stubborn chin. Wasn't it a coincidence, him being here?'

The girl was not making snide remarks, Averil decided, it was simply her own conscience nagging, telling her that this could not possibly be chance.

'He is a fighting man, not a courtier,' she said. 'Doubtless a prominent nose is no handicap at sea. Eat up, Waters, before your dinner gets cold.'

'Yes, miss.' Waters attacked the steak-and-oyster pie with relish. 'What sort of house has Lord Bradon got, miss?' she asked after a few minutes.

'He is the heir, so the properties actually belong to his father, the earl,' Averil explained, trying to recall the details. 'There is a large town house in Mayfair and then Kingsbury, the country seat in Buckinghamshire. And I believe there is a shooting box somewhere as well.'

'And one day you'll be the countess.' Waters pursued a piece of carrot round the plate. 'That's wonderful, miss.'

'Yes.' Indeed it was. Her great-grandfather had sold fruit and vegetables, her grandfather had opened a shop selling tea and coffee and her father had built on that start and become a wealthy merchant with a knighthood. Now he wanted connections and influence in England for his sons, her brothers. Mark and John were not expected to soil their hands with commerce but to become English landed gentry. With her help they would make good marriages, buy estates, become part of the establishment.

Averil had never had to do a hand's turn of work in her life, only to live in the lap of luxury and become a lady. Now it was her duty to make her contribution to the family fortunes. But she could not take marriage vows and deceive her new husband.

A tap on the door heralded the servant who cleared the plates and dishes and left an apple tart and a jug of cream in their place. Averil ate, absently listening to Waters's wistful hopes that Lord Bradon might have a place for her in his establishment.

The door behind creaked open. 'Thank you, we have finished. You may clear now and bring a pot of tea in about an hour,' Averil said as she folded her napkin and stood up.

There was no sign of the servant. Luc stood in the open doorway, filling it.

Chapter Fourteen

'Captain d'Aunay. Is there something you wish to say to me?' How calm she sounded. It was as though someone else entirely was speaking, not the woman whose pulse was racing and whose mouth had suddenly lost all moisture.

He smiled and the maid jumped to her feet. 'I'll go and—'

'Stay here, Waters.' Averil gestured to a chair on one side of the empty fireplace. 'Sit there, if you please.'

'Yes, miss.' Eyes wide, Waters obeyed.

'I merely wished to see whether you are comfortable, Miss Heydon.' Uninvited, Luc strolled into the room and let the door swing to behind him. He filled the cosy, slightly shabby, space just as he had dominated the old hospital hut.

'Perfectly, thank you, Captain. I was on the point of saying to Waters how pleasant it was to have a room to ourselves where we could lock the door.'

'Indeed, that is why I thought you would like this one.'

'You would have me believe you selected this especially for me?' She wished she could sit down, but she would have to invite him to as well and then how would she get him out?

'Of course. Sir George's secretary showed me the inns he had noted for the postilions. I thought, given how busy the roads to London from the ports are, that it would be as well to keep an eye on you if I could.' Luc propped one shoulder against the window frame, quite as comfortable as he would have been in a chair, leaving Averil standing stiffly in the middle of the room.

She sat down and fixed him with a chilly smile. 'Most kind, but I would hardly wish for your assistance when you have your duties to perform.'

'How fortunate that pleasure and duty do not conflict,' Luc said, so smoothly that her fingers itched to wipe the assurance off his face. 'We made good time to Plymouth, I spoke to the senior officer there and was ordered up to London to report to the Admiralty.'

'Then should you not be on your way?'

'I was not required to gallop,' he said. 'Merely to present myself with due despatch to their lordships. Would you care for a stroll to take the evening air, Miss Heydon?'

It was on the tip of her tongue to refuse him, but the room was stuffy, she was stiff with sitting and she had a maid with her. A walk would be very welcome. But if Luc thought she would consent to vanish into the woods with him for further, highly educational, dalliance that would shake her tenuous composure even more, he was much mistaken.

'Thank you, Captain. That would be delightful.'

Oh, yes, that was precisely what he had thought she would say. It was incredible how those cool grey eyes could heat into sensual invitation.

'Come along, Waters, fetch your bonnet. And my bonnet and shawl, please.'

'You think you need protection from me?' Luc asked softly as the maid went into the bedchamber, leaving them alone.

'From the moment my feet touched the mainland I think I have re-entered reality. And my reality is one of respectability, Captain.'

'I see. And you think Lord Bradon will appreciate these geographical boundaries on behaviour?'

'I have no idea, but I will not insult him by risking being seen behaving in any way that is not proper—not here, where I might be recognised later by one of his acquaintance.'

'One hopes Lord Bradon appreciates the sensitive honour displayed by his betrothed,' Luc said as Waters emerged with Averil's bonnet in her hand, the shawl over her arm. Gloves were one thing that she had not been loaned. It was most unladylike to go out without them, but it could not be helped.

'Indeed. Honour is such a very subtle subject for gentlemen—so difficult for a lady to decipher.' She tied her bonnet strings while she spoke and Luc took the shawl from the maid and arranged it around her shoulders, his fingers carefully touching fabric, not skin. The shiver could only come from her imagination. The ache, as she knew well by now, was sheer wantonness.

When they reached the yard he offered his arm. She placed the tips of her ungloved fingers on it and they strolled towards the street, Waters close on their heels. She was within earshot and Averil intended that she stayed there.

It was an effort not to let her mind run round and round their last encounter, like a squirrel in a cage. 'This is the first English town I have seen properly,' she said, determined to pretend it had not happened and this man had not caressed her intimately, brought her wicked delight, seduced her into sin. 'I did not feel I could walk out in Penzance or Okehampton without an escort. Is it usual for so many buildings to be of stone?'

'In parts of the country with good building stone, yes,' Luc said. 'It is the same in France. Otherwise there are brick or timber-framed houses, like that one. It can change within a few miles, depending on the underlying rock.' They strolled on a few more paces. 'The market square,' Luc observed. 'An historic feature, I have no doubt. How genteel we sound. I had no idea a small town could provide such innocuous subjects for conversation.'

'And how fortunate that is,' Averil returned, studying the open space. 'Markets in India are very different. On the way we moored at Madras and I visited the market to buy Christmas presents with Lady Perdita and Lord Lyndon. There was a mad dog and Dita saved a child from it—and me, too. Then Lord Lyndon saved Dita.'

The square was warm with evening light and people going about their business. They moved slowly now, at the end of the working day, stopping to talk with neighbours, to wait for a child's lagging steps.

'How calm and ordered this is. I was so afraid in that market, and I did nothing, just allowed myself to be bundled to safety.' She shivered, seeing a small boy fetching water from the pump, fair-haired and red-cheeked and laughing with his friends, so unlike the small Indian child who had run screaming in terror.

'And you blame yourself for not being in the right place to act,' Luc observed. 'Of course, I have seen how timorous you are, how cowardly, so perhaps you are right.'

'You are teasing me,' Averil observed. There was a warmth in his look that told her it was more than teasing. He thought her courageous? Thinking about it, perhaps she had not done so very badly in the face of shipwreck and capture and a fight at sea.

'As you say,' he agreed with a chuckle. 'Where shall we go now?'

'The church?' That seemed an innocuous destination. If she had been alone she would have liked to go inside and sit for a while, but she felt awkward asking Luc to wait. 'Oh. It is very large, is it not? And a tower with those pointed things on the corners. How interesting— this is the first English church I have seen close to.'

She looked over the wall into the churchyard. 'And so green! In Calcutta, where I used to live in India, there is a big cemetery for the English with massive tombs and dusty paths and trees that look nothing like these at all. And birds and little squirrels and… Oh, dear, I have become quite homesick. How foolish, I thought I had got over that.'

'Come and sit down.' Luc led her into the church-yard and found a bench. Waters perched on the edge of a crumbling table tomb and watched Luc with interest.

She finds him attractive, Averil thought as she caught an errant tear with her handkerchief and straightened her shoulders. *And who am I to blame her?*

'When my mother and I returned to England my English grandfather, the Earl of Marchwood, thought it was best I go to university and then into the church,' Luc observed. He took off his cocked hat, leaned back with his hands clasped behind his head, stretched out his long legs and gazed up at the tower.

'Into—you mean, become a clergyman?' Averil collapsed into unladylike giggles. 'You?'

'You have a very unflattering opinion of me, by the sound of it,' Luc remarked. He appeared lazily indifferent to her mockery. 'Grandpapa was not best pleased to discover that I held the same rationalist beliefs as my father. By the time he had stopped spluttering and threatening me with hellfire and eternal damnation I had joined the navy.'

'You are an atheist?' She had never met one of those dangerous creatures.

'A sceptic with an open mind,' he corrected her. 'I am perfectly comfortable reading services at sea or turning out for church parade. Does that shock you?'

'No,' she said and heard herself sound as doubtful as she felt. 'But you wanted to join the navy?'

'Not particularly. I wanted to kill revolutionaries. I wanted to kill the people who had taken my father's life and my home. It was the navy or the army and I found the Admiralty first.' He shrugged. 'It was fortunate, I suspect. The navy is far less snobbish about foreigners without much money than the army is. Now I have the money and it doesn't matter.'

'Where did you get it from?' A most improper question, she knew. Ladies did not discuss money.

'Prize money and then an inheritance from my mother's side of the family,' Luc said. 'I will need a great deal when I get my hands on my estates again. But there is enough to finance my pleasures very adequately,' he added, so blandly that Waters, swinging her heels and watching the verger locking the church, did not seem to notice anything untoward.

Luc's fingers curled around hers and he began to make circles in the palm of her hand. As Averil stiffened and tried to pull away he half turned on the bench so his shoulder was to the maid and lifted her hand to his lips.

As she tugged he opened his mouth and sucked the length of her index finger right in.

His mouth was hot and wet and the suction was strong enough to make her gasp and his eyes were sending her the wickedest of messages. Her other fingers were splayed against his face, the evening growth of beard bristling under the sensitive pads. Then she realised what this was mimicking and her cheeks reddened and his lids lowered as if he was in a sensual dream.

Averil tugged again and he closed his teeth, gently. 'Let me go,' she demanded. 'It is indecent!'

He released her and smiled. 'Such a naughty imagination, Averil,' he murmured and licked his lips. 'Whatever can you mean?'

She got to her feet. 'Waters, come along and stop day-dreaming!'

'Yes, ma'am.' The girl scrambled down from the tomb and Averil felt a stab of guilt for snapping at her.

'We must go back now. We have a long day tomorrow. Thank you, Captain d'Aunay, but I am sure we can find our own way to the inn.'

'You will accept my escort, I hope. My intention is to protect you.'

'Your intention is to seduce me,' she hissed as she took his arm. It would create a scene, and questions in Waters's mind, if she made an issue of walking with Luc.

'To protect and seduce,' he murmured back as he opened the gate out of the churchyard.

Averil laughed in the hope that the maid would not realise they were arguing. 'You attempt to reconcile opposites, Captain.'

'Not at all. I believe I know where your best interest lies, Miss Heydon.'

'Then we must agree to disagree. My mind is quite made up on the matter.'

'I had noticed how very stubborn you are, Miss Heydon, and to what lengths you will go to get what you want.'

'What I think is right,' she corrected him. 'For you to lecture me for being stubborn is, I venture, a case of the pot calling the kettle black.'

Luc was silent as they crossed the market square. Averil let herself feel the texture of his uniform jacket under her palm, the rough edge of the gold braid at her fingertips, hear the sound of his boots crunching over the dusty stones.

It felt right to have him by her side, as though they were a respectable married couple walking back to their comfortable home after a church service. There were unspoken words between them, a sensual tension that left her short of breath as though she had been hurrying, yet there was a comfort in being together. Would it feel as natural to walk with Andrew Bradon? Would it be as easy to stroll in companionable silence without the need to make conversation?

The words were there, though, even if neither uttered them. *Kiss me, touch me, stay with me.* They were in the slight pressure of her hand on his arm, in the way he watched her profile, their lagging steps that got slower as they neared the inn.

It had to stop, she knew that, or they would drift upstairs and then—who knew? And even though she could rely on Luc to save her life, she could not trust him with her virginity. Or perhaps it was herself she did not trust.

'Thank you so much, Captain,' Averil said in her

brightest society voice as they reached the inn yard. 'I feel better for the fresh air and the exercise.'

'You will set out early tomorrow, I imagine. It is a good twelve hours to London.' Luc stood, hat in hand, showing no sign of wanting to inveigle his way upstairs. Was it all her imagination and he just wanted to flirt?

'Yes, the postilions said we should leave at half past seven. I shall be very glad to arrive, I must confess.' The prospect of stopping this endless travelling, of reaching somewhere—anywhere—permanent after four months, was almost enough to overcome the apprehension about meeting her betrothed.

'Bruton Street, I believe,' Luc said.

'How—how did you know?' A cold trickle ran down her spine. He had promised not to speak to Lord Bradon—surely he would not break his word?

'I checked. Don't look at me like that, I shall not interrupt your arrival with an ill-timed call, believe me, Miss Heydon.'

'Of course. Thank you. It may be a little…strained at first, getting to know each other.' His silence spoke volumes about how strained he expected it to be. 'Well, good night, Captain d'Aunay. I wish you well at the Admiralty.' She held out her hand and he took it, bowed over it and stood aside for her to enter.

'I think the captain's better looking, now I'm used to that nose,' Waters remarked as they climbed the stairs.

'Shh! For goodness' sake, girl, he'll hear you!'

'He didn't come in, Miss Heydon.'

'Oh.' Good. Excellent, in fact. That was that then. She would not see him again, perhaps not for years and when she did she would be Lady Bradon, a respectable society matron and Luc would be a count, or an admiral or ambassador for a royalist France. They would meet and smile and part again and all this agonising would seem pointless.

Unless Lord Bradon rejected her. The cold shiver came back. He was not going to be pleased, that was certain. But he might be a wonderful, warm, understanding man who would forgive her adventure and she would forget Luc. No, never forget him. He would always be part of her memories: his courage, his pride. His lovemaking.

'Time for bed, I think, Waters. Please ring for the hot water.' On an impulse, she said, 'What is your first name? Waters seems so stiff.' Probably it was how Lady Bradon should address her maid, but it was not comfortable.

'Grace, miss.'

'How pretty. I will call you that if you do not feel it lowers your dignity.'

'*My* dignity, miss? I think calling me by my surname is because you'll be a great lady and I'm supposed to be a *superior* servant.' She said it with such a comical expression that Averil laughed. 'Only I don't think I'm cut out for being a superior abigail.'

She was rather dumpy and snub-nosed, Averil thought, thinking of her aunt's descriptions of how a suitable dresser would look and behave. But she was warm and sensible and cheerful. Averil decided she would do her best to keep her—warmth might be in rather short supply at Bruton Street.

'I think you will do admirably, Grace. I cannot promise anything, because Lord Bradon may already have employed someone as dresser, but if he has not, then I hope you will stay with me.'

'Oh, Miss Heydon, thank you.' Grace beamed. 'Oh, and, miss, that means I'll sit with the upper servants, right up at the top!'

And so she would, Averil thought with an inward

smile. Ladies' maids and valets took their employer's rank as far as the hierarchy of the servants' hall was concerned.

Grace was still bubbling with excitement as they took their seats in the post-chaise at just past seven the next morning. The yard was busy already with two private coaches ready to leave and another post-chaise with the ostlers backing the horses between the shafts.

Averil made herself as comfortable as possible and wondered if she would be able to sleep, something that she had signally failed to do the night before, except in snatches. Long intervals, marked by the church clock—which might as well have been the church bells tolling—were spent tossing and turning in an effort to stop imagining scenarios for her arrival in Bruton Street.

What would it be? A warm, understanding welcome, chilly reserve but acceptance or downright anger and rejection? She rehearsed, over and over, what she would say, how she would explain those nights in the company of a gang of condemned men and a half-French officer.

Then, when she did fall asleep, her dreams were full of Luc who was making love to her, fully. And then he appeared in the Bruton Street drawing room and explained that he had to do it, even though she was so inept and naïve in bed and then, somehow, he and Andrew Bradon were standing facing each other with duelling pistols raised and… And Grace had shaken her awake because she was having a nightmare.

The breakfast bacon was sitting uneasily in her stomach. It would be best to be very careful what she ate on the journey, she decided as the postilions swung up and the chaise lurched into motion. It would not do to arrive in fashionable Mayfair travel sick as well as crumpled and uneasy.

As she thought it they passed the other chaise and its occupant who was just settling into his seat. Luc. 'Goodbye,' she mouthed and lifted her hand.

He said something in response and she tried to read his lips. *'Au revoir.'*

Chapter Fifteen

March 29th, 1809—Bruton Street, Mayfair, London

Light flooded out as the front door opened. Luc slowed to a stroll on the corner of Berkeley Square and watched the post-chaise drawn up at the kerb. Averil walked up the steps, paused. There was discussion, too far away for him to hear, then she and the maid went in and a pair of footmen ran down to take their bags.

She was inside, but he had expected that. How long would she stay? That was the question. If she was determined on being utterly frank with Bradon, then what would the man do? He could ship her straight back to India, he supposed, although that would involve cost and Luc suspected that the family was not given to paying cash on the nail for anything if they could avoid it. He might simply throw her out. Or he might accept her.

That would be the action of a trusting, forgiving man. Or a man who wanted Averil's money more than he was concerned about her honour. Luc paced slowly around the periphery of the big square, past Gunther's, past the huge old plane trees, back up the eastern side to the corner.

Well, she wasn't out on the pavement with her bag at her feet so he should take himself off to his chambers in Albany, five minutes' walk away, and try to be pleased about it. Best not to walk along past the house; she might be looking out and feel pursued.

Which was exactly what he was doing, although he did not want to distress her by doing so. Somehow he could not keep away. Perhaps Mere had been a mistake, or simply unkind. He had wanted to help her, make the long, fraught, journey easier. But he had also wanted to see her, touch her, steal a kiss if he could. Like an infatuated schoolboy, Luc thought with a wry twist of his mouth as he strode up the slope of Hay Hill and right into Dover Street.

Bradon would be a fool to spurn Averil. She was rich, lovely, intelligent and patently honest. He would believe her when she told him she was a virgin, surely?

Luc turned left out of Dover Street into the bustle of Piccadilly, his mood sliding towards grim. Averil was not going to be his, it was not right that she should be, and to wish that she would be forced into that position was selfish.

All right, I'm selfish. But I didn't cast her up on the beach at Tubbs's feet. I didn't keep her bedridden for days. Yes, but I could have locked the damned door and slept with the men; his conscience riposted. *I needn't have slept in her bed, kissed her, shown her what lovemaking could be like, taught her desire. But I did not take her virginity,* he thought. *I could have done, and I did not. I could have seduced her.*

It was the same conversation he'd been having with himself since he had left Plymouth. He supposed it was partly mild euphoria to blame for his reckless decision to try to find her on the London road. But the admiral had been enthusiastic about the mission, he was assured of a good reception at the Admiralty; his life, it seemed, was back on course, his honour restored. Porthington, he had been informed by a secretary with a very straight face, would be offered a posting in the West Indies. A long way away, and unhealthy with it, the man had added.

So now Luc would have more than enough to keep himself occupied until their lordships decided where to post him next. There would be work to be done to tie up the Isles of Scilly leaks, news to catch up on and the Season was in full swing. He could make an effort and start a serious quest for a wife. And he would wait and watch Averil as she ventured into her new life, his hands outstretched to catch her if she slipped from Bradon's grasp.

The image of Averil tumbling into his arms was enough to make his mouth curve into a smile. He walked into the cobbled forecourt of Albany, nodded to the door-man and climbed the stone stairs to his chambers to see what was awaiting him after more than two months away.

At the door he paused, hand on the knob, as a shiver ran down his spine. He was tempting fate, instinct told him—the same instinct that had saved his life at sea before now. He thought he was stepping back into his old life, but in a better, more purposeful way. But now there was someone else to consider—he was not alone any more.

She isn't yours, he told himself and opened the door. *You have to let her go.* The pain was sharp, just as he knew it would be if he was ever careless enough to care about someone. *Too late now...*

'Hughes! Send out for a decent supper. I'm back.'

* * *

'Miss Heydon. The earl and Lord Bradon are expecting you. Her ladyship also,' the butler added. His eyes flickered over her travel-stained, borrowed gown, the two small valises, Grace's dumpy figure. 'This way, if you please. The family is in the—'

'I would not dream of going to them in my dirt,' Averil said. 'Perhaps someone could show me to my room and have hot water sent up. And please tell the family that I will be with them directly.'

The butler's gaze sharpened into something like respect. 'Very good, Miss Heydon. This is your woman?'

'Waters is my dresser, yes. When I have something other than borrowed garments, that is,' she added. 'Doubtless there is a room for her?'

'Yes, Miss Heydon. John, show Miss Heydon to the Amber suite. Peters, water at once and have Mrs Gifford send one of the girls up to assist Waters.'

'Thank you.' Averil straightened her shoulders, sent a firm message to her wobbly knees and followed the footman up the stairs. *Start as you mean to go on*, she told herself. And being intimidated by the upper servants would not be a good beginning. Nor would appearing before her future mother-in-law looking like a hoyden.

''Strewth, miss,' Grace said as the footman left. 'It's a bit grand, isn't it?'

'Indeed, yes.' Averil turned on her heel to admire the heavy golden-brown hangings, the tassels, the gilt-framed pictures, the marble overmantel. None of it was new, she could see that, and all of it, in her honest opinion, needed some loving care. It was not exactly shabby, but it was definitely worn.

Hot water came with exemplary speed, brought by

a pretty maid with freckles who confided that she was Alice and would Miss Heydon like a cup of tea?

'We both would,' Averil said firmly as Grace attacked her dusty hem with a clothes brush. A large glass of wine would be even better, she thought as she washed her hands and face and began to unpin her hair. But she was going to need all her wits about her now.

'Thank you, Rogers, I am ready now.' The butler looked up as she came down the stairs and she congratulated herself on thinking to ask his name.

He opened a door and announced, 'Miss Heydon, my lady.'

Averil found herself in cool, glittering elegance. White silk walls, gilt details, marble, a pale lemon-and-cream carpet that stretched like an ice flow across dark glossy floorboards towards the chairs and a sofa arranged in a conversation-piece setting at the far end.

Two men got to their feet from the armchairs as she began the interminable walk across the carpet. The taller must be the Earl of Kingsbury, she realised. His brown hair was grey at the temples, his thin face lined more with experience than age. Beside him was his son Andrew, Lord Bradon. Her betrothed. The man she was going to spend the rest of her life with—if he would take her. Shorter than his father, plumper, with the same brown hair and brown eyes. A comparison with another man of the same age flickered through her mind and she forced a smile.

She arrived in front of the sofa and the woman who sat on it. Small, birdlike, dark-haired and dark-eyed: the countess. Her steady regard changed suddenly into a bright smile. The two men bowed. Averil curtsied. *We're like automata*, she thought wildly. A clock would chime at any moment.

'My dear Miss Heydon! What an adventurous journey you have had to be sure. Come and sit beside me. Bradon, ring for wine—we must drink to Miss Heydon's safe arrival.'

Averil sat, expecting an embrace, a kiss or at least a pat on the hand. Nothing. The men resumed their seats, the countess sat beside her, straight-backed, hands folded in her lap.

'You left your family in good health, I trust?'

'Yes, ma'am. My father sends his good wishes and regrets that he was unable to accompany me.'

'Business pressures, no doubt,' the countess remarked and the earl smiled. Rogers brought in a tray with champagne already poured. Averil curled her fingers around the fragile stem of the flute and made herself focus on not snapping it.

'Er. Yes.' No one appeared about to make a toast so she sipped the wine. It fizzed down into her empty stomach. *Mistake. I don't care.*

'And it was an uneventful voyage until the shipwreck, I trust.'

'Yes, ma'am, thank you.' She doubted that her future mother-in-law wanted to hear about mad dogs in Madras, Christmas festivities on board or a joint attempt by the younger passengers to write a sensation novel.

'And the ship was wrecked on the fifteenth of last month, I understand?'

Why were the men so quiet? Averil addressed her answer to Andrew. 'Yes, that is correct. At night.'

'But the letter from the Governor was dated the twenty-first, six days later.' The countess frowned. 'That was very remiss of him, I fear.'

'I was unconscious for three days, on one of the outlying islands. They did not know who I was.' The Governor would have told them that already—her skin began to prickle with apprehension. They were already suspicious. She would tell Andrew what happened tomorrow; she could not blurt it out now, not in front of his parents like this.

'Oh. I see. You were cared for by respectable people, one hopes.'

'A secret navy mission. They rescued me when I was swept on to the beach.'

'Men?' The countess might as well have said *Cockroaches?*

'Yes, ma'am.' Averil took another sip between gritted teeth. She had known this was not going to be easy, but why did her betrothed not utter a word? The earl was watching her from under hooded lids: a calculating, predatory stare. 'I really cannot say much more about it just now—it was very confidential. I will explain all about it tomorrow to Lord Bradon.'

He spoke so suddenly that she jumped. 'I am sure you will.' He might as well have been referring to details of a shopping expedition to buy a new hat. 'Ah, here is Rogers. Dinner at last.'

'You slept well, my dear?'

'Thank you, yes. My lord.' Andrew Bradon had not asked her to use his given name, so she did not presume. The study was very masculine, very *English*. Was it his taste, or his father's? The earl had excused himself after dinner and she had not seen him since. She suspected that he was not much at home.

The chair Brandon offered her was comfortable, they were alone, his expression was pleasant. What, then, was making her stomach tie itself into knots? This was much worse than she had imagined when she had woken that morning in a bed that seemed far too large and soft and lonely.

'I believe there is something you need to tell me about the shipwreck.' He settled back in his own chair behind the desk and nodded encouragingly. Why, then, did feel she had been called in to explain breaking the best china?

'About the aftermath and my rescue, yes.' This was the right thing to do. Averil took in a breath. 'I was washed up on the beach of an island that is normally uninhabited. I was found by a group of men who were part of a secret mission to intercept messages being sent to the French by a traitor in the islands. Their captain assisted me to shelter in the old isolation hospital on the island.'

'And why did he not return you immediately to the main island?'

'Because I was semi-conscious. He had no way of knowing whether, when I awoke, I would say anything about their presence there. At that point no one could be trusted.'

He did not say much, this man. No exclamations of sympathy or anger, no reaction at all save for a pursing of his lips. Averil guessed he was waiting for her to prattle on out of sheer nervousness and rather thought he was succeeding. 'I was unconscious for two days.'

'Three nights.' Of course, he had to pinpoint the number of nights. 'Who nursed you?'

'He did. The officer.'

'Did he rape you?' Still the same calm, pleasant tone. 'No!'

'Really? Are you certain? You say you were unconscious.'

'I would be able to tell. And besides, he is not that kind

of man.' She tried to keep the passion out of her voice, offer an objective assessment, but she was not at all sure she succeeded.

'Did he take liberties of any kind?'

'He kissed me. I slept in his bed.' There, she had said it.

'In his bed?' Everything about Bradon's rounded features sharpened as though he had suddenly come into focus. 'In his *bed*?'

'It was that or sleep outside with the men who were a rough crew sleeping in makeshift shelters.'

'And you kissed him. Did you enjoy it?' He was coolly objective again.

'I have nothing to compare it with. I am a virgin, my lord.' *And I am blushing like a peony and ready to sink.* It was so much worse than she had expected, even though he was so calm and dispassionate. Perhaps because of that. Why was he showing no emotion?

'So you say.'

Averil found she was on her feet. 'I give you my word! Why on earth should I tell you this if it was not out of a desire to be honest with my betrothed?'

'Because you fear you may be with child, of course.' He steepled his fingers and regarded her over the top of them.

'With child?' For a moment it did not make sense. What was he talking about? She could not be pregnant because Luc had not… Then the anger came. He did not believe her. 'It would have to be an immaculate conception then, my lord.'

'Do not blaspheme!' Finally, some emotion.

'I am not lying. I am not pregnant because it is impossible that I should be.'

'Indeed, I hope you are telling me the truth. I will not tolerate a lying wife.'

He was going to throw her out. Something very like relief flooded through her. Averil shook her head. Relief? This was a catastrophe. 'I understand that given the possibilities for scandal you would wish to reconsider the marriage contract. But it was a secret mission, you may rely on nothing of my presence coming out. The Governor gave his assurances that he would say nothing.'

'How you do run on, my dear.' Bradon brought his hands palm down on to the desktop and studied her. 'I did not seek to marry you for your virginity, when all is said and done. We will simply wait and see for a month.'

'Wait? And if I am not with child, you marry me?'

'It seems prudent, would you not say?'

It seemed incredibly cold-blooded. Averil struggled to say so, with tact. 'You do not trust my word or you would not insist on this stratagem. Does it not concern you that I might have lied to you, that I am not a virgin, but I have escaped becoming pregnant? Is such suspicion any basis for marriage?'

'How very innocent you are, my dear—about life, if not in other ways. I am marrying you for the benefits of your very substantial dowry. My father is expensive, I fear. You are marrying me for a title and status. You appear to be a handsome young woman of good address and refined manner, as I was led to believe. What has changed? Has your dowry gone down with the ship?'

'No. Of course not.' So this was how it would be: polite cynicism. He would accept her because he would discover soon enough that she was not pregnant whether he believed it at this moment or not. She must accept him because he had given her no reason not to. He had not struck her or rejected her. He had not even raised his voice to her. She felt more cold than when Luc had carried her from the sea. This man simply did not care about her at all.

'Will it not appear odd that the marriage is delayed?' She tried to match his tone.

'Why, no. No one of any significance knows of it, after all. You are visiting us, we will introduce you into society. After a month I may—or may not—marry you. There will be no expectations, so no gossip, no unpleasant rumours.'

'How civilised,' Averil murmured and he looked pleased, although she did not know how he hoped to keep it a secret. Dita knew. Alistair Lyndon and Callum Chatterton knew. Her chaperon knew. She had made no secret of her reason for travelling to England when she had been on the ship. But something held her back from saying so.

Then she realised why. She welcomed this breathing space. It took little mental effort to calculate that she had three weeks' grace before her mother-in-law knew she was not with child; there was no possibility of hiding such things from the female servants.

'There are some practical matters,' she said. 'I require clothing and I owe Sir George Gordon for my travel here.'

'I assume your father made arrangements with his agents here for you to draw on funds?'

'Yes. Yes, he did.' So, Bradon was not taking on the responsibility of repaying Sir George. Was he mean, penny-pinching or seriously short of money? Her eyes strayed over the ornate furnishing, the silk curtains, the yards of leather-bound, gilt-embossed books. An aristocratic family wealthy in land and property and possessions without a silver shilling to spare, no doubt. The expensive father out pursuing his pleasures while the prudent son ensured the family finances.

Averil tried to keep the judgemental thoughts from her mind. It was not her business how they came to this. It was up to her to try and make sure they were towed out of the River Tick before her children reached their majority, that was all.

'Papa's bankers and lawyers are in the City. May I have a carriage to call on them?'

'Of course.' He got up and came around the desk to stand beside her. Averil felt compelled to stand, too. 'I will accompany you. I assume you will need someone to vouch for you, with all your possessions and papers gone.'

'Yes. I suppose I will. Thank you.'

He took her hand, lifted it, then brushed his lips over her knuckles. She forced herself to stand still and accept the caress, if that is what it could be called. 'We will set out after luncheon. The sooner you can replace your trousseau, the better. Mama will lend you her dresser to guide you to all the best places once you have some money.'

Averil spared a fleeting thought for the silks and muslins, the jewellery and shawls, the piles of linens that she had painstakingly monogrammed as they sailed across miles of oceans. All gone, all lost, along with her dreams.

'Thank you. I will go and put on my bonnet.' He released her hand. *And put any hopes I ever had of love and romance firmly in a box and throw away the key.*

Chapter Sixteen

Luc strolled up Bond Street and turned left into Bruton Street. He had no convincing excuse for coming this way, he admitted to himself. Yes, he was intending to visit Manton's to pick up some new pistols and try a little target practice, but this was a roundabout route by anyone's calculation. He could tell himself he was getting some exercise, but that was purest self-deception. He was worried about Averil and he was missing her like the devil.

He should walk on past and go about his business; there was nothing he could do in any case unless she appeared here and now on the pavement in front of him. However much he wanted her, he had given her his word that he would not turn up on the doorstep and precipitate a crisis.

But despite his resolve some demon had him turning right and then right again into the mews that served the smart houses. He had promised nothing about watching the house and now he grabbed at the loophole. *Damn it, but this obsession hurts. Where's your will-power, man?*

He didn't seem to have any, only a sick fear that he was not going to be able to bear it when she married Brandon.

An English gentleman would cut her out of his life: it was, after all, the honourable thing to do. A Frenchman, hot-blooded and passionate, would ignore his own promises and snatch her. But he was neither. God, was he ever going to find where he belonged? What if Napoleon was never defeated and he was stranded here, belonging to no country?

Stop it! Luc exerted years of hard-learned discipline and got his thoughts under control. *Just deal with it, day by day, just as you always have. Concentrate on Averil and whether she is all right.* He forced his attention back to the mews.

It was quiet, so presumably the carriages had gone out for the morning. A man whistled as he came out of a stable with a bucket, nodded to Luc with no sign of curiosity, and strode off.

Luc walked along, counting until he got to the back of the Bradons' house. Where was she? He leaned a shoulder against the wall and eyed the gate that led into the garden as though it could answer the questions that so preoccupied him.

Averil would not be installed in Bradon's bedchamber yet, of that he was certain. The family would do this properly, although without any great fuss, given the bride's connections. But the man might be making love to her even now. What was there to stop him? And unless Bradon was made of stone, he would want her. Jealousy lanced through him. The bastard would take her innocence and that belonged to him, no one else.

As he watched a window opened on the second floor and there was Averil, as though he had called to her. She leaned her elbows on the sill and leaned out, a most unladylike thing to be doing. Luc smiled, the dark mood evaporating like mist under sunshine, and lifted a hand.

For a moment he thought she had not seen him, or perhaps did not recognise him in civilian dress, then she made a flapping gesture with her hand as though trying to shoo chickens. Amused, Luc stayed where he was. He could almost hear the huff of exasperation as she slapped both palms down on the sill and stared at him across the length of the garden and the low roofs of the mews buildings. Now what would his Averil do?

Her face changed and he realised she was mouthing something, although from that distance it was impossible to tell what. *Go away*, probably. They stared at each other for a while, then she ducked back inside and pulled down the window. Luc grinned; she was wearing a pale gown and the glimmer of white behind the glass showed clearly that she was standing watching him. He tipped the brim of his hat down, shifted his shoulders more comfortably and set himself to look like a man with nothing better to do than prop a wall up and watch the world go by for the rest of the morning.

It took ten minutes before the gate opened and Averil appeared. 'Go away! What on earth are you doing here?'

Luc straightened, came across and stood next to her under the shelter of the garden wall. No one looking out of the windows in the house could see them there. 'I wondered how you were.' *I needed to see you so much it hurt.* No, he could not admit his weakness to her. Instinct warned him to hide his vulnerability.

'I was perfectly all right until I saw you,' she retorted. 'I almost had a heart stroke.' She was looking delightfully flushed and flustered, but he saw the dark smudges under her eyes and wondered how much sleep she'd had the night before. Had she been thinking about him, or worrying about Bradon?

'You recognised me.'

'I could think of no one else your size who would be lurking in back alleys.' Despite her tone he suspected she was glad to see him. He hoped she was.

'How was it? What is he like?'

'Lord Bradon is perfectly charming and his parents are delightful. I could not be happier.' Her green eyes were dark and shuttered.

'Liar,' he said. 'Something is wrong. Tell me the truth. Did you confess what had happened?'

'I told Lord Bradon this morning. About the shipwreck and being washed up and being in the hut with you for those days and nights. I did not tell him I was naked, or about…about the summer house in the Governor's garden. He was very calm about it. He is—oh, I don't know!' She threw up her hands and for a moment Luc thought she was going to cry, then she tightened her lips and controlled herself. 'He is very emotionless, very cool. They all are. There is no feeling or warmth. But I expect we will get used to one another soon.'

Luc put his hand on her arm. It was good to touch her and hell, too. He wanted to yank her into his embrace and kiss her senseless. She shook her head. 'No, do not do that.' He took his hand away, feeling absurdly as though she had slapped him. 'I do not need sympathy. I will be all right.'

'So what did Bradon say? About us?'

'I told him nothing about you. I told him that I could reveal nothing about the identity of the officer involved because of the secrecy required for the mission. He appeared to accept that.'

'And you are still here. So he believes you are a virgin.'

'No. Not exactly. He either does not trust my word or thinks me too ignorant to know if something had happened while I was unconscious. For a month, until he is certain that I am not with child, it will be put about that I am merely a guest of the Bradons. Once he is sure, then we will become betrothed.'

'My God. The cold-blooded devil. You will not stay with him, surely?'

'Why not? What has changed?' She shrugged and he felt a spurt of anger. This was not Averil, not his Averil, this obedient, long-suffering puppet. 'I did not behave well on the islands, I should have been stronger willed. There is a contract. My family—'

'Your family can shift for themselves!' He fought to keep his voice below a quarterdeck bellow. 'They are adult men, the lot of them. You can't behave like a virgin sacrifice, Averil, and they should not expect it of you.'

'Can't I? What will your wife be? She will not be agreeing to a love match, will she? She will be marrying a man who wants her for her bloodlines and her deportment. Will you lie and pretend to a warmth you do not feel while all the time you sneak off to your mistresses?'

The temper and the shreds of restraint that he was hanging on to by his fingernails escaped him. Luc hauled Averil into his arms and lost track of what he was about to say, let alone what he was thinking. She was soft and yet resilient as she pulled back against his arms, she smelled of a meadow in springtime and his mouth knew what her kiss would taste like.

'I do not sneak,' he snapped. 'And I am not such a damned cynic as this money-grubbing Englishman you are throwing yourself away on either.'

'Luc, please…' *Please go,* she meant. Her mouth was soft and under his hands, her body trembled and he knew he should either release her or just hold her, give her the comfort of some human warmth and care. But the devil that had brought him here was strong and the feel and the scent of her was making his head spin with desire so he took her mouth and closed his eyes on the hurt in her green, exposed, gaze.

She was quivering with anger and desire and vulnerability in his arms. She tasted of his dreams and she felt like heaven and he ravaged her mouth even as she twisted in his arms and kicked at his booted shins with her pretty little slippers.

When he lifted his head she stared back, holding his eyes despite the confusion in her own. He remembered the way she had looked deep into his eyes on St Helen's as she searched for the truth in his words.

'Damn it, Averil. Be mine. Come with me—I'll give you all the warmth you'll ever need.'

'You'll ruin me for your own desires, you mean,' she said flatly. 'Let me go. Promise me you will stay away from me.'

Sick at what he had just done, at the look in her eyes, Luc opened his hands and she stepped back. 'There. Free. But I will not stay away, not while you need me. Not while you want me.' *Not while this madness holds me.*

'You—' The effort it took to regain her poise was visible, but she managed it. 'You are arrogant, Monsieur le Comte. I neither need nor want you. Only your absence. Goodbye.'

Luc opened the gate for her and she went past him a swish of skirts without looking at him. He waited until she was through and said, 'Convince me.' The gate shut in his face and he heard the unmistakable sound of a bolt being drawn across. He should leave her to Bradon, forget her. He ran his tongue over his lips and tasted her—passionate, feminine, innocent—and knew he could no more do it than fly.

'That was reasonably satisfactory.' Andrew Bradon replaced his hat and frowned at the traffic fighting its way up and down Cornhill. There was no sign of the carriage. 'Where has that fool got to?'

'There does not appear to be anywhere he could wait.' Averil stared at a flock of sheep being driven down the middle of the street; it was like Calcutta but cooler and with sheep, not goats. Sheep were easier to think about than what had happened this morning. Two men: ice and fire. They both burned the skin.

'He should have kept circling.' Still fuming about his coachman, Bradon extended his crooked elbow. 'Take my arm.'

'Thank you.' She had fled upstairs from the garden and washed her face and hands, brushed out and redressed her hair, afraid that he would somehow scent Luc on her.

'I do not understand why that lawyer wants all your bills sent to him to settle. He could have entrusted a sum to me to deal with on your behalf.'

'Doubtless Mr Wilton will need to give Papa an exact accounting for the purposes of insurance after the shipwreck.' *And I am going to have to go through my married life being this careful and tactful. Mr Wilton saw no reason to put the money into your hands until he was forced to by my marriage. He is a canny man.*

But he was also a dusty, dry and unimaginative man, she decided. She wondered whether to write to Papa and mention this. Wilton seemed to be the sort of person who would carry out orders even if they made no sense—there was a feeling of unyielding rigidity about him. On the other hand, he did appear to be utterly devoted to Papa's interests. Sir Joshua's word, it seemed, was law.

There was a navy blue uniform and a cocked hat in the crowd pouring out of the Royal Exchange. Averil told herself not to be foolish. The City must be full of naval officers; besides, he had been wearing civilian dress. *Oh, my God. It is him. Luc—*

'My dear? What is wrong?'

'That crossing sweeper—I thought he was going to be struck by the carriage with the red panels.'

And Luc was crossing the road, coming towards them. Her heart beat so hard she thought she would be sick. *No!* He was going to speak. He was going to betray her in some way, make Bradon suspicious and her own position more precarious so that she would be forced into his arms. Averil closed her eyes and tried to banish the memory of just how those arms felt around her and how much she wanted to be in them.

'Excuse me. I think you have dropped this?' Luc stooped and straightened with a man's large linen handkerchief in his hand. He made a polite bow in her direction, but his eyes passed over her with no sign of recognition and his enquiring gaze fixed on Bradon.

'What? No, not mine. Obliged, sir.'

'Not at all. Lord Bradon, is it not?'

'Yes.' Bradon pokered up, whether because he objected to being addressed by a stranger or because he was suspicious of anyone in naval uniform after this morning's revelations, she could not tell.

'Forgive me, but someone pointed you out to me the other day as a considerable connoisseur of porcelain.' Under her palm Averil felt Bradon relax. It was a miracle that he could not feel her own pounding pulse.

'You are interested?'

'As a mere amateur. I was able to pick up some interesting Copenhagen items when I was in that area recently.'

'Indeed? I do not believe we have been introduced.' Bradon's manner became almost cordial.

'Captain le comte Luc d'Aunay.'

Averil managed to breathe. Bradon would not suspect a count of involvement with an undercover operation and, thanks to the remark about Copenhagen, he now had a mental image of Luc being posted somewhere in the North Sea. And Luc was very properly not acknowledging a lady to whom he had not been introduced and not, as she had feared, doing anything to make Bradon suspicious. Perhaps this was a coincidental meeting. Had he recovered from that morning's madness?

'...interesting dealer off the Strand,' Bradon was saying as she pulled herself together to listen to the two men. 'Feel free to mention my name.'

'Thank you, I will certainly do that. Good day.' Luc raised his hat, his gaze focused on Averil for the first time. His expression was perfectly bland with just the hint of a query.

Her escort seemed to remember her presence. 'Er, Miss Heydon, from India.'

'Ma'am. India? I thought I had not had the pleasure of seeing you in town before.' The bow was perfectly judged: polite and indifferent with just the hint of masculine appreciation that would be expected.

'Captain.' She inclined her head. 'Lord Bradon's family has kindly asked me to stay with them for a month.'

'I will not delay your sightseeing any longer. Thank you for the recommendation, Bradon.'

As Bradon turned to hail their carriage Averil glanced

back, but Luc was gone, swallowed up by the crowds. What had he been doing there? Surely not following her? He had work to do at the Admiralty, she was certain; it would do his career no good if he neglected that in order to dog her footsteps in the hope she would throw her bonnet over the windmill and decide to become his mistress!

'We will return to Bruton Street,' Bradon said as they settled into the carriage. 'Mama will have given Finch her instructions on where to take you and what you will need. We must have you creditably outfitted before anyone else sees you in that hand-me-down gown.'

'Yes, my lord.' Averil bit her lip and reminded herself of her duty and that tumbling out of the carriage and running up Cornhill in search of Luc would be madness.

Luc took one of the side alleys, went into the George and Vulture, the first tavern he came to, and sat at an empty table in the taproom. 'A pint of lush,' he said to the girl who approached, wiping her hands on her apron. Brandy was tempting, but strong beer was prudent.

He still could not credit that Bradon was waiting a month to see if she was with child. Calculating devil. At least he had seen him now. After what Averil had said that morning he could not rest until he had seen her with her betrothed, seen how the man was with her. The tankard came and he took a swallow. Good London beer, full of hops and dry in the mouth; he had missed that.

Yes, he was a calculating devil who did not believe Averil when she told him she was a virgin. Luc realised he was angry and drank again while he sorted that out in his head. Bradon did not believe her; in fact, he thought she could well be lying. He deserved to be called out for that alone, Luc thought as he drained the tankard.

Getting changed, visiting the Admiralty, had distracted him not an iota from the anguish and confusion that morning's encounter had caused, but he had not had time to think too deeply about the workings of Bradon's mind.

Damn it, Averil was so patently honest, he thought now. Didn't the fool realise that she could have spun him any number of yarns—with the full support of Sir George and his sister? Bradon did not deserve her, but the very fact that he was keeping her, for a month at least, proved that he wanted her, or her dowry, more than he cared about her maidenhead and his own honour.

In a month, possibly much sooner, he would realise that she was not with child and then the marriage would go ahead. She would become Lady Bradon and be lost to Luc for ever.

The fantasy that had been sustaining him since he had sailed from Scilly, of Averil spread beneath him on a wide bed, gasping his name as he drove them both to ecstasy, gripped him afresh, only this time not with a wash of pleasurable anticipation, but with claws of frustration. He snapped his fingers for another tankard. Frustration and loss, if he was to take her at her word and leave her to the other man. Damn it, but he needed her. Where else would he find that enticing mixture of courage and sensuality, beauty and honesty, innocence and spirit?

A group of clerks came in, loudly discussing a prize fight, and called for ale and food as they settled at the next table. Luc nursed his beer and let their argument wash over him until the arrival of their pie reminded him that he had been up since dawn working on his notes about the Scillies traitor. Then he had found his feet leading him to Bruton Street to watch for Averil and to try to find out what had happened with Bradon.

Now he knew. Bradon would marry her and she had

accepted that, and his lack of trust in her. The meek way she had stood there just now, her hand on his arm, ignored by the men, waiting to be acknowledged, made his blood boil. Bradon would be satisfied with his bargain, that was for sure, but he doubted it would give Averil any joy.

But her joy, or lack of it, was no longer his business, it seemed. He ordered pie and told himself that he had to stop thinking about her. He had a wife to find. A home to build. Somehow it no longer seemed so straightforward or desirable.

For two days Averil shopped, with Finch the stiff-backed dresser at her elbow and Grace, almost bursting with the effort to behave with as much decorum as Finch, at her heels. She wrote to Mrs Bastable, her chaperone on the *Bengal Queen* and another letter to her father. She wanted to write to Dita, who must now be safe at home in Devon with her family, recovering from her ordeal. But she could not risk to writing what she had to confide to her friend; she must just hope Dita would come up to London soon. She needed her so much.

She took delivery of her new clothes and supervised her borrowed ones being cleaned, parcelled up and returned to Miss Gordon along with a letter of thanks and the assurance that her banker was dealing with the money she owed Sir George.

She arranged flowers for Lady Kingsbury and suffered her purchases to be examined and approved. She thanked her future mother-in-law for the loan of a pearl set and some garnets and sat and addressed invitation cards for a *soirée* in a week's time and she felt as though her heart was weeping in sympathy with the rain that was pouring down outside.

As they drove back from church on Sunday Lady

Kingsbury was graciously pleased to compliment her on her walking dress and bonnet. 'You dress with taste, Miss Heydon.'

There was no sign of the earl—he appeared only at dinner and then left. The countess did not appear remotely discommoded by his neglect. Perhaps she was glad of it, as Averil might become glad of Bradon's absence once she was married to him. She shivered.

'Thank you, ma'am.'

'You will accompany me to the Countess of Middle-hampton's reception on Tuesday evening. That will introduce you to a number of people of influence without the necessity to concern ourselves with dancing yet. You can dance, I trust?'

'Yes, ma'am. I enjoy it.'

'Excellent. Tomorrow I will review your new wardrobe with you and give you some guidance on who you will meet in London this Season. Do feel free to ask me any questions about matters of etiquette—I am sure things are different here from what you are used to.'

'Thank you, ma'am.' So, she was to be assessed to make certain she would behave the right way. Averil had no way of telling whether Bradon had told either of his parents the shocking tale of her rescue. She saw virtually nothing of the earl, and Lady Kingsbury, she suspected, would remain poker-faced and cool if she found herself in the midst of the Cyprians' Ball.

Her spirits rose despite the thought of Lady Kingsbury's critical assessment. It was frivolous, but a reception would mean new people to meet, entertainment, a change of scene, noise, human contact, warmth. She needed warmth as a drooping flower needed water. She needed, more than anything, someone to put their arms around her and simply hug her.

Chapter Seventeen

The Middlehampton reception delivered as much noise, heat and distraction as Averil could have hoped for. For the first time since the *Bengal Queen* had entered northern waters she felt warm enough.

Lady Kingsbury introduced her to a number of other young unmarried ladies and drifted off to gossip with her own cronies while Lord Bradon vanished in the direction of the card rooms. That suited Averil very well indeed. She smiled and chatted and one young lady introduced her to another and so on until her head was spinning with the effort of remembering names. Many of them had beaux and the young men flirted with Averil and the girls wanted to know about Indian silks and they all wanted to hear about life in the East and she found herself laughing and talking as if she was back in Calcutta with her friends.

She turned, gurgling with laughter over Mr Crowther's tale of how he had encountered an elephant at some eccentric house party in Hampshire and had been prevailed upon to mount on to its back—'Into a howdedo'—

and had fallen off and his hat had been eaten by the elephant. 'They brought it back to me three days later,' he finished mournfully. 'But it was never the same again.'

There was an elegant girl reflected in one of the long mirrors, her face alight with amusement, her gown just like Averil's. *It is me! My goodness. How very* au fait *I look.* And then a figure in a blue tailcoat with gold lace and white collar tabs appeared in the glass behind her and the laughter fled, leaving her wide-eyed and breathless.

'Miss Heydon. Do you remember me? We met in the City five days ago.' Luc stood there, *chapeau bras* tucked under one arm, dress sword at his side, the picture of the perfect naval officer. *Which he is,* she thought, her stomach swooping.

'Of course. Captain d'Aunay, is it not? May I make you known to Miss Langham and Miss Frederica Arthur? And Mr Crowther, who has had much more exciting experiences of elephants than I ever had in India.' She had an instinct to hide him in a mass of other people, even though she wanted him all to herself, alone. If Bradon saw them together he could find no blame if they were part of the crowd, surely? After all, he had introduced them himself.

Lady Kingsbury walked past as the two of them stood talking to half-a-dozen others, separated by the vivacious Miss Langham. She scanned the group with a critical eye and inclined her head in approval.

'That's your mama-in-law to be, I gather.' Luc had come back to her side.

'Yes.' There was so much noise that although they stood just a few paces away from the nearest group they would have had to have screamed before anyone would have picked up their words.

'She looks a cold fish.'

'She is.' Averil shivered. 'They all are.'

'I still have trouble realising that he proposes this month's trial to make sure no little mistake is in the offing.' He sounded comfortingly outraged on her behalf.

'Yes. I was…surprised. I thought that if he did not believe me, the fact he thought I was not…you know… that would be enough to reject me.' Part of her, madly, wished he had. Then she could be with Luc. And ruined, she reminded herself. 'I suppose I have too much money for that.'

'And yet you stay.'

He sounded cold and angry and she bit her lip against the hurt of it. 'Of course. There is an agreement. Why did you follow us into the City? Do you want to risk everything?'

'I had to see you with him. You looked beautiful, but you are unhappy.' Luc moved a little closer, his back to the room, and she found herself in an alcove. It was all right, she told herself, there was no curtain, she could be seen by anyone who looked and all they were doing was talking.

'I never expected happiness exactly. I did not know him after all, let alone love him. Contentment will come—it must. But, oh, I long for some warmth, to be held.' Her voice trailed away. Luc stood like a statue and then reached for her hands. 'No. I cannot. We must not. If there is the slightest suspicion of us, it would be a disaster. I am simply being feeble, I think.' She put up her chin and smiled a determined smile.

'Feeble? My God,' Luc said with a sort of suppressed fury. 'I could shake you, you idiot girl.' He spun on his heel and stalked off. Averil followed the dark head until it vanished through the double doors that opened on to the hall. He had gone and he was obviously angry with her, which was so unreasonable of him. She was doing her best to be brave and dutiful, although that appeared to anger him, and he must realise that she could not flirt, let alone permit anything more intimate.

She had thought that he cared for her, wanted what was right for her, but it seemed that all he wanted was her in his bed until he tired of her and frustration was making him irritable.

Well, she was frustrated too. She almost wished Andrew Bradon would take some liberties, just so she could be held and kissed. But she wanted Luc and it was so unfair of him to teach her to feel passion and then... Then what? He had done what she asked of him and let her go to Bradon instead of abducting her in a thoroughly shocking and romantic manner. Which is what, she very much feared, she had wanted him to do.

Thoroughly exasperated with herself and Luc, and Bradon, Averil swept out of the alcove and rejoined the party. Frederica Arthur came over and linked her arm though hers. 'Oh, has that handsome naval captain gone already?'

'You think him handsome?'

'Well, not conventionally, perhaps.' Miss Arthur lowered her voice. 'But he is very manly, do you not agree?'

'It is the uniform,' Averil said repressively.

'Perhaps.' Her companion's eyes twinkled with mischief. 'And I do so enjoy flirting and making my poor Hugh jealous.'

'You are betrothed?'

'To Sir Hugh Malcolm—see, over there, the tall man with blond hair by the potted palm. We will be married next month. I cannot wait.' The mischief left her face to be replaced with a tender look. 'I want to start a family as soon as possible. I love children, don't you?'

'Yes. Yes, I suppose I do.' Averil realised she had never thought much about the matter. Children were part of family life, part of her obligation to Bradon. But, listening to Frederica's happy plans as the other young woman chattered on, she realised that just because she had taken the idea for granted did not mean it was not important. The abstract concept of children became an image of a real child, a baby. How wonderful. Andrew Bradon seemed steady and responsible, even if he was not demonstrative and his approach to their marriage was coldly practical. He would be a proud father, she thought. A good father.

'There you are, my dear. I was looking for you to take you in to supper.' Andrew Bradon was looking positively animated.

'You have had luck at the card tables?' Averil enquired as he steered her towards the supper room. She realised now that his father was a serious gamester and that was where much of the family fortune had gone. She was not pleased at the thought that her dowry, and their children's inheritance, might be frittered away by her husband.

'Very gratifying. I only play for low stakes, you understand. My father is the gamester in our family.' He found a table and pulled out a chair for Averil. 'You do not play cards, I trust?'

'No, I do not.' She smiled up at him and saw a glimmer of answering interest. 'I am so glad you only play moderately.'

He was still unusually animated when he returned with food for her. 'You look very well, this evening, my dear. In excellent health and looks. Your appetite is good, I trust?'

'Oh, yes, I feel very well, thank you.'

For a moment she did not understand, then he patted

her hand and said, 'Excellent', before attacking his own selection of patties, and she realised he thought her robust health indicated that she was not in a delicate condition.

Perhaps he is just shy and hides it behind a façade of indifference, she thought and watched him from beneath her lashes. He would never be Luc—that was wishing for the moon—but perhaps she had misjudged him. *I will be happy. I will forget Luc,* she vowed, and smiled at Andrew again.

Chapter Eighteen

'The reception went very well,' Lady Kingsbury pronounced as they drove back to Bruton Street. Averil could still not think of it as *home*. 'You have already made a number of most suitable acquaintances. We will attend the Farringdons' ball tomorrow night, I think. Brandon, I trust we may count on your escort?'

'Of course, Mama.'

'Unfortunately it is a Wednesday, but we will visit Almack's next week. There are certain to be several of the Patronesses at the ball. I will secure a voucher for you.'

'Thank you, ma'am. Is the fact that it is Wednesday relevant?'

'Of course. A ball and supper every Wednesday during the Season. Do you not know about Almack's?'

'Oh, yes, ma'am. My friend Lady Perdita Brooke told me about it on the ship, I just did not understand about Wednesdays.'

'Perdita Brooke? You know her well?'

'Very well. She is my particular friend. You may

imagine my relief when I discovered that she, too, had survived the wreck. She was saved by Viscount Lyndon.'

'He is now Marquis of Iwerne. That is not an acquaintance I would wish you to pursue. The man is a gazetted rake and as for Lady Perdita, there was considerable talk before she left for India. Shocking behaviour. She eloped and was some time in the company of a most unsuitable young man.'

'But, ma'am, she is my friend! And Lord Lyndon, I mean, Iwerne—I have something of his that was washed up after the wreck. I was going to write and send it to him.'

'I forbid you to correspond with either of them,' Lady Kingsbury said. 'We cannot be too careful under the circumstances.' *So she does know her son believes I lost my virginity.* 'You will promise me, Averil.'

It was the first time the other woman had used her first name. 'I will not write to Dita, if that is what you wish, ma'am.'

'Then that must be the end of it. Yes?'

'I promise.' But Dita would come to London soon; she had not promised not to meet her, only not to write. And somehow she would return Dita's gift to Alistair, that would not be *corresponding.* She could do that without breaking her word.

Averil was enchanted by the Farringdons' ballroom with its swags of spring flowers, fountains and little sitting-out alcoves created with the cunning use of striped canvas. The whole room resembled a *fête champêtre* on a sunny day.

'How delightful! I do not think I have ever seen anything so fresh and pretty.'

'Hush, my dear. One should not appear gauche and

over-excited. Do try for more decorum,' Lady Kingsbury reproved as they made their way from the receiving line into the throng in the ballroom. Arriving too early was another fault to be avoided, apparently. Averil felt decidedly provincial.

There were scarlet jackets in abundance amongst the severe black and midnight-blue tailcoats, and several groups of naval officers as well. Averil scanned them and then tried to decide whether she was pleased or not that Luc was absent.

'Ah, there is the dear Duc de la Valière,' Lady Kingsbury said, nodding towards a group on the far side of the room. 'In fact, half the *émigrée* community appears to be here this evening.'

With tacit permission to stare, Averil studied the dozen or so people in conversation around the plump figure with his chest covered in decorations and orders. The ladies were all dressed in what she had come to recognise already as the latest stare and she looked with envy at one particular gown of pale sea-green with azure ribbons.

Its wearer was deploying her fan with her eyes fixed on a tall, dark gentleman next to her. The group shifted a little and Averil found herself staring at Luc wearing civilian evening dress.

Every good resolution to forget him promptly flew out of the window. Averil let out a long breath and tried to understand how she was feeling. Happy, apprehensive, aroused—oh, dear, he still made her ache when she saw him and there were flutters of wicked sensation in the most embarrassing places. Her nipples hardened against the muslin of her chemise. But most of all, seeing him made her happy in a strange, painful way. She wanted to be with him.

'What lovely gowns the French ladies have,' she remarked, searching for a reason for her close interest.

'Smuggled silks and lace,' Bradon said. 'Come, I will introduce you to the *duc*. One meets him everywhere, you know—a great crony of Prinny's.'

It was hard not to look at Luc as they crossed the floor. Averil made her curtsy to the *duc*, salvaged enough of her unreliable French to reply to his rather effusive compliments and stepped back while Bradon continued to talk to the older man. The effort not to look at Luc was making her feel awkward. In fact, she thought, as she felt her whole body stiffening up, she probably looked as though she was too shy, or perhaps too stand-offish, to look at any of the others in the group.

'Miss Heydon?'

Averil gasped, dropped her fan, reticule and dance card and felt herself blush peony-pink as she bent to scrabble them up. 'Ouch!' Her head made contact with another and she sat down, hard, on the floor.

'Miss Heydon—'

'Averil!'

Hands seized each arm and she was pulled to her feet feeling like a cross between a rag doll and a small child. On one side Bradon was a picture of disapproval, as well he might be. On the other Luc was biting the inside of his cheek in an effort not to laugh. At least the irritation with her that had gripped him last time they met appeared to have gone. She smoothed her skirts while she fought for composure.

'Miss Heydon, I do apologise.' At least he was speaking English, thank heavens. She did not think she could cope with this in French. 'First I make you jump, then I almost knock you out. May I fetch you some lemonade, or help you to a chair?'

'Miss Heydon will be quite all right with me, Captain d'Aunay,' Bradon said, cutting across her own response.

'Thank you both, I am fine, I assure you.' She spoke to a point in the air midway between the two men. 'It was the merest bump.'

'In that case, Miss Heydon, might I ask for a dance?'

Beside her she felt Bradon shift as though he was about to intervene, then he relaxed and she breathed out. He could not have it both ways, she thought with a spurt of amusement. Either she was his betrothed and he could legitimately bristle at any man wanting her attention or she was merely a guest and, provided she was not accosted by an undesirable partner, he really had nothing to say on the matter.

'I would be delighted, Captain. Or should I say Monsieur le Comte, as you are out of uniform?' she asked as she proffered her rather crumpled dance card. Of course, if Bradon only knew it, Luc was absolutely the most undesirable partner for her.

'Captain is less of a mouthful,' Luc said, his eyes smiling into hers as he looked up from filling in the card in a way that brought the blush back to warm her cheeks. 'I have taken the liberty of marking two sets including the supper dance.'

Bradon stiffened again, then remarked, 'Your very first partner at your first English ball', in such an insufferably patronising tone that she wanted to hit him.

'Oh, no, not my first partner,' she said, smiling wide-eyed at him. 'See.' She turned the card so he could see Luc's initials against the third set and the supper set. The first two sets were free.

'Then allow me.' Bradon whipped the card from her hand, frowned at it, then put his initials against the first set and another after supper. Luc lowered one eyelid in what might have been the ghost of a wink and turned back to the young lady in sea-green, who was, of course, speaking French.

She had auburn hair and was quite lovely. She also appeared to find Luc fascinating. In fact, it seemed mutual, judging by the intensity with which they were making eye contact. Something tightened inside Averil, an uncomfortable twist of what was almost apprehension.

For goodness' sake! Why should Luc not enjoy talking to a pretty young woman? He was, she reminded herself, looking for a wife. A French wife. It would be foolish indeed of her to expect him to reject the company of other women simply because she was not going to become his mistress.

He had probably already taken a new mistress, she thought, sliding even deeper into gloom at the thought. He was not a man to stay celibate for long, she was sure.

The scrape of bowstrings caused the chattering guests to turn towards the floor and the first chords from the orchestra on the dais brought the dancers on to the floor to make up the first set, the country dance that was opening the ball.

Bradon took her arm and steered her into the line of ladies before taking his place facing her. Lady Farringdon, a sprightly blonde, took the head of the line, called the first figure, and they were away. Averil was too occupied in concentrating on her steps to do more than follow Bradon's lead for at least the first fifteen minutes, then they were safely down the line, had executed a complicated figure without her falling over and disgracing herself again and she began to relax a trifle.

Luc was halfway down the line, partnered by the girl in sea-green, who was, of course, dancing with grace and confidence and managing to talk at the same time.

He was courting her, it was obvious in the way he moved, the way he looked at her, the way she coyly avoided looking at him. The sensation in Averil's stomach stopped being a vague discomfort and became a pain she recognised, even though she had never felt it before. It was jealousy. Full-blown, green-eyed, savage jealousy. She should be ashamed. But she was not.

I love him, Averil thought, and turned blindly to follow Bradon's lead through the next figure. *I love him.* It was not simply desire, or gratitude for her rescue. She wanted him body and soul and heart, even if he never touched her or kissed her again. She wanted him as the father of her children. She wanted to grow old with him.

Appalled, Averil looked at Bradon, the man to whom she would be tied for life, who would be, if she was blessed with them, the father of her children. And she could feel nothing except a vague pity for his coldness.

He was well-enough looking, there would be nothing to actively repel her when he came to her bed. He seemed intelligent enough. Until a few minutes ago the fact that she did not love him had not mattered one iota—she had not expected ever to experience that emotion. Now she was dizzy with despair because she knew what it felt like to love a man and she could never have him.

'Are you quite well, my dear?' Bradon bent to murmur in her ear as the measure brought them to stand side by side. 'You have gone quite pale.'

'It is very warm in here,' she lied. Her limbs felt numb with cold.

'I would have thought that after India you would be accustomed,' he said with a frown. 'You are not... unwell?'

'No, I am not,' she almost snapped back. 'And I have been out of India's heat for months now, my lord.'

'We had best sit out the remainder of the set, I think.' He took her arm to guide her out of the line, but Averil resisted. She did not want to have to sit with nothing to do but think, nothing to look at but Luc and the French girl, so absorbed in each other.

Somehow she got through the set, and the next, a cotillion where she was partnered by a shy young man who hardly managed to articulate his request for the dance. Without any need to converse Averil was left to work her way through the complex figures and to brood on Luc.

Even if he knew she loved him he would not marry her. He had made his requirements in a bride quite clear. She must be French and even Averil's spoken French was inadequate. She must be of aristocratic breeding and Averil's grandfather had been a shopkeeper. There was nothing except a physical attraction to make him want her and she had a sinking suspicion that once he had made love to her fully and satisfied that urge, then she would hold no further attraction for him. She was hardly skilled in the arts of love. How long, she wondered gloomily, would he have kept her if she had yielded to his desire and become his mistress? A week, a month?

Shy Mr McCormack delivered her back to Lady Kingsbury with mumbled thanks. The orchestra stopped to retune, the volume of conversation rose. At any moment Luc would come to claim her for the next set and she had not the slightest idea what she would talk to him about, or even if she was capable of conversation.

She was so lost in painful thought that when he appeared in front of her in the flesh she gasped.

'Am I startling you again, Miss Heydon? I do apologise.' Luc stood there, elegant and groomed, a thousand miles from the piratical figure who had hauled her naked from the beach on St Helen's. But that man was still there with the dangerous fire in those deep grey eyes, the jut of that arrogant nose, the set of the determined chin. And the lean figure, all hard-toned muscle and long bones that made her mouth dry with desire when she looked at him. Those were the same.

And so was the mouth that could thin into a hard line of anger or curve into a smile that made her want to follow him into sin and back, that could bark orders in one breath and breathe promises of those sins with another.

'I was momentarily distracted, Count,' Averil said. She got to her feet without a stumble by focusing every ounce of concentration on her deportment. *I stand just so, my hands like this, my back straight and shoulders down. Head up. Fan and reticule—both under control. Chin up. Smile. Put out my hand to him...*

She thought she was succeeding admirably until they took their places for the quadrille. 'What is wrong, Averil?'

'A headache, that is all.' The smile became brighter.

'You no more have a headache than I have. Is it your thoughts that are painful?'

'Perhaps,' she admitted. 'It is not such an easy thing as I thought it would be, to travel so many miles and to learn to live with strangers on such terms of intimacy.'

'Do you think Bradon will become easier with acquaintance?'

'He is not a man who finds it easy to give expression to his feelings,' Averil said, choosing her words with care.

'If he has any,' Luc countered.

There was a slight confusion in a far corner of the dance floor. A young lady had fainted, it seemed. Partners relaxed and began to talk quietly to each other while chaperones bustled about.

'His reactions so far do argue a lack of trust,' Averil said. 'But then, he knows as little about me as I do of him.'

'It is not simply a question of trust.' Luc frowned. 'There is a practical expediency about it that I do not like—it does not seem to matter to him whether you told the truth or not, merely whether there would be consequences if you had not. I could understand him deciding that he would not marry you because you had been compromised, but this is having his cake and eating it, too.'

'I suppose any man might be concerned about such consequences,' Averil murmured. 'You would, surely, if it was a question of the charming young lady in sea-green?'

He looked across the room. 'Mademoiselle de la Falaise? Perhaps I would.'

Indeed you would. 'Is she the one?'

'Perhaps,' he said again. 'She is very lovely, very well bred. Her mother is a distant cousin on my father's side. Her father's estates are in Normandy also.'

'Perfect.' It was true, what they said: the heart did break and you could feel it, a hard, sickening pain like the crack of a bone splintering.

'Time will tell. I do not know if there is any depth or spirit under the elegant little tricks and she does not know me at all. And her father is suspicious of the half-breed naval captain. He, too, wants to return to France, to take his place back at court, to be what he once was. He must choose his sons-in-law with care. Am I French enough for him? Where do my loyalties lie? Am I a dangerous constitutionalist like my father? He wonders about those things.'

'Do you wonder? You sound very French now,' Averil said. Her lips felt numb, but she kept smiling.

'Really?' Luc's voice was sombre. He added something half under his breath and she strained to catch it as the band struck up again and couples straightened up and resumed their positions. *I wish I knew where I belonged, what I was.* Had he really said that? But he seemed so assured, so certain about his desire to return to France.

'Oh, yes. Your intonation has changed, there is the faintest accent. It is most attractive,' she added lightly, testing her own composure by being a trifle daring.

'And you,' Luc said as he took her hand and the first steps of the dance brought them almost breast to breast. The dark mood seemed to have fled as fast as it had arrived. 'You are even more lovely than you were on my desert island, *ma sirène.*'

She could translate that: *my mermaid.* 'You should not flirt with me while you are courting Mademoiselle de la Falaise.' And that was all it was, flirtation. It came so easily to him, so hard to her. Or perhaps the difference was simply that her feelings were engaged and his were not.

'I do not know how to flirt with you, Averil,' he said as the dance parted them for a wide circle. As they came back together he was frowning. 'With you, I can speak only the truth, it seems.'

'Then you should not speak such truths,' she said and looked up into his eyes. His expression changed, sharpened, and too late she realised that she had done nothing to shield her own. What had he seen in her face, in her gaze?

'Averil, leave him. It is not too late.'

She was silent. The other couples were too close, her heart was beating too hard to find breath for words. When, minutes later, the music stopped and with it the end of the first dance, she stepped off the floor and into one of the little striped tents that were scattered around the room.

'Leave him? For what? My ruin, if you are still asking me to be your mistress.'

'Come to me. I will deal honestly with you, Averil.'

She sat down in a swirl of peach silk and gauze and he stayed on his feet facing her, sombre. Anyone looking in would think, perhaps, that they had intruded on a proposal. And that, of course, was just what it had been. A dishonourable proposal.

'Then let us be entirely honest, shall we? You seek a bride, quite coolly, as though you select the right horse for your carriage.' She paused to get her breathing under control. She must not let him see how this affected her. 'You chose one who will restore the part of you that is not French because, somehow, your identity is compromised by your English blood. You want me, for reasons I will not explore here, and so, just as coolly, you offer me my ruin. Because I am a merchant's daughter, and English, and therefore fit for nothing else. You call Bradon cold and practical. Have you looked in the mirror? That description fits you just as well, I think.'

'You want to marry me?' Luc asked, looking at her as though he had never seen her before.

'I think,' Averil said, finding her anger and with it breath to continue, 'that you should remove yourself before I forget that I am a lady—insofar as a daughter of trade can be, of course—and throw one of these flower arrangements over your arrogant, smug male person.'

Chapter Nineteen

Luc turned on his heel and walked away, not because he feared a bouquet being thrown at his head, but because he was so strongly tempted to turn Miss Averil Heydon over his knee and… Or, strangle her. Or shake some sense into her. But it was he who needed sense knocking into. What had he said? That had almost been a proposal.

Louise de la Falaise saw him from across the room and made a pretty little gesturing motion with her fan. He bowed and walked on. She was very lovely and intelligent, too, as far as he could tell, with her every move and word being supervised by her mama. He should desire her, but he did not, even though she was probably the woman he would propose to. He desired one woman only and she was impossible.

Averil was English. His father had married an Englishwoman and their only child had never known where he belonged, where his loyalties lay, which identity was his. When the time had come to make a decision and take a stand, he had not had the strength to stand up to his mother and to remain in France with his father. The fact that he was just a boy made no difference. If he had stayed, he supposed that now he would be long cold in his grave.

But he had made his choice, he lived and now he had made a decision: as his father's son he could make no other. He had lands and responsibilities to resume and to hand on to a son who would at least be three-quarters French.

Averil was…impossible. The scandal if she left Bradon would be shocking; he could not believe the man would take the loss of such a dowry lying down. She was wrong for him, as wrong as a dangerous drug would be. And he must not compromise her. Bradon had accepted her, she had accepted Bradon for what he was. It would be the action of a blackguard to seduce her away now.

There was Bradon now, talking to a striking brunette. He felt a wave of dislike run through him. The man bristled proprietarily when he saw Averil with another man, but he made no move to touch her except to take her arm formally. His eyes did not follow her with anything in them except a cool assessment. He did not even desire her person, it seemed.

Luc stopped, then swung back, apologising to the officer he almost flattened with the suddenness of his movement. He passed a footman with a tray and lifted two glasses from it as he went. Averil was still sitting in the gay little tent, just as he had left her, her face calm, her hands folded decorously in her lap, her eyes blank.

She looked up as his shadow fell at her feet and went a little pale, but she made no move to throw the arrangement of hothouse lilies on the table beside her as she had threatened.

'Here.' He thrust the glass into her hand and drained

his own. 'Does he make love to you?' He sounded like a jealous fool. He did not care.

'Bradon?' Averil looked at the glass as though she had never seen one before. 'No.'

'Does he kiss you? Caress you?'

'No. He kissed my hand, once. He shows no affection and no desire. Why do you ask?' She took a mouthful of the champagne, swallowed. 'What possible business is it of yours what my betrothed does? Please do not tell me you are jealous of him—what right have you?'

'I saved you on that beach and then made a decision that could have—may have—ruined you. I—'

'Oh, so now you are going to tell me again that you feel responsible for me?' Averil got to her feet in an inelegant scramble, tossed back the wine with a reckless hand and stood toe to toe with him, glaring up. 'Well, you are not. I may have been innocent, but I was not addled—I am responsible for the decisions I made. And if you think I should be grateful to you—'

'I think that you are just the right height for me to kiss,' Luc said, ignoring the music and voices and laughter at his back, ignoring her anger. All he could see was her face, all he could smell was the fresh sweetness of her skin, all he could hear was his own blood pounding in his ears and the madness of a need he did not understand, that was so much more than lust, sweeping through him.

'No.' Averil stepped back and the pain deep in her eyes stopped him as abruptly as if she had slammed a door in his face. 'No. I cannot bear this. It may all be about physical pleasure, the fun of the chase, for you. But it is not for me. For me it is a torment. I am not one of your sophisticated matrons or headstrong daughters of the aristocracy. I am a merchant's daughter and I was not brought up for these games. I was brought up to keep my word and to respect and honour my husband.'

'Averil, I am sorry—' He would cut out his heart and lay it at her feet if that would help. It could not hurt any more than the pain in it now.

'Oh, I do not blame you,' she said bitterly. 'You flirt and make love like a hound chases a rabbit—on instinct. If I had not been so weak, Bradon would still have cause for suspicion, but at least I would have a clear conscience and I would not have to be fighting the temptation to give in to you.' She gave a little sob that turned the knife in his heart. 'I would not have known what it was to be made love to as you made love to me, I would have known only him.' Appalled, Luc reached for her. She batted his hands away. 'Go. If you have any concern for me at all, *any,* go and leave me alone.'

Hell. What had he done? She was right, she did not know how to deal with the likes of him and he had no idea how to deal with her, except in his bed. Her chin came up and he could see the effort it was costing her to stand there and confront him like this. His temper, for some reason never far below the surface these days, flared. He wanted to hurt someone, to share the pain that racked him.

'Yes, I will go. As you say, Miss Heydon, I should not be toying with someone who does not understand the rules these games are played by.' He held up his hands in a gesture of surrender. 'Your virtue has defeated me.'

He knew he sounded ungracious, angry, sarcastic, all the things he had no right to feel. He expected her anger in return, was braced for tears. What he did not expect was for the well-behaved Miss Heydon to scoop up the vase of lilies and throw it at his head, just as she had threatened.

Luc caught it before it hit him, but water and lilies went everywhere, showering his immaculate evening clothes. Averil gasped, then turned and slipped through the flap at the back of the little tent, leaving him to shake himself like a wet dog. Lily pollen stained his shirt front as he batted petals from his lapels and water ran down his nose and dripped to the floor.

Behind him the flaps of the tent shifted. 'Ah, there you are!' said Mademoiselle de la Falaise in French. 'It is our dance next, *monsieur.*'

He turned and she stared, her mouth open. '*Mon Dieu!* What has occurred?'

'I was unaccountably clumsy,' he said. 'I tripped. Obviously I cannot stay at the ball. You will excuse me. I regret greatly that I must forgo our dance.'

'I also, but there is nothing to be done.' She shrugged with rueful charm. 'I must go and find a dry gentleman. Goodbye.' Her lips were twitching as she turned and left.

'Goodbye indeed,' Luc muttered. That had done his dignity with the woman he was thinking of courting a great deal of good to be sure. Now what? He could hardly walk out on to the dance floor looking like this. Where had Averil got out? He investigated the back of the tent and found it opened out on to a corridor under the orchestra gallery and it was mercifully empty. Luc gritted his teeth and stalked off to the front door.

'I thought you were engaged for the supper dance, my dear.' Bradon appeared in front of Averil as she sat on a gilt chair in the furthest corner from the little striped tent.

'I was. I gather Captain d'Aunay had an accident and had to leave.'

'I trust he is not badly injured. If no one else has

claimed you, perhaps you would care to dance with me.'
He held out his hand and Averil put hers into it.

'Thank you, I would prefer that in any case.' He
smirked a little, she noticed. She fixed a bright smile
on her own face. It was time to face the future as Lady
Bradon and convince her betrothed that she was indeed
the wife for him. After all, the man she loved was an
unscrupulous scoundrel who lost his temper when
thwarted. Andrew Bradon's cool equanimity was positively soothing after that scene in the tent.

She wondered what had come over her as she tried
to feel remorseful for losing her temper so thoroughly
and with such violence. What if she had hit him with the
crystal vase?

He deserved it, the angry little voice inside her said.
Just fall out of love with him, that is all you need to do.

Of course. Fall out of love. She smiled up at Bradon
as they took their places. It was a matter of will-power.
'Six days of our month have gone already, my lord,' she
said and saw his pupils widen. He was not as indifferent
to her as she thought.

'You are a formal little thing, aren't you?' he said.
'You should call me Bradon.'

'Yes…Bradon.' Was she supposed to have known that
would be acceptable without being asked? No matter.
Provided she made no major breach of etiquette he
seemed to like putting her right. Being patronised was
just something else she must add to her list of things to
become accustomed to. Somehow it no longer seemed of
importance, she was so unhappy. The pain could not stay
this acute for ever, Averil told herself as she stumbled and
Bradon steadied her. When it became a dull ache then
she would manage better.

'I am so looking forward to Almack's,' she said.

'Ah, yes, Mama has secured you vouchers. She will explain the rules to you—there is no need to be nervous about it.'

'I wasn't,' Averil said and he frowned.

'You should be. Pay great attention to what Mama tells you—making a good impression at Almack's is vital.'

'Yes, Bradon,' she said meekly and told herself he was only concerned that she was not embarrassed.

Resolutions were all very well, Averil realised at one in the morning as she sat up in bed and lit a candle. She should have gone to sleep half an hour ago when she climbed into bed, but her eyes, hot and heavy, would not stay closed and her mind would not settle.

I love him and I cannot have him. I should not want him. I must learn to forget him. How long would it take? If only she could marry Bradon now, or in a few days' time. Then perhaps her foolish heart would give up, because then being with Luc would be an impossibility.

But it would be another two weeks before the arrival of her courses convinced his mother that there was no danger of her carrying another man's child. Then there would be all the necessary preparations to be made, her drowned trousseau to replace, arrangements to be made. Another month at least.

Averil tossed and turned and finally gave up. The soft pile of the carpet cradled her feet in luxury as she slid out of the high bed, reminding her of her new circumstances. She would go down to the library and find a book, or a fashion journal or something to distract her mind until she could sleep.

The house was quiet as she padded downstairs in bare feet. Her ghostly reflection in her white robe made her jump as she came face to face with a mirror on the first landing and her heart was still thudding as she walked across the hall to the library door.

The fire was burning low in the grate, but candles were still lit and she found the pile of journals on a side table easily enough. Fashion and frivolity to distract her or something serious, sermons perhaps, to make her concentrate?

As she stood with the journals in her hand she became aware of voices. The door to the study was slightly ajar and at least two people were talking in there. Eavesdropping was unladylike and irresistible. Averil put down the *Lady's Monthly Museum* and walked soundlessly to stand by the door.

'...better than I could have hoped. Inexperienced, of course, but there is no vulgarity and she has a certain style. I have high hopes of her once she acquires a little town bronze.' It was Lady Kingsbury and she was talking about her. Averil tried not to bridle at the presumption that she might have been vulgar. 'I just hope that our fears are unjustified and she is not breeding. My instincts tell me that she is not.' Averil rested her hand on the door jamb and leaned closer.

'It will be a pity if she is. The girl has potential, as you say, and of course, there is the money,' Bradon remarked.

'I have been thinking about that, and I agree with you, it would be regrettable to lose her and the money both. If she is carrying a child, then it is not an insurmountable problem, we can deal with that.'

Averil clapped her hand over her mouth to stifle the involuntary gasp.

'End the pregnancy, you mean?' Bradon said conversationally. 'There's that woman in Charles Street that I sent my mistress to when the careless little slut got herself in pup, if you recall.'

Averil dropped her hands to cradle her belly as though there was a real child into there that they were threatening. *That poor girl. He takes no responsibility, he sounds as if he hates her for it.*

'I did think of that, but we do not want to risk anything that might harm her future childbearing,' Lady Kingsbury said with as much sympathy as if she was talking about her lapdog. 'There is always such a risk of infertility and the last thing you want is to find yourself tied to an otherwise healthy young wife who cannot bear a child.'

'She might not stay so healthy in that case,' Bradon said in such a matter-of-fact way that it took Averil a moment to realise he was suggesting murder. Her murder. Soundlessly she slid to the thick carpet, her legs incapable of supporting her.

'Better not to complicate matters,' his mother said with chilling practicality. 'If the chit has got herself with child, then we send her off to the country somewhere for about ten months and *then* you marry her. We can always say she came down with an illness as a result of the change of climate or some such excuse. And at least you will know she is fertile. We can find some couple to take the child.'

'Rather a risk, don't you think? They might talk. But then, small babies are so fragile. It would be best to make sure it never became a hostage to fortune.'

'Yes, that would be best, and so easily done with a newborn babe.'

Averil stuffed her knuckles into her mouth against the rising bile. Oh, God, what had she done? She was trapped with people who would kill without the slightest compunction simply for money. A baby. An innocent babe. How could they even contemplate such a thing? And then to solve the problem of an infertile wife by murder—how long would they give her to conceive before they decided she was not use to them? A year?

The urge to retch almost overcame her. With painful slowness Averil crawled back away from the door until she could haul herself upright.

She made herself tiptoe across the floor, not run, screaming, as she wanted to. Somehow she remembered not to slam the door, then she fled upstairs, not stopping until she was huddled shivering in her own bed again.

She had thought him cold-blooded to insist they wait a month, but this ruthless expediency, the cold disregard for anything except their own greed and needs was breathtaking in its awfulness.

To send her away and insist the child was given to some kind couple who would love it—that she could understand, even though she would never have agreed to it. But to hope that the infant would die, to help that to happen... They probably did not even think of it as anything worse than letting nature take its course, she thought numbly, hugging herself as though to protect a real child.

Then to contemplate disposing of her like a useless animal... No, that was cold-blooded evil. If there was no excuse for that, then there was no excuse for the other. They were murderers.

If she had not gone downstairs and heard that conversation, she would have made herself marry Bradon and perhaps she would never have understood just what manner of man he was. He would probably be a perfectly good father to his own children, Averil thought. It was just some poor little inconvenient scrap of humanity who got in his way that would be disposable. Only women who were of no use to him who could be discarded like rubbish.

This changed everything. She could not bring herself to speak to Bradon again; even the thought of seeing him filled her with sick horror. It did not matter that no child was at risk, he had revealed himself in his true colours and she would never be able to forget, never be able to trust him. She would never be able to let him touch her without recoiling.

Papa would not expect her to marry a man like that, nor into a family so callous and calculating and criminal. Bless him, she thought fondly. He was ambitious for the family, but he would protect a grandchild, even a scandalously illegitimate one, with his life.

She would have to go home to India, there was no other solution—and to do that she needed enough money for the return journey. Her courage almost failed her at the thought of another voyage with all its dangers, but there was nothing for her here in England. Nothing.

In the morning she would go to the City and Mr Wilton's office and he would give her the money for her passage. Perhaps Grace would go with her. She must pay her off in any case, and find respectable lodgings while she waited for a ship. She would manage somehow and she would get home to people who loved her and hope they would forgive her for her imprudence.

Her mind was in turmoil. If she had never been shipwrecked, she would not have met Luc. She would not have been compromised and Bradon would have married her and she would have been tied to a ruthless, heartless man. It was the luckiest of escapes, it might even have saved her life. But then her heart would not have been broken and she would never have known what it was to love a man.

Dry-eyed, Averil curled up under the covers and waited, sleepless, for dawn.

Chapter Twenty

'I do not understand. Why can you not give me money to return home?' Averil looked around the dark panelled walls of the office as though she could find some explanation of the man's adamant refusal pinned to them.

'Because I am not authorised to, Miss Heydon.' The lawyer looked over the top of his spectacles at her as though she was a rather stupid new office clerk who could not add up. 'Sir Joshua instructed me on the disbursement of funds for your dowry on the occasion of your marriage to Lord Bradon and for reasonable expenses in the days before your marriage.

'The additional expenditure resulting from the tragic loss of the ship is necessary to accomplish the marriage. But Sir Joshua intends you to marry Lord Bradon, not to return to India on a whim. It is, of course, highly regrettable that you are feeling homesick, but really, Miss Heydon—'

'You do not understand, Mr Wilton. Lord Bradon is not what I thought. I cannot marry him. This is not a whim.'

'Indeed? A false representation has been made?' Mr Wilton sat up straighter and pushed his glasses more firmly on to his nose. 'He is already married? Not of sound mind? Fatally ill?'

'No, none of those things. There is no legal reason why I should not marry him. But I cannot like him.' She could hardly accuse Bradon of a hypothetical murder of a child who did not exist or of threatening her life.

And she could not say either that she loved another man, that she was compromised. Instinct told her that the lawyer would be entirely in sympathy with Bradon's solution to the problem, at least as far as secretly removing the child was concerned, and that he would dismiss her tale of what else she had heard last night as feminine hysterics.

'Really, Miss Heydon, you cannot in all seriousness expect me to disburse a significant sum of my client's money and to overturn almost two years of discussion and negotiations simply because you cannot like your future husband! On what grounds?'

'He is cold.' The lawyer did not say, *And what does that matter?* But his expression said it for him. 'He is not kind.'

'He has threatened you? Struck you?'

'No…' She had no evidence, only an overheard conversation in the middle of the night with no witnesses. How could she make this practical, unimaginative man understand? She could not, she realised.

'You will forgive me, I trust, Miss Heydon, for my plain speaking. But I would be negligent in my duty to your father if I did anything to encourage this fancy of yours. Young ladies in your position do not marry for love, like the heroine of some fantastical romance novel.

And no doubt halfway back to India you would change your mind again on another whim.'

'But what am I to do if I cannot go home?'

'Why, Lord Bradon's house is your home now, Miss Heydon. You can, and must, return there.'

'I will not—'

'Then I will have to inform Lord Bradon that you appear to be suffering an affliction of the spirits and require medical attention. In fact,' he said, frowning at her, 'I wonder if I should not go back to the house with you and speak to his lordship. I am really most concerned. Perhaps you are suffering a brain fever brought on by delayed shock after your ordeal during the shipwreck. Yes, indeed, that must be it.' He got up from behind the desk. 'Now, I will call my carriage and we will get you home at once, my dear Miss Heydon.'

'No!' Averil saw a vision of herself trying to explain to the outraged Bradons why she had run away. She could imagine the scene all too clearly. They would be calm, appear concerned, they would assure Mr Wilton that they had no idea that she was unwell. How sorry they would be that by plunging her into the social whirl they had so distressed her poor, fragile mind. And the moment the door was closed behind the lawyer she would be a prisoner until they discovered it was safe to marry her to Bradon.

'No,' she said, conjuring up every ounce of control she possessed. 'That is very kind, but I have my maid and a carriage.' She pulled a handkerchief from her reticule and dabbed her dry eyes with it. 'You are right, I must be unwell. I have not slept well since the wreck… Such nightmares. Perhaps they will allow me to go to the country estate and rest.' She managed to make her voice tremble a little. 'It will all seem better then, will it not, Mr Wilton?'

'Of course, my dear, of course.' He subsided back into his chair, his relief obvious that she had become a tremulous, biddable female relying on his superior judgement. 'I will ring for a small glass of sherry wine for you. I do not as a rule approve of females consuming alcoholic beverages, but in this case, it may be wise.'

'Thank you,' Averil murmured, wielding the handkerchief again as she sank back into the depths of the chair. At least it would give her a few minutes to think. What on earth was she to do now?

She could go to Lady Perdita Brooke—but Dita's parents would never countenance her sheltering a runaway, especially when Dita herself had a recent scandal to live down. Nor could she ask Dita for a loan, not of the amount of money she would need for lodgings until the ship sailed, the fare, money for three months and wages for Grace, whom she could hardly abandon.

There was one possibility, so shocking that when the sherry came she gulped it down and almost made herself choke. Was it her only option or was it what she wanted to do and she was finding excuses, telling herself she had no other choice?

It took several minutes to shake Mr Wilton off, to assure him she did not require handing into her carriage—which was a good thing as she had come in a hackney—and that she felt much more calm and rational now. She had a sinking feeling that he might write to Papa, but if her plan worked she would be home in India at the same time as any letter.

With the patient Grace beside her she stood on the pavement and looked for a hackney. 'Grace, I need to talk to you, in confidence, about something rather shocking. If you feel you would rather not be involved I quite understand, but in that case we had better go back to Bruton Street now and I will drop you off. All I ask is that you say nothing about it for as long as possible.'

'Of course I'll come with you, Miss Heydon,' the maid said. 'Look, there's one.' She darted to the edge of the pavement and waved down a cab. 'Is it an elopement, miss?'

'No. Not quite.' The driver leaned down for directions. 'One of the main shipping agents, please. I want one who handles the East India ships.'

'Oh!' Grace's eyes were wide as they settled on the worn seats. 'Are we going to India?'

'I am, but not you.' The girl's face fell. 'It is a three-month voyage, Grace. And dangerous—look what happened to me on the way here. And India is hot and unhealthy.'

'I'd like to go,' Grace persisted. 'I've always wanted to travel, honest, miss. If I can survive all the things you can catch in the Rookery, I can manage in India, I'll be bound.'

'I might not be able to pay you for months,' Averil admitted. 'I may not even be able to pay for the two weeks you have been working for me already. I am going to do something very shocking, Grace. I am going to put myself under the protection of a gentleman and hope that he will fund my passage and your wages.'

'I knew it! I knew this valise had more in it than a gown to be altered like you told her ladyship. It's too heavy.'

'It contains everything I own,' Averil admitted. 'Which is not much. And then there are your things—I did not dare tell you about it in the house in case anyone overheard, and I did not know how we could get two valises out.'

'Not to worry, miss.' Grace showed no sign of shock or alarm at Averil's explanations. 'When we find out whether he's up for it I'll take a hackney back to Bruton Street and sneak my stuff out the back way.' She sat in silence for a while. 'You don't want to marry Lord Bradon, miss? Can't say I blame you. Nasty bit of work he is, if you ask me. Like a dead flounder.'

'Grace!' Averil choked on a gasp of laughter.

'Well, he is. He's got hands like one, too.'

'How do you know? He has not made advances to you, has he?'

'Sort of pats and gropes when he's passing.' The girl shrugged. 'Nothing I can't cope with. Some of the gents is like that—they fancy a servant girl because we don't answer back—mostly. Yes, me lud, no, me lud,' she mimicked savagely. 'Lie on me back with me skirts up if you like, me lud. I don't stand for it myself.'

'I am so sorry, Grace. I had no idea—how dreadful.' The hypocrisy of it! Lecturing her on virtue while all the while he was harassing the servants.

'Your gent's not like that, is he, miss?'

'No,' said Averil. 'He asks for what he wants and he takes *no* for an answer.' More or less. 'I think this must be the shipping office.'

They climbed down into the bustling street. It was closer to Calcutta than Mayfair, Averil thought, finding to her surprise that she could smile. The noise and smells and the mass of carts and porters and hawkers were familiar and unthreatening. 'Wait please,' she called up to the driver. 'We will not be long.'

'Two weeks,' Averil said as they sat back in the hackney fifteen minutes later. She studied the printed sheet in her hand. The *Diamond Rose* for Calcutta. Cabins close to the Great Cabin that would accommodate the two of them were still available, but at a price that was quite impossible to meet unless Luc helped her.

Would he pay that much, plus Grace's wages and some money for her expenses on board, in exchange for her virginity and just two weeks of her unskilled lovemaking?

'Do you love him, miss?' Grace asked as the cab turned into Piccadilly. Averil felt her chest tightening so that she could scarcely breathe.

'Yes,' she said. 'But he does not love me and he does not know how I feel about him. And he must not.'

Grace did not answer, but she changed seats to sit next to Averil and squeezed her hand. Her lover had jilted her, Averil recalled, and squeezed back. The pressure in her chest eased a little.

The hackney swung through a tight opening into a cobbled yard. 'Albany!'

'Veil, miss!'

Averil pulled down the coarse veiling as she climbed down. A porter came out as Grace lifted the valises out.

'Can I help you, madam?' It sounded like, *Go away, we don't welcome your sort here.*

I am a fallen woman, Averil realised. *Or, at least, I am falling.* 'Thank you. Captain d'Aunay's chambers, please.'

The porter went back inside with a curt nod, leaving them standing on the cobbles. After five minutes Averil squared her shoulders and walked towards the door; she could hardly stand there until Luc happened to go in or out.

A dapper little man appeared on the step as she reached it. 'Madam? The captain is not at home at the moment.'

'He told me to send to him here if I ever needed help,' Averil said.

'Ah. Yes, indeed, ma'am. Will you follow me?'

They walked after him down a passage that seemed to Averil as long as a rope walk. The man opened a black door and ushered them into a sitting room. 'If you will make yourself comfortable, ma'am, I will see if—'

'Hughes!' The shout was unmistakeably Luc's voice. 'Something for my damned head and get a move on. I think I'm dying.'

'He's awake. Excuse me.' The manservant vanished through a door at the rear of the room.

They could hear his voice, low and soothing, then, 'A *what?* Who?'

'Hangover,' Grace observed. 'Does he drink much?'

'I have never seen him even tipsy,' Averil said. On St Mary's she had seen him drink and keep up with Sir George's not inconsiderable dinner time consumption, but he had shown no ill effects. In fact, he had made love to her afterwards.

There were more growls from the direction of the bedchamber. Oh, dear. He did not sound like a man who could be persuaded to part with a large sum of money in exchange for a novice mistress's inept caresses. The nerves that had been a flock of butterflies in her stomach turned into bats.

Hughes reappeared, seized a decanter from the sideboard and vanished again. Finally he put his head around the door. 'If your woman would care to join me in the scullery, ma'am, the captain will be out in a moment.'

Grace got to her feet, stopped, whisked off Averil's bonnet, patted her hair into place, hissed, 'Bite your lips. Good luck', and followed him out.

Averil sat watching the door as though a tiger might

emerge from it. Every carefully rehearsed sentence fled from her head. When the door did open she was ready to faint through sheer nervous anticipation.

Luc stopped in the doorway and studied her without speaking. His hair was wet and looked as though he had poured water over his head and then run his fingers through the black locks. There were purple smudges under his eyes, which were bloodshot. He was wearing a shirt, open at the neck, and pantaloons; his feet were bare.

'You look dreadful,' Averil said without thinking and stood up. He looked like death and she loved him. She wanted to take him in her arms and fuss over him and soothe his headache and kiss away the strain around his eyes and never leave him. Instead she clasped her hands tightly together and just waited.

'I have seen you looking better,' he rejoined. 'And worse, come to think about it. I am damnably hungover. I am probably still half-cut. Tell me what's wrong, just don't shout at me.'

'I won't.' Averil bit her lip. 'Hadn't you better sit down?'

He gestured at the *chaise* and sat in the chair opposite. 'Does Bradon know you're here?'

'No!' Luc winced. 'Sorry. No. I have run away and left no note. I cannot bear to marry him.'

'And so you have come to me.' The colour was returning to his face and the bleak look in his eyes seemed to fade. Whatever potion the manservant had given him must be working.

'Yes. But—'

'Ah. The *but.* Tell me the worst.'

The door opened to admit Hughes with a tray. 'Coffee, Captain. Your woman said you would take coffee also, ma'am.' Leaving her to pour, he left as quietly as he had entered.

She stirred in sugar, careful not to strike the porcelain and make a noise, passed a cup, black, to Luc and added cream to her own.

'I want to go home, to India. Bradon is a man that my father would not wish me to marry, once he knows the truth about him.'

'Tell me what he has done.'

Averil explained, not at all certain that Luc would believe her. Her father would, she was certain. But would another man?

Luc's face darkened. 'The man contemplates the murder of a woman and child as he might consider destroying a wasps' nest. It would do the world a service to remove him from it. And that harpy of a mother of his. But I suppose one cannot, not without evidence.'

'No,' Averil agreed. 'But you understand why I cannot marry him.'

'Of course. Thank God you ran before they discovered you had overheard.' He rubbed a hand over his face. 'Tell me the *but*.'

Averil bit her lower lip, struggling to find the way to express what she wanted. In the end she simply said, 'I will be your mistress for two weeks in exchange for my passage back to India, Grace's wages as my companion on the voyage and enough money to cover my expenses to Calcutta.'

He was silent, watching her with an impenetrable, heavy gaze over the top of steepled fingers.

'I know it isn't for very long, and it will be a lot of money and I won't be very good, although I am a virgin and men seem to set a lot of store by that, so I suppose that is something, and I will do my best…'

He held up one hand and she trailed to a halt, red-cheeked and breathless with embarrassment and nerves.

'What is your plan if I refuse?' He might have been discussing naval tactics in a meeting except that he had gone white under his tan.

'I have none.'

'So you are desperate and I am your only hope?'

'Yes.'

'Flattering,' he remarked.

But I love you! The words she could not say were bitter on her tongue. What could she say? That if she was not desperate she would still have come to him? No. Nor would she have seen him again if her father's lawyer had given her the money. She would have written to say goodbye, that was all. So he had every right to feel used.

'I am sorry. I thought you wanted me.'

'Oh, I do, my dear. Very much. I was hoping you would come because you wanted me, too—and for rather longer than two weeks.' He closed his eyes and she wondered if his headache was still very bad. 'For much longer,' he said and opened them again.

'But the ship sails then and in any case, the third week wouldn't be...' Her voice trailed away. Possibly it was possible to blush even redder, but she doubted it.

'In three weeks your not-to-be mother-in-law would have known you were not with child?' he enquired. 'There is no need to colour up like a peony, I am aware of how females work, you know.' Luc did not sound at all like a man who had just heard that his physical desires were to be gratified. 'Are you not afraid that two weeks as my mistress will leave you pregnant?'

Yes, it *was* possible to become more embarrassed. Averil studied her gloved hands intently. 'I overheard two married women talking at the reception. They have lovers, I think. And then I asked Grace about what they said and she told me that there is a way if the man...'

'I see. So I have two very expensive weeks teaching you how to make love and I have to withdraw every time?' His voice was flat; she could not tell whether he was furiously angry with her or disgusted and bored. Had she hurt him?

'Yes,' she said. A seam in her glove split and with it her nerve. 'I am sorry. I should never have come here, never have asked. It is quite unreasonable of me, I can see that. I will go away.' The wave of flat despair blacked out even the fear of not knowing what she could do now. All she could think of was that she would never see Luc again, never lie in his arms, never show him how much she loved him even if she could not say the words.

Chapter Twenty-One

'**A**veril.' She looked up as Luc knelt in front of her and caught her hand. The glimpse of pale skin through the split glove seam was deeply affecting. It was erotic, but it also made him feel a strange tenderness, almost enough to wash away the hurt that she had come to him not because she wanted him but because he was the only person she could sell herself to.

'It is not unreasonable, quite the contrary—it is quite delightful of you,' he said, instinct telling him to keep his voice light. He could not beg her to stay for ever, not when she was so desperate to leave that she would do this thing. 'I must admit that two months would be better and I do hope you will not ruin any more expensive gloves while in my keeping, but I agree to your terms.'

The hazel eyes that looked into his with such earnestness were dark and troubled. There was real fear lurking there. She must have been at her wits' end to have come to him, he knew that. He was her last resort. If he had not taken her in, what would she have done? The options were bleak and the least dreadful of them would be to return to Bradon.

Her desperation put her feelings for him in stark context: becoming his mistress was better than selling herself on the streets, better than throwing herself in the Thames and preferable to returning to a man who terrified and disgusted her. His pride kicked at the realisation. And there was something else, a feeling he could not identify except as an ache. He pushed the pain and resentment to the back of his mind; it was time to put his own feelings to one side and think only of her.

As he spoke her eyes lost focus and he realised she was near to fainting with relief. 'Drink your coffee. Have you eaten today?' She shook her head. Luc got to his feet and tugged the bell. 'Hughes, some food for Miss Heydon.'

As the manservant vanished to the scullery he contemplated his new mistress. His mouth felt dry, his loins were heavy with desire. *Not now*, he thought, willing his clamouring body into some kind of obedience. She was virginal, distressed, determined. Exhausted. He needed to get her safe so she could rest before he so much as kissed her fingertips. That did it all over again; he could only be grateful that she was too preoccupied to notice his rampant arousal and be alarmed even more.

'I'll go and get dressed,' he said as Hughes brought in a tray and began to set an omelette and bread and butter and preserves on the table. 'Eat, you'll feel better.'

In the bedchamber as he changed he worked through the list of things to be done while Hughes jotted notes. 'Book the best cabin you can get—no, make that two cabins, on the next ship for Calcutta. There is one in two weeks, apparently. Go for the best, even if that means settling for one bigger cabin rather than two—I'll leave that to your judgement. On the way call in at the agent for the Half Moon Street house and tell him I want to extend the lease for another month.'

'Staff, Captain? Footman, a cook-housekeeper and a maid?'

'Yes, that will do. Get them round there as soon as possible, I want the place clean and provisioned by tonight.'

He had leased the little house for a new mistress just before the crisis with the admiral blew up and it had never been used for that purpose. Now, although it was in Mayfair and possibly dangerously close to Bradon, he thought Averil would feel comfortable there. It was not as if she was going to be going out much. His body stiffened all over again and he jerked his neck cloth tighter.

'Uniform, Captain?'

'Yes, I need to go down to the Admiralty.' There was his finished report on the Scillies affair to present this afternoon, if he could manage to focus on that. Possibly they would have his new posting. If they wanted him to leave immediately, then they could think again. He found he could smile, his thumping headache beginning to melt away.

'Tell Miss Heydon's woman to make her mistress comfortable in here—she needs to rest.'

He buckled on his sword as he walked through into the main room. Averil had colour back in her cheeks and the plate was clean. She smiled at him as he stood in the doorway. 'How handsome you look in uniform.' She tilted her head to one side and studied him. 'I preferred your hair longer, though.'

Luc grinned at her. 'Flattering me? You do not have to, you know.' He was unprepared for the feeling that hit him when she smiled back. It was as though she had always been there, in his rooms, smiling at him. Only two weeks. Fourteen days. How did you stretch time to make it last for ever? What was the matter with him? He had never wanted to keep a mistress beyond a few months before.

'Do you feel better?' Averil asked. She stood up and came to stand in front of him, frowning a little as she studied his newly shaven face. 'Why did you get so drunk?'

Because he had decided to speak to the Comte de la Falaise today, ask his permission to pay his addresses to Louise, was the honest answer. Because he had contemplated married life and the prospect had filled him with nothing but gloom. An afternoon of brooding had failed to reveal why, when he was within an inch of achieving a major objective in his plans, he should feel so damnably flat and empty.

It was not as though he expected Louise's father to refuse his suit. The man had been unbending subtly over the past few days. He had hinted that he had heard good things about Luc's career prospects, he had made vague, but suggestive, enquiries about the d'Aunay lands in France.

And Louise would do exactly as her father told her. Not that there was any reason why she should not: she had never given any indication of disliking Luc. Nor, if he was honest, of favouring him above any of the other men who paid her the attention a pretty young lady received. She did not care, in effect. Which was exactly what he wanted, of course.

At that point in his mental processes he had begun drinking and had kept drinking, something he never did, not when he was alone. Burgundy had been succeeded by brandy, he recalled vaguely. Brandy had been followed by merciful oblivion and by waking with a head full of hedgehogs, a mouth full of dry hay and a stomach that was achingly empty.

And now he felt wonderful—and fearful, too. 'I had been working very hard to finish my report to the Admiralty about our little adventure. It was late, I was tired, I did not notice how much I was drinking.' He could not tell her about Louise and that proposal would have to wait. Wait until Averil had left, headed half a world away from him. Marrying a woman for whom he felt nothing would not matter then.

Averil sucked in her cheeks as though she was biting the inside of them to keep from saying something. When she eventually spoke all she said was, 'I hope you finished it before you became drunk, if that is where you are going now.'

'Yes,' he said and showed her the leather portfolio under his arm. 'All checked before I touched a drop. I am not going to disgrace myself.'

'Good.' She reached up and tweaked his neckcloth, her face absurdly serious as she inspected him.

'That is very wifely, my dear,' Luc said, enjoying being fussed over. The expression drained from her face.

'I beg your pardon, I had no wish to presume.'

'You are not. I enjoy being looked after. I—' He touched the back of his hand to her cheek and swallowed, forgetting what he had meant to say in the feel of her skin, the way her eyes widened, became greener, the soft catch of her breath. If he wasn't careful he would drag her into the bedroom and neither of them would emerge until tomorrow. And he must go to the Admiralty and she must rest.

'I must go. Hughes is making arrangements for a house for you. Meanwhile use my chamber. Sleep. You are safe here.'

'If Bradon finds out—'

'How should he? I will keep you safe, Averil.'

'I know, you always have.' Her smile vanished in a huge yawn. 'Oh! I am so sorry!'

'So tired, you mean.' He pointed at the bedchamber door. 'Go and sleep.'

The bed smelled of Luc, the familiar scent of him from their little bed on the island all mixed up with clean linen, leather and an elusive, citrusy cologne.

Averil closed her eyes, burrowed into the pillows and let herself relax, finally.

'I'll be outside,' Grace said. 'I won't go for my things until the captain's man comes back.'

That brought her back to reality with a jerk. 'No, go now.' Averil sat up and pushed her hair back with both hands. 'The longer you leave it the more suspicious they will be that I haven't returned. I'll be safe here.'

'Yes, you are right, miss. He's a good man.'

'He is. But he is going to marry a French lady. He has it all planned out. When Bonaparte is defeated he will go back to France and be a Frenchman again.'

Grace simply muttered something under her breath as she closed the door. Averil lay down again, breathed deeply and told herself that two weeks could seem like a lifetime if she lived it as if it was.

Through her thick veil the narrow hall was blurred. Averil pushed it back and looked around. 'This is all for me?'

'Yes, of course.' Luc was still in uniform. He tossed his hat on to the hall table, unbuckled his sword and propped it in the corner. 'Show Miss Smith's woman to the bedchambers,' he said to the footman who had opened the door to them.

At the back of the hall a thin woman bobbed a curtsy. 'Mrs Andrews, ma'am, the cook. And Polly is down in the kitchens and that,' she nodded towards the footman's back as he climbed the stairs, 'is Peter. I had the parcels sent up, ma'am.'

'Parcels?' Averil looked at Luc.

'I did some shopping. You can send your maid out for anything I have forgotten, but I suggest she goes veiled.'

'Of course. Thank you.' Now what? Should she offer him tea? Would he expect to have a conversation in the drawing room that she could glimpse through an open door to the right. Averil's heart thudded and her mouth felt dry. Perhaps she should brazenly walk upstairs to the bedchamber.

'Why don't we go and check what I selected?' Luc said and the amusement in his eyes told her he knew exactly what she was dithering about. 'Dinner for seven-thirty,' he said to Mrs Andrews without so much as a hint of embarrassment.

Presumably he kept all his mistresses here and the staff thought nothing of it. She set her expression into bland unconcern and mounted the stairs. As they reached the top Luc touched her arm and indicated a door that was already open.

Inside the footman was gathering up wrapping paper and Grace was putting away what looked like the contents of an entire shop. Or shops—there were gowns, underwear, shoes, bonnets in the armoire and the chest of drawers, a heap of toiletries on the dressing table.

'Luc, this is too much! Grace—' But the maid and the footman had vanished and the door shut with a soft click.

'No, it is not,' Luc said. 'But just at the moment you

are wearing entirely too much.' He began to unbutton his uniform jacket. 'And so am I.'

She had seen him undress before with a total lack of self-consciousness. *I have seen him naked. I have touched him,* she told herself as she tried to get her breathing under control. But this was different and the way he looked at her was different. *Let me do this right,* she thought. *Let me please him.*

She must not be passive, she thought. He had liked it when she had straightened his neckcloth; perhaps he would like her helping him undress. As Luc began to shrug out of the jacket she went behind him and eased it from his shoulders and hung it on the back of the dressing-table chair. Then she stood in front of him and pulled the ends of his neckcloth free and began to work on the knot. He went very still and she looked up to meet hot, dark eyes.

'Go on,' Luc said and made no move to touch her.

The neckcloth seemed endless as she unwound it. He bent his head, but even so she had to keep standing on tiptoe and her breasts brushed against his chest and her hands kept rubbing against the thick silk of his hair and by the time she had the length of muslin free she was as aroused as if he had been kissing her.

'Go on,' he said again as she turned from folding it on top of the jacket.

Her hands were shaking as she undid the shirt buttons and pulled it free from the waistband of his breeches. He bent as she tugged at it and it came off over his head, leaving him naked from the waist up and quite blatantly aroused.

'Touch me.'

'I don't know how.'

'What gives you pleasure? Men are not so very different.'

His hands on my breasts, his hands between my legs. She did not think she could touch him there, not yet. And men did not have breasts. But they did have nipples. Intrigued by the thought she touched the right one with a tentative finger. Hair brushed her palms and tickled, the brown disc crinkled, just as the aureoles of her breasts did. Luc caught his breath. She touched the other one with the same result. Her own nipples hardened and peaked and she gasped.

Averil used finger and thumb, squeezed, rolled and he clenched his fists, his eyes closed—and a startling shaft of pleasure caught her low in her stomach as though he had caressed her.

She moved closer, her hands flat on his chest, and lifted her face to kiss him and then he moved, his arms coming round her to crush her close, his mouth taking her proffered lips without hesitation.

The kiss was demanding, urgent, and his hands worked on her gown as he moved his mouth over hers and stroked his tongue into her mouth, setting up a rhythm that had her licking and nibbling back. Her gown came undone, he moved his hands, it fell off. There was a tearing sound and her chemise and petticoats followed it and Luc raised his head and stepped back.

'Nice,' he purred. 'Oh, yes.'

She was standing there in corset, stockings and garters. She felt ridiculous and exposed and vulnerable in a way that being naked with him had never felt. Averil tried to catch hold of the corset strings, but they eluded her. 'Leave it,' he said and caught her to him again, one hand on her buttocks so she was bent back, her belly against the jut of his erection, as he lifted her breasts free of the constricting corset.

'Aah,' she whimpered as he began to lick and suck and the sensitive, tight nipples hardened and her breasts swelled and ached. 'Don't stop, Luc.'

'I have no intention of stopping,' he said and she felt a deep satisfaction at the way his voice shook, even as he struggled to sound in control. 'I don't think I could if I wanted to.'

She found herself sprawled on the bed without knowing how she got there and Luc had got rid of boots and breeches and was standing over her aroused and magnificent and she wondered if she should feel fear, but all she could summon up of coherent thought was that she wanted him inside her, she wanted to surround him, hold him, be one with him.

He knelt on the bed between her spread thighs and she reached for him as he lowered himself over her. 'Averil, don't be afraid.'

'I am not afraid. I want you.'

He did not answer her in words, only with the caress of his hand as he opened her and the weight of his body as he came down on to her so that the hair on his chest fretted at her sensitive breasts almost unbearably and the heat of his mouth made her lips part, trembling even as she closed her eyes the better to feel and touch and taste him.

Her thighs cradled him and she remembered that moment in the hut when she had realised what her aunt's careful words of explanation had meant in reality and she smiled as he entered her, smiled through the discomfort that vanished into wonder and delight and she was still smiling as his mouth captured her lips and he began the slow, perfect rhythm that transformed the two of them into one striving, passionate creature and finally, finally, broke her into a million shards of pleasure.

She tried to hold him as she felt him leave her, then remembered why he had to and tightened her arms around Luc as he shuddered and groaned and the heat gushed on to her belly and he lay still in her arms at last.

I love you, I love you, I love you. The words kept running in her head as he finally rolled from her, stooped to kiss her and then went to wash. She was still thinking it as he came back with a damp cloth and cleaned her sticky skin. She should not be surprised he was so gentle with her, he had nursed her before. But now she was conscious.

Luc bent over her and brushed the tumbled hair back from her face. 'Thank you.'

'Was it—was I—all right?'

He closed his eyes for a moment and when he opened them the deep intensity matched the seriousness in his voice. 'You are everything I had dreamed you would be.'

'Really? I am so ignorant. I don't know all the things I should know to please you.'

'You do not need tricks to please me. You just need to be yourself and to do what comes naturally.'

'May we do it again?' He was ready for her. 'You cannot hide what you want,' she said, and, greatly daring, reached for him. So hard and yet so smooth. Finest kid leather over steel. She stroked along the length and then curled her fingers round, gauging the size with a purr of satisfaction.

'Wanton.' He did not look displeased. 'We will not do that again today, you will be sore.' She registered the look of satisfaction at her murmur of disappointed protest. 'But there are other things we can do. Let me show you,' he said, his voice husky as he knelt by the bed and pulled her towards him so her legs dangled over the edge.

'Luc?' He parted her thighs and the dark head bent closer. 'Luc!' She had thought she could not feel anything more intense than what she had already experienced. It seemed she was wrong.

Chapter Twenty-Two

'I had not understood,' Averil whispered as Luc leaned back on the *chaise* beside her after dinner and rested his head on the carved back rail with a sigh of repletion. *Sex or food?* she wondered. Perhaps both.

'What did you not understand? You don't have to whisper, no one can hear you.'

'I thought we would make love once or perhaps twice a day. I did not understand that we can do it over and over again.' She managed to raise her voice above a whisper, but it still seemed wicked to be talking about things like this outside the bedchamber. Luc turned his head and smiled that lazy, satisfied smile she was beginning to recognise.

'Am I wearing you out?'

'No, not at all. I still… It is very shocking.' And wonderful. She had not realised that she could speak of love without words, with her body.

'You still want more?'

Blushing, she nodded. How was it possible not to?

Perhaps one simply dropped from exhaustion after a while—or burned up with frustration if you had to stop.

Luc slid down until he was lying on the *chaise,* then he unbuttoned his evening breeches. 'If you want more—'

Of course she wanted more. But surely not in the dining room, on the *chaise.* 'The servants!'

'They will not come until we ring.' He had freed himself from his clothing and she could not help but reach for him as he shifted a little. 'Kneel over me, there is room either side of my hips.'

'Me—on top?'

'Then you can be in control, go as slowly and as shallowly as you like. I don't want to hurt you, Averil. You are very new to this.'

But not so new that he had to help her, she thought with a surge of triumph as she looked down at him. Gently she eased him into her warmth and felt the tears start in her eyes because of how perfect it was. She blinked them back in case he thought he was hurting her and bent forwards to kiss him. *Love you*, she murmured against his lips. *So much.*

'You had better stay in today,' Luc said over a very belated breakfast the next morning. 'I will do the rounds of the clubs and see if there are any rumours about your disappearance. I don't think I have done anything to make Bradon suspicious of me, but it will do no harm for him to see me around as usual.'

'I have no idea how he will react,' Averil said. But a cold feeling in the pit of her stomach said otherwise. He would be furious and ruthless, for he would be losing a great deal of money. 'Do be careful,' she added. 'What if he uses Runners?' But he merely smiled and reached for the coffee.

Grace had returned safely with her own possessions to report that she had mentioned to Lady Kingsbury's dresser Finch that Miss Heydon was lying down in her bedchamber with a sick headache. She had locked the door and taken the key away with her, she added with a mischievous grin.

There was a real world out there, Averil reminded herself. And Luc had to live in it—and he had to continue to live in it when she had gone. 'I should have asked before now,' she said, contrite. 'How was your report received at the Admiralty?'

'Well, I believe. They are interested in the methods of analysis I used to trace the leaks and focus on the source. They want me to teach them to a group of lieutenants who have an interest in intelligence work.'

'That is good,' Averil said. His mouth twisted wryly. 'Isn't it?'

'It is flattering and it means they aren't posting me to the far ends of the earth right away.'

'No, of course.' The cold knot inside became a stone. 'It will mean you can continue to court Mademoiselle de la Falaise.'

Luc put down his cup. 'I'm not courting the woman while I am with you! What do you take me for?'

'A man who wanted to set up a mistress,' Averil retorted. 'You have every intention of keeping one when you are married, have you not?'

'I—yes. Yes, I suppose so, after a few months, I suppose, if I am still in the country.'

'Well, then? How is this different?'

'You are different.' He frowned at her and she stared right back at him. 'Don't ask me why. I do not know.' Luc pushed back his chair and got to his feet. 'It just does not seem right.'

'It is less hypocritical to take a mistress after you have married and have taken vows than it is when you are simply courting a woman and making her promises by implication?'

'Damn it, Averil. You are hardly in a position to take the high moral ground on this!' He strode towards the door. 'You had a contract with Bradon that you set great store by, I seem to remember.'

'My father had. I had made no promises to Bradon and you know perfectly well why I could not marry him! I do not like breaking a contract—'

'Stop talking like a merchant!' He spun round and stalked back. 'This is not about some cold-blooded business deal.'

'No?' She found she was on her feet. 'It always was. A mistress provides her body in return for money, does she not? You were clear about that, back in the Scillies—you treat your mistresses well, you said. You provide for them. What would you have done about finding a wife if I had said *yes* then?' He opened his mouth and she swept on. 'You would have gone ahead and courted Mademoiselle de la Falaise and told yourself that she would expect you to have a mistress, that it was part of the expectations in that kind of marriage. And this, now—you and me—is about a financial exchange, so what is different?'

'I don't know, damn it,' Luc said as he came to a halt in front of her. 'It just is.'

'Well, I hope that your analysis of clandestine enemy activity is better than your understanding of relationships, or there are going to be some very confused lieutenants in the near future,' Averil said, standing her ground in the face of over six foot of infuriated male. Oh, but he was magnificent, grey eyes flashing, chest heaving; even that nose of his was designed for nostrils that flared. She wanted him…

He grabbed her by the shoulders and kissed her. He was furious, she could taste it, feel it and the excitement flared through her veins. What had come over her? She rocked back on her heels as he released her and she realised she was fizzing with energy and desire and excitement. All her life she had been well behaved and quiet and had avoided conflict like the plague. Now all she wanted was to rouse Luc to kiss her like that again.

'You brute!' Wanting to provoke, Averil picked up the first thing that came to hand, the coffee pot, and to her surprise Luc gave a bark of laughter.

'Oh, well done—perfect mistress behaviour! But you should choose something more valuable and then, when you have smashed it, you must wheedle an even more valuable replacement out of me—' He ducked as the pot flew past his head and splintered into shards against the door. 'Ah well, at least it was empty. That flower vase soaked me.'

With his amusement her own excitement ebbed away. Averil just stood there, her hands pressed to her mouth. What had she done? Twice she had thrown things at him, behaved like a hoyden, and now he was laughing at her as though that was amusing. She loved him and all she was to him was a convenient body, a female to amuse himself with, a predictable creature with grasping habits and a tendency to make scenes.

Appalled, she felt the hot tears welling up and running down her face, unstoppable.

'Averil!' Luc's feet crunched through the ruined coffee pot. 'Stop it. You do not cry, you never cry.'

'I don't mean to,' she said. 'They won't stop.' He

reached for her and she batted at his hands. 'Go away. Please, just go away.'

She meant it. Luc backed towards the door, reluctant to leave her with those great tears running silently down her cheeks, but he had no idea how to stop them or what to say without making things worse. How had their leisurely, contented breakfast turned into this? His crime, he decided as he picked up hat and gloves and let himself out, was that he was not continuing to court Louise.

As he cut diagonally across Green Park for St James's Street he puzzled over why Averil was not pleased that he was staying faithful to her. She had his undivided attention for two weeks—and she was showing every sign of thoroughly enjoying those attentions. There was something wrong, some hairline crack in the pattern of what Averil had told him and how she was acting, yet he could not put his finger on it. And what had made her cry? She had faced far worse on St Helen than a row over the breakfast table and yet she had never once given way to tears. Why was he able to untangle the subtle pattern of a spy's actions and yet he could not understand a woman who was sharing his bed?

His heartbeat slowed as he walked and his thoughts became more coherent. She was sharing his bed. He had got what he wanted, but at what cost? He had ruined her. That she seemed to enjoy his lovemaking mattered not at all. He had corrupted her.

But I have agreed to help her, the inner demon protested, but he thrust away the easy excuses. Now, the hangover gone, his lust slaked, he could see clearly. What he should have done was to install her in the house, buy her what she needed and protect her until the ship sailed.

He should not have laid a finger on her whatever either of them wanted.

Luc felt sick. Sick with guilt, sick with the knowledge that the moment he had her alone again he would not be able to stop himself from taking her again, caressing her, making love to her until they both collapsed with exhaustion. Sick with the knowledge that when she left him he had no idea how he would stay sane.

The walk was long enough, and brisk enough, for him to have regained a semblance of calm by the time he reached White's. Which was fortunate as the first person he saw as he entered was Lord Bradon.

'Ah, Bradon, this is well met. I have been hoping to run into you.' He kept his voice cheerful and his hands relaxed even though in his imagination he had the man by the throat and was pounding his brains out on the elegant marble floor.

The other man turned, his already frowning countenance turning darker when he saw who was addressing him. 'Were you, indeed!'

'Yes, although this appears not to be a convenient time to discuss porcelain. You seem distracted.'

'You want to talk to me about porcelain? Is this a joke?'

'Well, it might be a forgery,' Luc said. How interesting that Bradon should react so badly to seeing him. Given that Luc had done nothing to anger the man there could be only one conclusion to be drawn: he was suspicious that Luc might have something to do with Averil's flight. 'I am not experienced with Meissen and I wondered if—'

'To hell with Meissen.' Bradon shouldered past him and out of the doors.

'Damn bad form,' Percy Fulton remarked, strolling

past the porter's desk and joining Luc as he went into the library. 'He was prowling round here like a bear with a sore head last night and back he comes this morning, asking who had seen you. I suggested he went round to your chambers and had my head bitten off for my trouble and now that he finds you he doesn't want to talk. Done something to upset him? I'm always ready to stand as second, you know. Can't abide the man.'

'A misunderstanding, that is all. But thank you.' Luc retreated behind a copy of *The Times*. So, Bradon had put two and two together and come up with the only naval officer who had been paying Averil any attention. It never did to underestimate the opposition and it seemed that he had done just that with Averil's betrothed.

So now he had to be very careful indeed or he would lead the man to her doorstep and, while he had no objection to facing him at dawn over the matter, it would do Averil's reputation no good at all.

Half an hour later he realised that he had been thinking about Averil and had not given a thought to protecting her from Bradon. Restless, he got up and walked out, back up the long slope to Piccadilly and Albany. He turned into the court yard and caught a movement from the corner of his eye. A man in dark, ordinary clothing moved down the side of the yard and out on to the street. Nothing so unusual there, but the way he kept his head averted had the hairs rising on the back of Luc's neck.

He had felt like that before now and had found a sniper with his sights on him. 'Who was that?' he asked the porter.

Jenks shook his head. 'No idea, Captain. I've been out the back for a few minutes.'

'Hughes,' he said as he let himself into his rooms, 'I

have a problem. How do you fancy a game of hide and seek?'

'Has to be better than blacking your boots for the rest of the morning, Captain.' The manservant began to untie his green baize apron. 'What's the plan?'

Half an hour later Luc strolled out of Albany at a leisurely pace. If they couldn't keep up with this, they deserved to lose him. At the bottom of St James's Street, with the warm red brick of the Tudor palace in front of him, he opened the door of Berry Brothers and Rudd and walked into an atmosphere redolent of wax polish, coffee and wine.

'Captain, welcome back!' The wine merchant came out from behind the counter. 'Are you here to be weighed or to restock your cellar?'

'The latter.' Luc moved around the great swinging coffee scales that most of the aristocracy of the day were weighed on. 'I am deplorably short of Burgundy.'

'Not easy to get just now, as you no doubt know.' The man shook his head as he steered Luc towards the head of the stairs down to the cellars. 'We are buying up what private holdings there are in the country, but naturally, we cannot countenance smuggled wines…'

'Indeed not.' Luc paused and peered at racks as he passed. Behind him the bell on the door rang as someone came in. 'I have a long list, I'm afraid, Humphries.'

At the bottom of the stairs Hughes appeared, a valise in his hands. Humphries said, 'Mind the shop, John. I'll be a while with Captain d'Aunay', and a young man put down a ledger and hurried up the stairs.

Luc stripped off tail coat and pantaloons and changed into buckskin breeches, a riding coat and a low-crowned hat, then followed the wine merchant back through the labyrinth of cellars and up another set of stairs.

'There you go, sir.' Humphries heaved open a trapdoor. 'Pickering Place.'

'Thank you—there will be an order coming your way in the next few days.' Luc walked briskly down the narrow passage back to St James, round the corner into Pall Mall and signalled for a hackney.

Averil rang for the maid and apologised for the state of the dining-room carpet. The girl, Polly, seemed surprised that she should do so and went calmly about her business picking up the pieces and sponging the thick pile.

Presumably such tantrums were only to be expected of a kept woman. Averil bit her lip. That was what she was: ruined, wanton and an outcast from decent society and there was no point in deluding herself that this was simply an idyll with the man she loved.

She had sold herself to him. The fact that Luc seemed to like her and that he also appeared to find their love-making satisfying, was beside the point, she lectured herself as she walked moodily up and down the pretty little drawing room. He had appeared quite happy that this was a financial transaction. What had she expected? That he would refuse to sully their relationship with money?

He had been gone a long time, but that was only to be expected. He had business of his own and no incentive to hurry back to a mistress who treated him to scenes over breakfast.

At last, after picking at her luncheon and mangling some embroidery for an hour, she rang for Grace. 'I am going out.'

'Is that wise, miss? What if someone recognised you?'

'In a hackney and wearing a veil?'

'Very well, miss.'

With both of them shrouded in sufficient black veiling for heavy mourning the two stepped out on to the pavement. 'There's a cab,' Grace said, but as she stepped forwards another figure emerged from behind the railings and hailed the hackney.

'Ferret!'

'Afternoon, miss. You hop in now. Where are we going?'

'We?' Beside her Grace was taking a firm and threatening grip on Averil's parasol.

'Cap'n said I was to go with you everywhere, miss. What'll I tell the driver?'

'Round Hyde Park,' Averil said at random and climbed in.

'Miss Heydon?'

'It is all right, Grace. I know this man.' Ferret settled opposite her and began to peer out of the windows as the vehicle moved off. 'When did the captain say you were to go with me, Ferret? He didn't tell me.'

'About noon, it was. Turned up down at the docks at me auntie's beer house. We're all down there while he sorts out the pardons and work and ships for us. Says there's a gent means you no good, so we're to guard you.' He flipped back the front of his frieze coat to reveal a collection of knives and a small club. 'Don't you be worrying about anything.'

'I feel very safe,' Averil said, her mind reeling at the thought of Bradon confronted by Ferret. 'All of you?'

'Well, Tubbs and Dawkins are watching the Cap'n's lodgings to sort out the men who are watching that, and Bull's following the Cap'n to see who is following him.'

Ferret looked remarkably clean and tidy, although his gap-tooth grin was as disreputable as ever.

'What will they do with whomever they catch?'

'Sell 'em to the press gang, miss. Nice park, ain't it?' He settled back as the hackney began to trot along the perimeter track, but his eyes flickered from side to side and Averil did not believe for a moment that he was as relaxed as he pretended to be. Beside her Grace kept a firm grip on the parasol; it was not going to be a calming ride, but at least it had the charm of novelty. Then Ferret's words sank in. Bradon had someone following Luc—he was in danger and all he had to protect him were the rascally crew from the island.

Luc turned the key in the door of the Half Moon Street house with a degree of caution. In his experience once a mistress had acquired the taste for throwing things she was likely to retain it.

The sound of running feet had him bracing himself, but Averil threw open the drawing room door and cast herself on his chest with no sign of a weapon. 'Are you all right?' She looked up into his face and the worry drained out of hers. 'Oh, thank goodness, yes, you are. I was so worried when Ferret told me about Bradon.'

'Bradon can go to the devil,' Luc said and kissed her with enjoyable thoroughness. Life was hideously complicated but this, at least, was perfect in its simplicity.

'Yes, but how does he know?' Averil, most satisfactorily pink and flustered from the embrace, dragged him into the drawing room. How easily she had slipped into this role, into his life. And how easily she would leave it.

'The man is not an idiot. He knows you were compromised by a naval officer and the only naval officer who has been paying you any marked attention since you arrived in London is me. Once his suspicions were aroused it wouldn't take much to discover that I have been out of town for some time, that no one can be very positive about where I have been and I returned just as you arrived.'

She had gone very pale. 'Averil, there is no need to worry. The whole crew are covering you.'

'I am not worried about myself!' She turned on him, fierce and passionate, and his breath caught and something he did not recognise jolted, deep inside. Not lust, not desire, although they were there, too. This was something warmer and deeper, this was what had been churning inside him ever since she had walked into his chambers at Albany. Puzzled, he caught at her hands as she twisted them into an anguished knot.

'He could harm you, he is vindictive and calculating. He could have you stabbed in some dark alley or go to the Admiralty and make trouble for you there. I must leave, now.'

'Over my dead body!'

'That is what I am afraid of, you stupid man!'

Luc produced his best quarterdeck frown. He needed to distract her, and fast. 'Might I remind you that you are my mistress and as such I expect obedience and respect. You have twice thrown things at my head, you have ruined a shirt, my best evening coat may never be the same again, that coffee pot was Dresden and now you say I am stupid. That little catalogue calls for chastise-ment, I fear.'

'What? You do not mean that you would—no!'

Averil gave a scream of protest as Luc picked her up and threw her over his shoulder, just as he had that first day on the beach. This time she fought, drumming her fists on his buttocks and thighs as she dangled upside down, kicking her heels as he carried her up upstairs and into the bedchamber, but it was hopeless. He twisted her round as he sat down on the edge of the bed and she found herself face down across his lap.

'Let me go, you brute! You dare beat me! I'll...I'll...'

Cool air touched her thighs, her buttocks and the world went dark as her skirts flew over her head. One large warm hand spread over her exposed backside, lifted—and she was rolled on to the bed with Luc scrambling after her, tickling her until she screamed with laughter.

'Oh, you beast,' she murmured when they finally lay still, gasping and tear-stained and still hiccupping faintly with hilarity.

'I know. Shall I be more beastly still?'

'Yes, please,' Averil said. 'I would like that very much.'

Chapter Twenty-Three

Eight days had seemed endless when she was staying with the Bradons. Now thirteen seemed to have sped by. Tomorrow she would sail for India. Tomorrow she would say goodbye to Luc and never see him again, possibly never hear what became of him. She had counted off the passing days with the dread of a prisoner awaiting execution, prayed that this evening would never come, but of course, it had.

Ferret had escorted a heavily veiled Grace to do their shopping, but as that had been spread over many days it had been possible to pretend it was still not all complete.

The only thing that had changed with time had been Luc, she realised, watching him as he lay asleep beside her. It was three in the morning, the watchman had passed only minutes before, but the candles were still burning. They had been making love half the night.

As the days had passed he had become quieter, more introspective. She had thought at first he was worried about Bradon, but then realised that he was too courageous to let the other man bother him once he had put measures for her protection in place. Then she wondered if he was working too hard at the Admiralty, but he seemed to enjoy the sessions he was having with his students and returned energised from them.

His lovemaking had grown more intense, more passionate, as the days and nights had passed and sometimes she would catch him watching her, his eyes dark and troubled as though she was a mystery he could not solve.

Now he lay sprawled face down, naked except for a twist of sheet that did nothing for decency. Averil resisted the temptation to touch him again or he would wake and she wanted him to sleep now so she could look at him and fill her memory with the images that would have to last her for the rest of her life.

For the first time she wished she could draw. 'I love you,' she whispered, over and over. It was a delicious, heart-breaking luxury to be able to say it. 'I love you.' Her lids drooped and she wriggled down the pillows to lie close beside him, soothed by the scent of his skin and the musk of their lovemaking. If she could just stay awake, the night would never end....

Luc woke slowly, smiling as he seemed to every morning, waking next to Averil. Eyes closed, he reached out a hand to where she would be lying curled up, her hair in her eyes, warm and soft and sleepy. She would come to him, still waking and they would kiss and then—then his hand touched the hollow in the mattress and it was cold. She was gone.

Puzzled, he opened his eyes and remembered. Today was the day she was leaving. The ship was sailing, Averil was going home. Leaving him.

That was what they had agreed and he had deceived himself for days that time would stand still. But it had not and he knew she had been fretting for this morning to come; he had just not admitted it to himself. He had moved a book she was reading and a scrap of paper fell out, a page torn from an almanac with the days crossed off. She had grown quieter and yet more restless and there were dark shadows under her eyes.

He closed his eyes again. *Coward. Get up and face it.* But there was something else to face, the fact that he had taken her innocence, had used her as his mistress when he could have simply hidden her away, given her the money she needed. That it had never entered his head until it was too late was no excuse. Neither was the fact that Averil enjoyed their lovemaking and had suggested the arrangement in the first place any justification.

There were no excuses for seizing what he wanted without thinking about Averil. But he was being punished for it now. He was missing her already. *I've grown accustomed to her*, he thought. *Accustomed to her touch and her laughter, to her scent and her company, her courage and her kisses. Accustomed, that is all. She will be gone and I will propose marriage to the de la Falaise chit and find another mistress...*

He rolled over on to his back, eyes wide open now. It was barely light. No, when he married he would make himself be faithful. Averil would not approve otherwise. But what did it matter what she would think? She would be thousands of miles away making a new life, trying hard to forget him and the bargain she had made to free herself from Bradon. By the time she came back to England, if she ever did, he would be in France, being a Frenchman at last, with his French wife and his French children at his side.

He tried to sink into the familiar dream that had sustained him so often in the past. But for the first time he could not picture the scene. Instead of a vivid picture of the château and laughing children and an elegant chatelaine there was nothing, just the black-and-white ghost of the house as he remembered it.

With a curse Luc rolled off the bed, dragged his robe around his shoulders and went to look for Averil. She was sitting in the dressing room, folding small items, placing them in one of the trays that would fit into the trunk that stood open next to the clothes press. Her face was shuttered, intent.

Luc thought to stand there for a while and watch her, but she looked up and the scrap of silk and lace fell from her hands. 'I was finishing packing,' she said.

So eager to be gone. 'Yes, of course,' he said. 'You will be happy to see your father and brothers again.'

'Yes. I miss them.' She bent and retrieved the camisole. 'This will all seem like a dream. The voyage, the shipwreck.'

'Me.'

She nodded, not meeting his eyes. Yes, she could let it become a dream, find a husband in India, pretend none of this had happened. With any luck and a little acting the man would never know. He felt faintly sick and guessed that it must be jealousy of that unknown, unsuspecting man. She would make the choice herself this time, he knew. She would choose with care, someone she would get to know before she committed herself, someone she could trust.

'You'll marry,' he said, almost welcoming the knot of pain in his gut.

'Yes,' she agreed, picking another garment from the drawer. 'I would like children.'

'Come back to bed.' Luc heard his own voice, rough, demanding. Impatient. He could have kicked himself when Averil put down the garment she was folding and rose obediently to come to him. *Obedient to the man who is paying her.*

'Come,' he said, more gently and saw the tears glimmering in her eyes. The tears he had put there because he was selfish and thoughtless and had taken what he wanted. 'Come back to bed and let us say goodbye.'

At nine o'clock Averil stood on the dockside shielded from the press of the crowd by Tubbs's bulk behind and Tom the Patch at her side. Ferret was with Grace, making sure the last of the baggage was safely on board. The other men were scattered along the quay, watchful and armed.

She searched in her reticule for a hair pin and found the Noah's Ark box. She had forgotten all about it. 'Tom, can you write?'

'Yes, ma'am. Learned at dame school.'

'Then can you please make sure this is posted for me?' she asked and scribbled Alistair's name and title on a slip of card and handed them both to him. 'He is sure to have a town house.'

'No message, ma'am?'

'No.' She could not think of a thing to say. She could hardly think.

Her protectors clustered around her. The only person missing was Luc. He would be making himself visible in Mayfair, he had told her. 'I daren't go with you to the ship,' he said as he held her in his arms in the battered hackney carriage. 'I can't be veiled, I'm too big and I can't hide this damned nose of mine. You will be safe. Ferret will stay with you until the pilot is taken off at Tilbury.'

Of course she would and it was the practical, sensible

thing for him to do, she knew that. And Luc had probably had enough of her emotions by now and wanted to avoid a tearful scene on the quayside.

He was right to fear it. She had been on the verge of losing all control ever since she had woken. The urge to kiss him awake, tell him she loved him, had been so overwhelming that she had slid from the bed and gone to pack her last remaining things, just so she was a safe distance from him.

And then he had stood in the doorway and looked at her with something like anger in those dark grey eyes and the roughness in his voice when he had asked her to come back to bed had been like a blow.

But their lovemaking had been almost silent, slow, so tender and gentle that she thought she would weep and then found that she was and that Luc was kissing the tears from the corners of her eyes before they could fall. 'You never cry, Averil,' he said.

Now she thought he had drunk every tear. Her eyes felt hot and dry, but she managed a smile for Grace and Ferret when they came to say it was time to board and words of thanks for the men who were guarding her.

Then she was at the rail and the ship had cast off and was slipping down river on the falling tide and she searched the quayside for a tall man, a dark head, the face that she loved. The man who had cupped her face in his hands as he looked at her with something in his eyes that she had never seen before. '*Au 'voir, ma sirène,*' he said as he climbed out of the carriage without looking back.

'*Au 'voir, Luc. Je t'aime,*' she whispered now as the docks slid away and the river widened. Ferret and Grace left her alone. Ferret, she knew, was scanning the passengers, checking, double-checking for anyone taking an interest in her.

Time passed, London passed, the river widened into an estuary. Soon they would drop the pilot, and Ferret would go with him.

The clocks rang the half-hour. Luc stared blankly at the open newspaper in front of his face. *Diamond Rose* was casting off now. She would slip down the Thames on the falling tide leaving nothing behind to mark her presence, only the ache in his heart.

The print blurred and he blinked, appalled to realise there were tears in his eyes. What the hell was the matter with him? It felt as though something—someone—had died.

And then he realised. Something had. He loved her. He loved Averil and he had let her go, sent her out of his life. The image of the château came back, in colour now, and the children were there and the woman by his side and the laughter was Averil's and the smiles on the faces of the children were hers, too. He had killed that future, those children, and it was too late. Too late.

But he had to try. Luc threw down the paper, ran from the library and down the stairs into the hall of White's club, thrust past the indignant members by the porter's desk, out on to St James's Street. 'Cab!'

Behind him he heard the porter. 'Sir! Your hat, sir! Your coat!' but the hackney stopped. 'Get me to the nearest livery stables in five minutes and there's gold for you.'

It would be too late, but he had to try.

Averil watched the banks as Tilbury came into sight. In a few minutes it would be too late, there would be no turning back. Perhaps it was already too late and this was madness, but quite suddenly, she knew what she must do. And with the resolve the blanket of misery that had seemed to stifle every breath lifted. 'Ferret!'

'Yes, miss?' The little man materialised by her side.

'I am going back with you.'

'What—back on the pilot boat? To London? To the Cap'n?'

'Yes. To the Cap'n.' For as long as he wanted her, for whatever he wanted her as. She loved him, she was his. *Papa,* she thought. *Forgive me, but he is my life now. I ruined your plans the moment I left Bradon. I cannot live without Luc.*

'Right, miss. Don't know as we can get your stuff off again, though.'

'It doesn't matter, just so long as we don't forget Grace.'

'I wouldn't do that, miss,' Ferret said with an emphasis that cut through her preoccupation with Luc. *Ferret and Grace?*

It took some argument and several guineas before the captain agreed to put another two passengers and their hand baggage off, but at last, as the ship lost way and the pilot boat came alongside, she was scrambling down the ladder with Ferret's hands on her ankles guiding her safely. 'If you'll excuse the liberty, miss.'

'Of course.' And Grace seemed to be positively enjoying it when her turn came.

The cutter cast off and headed for shore. 'What's that?' the pilot said, scratching his head and pointing at an identical craft heading out towards them. 'Late passenger, I reckon.'

There was a man standing up in the bows, rock-steady, at home on a ship. A man she would know anywhere. '*Luc,*' she whispered.

Hands reached out to stop her as she fought her way

forwards amongst sailors and coils of rope. Then she was standing on the prow as he was and as the boats lost way and came together he reached out and caught hold of her and swung her across to him.

'Averil. You were coming back to me?'

'Yes. To you.' She stood there in the circle of his arm and everything vanished, the onlookers, the tossing boat, everything but him. 'You were coming for me?'

'I love you. Why did I not know before? I love you.' He looked down at her, and for the first time she saw real uncertainty on his face. 'Do you think you could…? You came back. I thought I would be too late. I rode harder than I ever have in my life and yet I thought I would be too late. But you are here for me…'

'Because I love you, too. More than anything, more than everything. I love you, Luc.'

'Thank God.' He closed his eyes and pulled her tight against him and she could hear his heart thudding as though he had been running. 'Let's go home.'

Luc was so silent beside her in the carriage on the long drive back from Tilbury that Averil wondered if he had changed his mind. But his arm as he held her against his chest was rock steady and his breathing was even, like that of a contented man. After a while she felt pressure on the top of her head and realised he was resting his cheek on her hair. She wanted to close her eyes and just luxuriate in being loved, but there too many things to worry about yet.

'Should I go into the country for a while until Bradon gives up looking for me?' she asked after twenty minutes.

'He is going to know soon enough,' Luc said.

'But he will call you out!' Averil wriggled free and twisted on the seat to look at him.

'He'll humiliate himself if he does—you were not known to be his betrothed, so if he fights me over you it will become common knowledge that he was jilted. If there was a chance he could get you back without a fuss, then that would be one thing—that was what I was afraid of, that he'd snatch you if he found you—but he won't be able to do that now.'

'But why not? We know he is ruthless and cold-blooded—'

'A married woman is of no use to him,' Luc said so calmly that for a moment she missed his meaning.

'Married? You mean to marry me?'

'Of course.' His smile as he saw the realisation hit her was pure, unclouded joy. 'There is no need to worry about banns—I can swear the allegation and get a licence from the vicar at St James's church just opposite Albany. I can prove residence easily enough, even though I am hardly a regular churchgoer. You do not mind St James's?'

'Mind? But you cannot marry me, Luc. You want a Frenchwoman. And my grandfather was a grocer, for goodness' sake!'

'So you came back to be my mistress?' It was his turn to stare now. 'You love me enough to do that?'

'Of course,' she said, impatient that he did not understand. 'For as long as you want me.'

'I want you for ever.' He shook his head, as frustrated as she by their mutual incomprehension. 'I did not understand what it was to be in love. I made all those stupid conditions, set up barriers that mean nothing. Yes, you are English, but you can learn French, we can divide our time so the children can grow up in both countries. Our first son, of course, will inherit the title, so he must always feel more French than English, but I know you will support me in that.'

'Children,' she murmured, and nodded, too moved for words. Their children. She wanted to kiss him because the look in his eyes answered every doubt she could ever have that he loved her.

'D'Aunays *do not marry trade,*' Luc said bitterly. 'I can just hear the words in my head. I was a fool, a prejudiced fool. Well, this d'Aunay will marry for love. All that matters is that I have found an intelligent, brave, beautiful woman whom I adore and who will stand by my side.'

It was a dream come true, and like all dreams, nightmare lurked on the edges. 'Bradon could sue you for alienation of my affections, the loss of my dowry.'

'Then he can have your damn dowry,' Luc said. 'How much does your father love you? Will he settle for a French count with a promising career in the navy while the war lasts and a foothold in two countries when it ends? Will he pay off Bradon if I do not ask for any dowry with you and settle my own money on you? He still gets a son-in-law with some influence and standing, after all.'

'You would do that?'

'Of course. I would hand over every penny I own to keep you. Averil, you have turned my life upside down. I thought I knew what I wanted and now all I want is you. You will marry me?' The sudden uncertainty in his voice caught at her heart. He was so strong, so confident and yet he was so unsure of her.

She swallowed, trying to find the right words to reassure him, but he got to his knees on the floor of the rocking carriage, caught her hands in his and said, 'Averil Heydon, I love you. Marry me and I swear you will never regret it. Marry me, because I do not think I can live without you.'

'I shall have to,' she said as she lifted their joined

hands to her lips and kissed his knuckles. 'Because I cannot live without you either. *Je t'aime.*'

'Now that,' Luc said as he sat down beside her and pulled her into his arms, 'that is all the French you will need for a long, long time.'

The carriage rocked on its way towards Piccadilly and the old church, but Averil did not notice it, for Luc's arms were strong around her and his mouth was tender on hers and the words he spoke, although she did not understand them with her head, she could translate with her heart, because they were all of love.

* * * * *

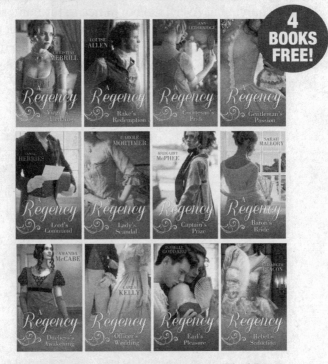